What critics are saying about the
AMBER FOX MYSTERIES:

"If you like Janet Evanovich's Stephanie Plum I think you will really like Amber Fox - I know I do."
~ Martha's Bookshelf

"Amber Fox is a modern, career-driven woman who seems to be a cross between Kinsey Milhone and Gracie Hart (Miss Congeniality). I enjoyed the great mixture of action adventure and slapstick. I found myself chuckling out loud and on one occasion snorting water out my nose."
~ Coffee Time Romance & More

"Amber Fox was hilarious with her tough as nails outer persona and her hysterical one-liners that were frequently laugh out loud funny. I definately recommend picking this book up!!"
~ The Caffeinated Diva reads…

"Amber Fox is the kind of strong lead female character with a great sarcastic wit that I love to read."
~ To Read, Perchance to Dream

FASHION, LIES, AND MURDER

SIBEL HODGE

"Three can keep a secret if two are dead."
BENJAMIN FRANKLIN

CHAPTER ONE

If life is like a box of chocolates, then mine is the mother of all coffee creams. You know—the ones that always get left in the box because no one wants them? Today I felt like a coffee cream, too. On the outside I was sleek and hard, but on the inside, I was just a lump of mush.

I sat in Brad's office, trying to ignore the queasy tingle that gurgled in the depths of my stomach. As he droned on about my assignment, I tuned him out and debated whether things could get any worse. I tried giving myself a pep talk, but I'm not sure it worked.

Come on, Amber, get a grip. It's no use wishing you could get the hell out of here. You can do this new job with your eyes closed.

Suddenly, something Brad said caught my attention and I snapped back to the conversation. "Hang on a sec. Let me get this straight. You want me to plant some bugs?" I asked, wondering if I'd misheard. "I take it we're talking about *bug* bugs and not the creepy-crawly variety." I shuddered at the thought. Spiders were a definite no-no.

Brad gave me a cool nod of agreement. The owner of Hi-Tec Insurance, Brad was a former Special Forces operative whom I'd known for years. He was also my former fiancé. I'd accepted a job as claims investigator at Hi-Tec after being let go from my position on the police force. Not the ideal situation, I know, but it paid the bills.

"Exactly why does an insurance company want to plant bugs in its client's offices?" I asked as I sat back in the chair opposite Brad's, my right leg jiggling up and down like a pneumatic drill.

"This is the twenty-first century. We're in the proactive insurance age now," Brad replied.

"So you're trying to avoid an insurance claim before it happens?"

"You've got it in one, Foxy. Claims are money, and if there's one thing I hate, it's losing money." An amused smile played around the corners of Brad's mouth as he looked at my knee aerobics. "Am I making you nervous?"

I stopped jiggling and gave him the eye roll to beat all eye rolls. "I think we're way past the stage of you making me nervous, Brad." He raised an eyebrow at that but continued, handing me a manila folder as he spoke.

"I've had a tip from one of my informers that this particular client is into something a bit dodgy—actually, a lot dodgy. I need to get a handle on the truth before I find myself involved in a multimillion-pound insurance payout."

I took the folder. "And what informer would that be?" I asked as I flicked through the file, watching out of the corner of my eye as he rolled up his shirtsleeves. The familiar action brought a reluctant smile to my face. A suit, dress shirt, and trousers didn't fit Brad. He was more at home in desert camouflage and chunky-soled boots. As I read the client's name, I knew my jaw had fallen to the floor but I couldn't help it. I barely heard Brad's response to my question.

"The usual—the seedy, underhanded kind."

"Umberto Fandango, the fashion designer? He's one of your clients?"

"Hi-Tec Insurance has a very diverse clientele, ranging from the scumbag lowlifes to the rich and famous ones." Brad rested his feet on his huge mahogany desk, looking pretty pleased with himself. He picked a piece of fluff from his trousers, examining it with distaste before depositing it in the trash bin.

"His bags are to die for!" Maybe being a claims investigator wouldn't be so boring, after all. "Have you seen the ones with—"

"Here." Ignoring my amazement, he tossed me a packet of black ballpoint pens.

Distracted, I examined the packet with interest. "What are these?"

"The bugs are cunningly disguised as pens. I just need you to go to Umberto's office, plant a few of these around the place, and leave the rest to me. To activate them, you just have to click the top of the pen. Do you think you can handle that?"

"No problemo. I'm Amber Fox, Miss Hot-Shit Investigator. I can do anything."

Brad glanced over at my leg, which was now bouncing up and down, space-hopper style. "I'd definitely agree with the 'hot' part." He arched an eyebrow. "Janice Skipper might agree with the 'shit' part."

I cringed. Janice Skipper was the reason I'd been let go from the force. She had carried a vendetta for me around for a long time, and had taken pleasure in making my life hell. To say Janice was a sore point for me was an understatement.

"Urgh! Don't mention that woman. If it weren't for her—"

"I know, Foxy—you wouldn't be here now." Brad stood up and moved around the desk. "Come on, I'll introduce you to Hacker. If you want anything technical done, he's your guy." He strode toward me, six feet of solid muscle that backed my five-foot-six frame into the wall. He stopped mere inches away from my face.

I caught a musky waft of his aftershave and sucked in a breath. A tingling sensation erupted in my stomach.

Calm down, Amber. Nothing to worry about. You've just got a case of gas, that's all. What else could that peculiar sensation be?

"It's good to have you back, Foxy," he whispered, staring down at me with haunting gray eyes. They're the kind that are lined at the corners, giving you just a hint that he's seen more in his forty years than most people would see in ten lifetimes.

I matched his stare pound for pound and swallowed hard, feeling goose bumps springing to attention on my skin. My throat felt constricted and dusty. "Don't call me Foxy," I finally managed to croak out.

"It's either Foxy or Sexy. You choose," he said. His words caused his breath to tickle my cheek.

"And Brad? You haven't got me back," I told him, hoping he couldn't see the pulse that was booming away at the base of my throat. Just when I thought I was going to have to do something to make him back off, he slowly leaned past me and opened his office door.

"We'll see about that," he drawled as he pushed away from me and went out the door, beckoning for me to follow him to meet Hacker.

A few minutes later, I rushed to the restroom. Cold water by the bucket load was in order. I leaned on the sink, staring into the mirror at my flushed face. My heart was still banging out a tribal drum beat. I hoped Brad hadn't seen it through my T-shirt.

Okay, so this probably wasn't a good idea, working for my ex, but then I hadn't exactly had many job offers in the last six months. No, scratch that. I'd had zilch, and I still had to pay my mortgage, so I didn't have a choice, really. The sensible part of me thought it was a positive and productive sign that Brad Beckett didn't affect me in the slightest anymore. By "affect" I mean I'd managed to get through a whole half-hour conversation with Brad without crying, fainting, or molesting him. Then again, maybe it was the crazy part of me that thought this was progress. It was definitely one of the two. I just hadn't worked out which was which yet.

Okay, Amber, this can work. I'd be professional about my job and just solve this one case for him before I found a new job. I wouldn't be here long enough to fall in love with him again. Anyway, my curiosity had been piqued so I couldn't quit straight away. I just hoped that curiosity didn't kill the Fox.

I took a deep breath, squaring my shoulders. Right, here we go, then. Onward and upward, and all that rubbish.

I turned on the cold water to splash onto my face, expecting a trickle. I shrieked with surprise as the water rushed out, tsunami style, splashing up and soaking the front of my T-shirt.

"Great!" I looked for some paper towels, but the restroom only had dryers. Before I could move to it, the door opened and closed behind me and I glanced up in the mirror. Brad was standing behind me, examining the reflection of my wet chest with great interest. I could feel my nipples straining through the tight fabric. And even worse, judging from Brad's smile, I knew he could see it happening.

"Nice look," he said, a husky note entering his voice.

I rushed to the dryer, frantically flapping my top underneath it. "What are you doing in the women's bathroom?" I hissed.

"Oh, didn't I tell you? This building has unisex toilets." He shot me an innocent grin.

A searing-hot tingle rippled through me. How the hell was a girl supposed to have any secrets around here if even the bathrooms weren't safe havens from his presence?

Brad winked at me. "There aren't any secrets around here."

It wasn't until I'd barged out of the restroom that I realized I hadn't actually said it out loud. So how did Brad know exactly what I was thinking?

* * *

The home of the Fandango Empire was a converted flourmill in Ware, Hertfordshire. According to the file, Umberto had a pretty impressive set of offices that took up the whole of the building, which included a runway for the models to practice on.

I cruised down Ware's high street in my blend-in-with-the-rest-of-the-world silver Toyota, silently rehearsing my fake spiel about how I needed to check and make certain his insurance coverage was meeting his needs, which was a laugh. What I knew about insurance could fit on the head of one of the pens Brad wanted me to leave. Still, I could BS with the best of them, and I promised myself that if I pulled this off, I'd be having a super-duper celebratory lunch afterwards—ooh, maybe I'd even throw in a monster chocolate muffin, too. My stomach gurgled loudly, although I couldn't tell if it was from nerves or hunger.

Squaring my shoulders, I pushed open the front door and stopped cold in the reception area. I looked around, soaking in the crazy décor. The theme seemed to be "If it doesn't move, leopard skin it." Don't get me wrong, I love leopard skin. I'm a real leopard skin kind of girl—as long as it's fake, of course—but a leopard skin reception desk, sofa, chairs, rug, curtains, and phone were a tad overkill.

Trying to act casual, I wandered over to the receptionist. "Hi, I'm here to see Umberto Fandango. I'm from Hi-Tec Insurance." With my hand in my pocket, I tried to look calm as I felt for the pens. Grabbing one, I covertly clicked the top to activate it and waited for my moment.

The receptionist looked around her computer screen at me, forehead pinched in a harassed frown. She appeared to be in her early twenties, and was attractive in a subtle way that probably went unnoticed in this kind of industry where obvious beauty takes center stage. "Do you have an appointment? I didn't see one for you in the book." She ran a finger down the page of a leather-bound diary in front of her.

"No, unfortunately not."

She glanced up at me again, the frown looking more harassed. "London Fashion Week is next week, and we're all very busy. Mr.

Fandango is rushed off his feet."

"Look, I'm sorry to just turn up like this, but I really need to talk to him about his insurance. We wouldn't want to find out he didn't have the coverage he needed for something, would we? It'll just take a few minutes." I flashed her a conspiratorial smile and placed my hand face down on the desk, willing her to turn her head for a second.

She sighed, seeing I wasn't going to give up. "Let me just buzz him, then. Hang on a sec."

Her momentary glance at the leopard phone was all it took for me to deposit the pen under her monitor.

"Thanks," I said.

While she spoke to someone on the other end of the line, I gazed toward the glass doors off the reception area, where an echoing male voice shouted out instructions. I followed the sound and moved to peer through the door to get a better look. Some female models with scary wigs stalked up and down the runway, covered in very spangly, glittery creations, as a tall woman stood yelling at them. On second thought, maybe the male voice I'd heard wasn't really male. Maybe it was just a giant woman wearing size-thirteen stilettos with a gruff voice. It was hard to tell. In the background, a woman who looked to be about five times over the required model weight limit of three stone sat at a desk, hot-fixing rhinestones to a white swimsuit.

A tall blonde woman, so thin she looked like she'd been photocopied, clicked her spiky heels in my direction. She eyed me from head to toe with disdain, studying my usual uniform of khaki combats, black T-shirt, and very comfy sneakers. "You're obviously not one of the models," she said as she tilted her head back. Her cheekbones were so sharp they looked like they could put out an eye, and I had to stop myself from leaning backward, just in case.

"Hi, I'm Amber, from Hi-Tec Insurance." I held out my hand to shake hers.

She ignored it and crossed her arms in front of her. Was it me, or was the atmosphere getting noticeably colder? I glanced over at the receptionist, who was chewing on the end of her pencil, a sympathetic look on her face.

"And?" the blonde woman said through lips painted a shade that Dracula would have been proud of.

"That's it, just Hi-Tec Insurance. There's no 'and' after it," I said.

The woman rolled her eyes. "What do you want?" Her voice sharpened, and she frowned at me; the really wicked, twitchy-eye, wrinkly forehead kind, except her forehead didn't wrinkle when she did it.

"Hey, you're fun! Isn't Botox amazing?" I asked, fascinated by her un-wrinkly forehead.

This earned me something eerily close to a snarl. "What do you want? We're very busy."

Properly chastised, I answered. "I just need a few moments with Umberto Fandango. It's about his insurance."

"What about it?"

Good question. Here comes the BS.

I cleared my throat. "I'm just checking out the business premises for security reasons. Obviously you have some very expensive and high-profile merchandise here, so I need to have a look around the entire area, as well as inspect your alarm system to make sure there's no possible breach of security. Don't worry, it's just routine information for our files." I gave her my most sincere smile, pulling out my camera to make my claim look authentic.

She weighed my words with an icy stare. "Hmm." A pause. Then: "Follow me." And off she clicked toward a corridor at the far end of the reception area.

I made use of my trigger finger, snapping off a few pictures as I followed behind her. We stopped when she paused outside a door at the end and punched in a sequence of numbers on a keypad.

The door clicked. "Wait here," she said. She slipped inside the room, returning a few seconds later. "Mr. Fandango will see you now."

I followed her into the ultra-modern office, which was decked out with a chrome and glass desk, chrome and leather chairs, a chrome lamp, chrome pen tidy, and a silver leather sofa. Wow, when this guy liked something, he really went to town. I quickly sneaked a peek at the pen tidy, crammed full of biros, as a man dressed in a purple smoking jacket stood from behind his desk and pumped my hand. I didn't think smoking jackets existed in real life, I thought it was just a myth, but no—they were alive and well and living in Hertfordshire. And this guy had to be in his fifties; far too young for a smoking jacket, in my opinion.

"I'm Umberto. What can I do for you, honey?" he asked in a weird, Lloyd Grossman mix of an American and English accent. He was on the short side, with thick, dark brown hair that was swept back with a touch of gel, dark brown eyes, and a spray-on tan that bordered on the Tango variety. Although he was clean-shaven, he had a hint of five o'clock shadow, and I suspected he would have to shave more than once a day to keep his beard in check.

I went through my spiel again and gave him a dazzling smile for good luck, all the while casually gripping one of the bug pens in my pocket.

"Knock yourself out. Just make sure you don't get in the models' way, or I'll have one hell of a catfight on my hands. Actually, I've got a few spare minutes, so why don't I show you around?" He flashed me a bleached-tooth grin and led the way out of his office.

In a split second, pen number two was secretly stashed in his pen tidy, and I was following behind him. The Ice Queen bared her teeth in an imitation of a smile, examining me like I was a piece of road kill stuck to her thousand-pound shoes as she sat down at the desk opposite Fandango's.

I resisted the urge to stick my tongue out.

As Umberto led me through the offices and the huge storage area upstairs that housed his fashion collection, I took notes and photos galore.

"So, waddaya think?" he asked as we entered the runway area, where the stiletto-heeled he-she was busy screeching at one of the models.

"I think I need to see the bags before I make my mind up," I told him. Maybe he'd give me a freebie while I was here.

"Beg pardon?"

"You know—those gorgeous handbags you make. Can I have a little peek at them? They're so cool. I love the ones with—"

"Sorry, honey, we don't make the bags here, they're all sent in from the States."

"Oh," I muttered with disappointment. Well, it had been worth a try.

"Waddaya think of the security, then?" he asked.

"It looks pretty secure to me."

"Aw, shit!" Fandango looked across the sea of prancing female models toward a dark-haired man in a crisp blue shirt and an expensive-looking suit. He was pretty hot, too. In fact, if I had to rate him out of ten, he'd be a nine and three-quarters. The man wore an air of expectation, and I watched as Fandango's demeanor changed abruptly. "Okay, that's your lot, honey. You need to leave now." As he made his way over to Mr. Hottie, I took the opportunity to drop a pen to the floor, casually kicking it under the runway. Based on the way Fandango had reacted, I assumed the man in the suit was a model.

A Kodak moment of a yummy model and a famous fashion designer seemed too good to miss, so I snapped a few pictures while I studied them through the viewfinder. They seemed to be involved in a heated argument about something. Maybe someone had forgotten to put all-white lilies in Mr. Hottie's dressing room, or the blue M&M's had been left in his chocolate selection by mistake. *Oh well*, I thought, *it's not my problem.* Operation Bug was complete, which was all that mattered to me. I smiled as I headed out of the building. *Way to go, Amber. Bring on the chocolate muffins.* My first assignment had been a success. Nothing could possibly go wrong now.

Could it?

CHAPTER TWO

I stumbled through the doors of Hi-Tec's plush Hertford office with my rucksack threatening to slide off my shoulder. I juggled two mochaccinos and four chocolate muffins with extra chocolate sprinkles in one hand, and two mozzarella paninis and a bottle of sparkling water in the other hand. I'll admit that the sparkling water was going a bit overboard, but this was a celebration after all.

After I made my way through the empty reception area, which was decked out in soft creams and browns with matching sofas, I swung a left down the corridor that ran past the busy underwriter's office. Hacker called out a "Yo" as I weaved past him and deposited my feast on my desk—if you could call it a desk; it was more like a slightly oversized coffee table. He sat surrounded by various monitors and computer equipment, arranged in an arc in front of him. It looked like something from the bridge of the Starship Enterprise.

Hacker had to be the least techy-looking guy I'd ever seen. He was black, six foot six tall, with two plaits sticking straight out from the top of his head and a goatee beard. He wore a hoodie three sizes too big and jeans that were so baggy they defied the laws of gravity, and he looked more like a gangster rapper than a computer expert. I'd heard that Brad met him when they were in the SAS together, and he was from somewhere like Haiti or Tahiti—I always got those two mixed up. Rumor had it that even though Brad had started Hi-Tec, he was still involved in his Secret Army Stuff from time to time. I didn't believe it was just a rumor, though. I knew firsthand about Brad disappearing for months on end.

"Yo back. Want a mochaccino?" I wiggled a cup in his direction.

Hacker stopped tapping on his keyboard and glanced over at my desk. "Don't you know that stuff will kill you? Your body is a temple." He circled his arms in the air and pressed his palms together, slowly bringing his hands to the center of his body, doing some kind of yoga deep breathing.

More for me, then, yay. "Sparkling water?"

"That's more like it." He grinned, and a gold tooth shone back at me. "How do you stay so thin, eating like that?"

"I guess I'm just lucky that I've got skinny genes," I said as I tossed him the water, which he caught with a swift flick of the wrist. "Is Brad here?" I glanced across the corridor to Brad's empty office.

"No, he's at a secret meeting," Hacker said as he fiddled around with a weird-looking electronic contraption in front of him, which looked a lot like a mixing deck one might expect to find in a recording studio. "He left those files on your desk."

I picked up the two folders. One was for a Callum Bates, and the other was for a guy named Paul Clark. I'd never heard of Clark, but Callum Bates was a very familiar name. I'd come across him in my days as a young police officer, way back before I'd joined the special operations team. If anything was going down in the area that involved car crime—jacking, theft, cloning, you name it—Callum was involved. I studied the file and chuckled. He'd recently put in an insurance claim for a stolen van. No wonder Brad wanted me to check it out to make sure it was genuine. Callum had probably nicked it himself.

Setting aside the Bates file for now, I perused the Clark information. Apparently, Mr. Clark had put in a claim for a disability insurance payout, asserting that he'd hurt his back in a warehouse accident and couldn't work again. Brad wanted me to do some observations on him to make sure Clark wasn't faking it. Okay, so the work wasn't exactly exciting special police operations, but at least I could afford my apartment now.

Standing up, I stuffed the files in my rucksack. I couldn't eat a celebratory lunch on my own, so I gathered everything together once again and struggled back out the door.

"Yo," Hacker said as I left.

I popped my head back around the door. "Does that mean hello or goodbye?"

"Anything you want it to mean. It's pretty universal."

You learned something new every day. "Cool. By the way, why isn't there a receptionist here?"

"Brad fired her. She kept making mistakes. He's looking for another one."

"Oh, okay. Yo, then."

* * *

After a slight accident of spilled mochaccino on my passenger seat, I arrived at my parents' house. Mum's sporty Mini wasn't in the driveway—no change there, really. She was always gallivanting off with her mates. Not that I blamed her, really. I mean, Dad had lived and breathed for his job as a police officer, and she had to find something to occupy her time all these years when he wasn't there. Just because he was now retired, she saw no reason to change her routine.

On the other hand, Dad's reliable old Land Rover was in the same position it'd been in since he'd retired from the force. He hadn't left the house for months, and it was getting just a little too weird now. An uneasy feeling crept up my spine and I remembered having read some survey once that said as soon as workaholic police officers retired, they tended to keel over and go to that big police station in the sky. Okay, maybe not *exactly* the day after, but it was pretty clear that the ones who were obsessed with work started to unravel as soon as they went back to a normal civilian life.

I let myself in with the key I'd had since I was a kid and dumped my rucksack on the floor, wandering into the living room.

"Dad?"

Once an energetic, confident man, Dad now spent his days slumped in his favorite armchair. He stared out at the neglected garden with blank eyes, a barely touched cup of tea held loosely in his hand. He looked disheveled and old, and he wore tatty slippers on his feet. I drew closer and grimaced at the sight of the stained cardigan he was wearing. God, what were those stains? Fried egg, I thought. At least, I hoped it was fried egg.

"DAD!" I repeated loudly as I unwrapped his hand from around the mug.

He turned toward me, as if noticing my arrival for the first time.

"Where's Mum?"

"Walking the dog," he said.

"What, in the car?"

He gave a helpless shrug.

"Right, first you're going to eat something, and then we're going to have a little chat." I waltzed into the kitchen, dropped off the mug, and grabbed a couple of plates. Back in the living room, I handed him a panini. "Here."

"I'm not hungry, love."

"Sorry, not taking no for an answer." I glared at him until he started nibbling around the edges, and soon he was devouring the sandwich.

"You need to get a hobby, Dad," I told him when we finished eating. "You can't just sit around the house all day moping. I know it's tough, giving up the job. No one knows that better than me, and I didn't even give it up voluntarily. But if I can get over it, then you can, too."

"And what sort of hobby am I going to do? I don't know anything else except policing."

I racked my brains, trying to think. "What about origami?"

"Boring."

"Tiddlywinks? They have tiddlywinks in the Olympics now."

He yawned.

"Cookery?" I said.

"Have you tasted my cooking?"

Hmm, probably not a good idea. Dad's cooking was so bad, he had even managed to burn the toaster somehow. No, not the toast—the actual toaster. My parents had been through about twenty toasters in my lifetime. "How about trainspotting? That's a bit safer."

"That would just remind me of the job."

"How would trainspotting remind you of the police?"

"When I was about thirteen, I used to go trainspotting with my old friend, Jeremy. I have such fond memories of us noting down all the train numbers. We would bet each other on whether the trains would be on time or not, wagering cookies, candies, and the like. Unfortunately, Jeremy had suicidal tendencies, and decided to impale himself on the front of the three-thirty to Paddington. Anyway, that was what made me want to join up, and why trainspotting reminds me of the job." He let out a heavy sigh.

I blinked. "Okay, well, what about…" I paused, looking around the room for inspiration. Flower arranging? No, too girly. Crocheting? No, too grannified. "Aha! What about this?" I grabbed a neighborhood watch leaflet. The group was advertising for volunteers. I waved it in front of his face.

He snatched it from my hand to prevent having his eye poked out with it.

"That's just what you need."

He read the leaflet slowly, a spark igniting in his sleepy eyes. "Yes!" He leaped out of the chair. "I can teach them proper surveillance techniques instead of the usual old twaddle they try and do. We used to make fun out of them down at the station, but beggars can't be choosers, eh?"

"See, there you go. You just need something to keep you active."

"Yes, I can see it now. This is going to be the best neighborhood watch program in…"

"The neighborhood?" I volunteered.

"Yes! Why don't we celebrate? I've got a nice bottle of bubbly in the fridge."

I kissed him on the cheek. "I'd love to, Dad, but I've got work to do."

"Right. Well, I'd better sort out my surveillance kit, then." He rushed off upstairs.

I let myself out to the sound of Dad banging around in the cupboards with excitement.

* * *

I parked my car outside Paul Clark's house, where I had a good view into his 1920s semi-detached house, and studied the photo in his file. Unless you looked closely, it was hard to tell the difference between Clark and the Honey Monster. The only distinguishing feature I could see was that his bushy beard and mop of hair wasn't quite as yellow as the Honey Monster's. He was huge—well over six feet tall—with bug eyes and a wide, gaping mouth. Apparently, he had five children—five, ouch!—and he'd worked at a warehouse for ten years before his accident. He had fallen off the forklift while unloading a pallet of baked beans, which caused damage to his lumbar vertebrae. A doctor's report said he wasn't able to work again, but for some reason, Brad had doubts. Was Clark telling the truth or not? That was what I was here to find out. I sat back in my seat and waited.

After an hour, and with no sign of life in the house, I decided to speak to the neighbors. Grabbing a clipboard and a cap with *British Gas* written on it, I made my way up to the other half of the semi and knocked on the door.

A young woman answered, a cigarette hung precariously between her lips. She was carrying a screaming baby on her hip.

"Aaaagh!" the baby wailed, loud enough to crack my eardrum.

"Shut up!" the woman snapped at the baby. "Bloody kids."

"Hi, I'm from British Gas." I smiled, even though the overwhelming smell of baby poop forced my throat to constrict. I eyed the full-to-bursting nappy on the baby's bottom. This was going to put me off peanut butter for life. "I'm looking for your neighbor, Paul Clark. Do you know where he is?"

She snorted. "What's he done this time? He's always up to something. Sneaky little buggers, those Clarks. Five kids they've got, and they can't look after any of them. If you ask me, his wife's a few pork pies short of a picnic, if you know what I mean." As she wiggled her lips, a lump of ash fell off the end of her cigarette and landed on her stained top.

"There's just a small problem with his gas bill payments, probably because he's not working at the moment. I just need to verify a few things with him."

"He is working. I've seen him going off to work every day."

"Oh, really? Do you know where?" I asked.

"Of course. He works at that big Asda supermarket in town. You'll find him stocking shelves somewhere."

"Great, thanks, you've been a big help." I nodded at her and hurried back to the car, where the air was clear of deadly toxins.

* * *

This was going to be a piece of cake. I would just sneak around, posing as an inconspicuous shopper, and snap a few pictures of Clark stacking shelves. Why had I been so worried about this job? It was ridiculously easy.

I heaved through the horde of shoppers, scanning the crowd for signs of any shelf-stocking activity. There was nothing going on in the fruit and veggie aisle, so I picked up a bag of bananas and wandered off in search of Clark. The bakery section was quiet and boring, except for the yummy smell of freshly baked bread. Ditto for the condiments aisle, the dairy aisle, and the cereal aisle. Maybe there was a special time of day when all the shelf stockers were let out in a frenzy, and I'd missed it.

I stood in front of the toiletries with the idea that if I stood there long enough, Clark would come to me. I could wait until closing time if need be, no problem.

As it turned out, I lasted about ten minutes. I was reading the directions on a box of teeth-whitening strips when I heard a rustling sound coming from my bag of bananas. Out of the corner of my eye, I saw the bananas begin to move.

Wait a sec, bananas don't move.

I stared at the bag as my hands shook. Nope, the bananas weren't moving at all. It was the ginormous tarantula inside the bag that was moving, tapping on the plastic with its hairy foot. I froze, hardly daring to breathe.

Omigod! Spider!

In my mental world, I was screaming my head off, but in the real world, I think my mouth was just wide open with no sound coming out.

I threw the bag on the floor and rocketed out to the parking lot faster than the speed of light—probably warp factor ten at least.

I did some deep breathing as I jumped in the car and locked the doors, just to be on the safe side. There was no way, absolutely no sodding way, that I was going back in there while that spider was on the loose. Paul Clark and Brad would just have to wait.

* * *

I sped all the way home, cursing my life, my new job, and humongous, ugly spiders that shouldn't even be let in the country. As soon as I pulled up outside my apartment, the heavens opened, sending cascades of water down the back of my T-shirt as I dashed into the building. I cursed that, too, running up the stairs to my apartment, which the estate agent had described as "cozy"—which really translated into "poky rabbit hutch."

The smell of fried garlic chicken greeted me as soon as I shoved the door open. That could only mean two things. One, Marmalade Fox, my ginger cat, was cooking his own dinner tonight, or two, Romeo Lopez, my boyfriend, was whipping up one of his culinary creations in the kitchen. I was hoping it was the latter.

As well as being an amazing cook, Romeo had other sterling attributes, as well. He had hazel eyes, cinnamon skin, and thick black hair, all courtesy of his Spanish father. He looked sexy as hell in just about anything, he knew which buttons to press on the washing machine, and he was pretty good at pushing my buttons, too. Additionally, he was one of the best cops I had ever worked with. All things considered, this put him firmly in the minority—people who are beautiful on the inside and the outside.

I kicked off my shoes, one of them nearly knocking over a giant terracotta plant pot by the front door that I'd never found a home for, and flung my rucksack down next to them. Dripping rainwater on the wooden floorboards, I walked the few steps from the hall to the lounge and ignored the wilted yucca plant on the way, promising myself I'd water it later.

Romeo stood in the galley-style kitchen, naked except for an apron. As I watched with appreciation, he poured two glasses of red wine and turned to me. "How was your first day?"

My temperature shot up a few degrees. "All the better for finding a naked chef in my kitchen." I smiled, took the glass, and stood on tiptoes to plant a kiss on his lips.

He grinned, nuzzling into my neck. "I aim to please."

"You wouldn't be doing this to persuade me to move in with you by any chance, would you?"

"Don't know what you mean, but now that you mention it…have you thought any more about my proposal?"

I flushed and glanced down at the floor, gnawing on my bottom lip.

"Well?" Romeo prompted me.

I gulped down my wine. "Wow! Look at that rain." I pointed out of the window behind him.

"Amber, you're avoiding this conversation."

"I am not!" I tried my best shocked voice. "I've never seen rain like it. It's so…droplettyish."

Romeo's steady gaze drilled into me. He raised an eyebrow. "Is that even a word?"

I feigned a sudden interest in my fingernails.

"You can't avoid it forever, darling."

"You practically live here anyway, when you're not working on special operations. Why do we need to make it so...official?"

"I like official." Romeo turned the nuzzling into feathery, light kisses that were designed to make me cave in. Just when it was starting to get interesting, my mobile rang. I groaned, slipping out of Romeo's grasp to answer.

"Foxy, why haven't you put those bugs in yet?" Brad's Australian twang sounded over the phone.

"What are you talking about? I did put them in," I replied, taking a swig of wine and holding my glass out for more.

"Did you activate them? I'm trying to listen to them, but I'm not getting any audio at all."

"Of course I did."

"Well, they're not working. You'll have to go back tomorrow and put some more in."

"Crapety crap!" I said, eyeing up Romeo's full moon as he tossed the salad.

"Let me know when they're in—oh, and Foxy...I need it done bright and early."

"Yes, boss." I hung up and frowned.

"Problem?" Romeo asked.

I didn't want to get onto the subject of Brad, so I deflected the conversation sharpish. "Nope, nothing to worry about. Hey, have you tidied up in here?" I glanced around the room. My haphazard magazine stack had been arranged in a neat pile on the coffee table. The fluffy cushions on my black leather sofa had been perfectly plumped. My DVDs had been re-stacked in my reclaimed wooden rack—in alphabetical order, no less—and my photos all stood to attention, marching in a perfect, ninety-degree-angled row across the bookshelf. "You'll make someone an excellent wife."

"Well, it's no use leaving the cleaning up to you. It would never get done. I even tidied up your toolbox." He nodded toward the small case that now closed perfectly, instead of having miscellaneous handles and

FASHION, LIES, AND MURDER

tools poking out willy-nilly. "So, how was your day really?" Romeo gathered me back into his arms.

"Somewhere in between rubbish and very rubbish." Where did I begin? My boss had come on to me on my first day, I had a suspicious-looking mochaccino stain on my passenger seat, I'd just bugged the offices of one of the most famous fashion designers in the world, and a tarantula had tried to eat me. And that didn't even include the toilet arrangements. God, my life was so doomed.

"That good, huh?" he asked, his voice full of sympathy.

"Insurance investigation is about as interesting as an anorak convention."

"Want me to make it better?"

"Only if you insist." I giggled.

Romeo's mouth widened into a lazy smile. "Hmm, let's start with your clothes, then. You're wet." With expert precision, he slipped my T-shirt over my head.

"No kidding."

CHAPTER THREE

The following morning I was ripped from my slumber by Romeo licking my foot. I could think of worse ways to wake up, but I'd never really been into toe licking in a big way.

"Get off!" I groaned, moving my foot out of reach and sinking back into la-la land.

A few minutes later he did it again. I sat up and saw Marmalade eyeing me with a naughty expression. Romeo was nowhere to be seen.

"You are gross," I said. Marmalade, who seemed quite pleased with that pronouncement, let out an ecstatic purr.

Getting up, I picked up my ginger furball, carried him into the kitchen, and poured some very stinky kitty biscuits in his bowl. I heaped a teaspoon of coffee into a mug and then added another for luck. I had a weird feeling that today was going to be a very long day.

After soaking in the shower for ten minutes, I dried my hair and went a bit overboard with some brown eyeliner and mascara. Even though my life seemed to be a bit crappy these days, it didn't mean I had to look it, right?

* * *

On my way back to the Fandango building, I realized that I was near Callum Bates's house, so I took a detour, hoping to cross him off my list of files.

When I pulled up at the address, I shook my head. You couldn't mistake his house if you tried. It was the only one on the dreary-looking street whose front garden looked like a car breaker's yard. At least the other residents had tried to spruce up their gardens with the odd gnome and hanging basket. I dodged past the dissected car parts and empty vehicle shells that sat abandoned on the drive, arriving at Callum's lime-green front door with only one drop of oil on my shoe. I thought that was pretty good going, all things considered, as I reached up and banged on the door a couple of times. A few slivers of peeling paint dropped off onto my shoes. I pulled a disgusted face and wiped them off.

After waiting a few minutes and not getting an answer, I peered through one of the windows, but I couldn't see anything other than some threadbare, yucky-looking brown curtains. I glanced around the outside of the house. There was a garage attached to the side, with doors painted the same lime color. Luckily, the garage doors had windows in the top section, which would hopefully make it easy for a quick peek inside. I'd just stepped over an old steering wheel when I heard someone calling out.

"Yoo-hoo," a voice said.

I looked around and spotted an elderly woman next door, standing on her front step. She beckoned me forward with the stack of mail she held in her hand.

"Are you looking for Callum?" Granny whispered.

"Yes, I'm from his insurance company. I need to ask him a few questions about the van he reported stolen." I smiled at her.

She looked up and down the street, scanning for any curtain twitchers, although something led me to believe that Granny here was probably the only curtain twitcher on the street. "Come in." She led the way into her house.

The unmistakable smell of ganja nearly blew my nose off as soon as I entered the front door. I coughed, looking around and taking in the sight of cannabis plants as far as the eye could see. Ashtrays sat on every surface, overflowing with joint butts. It looked like she was running a dope factory and smoking the proceeds at the same time.

Ignoring the illegal plants, I turned to face her. "So, did you see anything?" I asked.

"Yes, I did."

I waited, expecting her to elaborate, but she stayed silent.

"Callum reported that his van was stolen three nights ago, when it was parked outside his house. Did you see anyone take it?" I prompted her, wanting to get answers before I ended up hallucinating on the fumes.

"First of all, I saw Callum outside with a man."

"Okay, and what happened with this man?"

"They talked for a while, and then the man got in Callum's van and drove it away." She winked at me. "Fancy a smoke? It's good for arthritis." She waved a gnarled hand in front of my face. "It's legal for medicinal purposes, you know."

"Er…no thanks. My arthritis is tickety-boo this week. You're sure this was three nights ago?"

"Oh, yes. In fact, I wrote it down. Hang on a sec, love." She rummaged around in a stack of papers on the kitchen table. "Yes, here it is." She read from her notes. "Callum was talking to a good-looking man in his thirties. Actually, he was very good looking. A bit of a dish, really. My, if I was five years younger, I wouldn't kick him out of bed. Do you know, I haven't had a fella since nineteen-ninety—"

"The van?" I cut in before I got to hear a complete rendition of her life story.

"Oh, yes. The dish and Callum had a conversation—looked quite cozy, too—then they shook hands, and the man drove off in Callum's van."

"So, what color was the man who had this conversation with Callum?"

"Purple."

"Purple?" I raised an eyebrow. One word flitted through my mind: whacko!

"Yes," she responded.

I didn't really know what to say to that, but I thought I'd keep her talking just in case. Sometimes the most valuable witnesses are the ones you least expect. "Okay. Was he light purple, dark purple, lilac?"

She tilted her head and pondered my question for a few seconds. "Light purple, almost violet. That's good, you know. A violet aura is pretty good."

"Hang on a minute, let me get this right. The man that drove off in the van had a purple aura?"

She nodded. "I see auras. You're dark green. That's not good. It means danger. You should be careful."

Granny's brain cells must've taken quite a beating over the years, probably from the pot. I suspected she also saw little green men and pink fairies. Maybe a few flying pigs as well.

"Well, I have to be going now." I hastened toward the door. "Thanks for...the information."

I breathed a sigh of relief when I got back outside and made my way back to Callum's garage. Standing on my tiptoes, I gazed through the murky windows, looking for anything that would give me a clue. Finding his van inside would be a big one. Unfortunately, it was too dark to see a thing. So much for wishful thinking.

Maybe I could get inside and have a little look-see. I glanced up and down the street. No one was about. I tried the door handle, and it turned, but the door only popped open an inch. I pushed on the panel, but it wouldn't budge. Well, I certainly wasn't about to be beaten by a stupid garage door. I glanced around again, making sure the curtain-twitching brigade wasn't about, and heaved the door forward with my shoulder. It groaned and suddenly gave way, my torso crashing through the door with momentum.

Big mistake! The door slammed into a tall metal shelf that sat behind it, and a tin of lime-green paint toppled off, splattering its gooey contents straight onto my head.

No, that didn't just happen, I chided myself. I stood there for a moment, stunned, with my hair and shoulders dripping lime green rivulets of paint. "Bloody bugger fuck," I shrieked as it dawned on me that no, I hadn't imagined it, and yes, it had actually happened.

I touched my hair. Saturated. Clothes? T-shirt now looked like a hippie lime-green tie-dye explosion. Fan-bloody-tastic. And after all that, the van wasn't even in there.

I winced, dripping a bright green trail all the way down the drive to my car. The only spot of good news was that I happened to have an old blanket in the boot. Wrapping it around my head and shoulders, I drove home, wondering what the hell I was going to do if the paint didn't wash out of my hair.

* * *

I stood in the shower for the second time that day, washing my hair for the tenth time, trying to work up enough enthusiasm to go back to work. I found that I quite liked the idea of staying in the shower all day, but then the hot water ran out, and it didn't seem as appealing.

Toweling off, I surveyed the damage in the mirror that hung over the sink. Wow. That was a lucky escape. I was almost back to my normal chestnut locks. And I was probably the only one who would notice that my hair had a slightly green, crusty appearance.

Who was I kidding? Everyone would notice. I flopped onto the bed and stared at the ceiling.

"Why can't something good happen?" I asked Marmalade, then did a mental head slap. Of course he couldn't answer an open question. I'd have to put it in simpler terms. "Is my life destined to be boring from now on? Meow once for yes and twice for no."

Marmalade, somewhat confused by the instructions, just yawned.

"You're no help." I closed my eyes and sighed.

I stared at the clock an hour later in disbelief. An hour! Where had all the time gone? Trying to make up for the lost time spent procrastinating, I got dressed and raced to my car. I had just slid behind the wheel when my mobile rang.

"Hey, Foxy, have you put those bugs in yet?" Brad asked.

"I'm just on my way. You won't believe what happened..." It was then I noticed that someone had broken into my car. "I'll call you back." I disconnected and stared at the glove compartment, which hung open like a gaping mouth. It had been ransacked, and the contents flung to the footwell. I picked up the pens, maps, mini voice recorder, a chocolate Easter bunny that had melted and now looked like it had one giant eye—not sure how I'd overlooked eating *that*—and a moldy packet of chewing gum. The only thing that seemed to be missing was my heavy-duty flashlight. I flung everything back in the glove compartment, slamming it shut.

Could today get any worse?

"Speak," Brad said when I called him back.

"Why can't you answer the phone like a normal person?" I snapped, dropping my head back against the seat.

"What's going on, Foxy?"

"Not only have I been attacked by a tin of paint today, but my car's been broken into as well." I sighed, fighting the urge to scream my head off. Good job I'd had two teaspoons of coffee. Otherwise I'd be doing an extremely good impression of a wailing banshee right about now.

"Is there much damage?"

"No. Looks like a professional job. No sign of forced entry, but the strange thing is they didn't take the CD player. The only thing missing is my flashlight." I rested my elbow on the window and rubbed at the tension worming its way into my forehead. All right, so it wasn't the best thing to happen to me in a while, but at least they hadn't taken the whole car. And they'd left the Cyclops bunny, which was quite considerate.

"Okay, well, get your ass over to Fandango's, then. I'm hearing some rumors from my informant that he's gone missing. And that's the last thing I need."

"Missing? Missing how?" I asked, surprised.

"As in I've heard that Fandango is nowhere to be found, and there was blood all over his office this morning."

Yep, that would definitely constitute missing. "On my way."

* * *

The rear parking lot at the Fandango building was eerily quiet as I pulled up. Crime-scene tape, which had been placed across the front doors, flapped loose in the wind. I wandered up to the building and looked through the windows. An empty, dark reception area glared back at me. I didn't have a clue what had happened, but I knew how to find out.

"Hey, darling," Romeo answered his mobile on the second ring, his husky voice sending a chill across my skin. "How is the interesting world of insurance?"

"It may be about to get more interesting. What do you know about Umberto Fandango?"

"The mega-rich fashion designer?"

"That's the one. Apparently, he may have gone missing. I'm at his place now. The building looks empty, and there's crime-scene tape everywhere."

"Let me see what I can find out."

"Thanks—oh, and if the police found any bugs in there, they're Brad's."

He paused for a while. "How come you don't know what happened if Brad was listening to him?"

"Well, the bugs didn't work. It wasn't my fault, honestly. He must've given me some duds to plant."

He chuckled. "So, if I do this, what are you going to do for me in return?"

I smiled to myself. "How about I order some take-out when you get home, and we have a repeat performance of last night?" I flushed, thinking about our sex-a-thon session. "As long as you don't snore like a hippo again afterwards. I swear I'm going to put duct tape over your mouth when you're asleep."

"As long as I can put duct tape over your mouth when you're awake." He chuckled at my gasp of indignation. "Sorry, but I can't make it tonight."

I hesitated. "Is this because I won't move in with you?"

"No, I've just been assigned to a special operation, and I'm going to be out of communication for a while."

"Oh." I pouted, knowing I sounded like a spoiled brat but not caring. I really liked the sex-a-thon idea.

"Are you jealous?" He couldn't keep the amusement out of his voice.

"Me? No way!" I said, doing a damned good impression of not sounding utterly pissed off.

"You are so bad at lying."

"That's not true. Sometimes I can tell really good lies," I said.

"Like when?"

"Like the time you bought me that really horrible hookerish top."

There was silence for a while. "You said that top was nice."

"It is. If you're a hooker."

"I see. What about the terracotta plant pot I bought for your birthday, which you've just left by the front door for months, untouched? I distinctly remember you saying that was nice."

"No, I like that. I just don't know what to do with it."

"I don't know whether to believe you now," he said. It was his turn to try and not sound pissed off.

"Sorry, but I've got to go. We'll talk later," I said, not really wanting to get into a lying contest with him over the phone.

"This conversation isn't over yet. What about—"

"Great. Bye!"

I hung up and dialed Brad.

"Speak," Brad said.

"Once upon a time there was a princess, and she lived in a faraway land called Woogahumphta, with free clothes and shoes and chocolate that had no calories in it—"

"What are you on, Foxy?"

"Stop answering the phone like that, then." I pulled a face at him down the phone. "Do you want the good news or the bad news?"

He let out an impatient sigh. "What's the bad news?"

"Fandango isn't here."

"What's the good news?"

"There's lots of crime-scene tape everywhere."

"And why is that good news?"

"I guess it isn't," I said. "I just didn't want to say there was only bad news."

Brad sighed, and I could imagine him running his hand through his hair in frustration. "What was Fandango like when you saw him yesterday?"

"Short, hairy, wearing a smoking jacket, can you believe that? I didn't think they—"

"Did he seem nervous or worried about anything?" he broke in.

"Why?"

"There's one other thing that I didn't tell you before. Fandango may be connected to the mob. I'm trying to get some more information from my informant, but he's gone missing, too."

My jaw dropped. "The *mob* mob? Or another unrelated, totally nice kind of mob?"

"Right the first time."

I just had to think it yesterday, didn't I? What else could go wrong, indeed?

CHAPTER FOUR

Bad news always gives me an appetite. I had a huge box of fried chicken and fries spread over Brad's desk. Not quite a family-size bucket, but close. I sat opposite him, stuffing fries in my mouth and reading through the file he'd handed me when I sat down. It was another case he wanted me to look into.

"Have you done something different to your hair?" Brad asked as he peered at my head.

"No!" My hand shot up to my hair, smoothing down a wayward strand.

Brad raised an eyebrow, but shrugged, moving on. "What happened with Bates and Clark?" he asked as he picked up the greasy chicken box with the tip of his finger and plonked it down on my side of the desk.

"Just a slight hiccup. Nothing to worry about. I'm more interested in this." I stared at the information in the file. "The Cohen brothers are up to their old tricks, then, are they?"

Brad stretched his toned legs out in front of him and laced his hands behind his head. He leaned back in his chair while he answered. "I've heard there may be an accidentally-on-purpose case of arson on the warehouse they've got insured with us. I need you to find out what they're up to."

I pulled apart a steaming hot chicken breast and caught Brad staring at me. "Want some?" I held the box out to him.

"I never thought you'd be offering me a piece of your breast again, Foxy." He grinned.

Luckily, I was saved from answering by Romeo calling me back.

"Okay, here's what I've found out so far. Fandango is officially missing. His assistant says she was hit over the head and can't remember a thing. She's not going to be released from the hospital until sometime tonight. The detectives assigned to the case found blood at the scene and a couple of bullets on the floor in his office. It looks like his entire season's fashion collection is missing, too," Romeo said.

"Thanks. Anything else?"

"Yeah, don't go poking around at the scene until tomorrow. SOCO are backed up with jobs and can't examine the place for evidence until later on."

"As if I would," I said, mentally crossing it off my to-do list for the day.

"You need to be careful, because it gets worse. Fandango has apparently got some kind of connection to the mafia. I knew this was a bad idea, you working for Brad." He paused for a beat, and when he spoke again there was an undercurrent in his voice. I couldn't tell if it was jealousy or concern. "Don't you think it's a bit strange that he offered you this job? How did he even know you needed one when you haven't had any contact with him for years?"

I let out a nervous laugh. "I don't know," I said, although that wasn't strictly true. If Brad wanted to know something, he would always find a way to get the information. I cut my eyes to Brad, who watched me with interest.

Romeo hesitated. "You haven't had any contact with him for years, right?"

I moved to the corner of the room. "Of course not," I whispered into the phone. "Anyway, it's not like anything is going to happen, is it? It's all water under the bridge. I'm with you now."

"It's not you I'm worried about," he growled.

Remembering the scene in the unisex bathroom, I tried to camouflage my own concern as confidence. "There's no need to worry."

He sighed. "Okay. I still don't like it, though. Why don't you get Brad to do some checking about this mafia thing? He can do a different kind of investigation than I can."

"You mean like secret, illegal, Special Forces stuff that sounds much more interesting than your special operation?" I know, I know, it was a bit below the belt, but I couldn't help it. His lack of confidence in me had hurt.

Romeo didn't answer for a minute. "You know exactly what I mean. And be careful. People who get close to Brad have a tendency to end up dead. Look what happened to his business partner who owned half of Hi-Tec."

I snorted. "You mean Mike Cross? That wasn't anything to do with Brad."

"Cross disappeared under suspicious circumstances, only to turn up later in the River Lee under very dead circumstances."

"You didn't even work that case. It was my case. And the prime suspect, David Leonard, was an officer who'd served in the SAS with Brad and Mike in Afghanistan or Iraq, or some other hot, sweaty country in need of their help. Leonard developed some kind of mental disorder shortly after returning from armed combat and began killing members of his old unit."

"Yes, but Leonard was later also found in the River Lee with a single bullet to the head, execution style. And I don't need to point out that Brad is a trained killer who can cover his tracks pretty well."

I glanced at Brad. Oh, yes, he was dangerous all right. And not just for the bad guys.

"Just look after yourself, is all I'm saying," Romeo said, his voice suddenly distracted. A woman's voice sounded in the background. "I've got to go now."

"Hey, is that Janice Skipper I hear?" I yelled into the phone. "Shit!" I said when I realized I was talking to the dial tone.

"Well, well, well. Romeo is on special ops with Detective Chief Inspector Skipper." Brad folded his arms across his chest, his face watchful. A blind man could have heard the smile in his voice.

I picked up a packet of sticky notes off his desk and threw them at him, hard. He ducked as they sailed through the air toward his head, but I've got a pretty good aim. They hit the top of his head and bounced off onto the floor. I grinned and stalked out. I would've thrown the chicken, but I was still hungry.

* * *

With Fandango's building out of bounds until tomorrow, and his Ice Queen assistant tied up at the hospital, I turned my attention to the new case Brad had handed me that morning.

Lonnie and Lennie Cohen were in the import-export business. They liked to import goods into their possession without the rightful owner's consent and export them at a great profit to themselves. Mostly they dealt in high-quality, stolen-to-order vehicles, but pretty much anything was fair game to the Cohens. As the odd couple of the crime world, Lonnie was tall and skinny, and could easily double as a beanstalk. Lennie looked like he'd stopped growing at age twelve. Both of them had been hit by an ugly stick.

I drove down the Ware-to-Hertford road, trying to ignore the shriekingly purple Jeep that seemed to be following me. While it wasn't exactly strange for a car to be behind me on a main road, what was strange was that the woman driving it had slid in behind me as soon as I'd left the car park at Hi-Tec. She had stayed on my backside while I drove around the town center five times, which I did just to make sure it was a tail. I didn't know who she was, but it seemed safe to say that following someone in a car that stood out like the Purple People Eater was not the kind of thing a professional would do.

I pulled into an industrial park that housed about twenty large warehouses and some smaller storage units. As my eyes scanned the area for the Cohens' unit, I drove an entire loop of the site.

So did the Jeep.

I couldn't exactly do a recon with Miss Conspicuous behind me, so I slammed my brakes on, threw open the car door, and strode toward the Jeep.

She quickly crunched the gearstick into first and sped out of the park.

I hurried back to my car, jotted down her plate number, and drove around to a residential area that sat behind the industrial park. Luckily for me, the Cohens' warehouse sat at the very edge of the park. I parked and cut through an alleyway at the back of the houses, where I could observe the warehouse from the safety of a secluded wooded area.

It didn't take long to push my way through the oak and silver birch trees, and I made myself comfortable as I sat on top of a slope that overlooked the building. It was pretty average as far as warehouses go— a large loading bay at the side, a front door with a small window next to it, and windows on the top floor, which were probably offices.

I hoped I'd only have to sit there for a little while. Maybe I'd get lucky and a couple of thugs wearing Arsonists-R-Us T-shirts, carrying petrol bombs and flamethrowers, would appear, and that would be it. Case closed.

No such luck. Bummer.

Three-quarters of an hour later, the only exciting thing to happen was my ass falling asleep. I stretched and shuffled around a bit, and came to attention when I saw a gold Mercedes SLK Kompressor approach the warehouse. It drove up to the loading bay and the door opened. I scribbled down the plate number and tried to snap a couple of pictures, but my camera battery was dead.

"Crapping hell!" I watched the car disappear into the building, and the door rolled down again.

The same thing happened with a black BMW X5 and a silver Aston Martin DB9.

I suspected that the vehicles had already been cloned, and the registration numbers would come back to a legitimate car of the same type. In a few days, the chassis numbers would be ground down and replaced with seemingly legal ones, and the vehicles would be exported out of the country.

I had a dilemma. On the one hand, the people in the building were more than likely committing a crime. On the other, this wasn't my kind of problem anymore. I was only being paid to look for the possible arsonist. I could always pass on the info to Romeo and get him to check it out.

Satisfied with that plan, I decided to come back the next day with a camera that worked.

* * *

With the Cohen brothers taken care of for the day, Callum Bates was next on my list. I parked in front of his house and ran to his front door, banging on it loudly.

A glassy, bloodshot eyeball peered out at me as the door opened a sliver. Callum's young criminal life had obviously taken its toll. He had a nose that had been punched a few times, leaving it at a crooked angle. His hair was thin and greasy, his skin was spot-ridden, and his pallor was so gray, he looked half dead.

"Oh, it's the pigs again. I've already reported my stolen van to you lot and got a crime number." He tried to shut the door again. "So, not today thank you, Miss Piggy."

"I take it you don't want the insurance payout on the van, then," I said, trotting back down the path. "Fine by me."

The door flew open and Callum stuck his head out. "What do you mean? What's the insurance got to do with you coppers?"

I gave him a smug smile. "I'm not a copper anymore. I work for your insurance company, and I'm the one who gets to decide if your claim is legitimate or not. Anyone who calls me Miss Piggy instantly gets their claim denied."

Bates pulled the door open farther, leaning his short, scrawny body against the doorframe. His jeans hung frighteningly low over his skinny hips. I hoped they fought gravity for just a little longer. I didn't want to be around when they fell down.

"Is this a trick? I bet you're still a Miss Piggy copper, aren't you?" A blob of engine oil dripped off his crusty sweatshirt and plopped onto the doorstep.

"Nice top," I said.

"What are you now, the Fashion Police?" He smirked and tugged at a hair growing out of his ear. "Anyway, who says I get my insurance claim denied?"

"It's in the rules."

"What rules?"

"The insurance claim anti-abuse rules, number three. See ya." I gave him a wave and pulled my car door open.

"Hang on a minute," he yelled down the path.

"Yes? Do you have something to say?" I cupped a hand to my ear.

He mumbled something inaudible.

"Sorry, couldn't hear that."

"SOR-RY!" he screamed.

I grinned. "That sounded a tad insincere, Callum. Why don't you try again?"

His shifty eyes darted up and down the street. Eventually, he said, "I'm really, really, really sorry. Satisfied?"

I shut the door and retraced my steps over the obstacle course of car parts that lined his front path. "Now that wasn't so hard, was it? So what's all this about your van? Do you seriously expect me to believe that Mr. Gone-in-Sixty-Seconds has had his own van stolen?"

He bit a grimy fingernail. "It's true!"

"What, like the time I arrested you on Christmas Day for driving a stolen car, and you said Santa Claus must've delivered it to your house by mistake?"

"Yeah, Santa Claus is always making those kinds of mistakes. It happens every year."

I glared at him.

"But it's really true this time," he added quickly.

"Okay. Then how about you tell me about the other guy."

He stopped gnawing on his nail. "What guy?"

"The one you were talking to outside your house the night the van was allegedly stolen. The guy you shook hands with, who then drove off in your van."

"Have you been talking to that crazy old bat next door?"

I folded my arms and waited for an answer.

"I don't know what you're talking about. The van was stolen, and unless you can prove otherwise, I'm going to get my insurance money," he sneered at me, revealing teeth that looked like they hadn't seen a toothbrush in very long time.

"Okay, if it was really stolen, then you won't mind taking a lie detector test, will you?" I smiled and watched him squirm.

"They don't have them things here. They only have them in American films." His voice cracked slightly.

"Oh, yes, they do," I fibbed.

"Don't."

"Do."

"Don't," he insisted.

I rolled my eyes and yawned. "Boring!"

Suddenly his gaze sharpened. He peered at me closely. "Have you got paint in your hair?"

I touched my head. God, I thought it had completely faded by now. "Don't be ridiculous! Anyway, call me when you want to do the test." And I disappeared quicker than Doctor Who's Tardis.

* * *

I beamed up at the Hi-Tec office half an hour later.

"Yo-yo," I said to Hacker as I strolled in.

He glanced up. "It's only one yo."

I shrugged. "I'm saving time. I can say hello and goodbye together." I plugged my camera battery into a socket to charge, then picked up another camera from Brad's office and dumped it into my rucksack. Pulling my notebook out, I sat on the edge of Hacker's desk. "Can you check out these license plate numbers for me, please?"

"Your wish is my command," he said as I perched there, looking over his shoulder as he typed in the information.

I called Romeo while we waited for the results but he didn't answer, so I left a message asking him to call me back and hung up. The results finally popped up and Hacker pointed at the screen. The three cars from the Cohens' warehouse came back to legitimate numbers. No surprise there. The Purple People Eater Jeep belonged to a Celia James. I wracked my brain trying to remember whether I'd ever come across that name before. Nope, nothing doing.

"Who's Celia James?" Hacker asked.

"I don't know. But Fandango's disappeared, my car's been broken into, and Celia James has been following me. Methinks all this cannot be a coincidence."

CHAPTER FIVE

The next morning I woke up bright and early, raring to go. Now that I had something to sink my teeth into, I could feel the old familiar buzz of adrenaline surging through my veins. Amber Fox, Miss Hot-Shit Investigator, was well and truly on her way back!

I stood outside Fandango's offices, checking out the view as I waited for the business to open. There were two houses in the vicinity of the old flourmill that could have had a view of what happened. I needed to talk to the owners, but first I wanted to speak to Fandango's assistant, and I was betting that if it was London Fashion Week soon, they'd still have an immense amount of work to be getting on with, even though their boss was missing.

I didn't have to wait long. At eight thirty, she pulled up beside me in her spanking-new Beemer. I waited until she had poked her skinny legs out the car door before I got out of my own vehicle. She rolled her eyes when she saw me.

"Morning." I beamed at her.

"Hunh," she snorted, with an expression that clearly suggested I'd personally ruined her morning. Obviously the whack on her head hadn't improved her manners.

"I didn't catch your name the other day," I said, falling into step along side her.

A blank expression stared back at me.

"Your name?" I prompted.

"What's it got to do with you?" she asked, scowling.

I whistled. "Wow, that's a long name."

She muttered something under her breath.

"Well, since I'm investigating the disappearance of Umberto Fandango, I'd say it had quite a lot to do with me."

"Heather Brown," she finally snapped, frosty vibes rolling off her tongue in my direction. No, frosty was too warm a word. More like glacial.

"I need to have a look around, and to ask you a few questions."

She didn't bother to respond as she unlocked the offices and flipped on the lights. I hurried along behind her as she clacked her way toward the office she shared with Fandango, her Jimmy Choos sending out an unhappy snap with every step.

I studied her as she took a deep breath at the sight of the bullet hole in the doorframe, the dried smears of blood on the floor, and the residue of fingerprint powder that covered most of the surfaces in the office. She stepped over the bloodstains and placed her briefcase on her desk, glaring at me with defiant eyes. Ms. Ice Queen Brown didn't seem all that upset about the fact that her boss was missing and possibly dead. Then again, she didn't seem the type to let anything upset her.

"How's your head?" I asked, studying the angle of the bullet hole and taking in the rest of the scene.

"It's still there."

"Well, that's a bonus. Are you sure you're up to working?"

"I'm only staying for a few hours to sort out some things that can't wait." She shot me a dismissive look.

"So, what happened yesterday?"

She sighed and lit a cigarette. Tilting her head back, she exposed her scrawny neck and took a slow drag. Seeing I wasn't just going to move on, she blew a line of blue-gray smoke in my direction and answered. "I don't know. Someone hit me over the head. I got knocked out and I can't remember." She curled her lips in a nasty half-smile and leaned skinny forearms on her desk.

"How unfortunate," I said in a tone that implied I didn't believe her in the slightest, and as I waited for her to continue, she flipped open her laptop and stared at the screen.

"Did you see or hear anything before you were knocked out?" I sat down in front of her, starting to understand why someone would hit her over the head. Much more of this and I would be taking a swing at her myself.

"No." This time she didn't even bother to look at me when she answered. She rested her cigarette in an ashtray on her desk and typed away, avoiding my steady gaze.

"What's the last thing you do remember?"

"I was here, at my desk. When I woke up again, I was lying on the floor, there," she said in a flat monotone as she pointed to the space between the back of her desk and the wall.

"What time was that?"

"About seven p.m."

"Who else was in the building at that time?"

"It was just me and Umberto."

"Was the place locked up and alarmed while you were in here?"

"I don't know. I can't remember. The door alarms were probably on."

"And the entire fashion collection has been stolen from this building?"

"Looks like it." She shrugged.

"Any idea how they got in if the alarm was set?"

Her head swiveled around and she narrowed her blue eyes at me in a piercing gaze. "No idea. So maybe the alarm wasn't on after all."

I sighed, meeting her stare head on, while I thought. What I really needed was a good, nosy look at their computers. If anything suspicious had been going on, I was betting on the fact that there was a trail. There usually was. I reviewed my choices. I could ask Heather if I could take a look, but I thought she'd give me a big, fat no, and I didn't want to tip her off. The other choice was that I could come back after she'd gone.

"Can you think of anything else that might be helpful?" I asked.

"No."

I stood up. "Well, you take it easy, then."

I wandered around the runway area and checked the dressing rooms that were next door to it before I headed to the upstairs storage area. I wanted to check for myself that the fashion collection was gone. Sure enough, the only thing left in the space was a lonely rhinestone lying on the floor. I slipped it inside a clear plastic bag and put it in my rucksack. By the time I came back down to the main floor, the receptionist had appeared. She sat at her desk, sobbing into a damp tissue.

"It's terrible," she sniffed when she saw me. As she wiped her eyes, I sent her a sympathetic smile.

"The disappearance? I know. It's awful. Were you here when it happened?"

The question brought on a fresh burst of waterworks. "No." She pulled a fresh tissue from her bag and blew her nose hard. "I finish at six. It happened after I left. Gosh, I feel dreadful about this." She glanced at the bloody drips on the floor with a shudder. They trailed from Heather's office all the way past the reception area and out the doors. "Do you think he's been k-k-killed?"

"I hope not." I gave her shoulder a sympathetic rub and leaned in closer as she continued.

"Umberto was such a wonderful person. A true gentleman, you know? He wasn't one of those rich people where fame and money goes to their heads, and they forget about the little people. And he was such a good boss, too," she added hastily, but not before I had noted the adoration in her voice.

I wondered if she might be in love with him. And if so, were the feelings reciprocated? Because if they weren't, could this simply be a case of unrequited love? Could this young woman who sat crying in front of me have been so obsessed with Umberto Fandango that she didn't want anyone else to have him, and would see him dead before that happened? No. I dismissed the idea as soon as it popped into my head. This seemed far too elaborate a plan for a crime of passion.

Seeing that she had calmed down, I decided to try another tack. "What's his assistant like?" I asked, my voice dropping down to a whisper.

She looked me squarely in the eye. "She's a bitch."

Yes, that just about summed up my impression as well. I chatted with the receptionist for a few more minutes, but she didn't reveal anything useful.

As I left, I thought about what I knew so far. Fandango must've been injured and dragged out through the front doors. At the same time, the entire fashion collection must've been bundled into a large enough vehicle waiting in the parking lot. This had happened around seven p.m., so it would be dark by then, but possibly early enough still for someone to have heard the shots fired. There were streetlights outside the building, so it would've been light enough to see the vehicle leaving.

SIBEL HODGE

The occupants of the house that sat to the right side of the old flourmill hadn't seen a thing, so I tried the other large, detached house opposite Fandango's. As I rapped on the door, a black woman who looked to be in her mid-sixties answered.

"Hi, I'm Amber Fox, and I'm investigating the theft and possible kidnapping that took place last night at the old flourmill."

"I've already spoken to the police and told them everything. I was the one that reported it," she said, starting to close the door.

I held my hand out to stop her. "Actually, I'm from Mr. Fandango's insurance company, and we have to investigate any possible claim. Can you tell me what you saw?"

"I'd just finished dinner and I heard a loud bang. BANG!" she yelled, making me jump. "Like that."

"And then what happened?"

"I thought it was a car backfiring or something, but when I looked out the window, I saw a white van speeding away from the warehouse."

I turned around and looked from her front door across the street. She had a bird's-eye view of the parking area. "Did you get the registration number?"

"No, but I know exactly who was driving." She gave me a knowing smile and waited.

"Who?" I asked.

"Barack Obama."

My first thought was that I didn't know whether to laugh my head off or drag her down to the funny farm. "You're telling me that Barack Obama was driving the van? Don't you think he's a bit too busy for a little trip to Hertfordshire? I'm sure he's got lots of other presidential things to be getting on with."

If looks could kill, I'd have been a goner.

"I know perfectly well what I saw, and it was Obama. I've been waiting for a man like that to come to power ever since Martin Luther King got himself shot. He's a savior—and he's really cute, too."

"Did you notice anything else about him?"

She paused and screwed her eyes up in thought. "When he drove up the road, he threw a cigarette out the window, which I thought was a bit strange. I didn't think Obama smoked. I thought he was a bit of a health freak."

40

And then I got it. There's a big difference between what people think they see and what they really do see.

I thanked her and headed back to the car to phone Brad.

"Speak," he said.

"Have you ever wondered how construction cranes are erected? Does another crane have to put up the first crane? And if so, how did they make that crane? And so on and so on. It could go on forever, and—"

"Stop talking rubbish, Foxy," Brad said.

"Well, stop answering the phone like that, then!"

"What have you found out?"

"I've solved the crime already. Apparently, Barack Obama was driving the getaway vehicle. Can we contact the CIA and get them to pay a visit to the White House?"

A silent pause. And then: "Are you kidding me?"

"The driver wore an Obama mask, which seems a bit strange. I wouldn't have thought that the mob would be into wearing masks. Aren't they more into suits and trilby hats?" I asked. "Unless the modern mafia are members of the Democratic appreciation society, of course."

"Anything's possible these days. Did you get anything out of his assistant?"

"She's developed amnesia. I'm guessing it's selective."

* * *

I had a couple of hours to kill before I returned to Fandango's to try and check out the computers, so I decided to head over to Paul Clark's house. I called Romeo again on the way. It rang, and the tone echoed through my hands-free earpiece while I replayed our last conversation in my head. I'd distinctly heard the voice of my archenemy, Detective Chief Inspector Janice Skipper, in the background, and I had the nearly irresistible urge to go over to the police station and punch her lights out. I admit it sounds a touch drama-queenish, but I had something she wanted—Romeo—and somehow she just couldn't get over it. She'd been trying to get her pointy little claws into him for as long as I could remember. Just because we were together didn't mean she respected that or stopped trying, and there was absolutely nothing I could do to stop it.

As voicemail kicked in, I snapped the phone shut and said the F word in quite a few variations. By then I was in Clark's neighborhood, and I did a drive-by of his house, hoping to catch a quickie picture of him doing acrobatics in the front garden, but there was no sign of life. I headed over and did a quick once-over in Asda, with no success there, either. Eventually, I doubled back and drove toward the Cohens' warehouse. Maybe the other fish were biting today.

* * *

Wouldn't you know it? I'd been sitting in the same position as yesterday, overlooking the warehouse, ready and waiting with my finger poised over the snapshot button for an hour, and not a single hot vehicle had driven in. I was in the middle of deciding whether to call it a day when I heard a rustling sound coming from the woods behind me, and lots of "ahs" and "damns" in a high-pitched American accent.

I twisted around and saw Miss Conspicuous weaving her way toward me through the trees, trying to avoid the low-hanging branches.

It was too late to dive behind the nearest oak tree as she'd already seen me, so I leaped to my feet and hurried toward her before she could come any farther and completely blow my cover. In her glaring red top, pink leggings, and a furry bag, which could only be described as squashed squirrel color, she stood out in the woods like an eyesore. Hell, she would stand out anywhere like an eyesore. I bet her earrings alone cost more than my whole year's salary. If I had to sum her up in two words, I would use "serial shopper."

I grabbed her arm and yanked her back toward the housing estate.

"Hey!" she yelled in a voice loud enough to wake up the dead. "Get your hands off me, you crazy woman."

I ignored her and frogmarched her back toward the Purple People Eater, which was parked behind my car.

"What do you think you're doing?" I gave her my best nasty-eyed death glare as I sized her up. She was a fragile-looking thing, with blonde ringlets and not a hair out of place, despite her trek through the woods. She had a heart-shaped face, and her lips glossed in a shiny pink. I guessed she was in her early twenties. Her innocent-looking eyes, carefully enhanced with eyeliner and mascara, blinked back at me.

I stood there, hands on hips, pushing out my C cups as I waited for an answer. "Who are you and why are you following me?"

"I'm trying to find my dad."

"And who is your dad?"

"Umberto Fandango," she said, and then her face just seemed to melt. Her nose wrinkled up, her lower lip trembled, and she burst into noisy tears. She launched herself into my arms, her own going around my neck. Clinging on like a limpet, she blubbed all over my T-shirt.

As I awkwardly patted her on the back, I groaned. "Oh, God."

CHAPTER SIX

Ten tissues and a red nose later, we sat in Starbucks, eating lunch—well, I was eating. She hadn't touched hers.

"I thought if I followed you, maybe I could find out what happened to him," Tia Fandango said in between heartbroken sniffs.

"I didn't even know he had a daughter. There's never been any mention of you in the papers, and you're not listed in our files."

"Dad's a very private person. He likes to keep his life out of the limelight."

I peered at her over my mug of cappuccino. "You don't look like him."

"I must take after my mother's side." She looked up at me through damp eyelashes. "Do you think he's…dead?"

I reached out and rested my hand on her arm. "I don't know, but I'm going to find out, I promise you." Okay, so I wasn't a police officer anymore, but this was my case now, and I was determined to get to the bottom of it. I was going to seize every clue, however small, however insignificant it appeared, and pounce on it, keeping it in my grasp until I could put the whole picture together. Until I knew the truth.

I told her what I knew so far, which, as you can imagine, went down like a stripper at a vicar's tea party, and produced another round of blubbing.

She excused herself and fled to the toilets. When she returned, she had a determined glint in her eye. "I want to help you. I could work with you. I'm psychic, you know, and I think I can help you find out what happened. And if we work together, we've got a double chance of finding him."

I shook my head and pushed away my plate with the half-eaten sausage baguette. "That's a definite no-no."

"Please." Her eyes implored me.

I looked her up and down. "Look, Tia, I don't want to be rude, but you stand out like a psychedelic flamingo. You can help by telling me what you know. Who is Celia James?"

A surprised look registered on her face. "She's just a friend who loaned me her car. I've been studying at university in the States for a long time, so I don't have one of my own."

"Why not borrow one of your dad's? According to our file, he's got a couple of vehicles insured with us."

"I went to his house, but I couldn't find the keys."

"You said 'his house.' Does that mean you live somewhere else when you're not studying in the States?"

"Yes. Dad bought an apartment, which is in the company name, and I stay there when I'm in the UK." She scribbled on a napkin. "That's the address."

I took the napkin and looked at the address, and then pulled the Fandango file out of my bag to check it against the information I had. It was a match. Fandango had insured that apartment along with his home and business addresses. "If you're psychic, what's going to happen to me tomorrow?"

She shrugged. "I don't know."

"Okay, what are the winning lottery numbers?"

Tia shot me a slightly aggrieved look. "It doesn't work like that."

"So how does it work?"

"I just get flashes of things—feelings and stuff. I think Dad's being held in an Italian restaurant somewhere."

I had just taken a swig of coffee, and I nearly spurted it out at her words. "What?"

"I'm getting some kind of connection with pasta," she said.

"Pasta?" I raised a skeptical eyebrow.

She shrugged again. "I know, it sounds completely kooky, but that's what I'm getting."

"Even if you're right, that's got to narrow it down to about a gazillion restaurants in the world."

Her eyes welled up again and I sighed.

I slid a stack of napkins toward her. "Let's start somewhere else. Do you know if he had any enemies?"

She wiped her eyes and shook her head. "Not that I know of."

"How about any business problems or arguments with any of his staff?"

"I don't think so."

I thought for a moment and then plowed ahead. Why not? I had to ask it. "Was he involved in anything…illegal?"

A guarded look came over her face. "What do you mean?"

"Well, anything to do with the mob, for example?"

She gasped. "Are you talking about the mafia?" She began shredding the napkins.

"Yes." I sank back in the chair, observing her carefully.

She blinked at me, astonished. "No! Dad would never do anything like that."

"Is there a Mrs. Fandango?"

"No. Why?"

"Well, if anything has happened to him, I'm just trying to establish who stands to inherit his vast fortune."

She dabbed at her eyes with a tiny morsel of shredded tissue. "That would be me."

"Do you know where he kept his will?"

"Probably in the office safe, at his house."

"Do you know the name of his lawyer?"

She sniffled. "No…oh, wait a minute. I think the name sounded a bit like a cake." She pursed her lips together and stared into space for a moment. "No, sorry. I can't remember." She patted her eyes and looked down at the shredded remains of her paper napkin like she couldn't remember doing it.

"Well, can you think of anything else that might help?"

She thought long and hard, finally giving me a firm shake of her head.

I paid the bill and ducked out of Starbucks while Tia rearranged her makeup in the restroom, just in case she decided to follow me. Either she really didn't know anything and was genuinely upset, or she was a good actress. I hadn't made up my mind yet. For all I knew, she might not even be Fandango's daughter. I'd know more after I made a few phone calls.

* * *

It was late afternoon when I arrived back at the old flourmill. The car park was empty, and the building looked unoccupied. From my tour with Fandango, I knew all the security codes for the keypad entry system, so after checking to make sure the coast was clear, I let myself in.

My first stop was Fandango's office. I sat at his desk, switched on his computer, and had started rifling through the papers on the desk when I heard a door slam somewhere outside. I froze for a second in disbelief when I heard the familiar clack of heels on the floor outside the office. No doubt, they were coming my way. My heart flip-flopped around in my chest as I looked for somewhere to hide. The desk was made of glass, so, unless I could make myself invisible, hiding underneath it would be a dead giveaway.

Crappy-doo-dah! I was going to get busted. I frantically scanned the room, hoping for a big black hole to suddenly open up and swallow me. Two seconds later, it still hadn't, and I heard the beeps of the keypad lock on the other side of the door.

I launched myself behind the silver sofa as the door clicked and swung open. I could hear my breath rushing in and out and, as the heel wearer came into the office, I caught a whiff of the now familiar, otherwise unusual perfume. It was the same stuff I'd smelled earlier in the day.

Shooting up from behind the couch, I came face to face with Tia.

"Aagh!" she screeched, rearing back in surprise.

Three thoughts ignited in my brain. One, she was here to batter me to death with the furry rodent bag. Two, she was trying to cover her tracks by getting rid of evidence, or three, she was doing the same as me—trying to find the missing fashion designer.

"What the hell are you doing here?" I hissed.

"Looking for a clue," she hissed back.

"I thought I told you not to follow me!"

She looked like she was about to cry any second. I felt bad for even suspecting her of wanting to do me harm. I threw my hands up in the air in a hopeless gesture. "Well, seeing as you're here, you can stand guard." I sat back down at Fandango's desk and tapped away on the keyboard, looking on his computer for anything that said *clue* in big, bold letters.

"I can help you look." She picked something up off the desk. "What about this?"

I glanced over at what she held in her hand. "It's a paperweight, and that is exactly the reason you can't help me look. Just out of interest, what were you studying in the States?"

"Neurosurgery."

"You're kidding." Whoa, scary!

She did a snorty little giggle that sounded like a hyena with a blocked nose. "Yes, of course I'm kidding."

I breathed a mental sigh of relief for all the poor brains in the world. "Shh!" I pressed my forefinger against my lips.

"Sorry. I was studying fashion, of course," she whispered.

I screwed up my eyes and frowned at the computer screen. "Damn, all his files have been wiped. There's nothing on here." I turned it off and rummaged around in his desk. The only thing I could find was a file tucked right at the back that contained some papers that looked a lot like financial spreadsheets. I stuffed it in my rucksack and moved on to Heather's desk.

Her laptop was nowhere to be seen. I went through the desk from top to bottom, and the only thing I found that was of any interest was a piece of paper taped to the bottom of her top drawer. It had the words *CB £5 million* scribbled on it. "Does this mean anything to you?" I showed it to Tia.

"No."

I pocketed the note, and we checked out the other offices, but there was nothing out of the ordinary, so we called it a day.

"You gave me your number, Tia. I'll let you know if I find anything. Promise me you won't follow me anymore," I said as we got in our vehicles.

"Okay." She gave me an unconvincing smile, and I just knew I'd be seeing more of her before I was ready to.

CHAPTER SEVEN

I put my foot down on the way home, dying for food. I was so hungry that I started fantasizing about garlic bread with cheese, roasted chicken, jacket potatoes smothered in butter, boiled broccoli and cabbage—*ew*! Where did the broccoli and cabbage come from? I stopped thinking about food when I reached that point and started thinking about the note I'd found.

What could the letters *CB* mean? Someone's initials? Possibly, but that would only narrow it down to a gazillion people of the population. A password for something? Too short. The name of a boat? Unlikely. A company? Maybe. I figured I would come up with something once I got some food in me. I always thought better on a full stomach.

As soon as I flung open my apartment door, my appetite vanished.

The living room that Romeo had only just tidied was a complete wreck. Magazines were piled in a messy heap on the floor, the cushions had been ripped from their covers and scattered around the living room, and the contents of my toolbox had been emptied onto the dining table. Added to that, my yucca was now yellow and dead looking. I didn't know if it had died of fright, or because I'd still forgotten to water it.

My guts churned around on a spin cycle as I marched into my bedroom. My shoes looked like they'd been flung around the room by a desperate bargain hunter at a jumble sale. The dresser drawers hung open, all the contents chucked onto the bed. I seriously hoped whoever had broken in hadn't been rifling through my knicker drawer as well. Oh no. God, please not the kicker drawer. I nearly passed out with embarrassment as I had visions of sweaty, wart-covered thugs pawing through my lacy thongs and cutie knickers with their chubby little fingers—sniffing them, even. I felt lightheaded and weak at the very thought.

I sank down onto the bed, not knowing whether to scream or burst into tears. I was heading toward the tears when I suddenly remembered Marmalade.

I jumped to my feet. Where was he? Had he been catnapped? I'd almost given up hope when I discovered him snuggled up in the bathroom under a pile of towels, which had been dumped on the floor. I gave Marmalade a big cuddle and then succumbed to the tears.

"Who was it?" I asked Marmalade, burrowing my chin into his fur.

Marmalade purred, but didn't give me any useful information to go on, so I called Romeo.

I paced the five steps up and down the living room, gave an almighty sniff, and blinked back more tears as I listened to the phone ringing incessantly on the other end of the line. "Pick up, pick up!"

He didn't.

Where the hell was he, and why wasn't he returning my calls? I snapped the phone shut and threw it on the floor. An instant later, I picked it up and called Brad.

"Don't you dare say 'Speak,'" I announced in a voice slightly louder than I had anticipated, which I followed up with a coughing sniffle.

"Foxy, what's up? Are you okay?"

"No, I'm not okay, Brad. Someone's broken into my apartment." I increased my pacing tempo to a neurotic level.

"Have you checked to see whether they're still there?"

"They've gone." I gnawed on my thumbnail as my eyes flitted around the room like a mad woman's, not lighting on any one thing for more than a split second.

"Are you going to call the police?" Brad asked, the concern in his voice going a long way to make me feel better.

"No. I don't think anything's been stolen. It's just a mess. It looks like they were searching for something."

He paused for a moment before he asked the obvious. "What were they looking for?"

"I don't know." I racked my brain. "First my car, and now my apartment. It's got to have something to do with the Fandango case."

"Look, I don't want you staying there on your own in case they come back. Get over to my house. You can stay in my guest room." There was silence on both ends of the line as we both thought about his offer.

"Okay. But don't get any funny ideas," I warned him.

He laughed. "Foxy, the day I don't get any funny ideas, I'll be dead."

* * *

Brad's barn conversion was one hundred percent male. The downstairs living space was a large, open great room, which featured a stunning beamed ceiling and tall windows. This was a minimalist interior with a capital M. There were no personal knick-knacks at all, and there was very little furniture, which would have turned the empty expanse into a cozy living space. It was spotless, but somehow I couldn't imagine Brad dressed in a frilly apron with a can of furniture polish in one had and a duster in the other. The only furniture was a black leather sofa and matching armchair, and a humungous flat-screen TV on one wall. This area led into the kitchen, which was where we sat, side by side, at Brad's black granite breakfast bar, eating Chinese takeaway and sipping red wine. Actually, my sipping had turned into gulping after the first glass, and it had already gone to my head, but I didn't care. That's what stress did to you, right?

"You still haven't got any stuff in this place. Why not?" I glanced around the kitchen and into the living area as Marmalade wound around my feet, begging for scraps. "It's cold—sterile, almost."

"I've got stuff. I've got a stove, a sofa, a—"

"I mean *stuff* stuff. Things that prove someone actually lives here, and it's not just a show house. Why haven't you got any photos or personal stuff, or any clutter? That's so not normal." I swirled my wine around thoughtfully.

Brad shrugged and sat back, scratching Marmalade's head as he watched me. "I don't need it. 'Stuff' just complicates things."

"I like stuff. Stuff is good. Why haven't you got any pictures of that Australian guy?"

"What Australian guy?"

"The one who adopted you from the orphanage."

"He wasn't Australian. He was Aborigine."

"Okay, Aborigine. If he took you on walkabout when you were a kid and taught you all you know about survival techniques, he must have been a big part of your life, so why haven't you got any pictures of him?"

"People aren't defined by their possessions."

I gave him a wry smile. "Oh yeah? What are they defined by, then?

"Their actions."

I probably couldn't argue with that point, so I gave up. In between mouthfuls of prawn chow mein and barbequed spare ribs, I told Brad about Tia, the note, and the files I'd found at Fandango's.

"Why isn't Tia mentioned as a beneficiary on Fandango's insurance policy?" I said. "It just states the beneficiary as 'any legal heir.'"

"When Fandango took out the policy, we were having a lot of trouble with the receptionist who was doing the administrative duties. I can only assume that it must've been an administrative error on our part that was never followed up." He twirled his noodles expertly around his chopsticks and took a bite. "So, what's Tia like? Do you think she's got anything to do with this?"

"I'm not sure yet. My instinct tells me no, but I don't know enough yet to be sure." I put down my spoon and fork and attempted to copy Brad with the chopsticks, which really wasn't going to happen after so much wine.

"Well, the files can wait until tomorrow. You've had a shock. Why don't you just relax tonight?" Brad suggested as he gazed at me over the rim of his wine glass, practically oozing pheromones.

I carried on trying to scrape up the noodles, but every time I got the chopsticks close to my mouth, they slipped off and back onto the plate. I gave up, picking up my fork again instead. "Who are you and what have you done with Mr. Workaholic Tyrant Boss Brad?"

His mouth moved in something that could've passed for a grin. Then again, it could've been a mouth twitch, too.

"The note in Heather's desk said *CB £5 million*. Five million pounds is a lot of money. Maybe CB, whoever he is, paid Fandango to disappear for some reason, or paid Heather the Ice Queen to develop a case of amnesia so he could run off with Fandango's fashion collection." I drained my glass and poured another. "And what's the mob's involvement in this? I doubt if there's much call for fencing a stolen fashion collection in the mafia business these days, unless it includes rhinestone-encrusted concrete boots."

Brad rested his elbows on the breakfast bar, his muscled shoulders straining against the perfectly tailored shirt. "So what have you got that they want?" He gave me a slow, lingering look up and down. "Apart from the obvious."

"Hey! No funny business." I gave him a playful slap on the arm. "I've got no idea what they could be after. Maybe it will all become miraculously clear when I go through the spreadsheets I found."

"Where's Romeo tonight?" A glint of amusement danced in his eyes. "Why didn't he stay with you?"

"I haven't been able to get hold of him for days. I wanted to tell him what was going on at the Cohens' warehouse, too, but he hasn't rung me back."

"Well, that's your call. Exporting a bunch of stolen cars isn't my concern, unless I've insured them. I'm only concerned about a possible arson payout on the warehouse." He reached over and twirled a stray wave of my hair around his fingers. "So, where is he, then—since he isn't with you when you need him?"

I gulped as my pulse disco-danced around in my body. This was not good. Pulling my hair free, I shot off my chair, picked up the plates, and deposited them in the dishwasher. When I finished, I leaned against it, staying well out of finger-twirling range.

"Maybe he's tied up, doing this secret operation with Janice Skipper," Brad said.

My spine turned to a block of ice at the mention of her name. I threw a dishcloth at him, which hit him on the head and then slid to the floor.

He threw his head back and laughed. "Just think, if you hadn't shot her in the ass, you wouldn't have been thrown off the force, and maybe you'd be working with Romeo tonight instead of her. Not that I'm complaining, of course. It means you're here with me instead."

"It was an accident—kind of—and anyway, I didn't get thrown off the force. I resigned."

"I thought it was more a case of resign or get fired." He stood up and strolled toward me. "And how do you kind of accidentally shoot your boss?"

I avoided his gaze and took a bigger swig of wine. "It was her fault. She shouldn't have pissed me off."

Brad leaned his weight against me, pinning me in between the dishwasher and his hard thighs.

On second thought, maybe that wasn't his thighs.

"What will you do to me if I piss you off?" He cupped my chin in his hand and locked his gaze on mine.

Uh-oh! Hot flash coming up. My skin tingled and I worried that it might actually be on fire. Why did he have to be so heart-stoppingly gorgeous?

Then he brushed his lips against mine, and the next thing I knew, we ended up in a full-blown, pretty damned sexy kiss, with lots of tongue action. It was dangerously sexy, in fact. He plunged his hands into my hair, and I could feel his heart beating against mine. I felt as though I was drinking him in—his heart seemed to be beating inside of mine, not outside. Everything else in the room seemed to vanish. It was just me and Brad, the kiss and one heartbeat.

My brain screamed a warning at me, but the rest of me turned squidgy. I decided to go with the warning and pushed him away. "You did piss me off, Brad. Don't you remember when you disappeared for three months without a word?" I moved to the other side of the breakfast bar in order to get some distance between us.

"I was doing a job for Special Forces, you knew that." He frowned and looked genuinely hurt. Either that or he was doing a good impression of hurt.

"I didn't know that until you came back. I thought you were dead, for God's sake." I folded my arms and gave him my best cool, detached look. "Anyway, it's ancient history. I'm with Romeo now."

He rubbed the bridge of his nose and looked down at the floor with an expression that I couldn't quite work out. "I know, Foxy. Believe me, I know."

"I'm going to bed," I told him before the conversation ended up heading somewhere I didn't want it to. "In the spare room," I added hastily, climbing up the open wooden staircase to the room next to Brad's, with Marmalade hurrying along behind me.

I quickly got ready for bed and crawled in between the Egyptian cotton sheets, but I couldn't sleep. I touched my lips. I could still feel Brad's mouth pressed against them. A warm glow pulsed in my cheeks, not to mention other parts. I felt shaky with yearning. What would happen if he did something freaky in the middle of the night? Oh no!

Even worse, what if I enjoyed it? Would that mean I didn't love Romeo? Or was it really possible to be in love with two people at the same time?

The rest of the night, I tossed and turned. My brain felt overloaded, and I didn't sleep except for fits and starts. Giving up, I rolled over for what felt like the hundredth time and glanced at my watch with a groan. Five a.m.

This is pathetic, Amber, you're a grown woman. Stop being so ridiculous. Nothing is going to happen.

Even so, Marmalade and I slipped out of the house at that point, heading back to my apartment to have a cold shower and tidy-up before I lost all power to reason.

CHAPTER EIGHT

I sat at my coffee-table desk in the Hi-Tec offices, the financial spreadsheets from Fandango's office scattered out in front of me. I sipped on a super-strength, caffeine-laden coffee, trying to make sense of what I was seeing in front of me. On first glance, the documents looked like legitimate records for sales of Fandango's fashion collection. The sales had been made to respectable, legal companies, but six months ago a new client popped up, referred to only as EF.

"What do you make of these?" I handed them to Hacker.

He studied them for a while, and then closed his eyes and did some deep breathing. He stretched his arms out in front of him and cracked his knuckles.

"What are you doing?"

"I'm centering my chakra. You have to let it flow. It gives you better concentration." After a moment or two, he turned back to his computer, and his fingers whizzed across the keyboard.

I tried the deep breathing and knuckle thing, but it didn't do much except give me a hand ache.

"Mmm," he said as he brought up one program after another, scrolling down and studying them with intense eyes.

"What's that?" I eyed his screen.

"This is Fandango's bank account."

"You can get into his bank accounts? Cool."

"This is just one of them. There may be more. I'll keep checking, but look at this." He pointed to the screen.

For the past six months, a company called Longshore Holdings had been making payments into Fandango's account. There were hundreds of them, each for ten thousand pounds, and they matched up with the payments filed under EF on the spreadsheets.

"Smurfing," I said, nodding and smiling. It all made sense now.

"Huh?" Hacker looked over his shoulder at me like I was mad.

"It's a kind of money-laundering scheme. If transactions go over a certain amount, there's a statutory limit that requires banks to report the transactions. It's basically a way of monitoring international financial transactions for the purpose of investigating money laundering," I said. "Anything over that limit gets reported to the government. Guess what the limit is?"

"Ten thousand pounds?" he asked with a smile.

"You got it in one." I grinned. "The bad guys keep the payments to ten thousand pounds instead of making larger payments, and they can get away without setting off alarms, and therefore an investigation."

Hacker stared at the screen, stroking his goatee. I half expected him to break into an excited rap.

"So, Fandango is into money laundering?" he mused.

I shook my head. "I don't know yet. It's possible that someone in Fandango's organization is using him as a blind. Longshore Holdings probably are money laundering, but who are they?"

"I don't know. But give me some time, and I'll find out."

"Can you try and find out who this EF is, and look to see if you can find out what CB means?"

"No problem. I'll let you know when I come up with something."

As he bent back over his keyboard, Brad silently crept up behind us like a stealth bomber. "Hi."

I jumped and bit my lip, feeling hot and flustered as I remembered what happened in the kitchen last night.

"Yo," Hacker said, engrossed in his work. Brad answered him back and then turned to me.

"What have you found out?" he asked.

"Smurfs," I said.

"What?" Brad looked at me like I'd just been let out of a mental home for the day.

"You know—little blue creatures who live in Smurfsville and wear white trousers and itsy-bitsy white caps. Some of them have funny little—"

"Foxy, have you lost it completely?"

I fought the urge to whack him over the head and filled him in.

"So, Longshore Holdings is laundering money by paying Fandango for a fashion collection?" Brad asked.

"That's certainly how it looks, but if you really think about it, something about the whole situation just feels off. Because if that was the case, why steal the collection and kidnap Fandango?"

Brad frowned, looking as puzzled as I felt. "Did you find anything on the computers in his office?"

I pulled a face. "They've been wiped."

"Mostly people just think they've wiped off the files, but usually the information is still stored on the hard drive somewhere. If there's anything on it, I can find it," Hacker said. "I'll go back with you later, and we can check."

"Okay, it's a date," I told him, impressed. I turned to Brad. "Have you got any night-vision goggles?"

"No, I'm fresh out of them this week. Why?" Brad asked.

"I need to check out the Cohens' warehouse at night, and it would be easier to see things with some goggles." Then I had a sudden flash of genius. "It's okay, though. I know someone who might have a pair."

* * *

I had three choices, none of which were particularly appealing. I could go back and hassle Callum Bates about his far-fetched insurance claim, I could stake out the Cohens' warehouse, or I could try and find Paul Clark. I didn't fancy another run-in with a tin of paint, and I figured that nothing much would be going down at the warehouse during the day, so I decided to go with Clark. That way I could pick up something to eat as well, and kill two birds with one stone.

My goal set, I entered Asda from the end opposite the produce section, figuring it was better to be safe than sorry. I grabbed a basket and stuffed it with custard donuts, cinnamon donuts, and chocolate donuts. I was of the firm opinion that a girl could never have enough donut. I had just approached the large deli counter when I saw Clark. He was straight ahead of me at the opposite end of the store. I had a clear line of sight as he worked stocking shelves. As I watched, he moved, twisting sideways to the big pallet of canned corned beef that sat next to him, and back again to load the cans on the shelves. If he had a bad back, then I was a chocolate teapot.

I grinned to myself, rummaging around in my rucksack for the camera. It was about time.

One minute, I was standing there, camera in one hand, basket in the other, inching my way toward Clark with the element of surprise and a guaranteed slam dunk in my sights. The next thing I knew, a boy of about twelve ran around the corner of the aisle and bumped into me. The collision sent me flying headfirst into a cardboard display stand that was crammed to the brim with condoms.

Aagh! Condom explosion. Packets shot everywhere.

I gasped as the *Are you having safe sex?* banner sailed through the air, landing face up on the floor next to my head with a loud slap. As I lay there, sprawled among the condoms, I closed my eyes and desperately hoped it was all some kind of bizarre mind-trick. I was really fast asleep, tucked in bed, just having a very peculiar dream, wasn't I?

"Are you okay?" a voice said over the mutterings of nearby shoppers.

I pried one eye open, gazing up at Paul Clark, who was looming over me with his huge bug eyes.

Shit. Not a dream.

I breathed out a heavy sigh. So much for the element of surprise. I could hardly catch him out now, could I?

"I think so," I mumbled.

"Here, let me help you up." He held out his arm for me to grab on to as I maneuvered myself up, much to the entertainment of an audience of shoppers and store workers alike. They started clapping when I got to my feet.

A hot glow of embarrassment crawled up my neck.

"Er…thanks." I stood up, wobbling slightly, and pushed away the hair that was now matted to my sweaty face.

"Do you need any more help?" Clark asked.

"Donuts," I said, and headed, somewhat dazed, through the crowd of people, straight to where my basket now lay, in serious need of a sugary donut rush.

* * *

Well, Amber, that went just brilliantly, didn't it? How hard could it be to take a bloody photo, for God's sake?

I sat in my car, cramming donut in my mouth until I felt better. It took four, which was pretty high on the sugar scale. I wiped the crumbs off my top, cranked the engine, and motored toward my parents' house. It was definitely time for some unconditional parental love.

I spotted the white Ford Explorer SUV in my rearview mirror as soon as I left the parking lot. This time the tail was more covert, sitting a few cars behind me as I drove around the industrial area, the town, the hospital car park, and then headed toward the A10. It stayed with me all the way, growing bolder the farther I drove. Now it was right behind me. Two mean-looking guys sat in the front, glaring out. One was bald, and the other had bushy black hair.

After driving up the A10 to Ware and back again, I turned off at the Hertford exit, drove around the roundabout six times just to piss them off, and headed down the hill with them sitting on my bumper. I swung a nifty right into the police station parking lot and watched as they sailed past me and carried on down the road.

I parked and stared at the large building, wondering if Romeo and all my ex-colleagues were inside cracking drugs rings and investigating murders instead of traipsing around, being attacked by paint tins, condom displays, and large arachnids. I fought the urge to go inside and look for Romeo, but stayed put since I didn't particularly fancy a run-in with Janice Skipper. I was buzzing on sugar, and there was no telling what I might do.

I sat tight a little while longer, making sure the ugly goons had well and truly gone before I edged out of the parking lot, keeping an eye out for the SUV the entire drive to my parents' house.

* * *

Dad opened the door wearing a baggy, flowery blouse over black leggings, his head topped with a long, blonde curly wig. I had to do a double take to make sure he wasn't Mum, until I noticed what I hoped was a gun stuffed down the front of the leggings.

"Amber! What do you think of the outfit?" He did a twirl.

My jaw hung open. It didn't quite hit the floor, but it was close. How strange. All my life people had commented on the fact that I looked so much like Dad. I had his small ski-slope nose, his huge cow eyes, and the same color uncontrollable hair. Not now, though. Now, Dad looked a lot like Mum.

"Impressed?" he asked, hopeful.

"That would depend on what you're trying to achieve," I said slowly, following him into the living room.

"Surveillance disguise." He sat down, crossed his legs, and squashed his gun between his thighs with a grunt. "The neighborhood watch group is lapping it up. They didn't have a clue what they were doing before I got involved. And now there won't be a crime within a five-mile radius of my patch. I can guarantee it."

I heard the front door open, and Mum's dulcet tones echoed down the hall. "Amber! Are you here?"

"Yes," I shouted.

"How are you, hon?" She came in and gave me a hug, then moved to stand next to Dad. The resemblance between them now was uncanny, apart from Dad's bowed legs.

Sabre, Dad's giant German Shepherd, an ex-police dog with slightly schizoid tendencies, bounded into the room and jumped up on me, knocking me to the floor.

"Get off!" I tried pushing him away to avoid being licked to oblivion, but he didn't feel like moving. After what felt like an eternity, he finally gave up with the licking and just lay on me instead.

"Sabre, come," Dad said.

Sabre growled, gave Dad a filthy look, and decided a little more licking was called for.

"Sabre!" Dad repeated in a stern voice. "Bloody dog. No wonder he was a police reject." Dad fumbled in his pocket, pulled out a dog biscuit, and threw it across the floor.

Sabre's eyes lit up, and he made a weird whining grunt before he jumped up and bounded off in search of the biscuit. When he finished, he made his way over to Dad, where he eyed Dad's foot like it was an industrial-size packet of doggy treats.

"What do you think of his outfit?" Mum asked as she cocked her head in Dad's direction. "Don't you think he needs to accessorize more?"

"Er," was all I could manage as I rolled onto my side and sat up. This place was a nuthouse. No wonder I had issues.

"Hang on, I'll show you." Before I could stop her, Mum dashed out of the room.

"How's the job going?" Dad asked.

"Actually, that's why I'm here. Have you got any night-vision goggles I can borrow?"

"I've probably got a pair somewhere. Let me have a look." He moved across the room and opened a huge chest. I watched as he pulled out a Kevlar bullet-proof vest, a couple of old-style straight police batons, a side-handled baton, a few pairs of handcuffs, and a large flashlight. He rummaged around at the bottom. "Here we are." He pulled out a pair of night-vision goggles and handed them to me. "Why don't you take the flashlight, too?"

I took both. "That would be great. Mine's been stolen."

"Who by?"

"I don't know."

He held my gaze for a minute, sensing my uneasiness. "So, how is it really going?"

I looked away. "Okay, I suppose. Today I was followed by a couple of thugs, so I guess that means I'm getting to close to something."

"Don't give up, Amber. You'll be great at this job." He paused for a moment. "I'll just put some new batteries in the flashlight for you." He took it upstairs, giving me a moment to think about his words, then returned a few minutes later and handed the now-working light to me.

"Thanks." I smiled.

"Now, what do you think of this?" Mum came back in, carrying dangly clip-on earrings and a chiffon scarf. She held them up next to Dad and turned to me with a huge smile. "See, that's much better, isn't it?"

CHAPTER NINE

"What's new in the world of hacking?" I asked as I breezed into the office.

"Not much. I'm still looking into Fandango's bank accounts," Hacker replied.

I dragged a chair over to his desk and sat next to him. "Are you ready to go to his office and look at the hard drives?"

"I am." Tia suddenly appeared behind us.

"I thought I told you not to follow me," I said to her as I turned, astonished.

"I'm not, silly." She did the snotty hyena laugh again. "If I was following you, I'd be behind you."

I arched an eyebrow. "Tia, you are behind me."

"Oh, yeah." She put her hand over her mouth and giggled. "Hey, who's your friend?" She gave Hacker a shy smile.

Hacker gave her a huge smile back. "Yo," he said to her. "I'm Roderick."

It was my turn to giggle. He didn't look like a Roderick.

Seeing my surprise, he scowled. "But no one calls me Roderick. You can call me Hacker."

"Yum—I mean, yo." She beamed at him. "Your plaits are way cool."

"Way," I agreed, but they ignored me and kept on staring at each other. "I saw a Tyrannosaurus Rex last night in my flat." That didn't get them moving, either. I cleared my throat. "Ahem."

They crash landed back to reality and looked at me like I'd spoiled all their fun.

I grinned at them. "Anyway, where were we? Oh, yes, we were about to go hard-drive hunting."

"Can I tag along?" Tia asked me.

"As long as you don't do anything," I said.

"Does that include breathing? I'm allowed to breathe, right?"

I didn't bother responding as I strode out the door, Tia and Hacker struggling to catch up.

* * *

It was eight p.m. and already dark when we arrived at Fandango's office. Not that the darkness bothered me; I was beginning to feel that I could make the journey blindfolded. As we crept into the unlit building, few stars shone above like pinpricks in the inky blackness.

"It's spooky." Tia clutched Hacker's arm.

"Don't you worry about that," he said, pulling out a necklace with what looked to be a chicken's foot on it from underneath his hoodie. "I've got something to protect us from hexes." He waved it at her.

She peered at it. I didn't know if she was going to laugh with relief or cry until she smiled up at him. "Do you practice voodoo?"

"I'm Haitian. Of course I do." He puffed out his skinny chest.

"Oh my God, we're made for each other! I'm psychic."

Call me strange, but I thought that a dead chicken's foot hanging around your neck was far spookier than a building with no lights on. That being said, I did flip the lights on pretty quickly at that point. There was a collective gasp as we took in the disaster.

"What the..." I glanced around the reception area, which looked like a hurricane had whipped through it. The place had been searched, probably by the same untidy, inconsiderate scumbag who had been to my apartment.

"F—fudging hell," Tia said.

"This is bad." Hacker got out his chicken's foot and waved it around again. "I can feel bad karma here."

"Come on, let's look at the computers," I said.

"Can you turn people into zombies?" Tia asked Hacker as we rushed toward Fandango's office.

"I tried it once, but it's a bit messy. It's much easier to just shoot people."

"If you ever try it again, I've got a few people in mind," I said. "What about voodoo dolls, you have any of those?"

He tutted. "Voodoo dolls are some nasty shit. If you start that, you gonna get it back three times over."

"Damn," I said, pulling the door open. "Are you sure?"

"Sure, I'm sure."

"Can't you just do something small, like make Janice Skipper's teeth fall out, or give her permanent spots, or maybe herpes?"

"Nope."

Fandango's office hadn't fared any better than reception. Paperwork and pens lay scattered across the floor, desk drawers had been emptied, and, more importantly, the computers, including hard drives, were gone.

"Great!" I said.

Tia's eyes welled up with tears. She fanned at them. "That means we can't get any information, then." She stamped her foot.

"I'm good, but not that good." Hacker draped an arm around her shoulder.

"What are we going to do now?" Tia flopped onto the silver couch and wiped away a stray tear.

I rested a hand on my hip, deep in thought. "Have you had any ransom demands?" I asked her.

She shook her head. "Is that good or bad?"

"Well, normally the chances of finding someone alive decrease every day they're missing, but I've just got a feeling that your dad is still alive."

"I know he is. I can feel it," she said. "I know you don't believe me, but there's some kind of connection with pasta going on."

"I didn't say I didn't believe you. It's just that it doesn't really help." I sighed. "I don't know about you guys, but I could do with a drink."

* * *

I poured two glasses of Zinfandel rosé for Tia and me, and an orange juice for Hacker, who mumbled something about his body being sacred. I kind of had an ulterior motive for inviting them back to my apartment. We all sat squashed together on my tiny sofa in my tiny but freshly tidied living room, lost in our own thoughts. Not that I was scared or anything. I'd cracked a few nuts and broken a few noses in my time, but

I had a funny kind of vulnerable feeling now that someone had been in here, and I didn't like it one bit. All right, I admit it. Maybe I was a teensy bit scared. It was nice to have someone else there, in case whoever had broken in came back.

I slapped the palm of my hand on my forehead. "Think!" I muttered. "Does EF mean anything to you?" I asked Tia.

She frowned for a second, and then a light bulb lit up behind her eyes.

"What?" I asked.

"I'm getting some kind of feeling. I think it's connected to the pasta thingy-bob," she said.

I groaned.

She grabbed my arm. "No, really."

"What about Longshore Holdings, does that ring a bell?" I asked.

She shook her head.

"Why would the mob steal the fashion collection if they were already receiving it in exchange for money laundering?" I wondered out loud.

"Maybe the mob didn't steal it." Hacker sipped his juice.

"Those guys who followed me today had *mafia* written all over them in orange neon," I said as I stood up and strolled around the room, head tipped to one side, mentally speculating.

"There's no way Dad would be involved in something like money laundering," Tia said.

"Well, he was involved in something. I just don't know what," I said.

Tia gulped. "Maybe they didn't really want the collection. Maybe they were just after Dad."

"Why, though?" I asked.

"I don't know," she said.

I glanced over at Hacker. "Got any crystal balls tucked in your hoodie?"

"Balls I got. They're just not crystal."

They left after we'd downed the bottle of wine, and I crawled under the sheets, expecting to nod off as soon as my head hit the pillow. Instead, I had another restless night—only this time I wasn't thinking about Brad, I was thinking I could hear noises coming from the kitchen.

I tried to ignore the scraping sounds for a while, pulling the duvet over my head in denial.

Had I actually heard something or was it my mind working overtime?

I pulled the duvet down to my nose, straining to listen as blood pulsed around in my ears. Then my blood froze mid-pulse. No, I could definitely hear something.

I bolted upright in bed. There the sound was again, but this time it was a clanking noise. Beads of sweat pricked at my palms, and my heart skipped a beat.

I shot out of bed, grabbing the first thing I could find in case I needed to defend myself, which happened to be a can of hairspray.

Padding barefoot through the darkened living room, I could hear the clanking sound again, louder now. It was coming from the kitchen. I jumped through the kitchen doorway—finger poised on the nozzle for maximum spray effect—and flicked the light on.

Then I clutched my chest with relief. My "intruder" wasn't an intruder at all. It was Marmalade, in the kitchen, with a wrench. I'd apparently missed it when I cleaned up the spilled tools earlier.

The wrench wasn't the only thing he was playing with, however. Obviously in a naughty mood, Marmalade had pulled out the contents of my rucksack, which now lay scattered on the wooden floor. The rhinestone from Fandango's offices glinted in the light, seeming to almost be taunting me to solve the case.

"You're grounded," I told him as I shoveled everything back into my rucksack.

Marmalade rubbed his head around my ankles, purring apologetically, but I ignored him. My mind was elsewhere. A weird feeling was hovering in the periphery of my brain, struggling to turn into a fully fledged thought. What was it?

I couldn't shake the idea that I was missing something obvious. It was something I should know, and it still hadn't come to me hours later, even after staring at the shadows on the ceiling above the bed all night.

CHAPTER TEN

The alarm clock jolted me awake at seven thirty a.m. after finally falling asleep around six. My eyes felt like I'd been staring into a sandstorm all night, and I was sure someone was banging a drum kit in my head.

I rolled out of bed, head clutched in my hands, and headed straight for the painkillers in the kitchen drawer. Fumbling the bottle open, I shook out several, downed some water, and swallowed, but the stupid pills got stuck in my throat.

My eyes watered as I coughed loudly, clutching the sink for dear life and trying to breathe at the same time. That didn't work, so I had a full-scale panic attack, gasping for breath, thrusting my torso back and forth as my throat made scary gurgling sounds. Just as I was having visions about trying to do a self-inflicted Heimlich maneuver, the pills dislodged themselves from my throat and propelled out of my mouth, landing in the sink.

I wiped at my streaming eyes and struggled to suck in as much air as possible. The bad news was that my throat felt like I'd swallowed a piece of sandpaper, and the drum kit had been joined by a couple of cymbals clanging around. The good news was that I was still alive.

Always a glutton for punishment, I tried another couple of painkillers with my cup of coffee and managed to get them down the hatch with no more problems. I took the success as a good sign, because today I was determined to catch the elusive Clark, and I knew I'd need all the luck I could get.

I rummaged around in my wardrobe, deciding what to wear. After the bad start to my morning, I decided today was definitely a black day.

I pulled on a black T-shirt, black combats, and tamed my bad-hair-day curly waves into a black scrunchie.

* * *

I had just parked outside Clark's house when I noticed the Purple People Eater in my rearview mirror, pulling up behind me. I groaned and scooted down in my seat, hoping that would suddenly make me invisible. Strangely, it didn't seem to work, because within moments, Tia tapped on my window.

I yanked open the door and climbed out.

"Awesome! We're twins." Tia grinned at my clothes. She also happened to be having a black day, and we were wearing almost exactly the same thing. However, her trousers were tailored and expensive looking, and her T-shirt was a Fandango classic. Mine were off the rack.

I folded my arms and tilted my head. "What are you doing here?"

"I thought I'd help you look for clues."

"I'm working on something else. You have to go now."

"Well, maybe I can help you, and then we can get finished quicker."

I narrowed my eyes at her. "Tia, there is no 'we.'"

Tia's mouth moved, but I'd stopped listening. I was too busy watching a big, round woman storm down Clark's path, heading straight toward us. Actually, big and round was being quite polite. Each boob must've weighed about five stone.

"I hope you've come to fix it this time." She scowled at us.

"Pardon?" I said.

"I recognize that uniform; it's what the other useless man was wearing the last time he came," she said.

"What man?" Tia asked.

I glared at Tia, a silent order for her to be quiet.

"The washing machine repair man. You've come to fix it, haven't you?" Mrs. Clark asked us.

"Yes." I grinned, hoping this was my opportunity to catch Clark doing a spot of DIY inside—or even better, weightlifting.

"No," Tia said at the same time.

I shot Tia another warning look.

"Well, you'd better do it properly this time. I've got five kids, you know, I can't do without a washing machine," she screeched in my ear.

"Come on, then. What are you waiting for?" She turned around and waddled back up the path.

"I'm just going to get my tools," I said, opening the boot and reaching for a small toolbox I had in there.

"What are we going to do?" Tia's eyes widened. "I don't know how to fix a washing machine," she whispered.

I shrugged. "Neither do I. Just keep your mouth shut and don't speak."

"Yes, but—"

"You're speaking!" I made my way up Clark's path.

"It's in here." Mrs. Clark led us into the kitchen, piled high with laundry.

I gawped at it. You could hardly move in the tightly packed room. "How long's it been since it stopped working?"

"A week. You've got to fix it today."

I didn't have this much laundry in a year, let alone a week. "Well, what seems to be the matter with it?"

"It doesn't work. That's what the matter is."

"Where's your husband? Can't he fix it?" I asked, fishing for information.

"That useless idiot. He said he was going to the launderette, but I think he's probably down the bookies."

Damn, no Clark. "Maybe he's popped into work to do a bit of overtime, so he can buy you a new washing machine. What sort of hours does he work?" Hint, hint.

Mrs. Clark shrugged. "I don't know, he doesn't tell me. We're supposed to be getting a big insurance payout soon. He told me I can get a top-of-the-line washing machine then."

"Oh, really?" I faked ignorance. "That sounds handy. What's sort of payout?"

"Oh he pre—" She slapped a hand over her mouth. "I'm not supposed to talk about it in case someone comes to investigate him."

"Ooh, it's a good job we're just plain old washing machine repair people then," Tia said, getting into the role, sounding like she actually believed she was.

I gave her a silencing glare. "Well, what did the other repair man say?" I asked her. Maybe I'd get a bit of a clue so I could fix it and make a speedy getaway, seeing as Clark wasn't here.

"He said it was the dongle sprocket or something." She frowned.

I nodded my head. "Right. Yes, the er…dongle sprocket is a bit temperamental on these models." I pulled a screwdriver and wrench out of my toolbox to get in keeping with my part and placed them on top of the kitchen worktop.

"Well, get on with it, then. I've got about forty loads to catch up with." She stood watching me.

Tia scratched her head.

I turned the socket on at the wall switch and an LED light came on the washer. "That's good."

"What is?" Tia asked me.

"The electric's working," I said.

"I know it's working. Fix the dongle!" Mrs. Clark's sigh was loud enough to hear in Outer Mongolia.

I pressed the start button on the washing machine. It made a chugging noise and then died.

"It's quite technical, isn't it?" Tia gazed at the machine in awe.

I suspected she'd never had to use one in her life.

I pressed it again a few times. A light flickered on the front panel and then faded away. "Hmm."

"Is that bad?" Mrs. Clark asked me.

I pursed my lips together in concentration. "Could be."

"Oh my God!" Mrs. Clark collapsed onto a nearby chair, rocking back and forth. "I can't cope with this. I NEED MY WASHING MACHINE! Promise me you'll fix it."

"Oh, you poor thing. It must be really hard having five kids." Tia put an arm around her. "Shall I make you some tea?"

Mrs. Clark stared at the washing machine with a blank face, nodding at Tia's offer.

"I think she's in shock," Tia whispered to me as she made Mrs. Clark some tea and spooned in about ten sugars while I dragged the machine out from underneath the worktop.

"Maybe your filters are blocked." I unscrewed the water pipes from the mains tap. "Oops," I said as water gushed out of the pipes. I glanced over my shoulder at Mrs. Clark, who looked like she was about to have a coronary on the spot. "Where's the shutoff?"

"Under there." She pointed to the sink.

Tia rushed to grab a bundle of dirty laundry, and pressed it onto the main pipe to stanch the flow while I located the shutoff and turned off the water.

"Phew, that was close." I looked at the filters. "Nope, these look clean." I opened the front panel and noticed a stray wire hanging out. "Ah, looks like this could be the problem. Where's my screwdriver gone?"

"Here it is. It must've fallen off the worktop." Tia grabbed it from the now wet floor and poked it into the wire. Instantly, we heard a loud bang as the wire caught fire. "Uh-oh."

"Oh, God." I grabbed Mrs. Clark's tea and threw it at the washer's electrical panel. The fire sizzled and went out, leaving the stench of burned plastic and tea in the air. For a moment, we all just gaped at the washer.

"You've blown it up." Mrs. Clark stared at it in frozen horror.

"Sorry about that," I said.

"But…you've blown it up."

"You'll have to ring up the customer service line and get someone else to come out. It's definitely faulty." I grabbed the toolbox and Tia's arm, and dragged her out the door. "I told you not to speak, let alone blow things up," I ground out as we rushed down the path.

"It wasn't my fault."

"Whose fault was it, then?" I yanked open my car door and got in.

"Where are you going?"

"Starbucks. I need caffeine." I slammed the door and whizzed off with Tia close behind me. I didn't even want to think about what Brad would say when I told him about the washing machine.

* * *

"I can't believe you did that," I said to Tia in between mouthfuls of roasted vegetable sandwich and cappuccino. I looked past her out the window, wishing I could crawl back into bed with an ice pack on my throbbing head.

"Well, technically it was the screwdriver that did it," she said.

"If you were really psychic, you would've known that was going to happen."

"I am really psychic, Amber. How else would I know you're going to get three phone calls in a minute?" She glanced at my phone, which was sitting on the table between us.

I snorted with disbelief. And then my phone rang.

A shiver danced up my spine as I answered it.

"Hey, Miss Piggy, when am I going to get my insurance money?" Callum Bates said.

"Sorry, there's no one of that name here," I said.

"Oh, sorry, I meant Miss Porky." His laugh cackled over the connection.

"La-la-la-la! I can't hear you." I hung up. "That was weird," I said. Then just as I threw my phone in my rucksack, it rang again.

"Hello?" I answered, looking at Tia, who had a knowing grin plastered to her face.

"Hi, Amber, can you pick me up a pair of brown stilettos in size nine while you're in the town? The outfit I'm wearing doesn't really go with the ones I've got."

I rolled my eyes. "Dad, are you sure you want stilettos?" Even I couldn't walk in them, never mind Dad.

"Yes. My disguise has to look authentic if I'm going to fool people. I can't wear size-nine hiking boots with a skirt. It would look too obvious."

"Good point. That would be a dead giveaway. What about wedges, then? They're much more comfortable."

"Good idea."

"Okay, will do—oh, and Dad, how did you know I was in town?"

"I've known you for thirty-five years, Amber. I knew you'd be in Starbucks."

"Another good point." I hung up again.

"Told you," Amber said.

"That was just a lucky guess. Anyway, you said three calls. I've only had two—"

And then it rang again.

"Yo," Hacker greeted me when I picked up.

"Yo-yo," I said.

"I have some interesting information for you," he said. "Can you swing by?"

I looked at my watch. "I'll be there in half an hour."

CHAPTER ELEVEN

I took a detour to Shoe World and perused the aisles. The only brown wedges I could find were a very fetching pair with pink butterflies on them. I saw a stunning pair of black ones that had my name on them, but my credit card was pretty much maxed out, and I couldn't justify any unnecessary expenditures until I got my paycheck. And in order to get my paycheck I had to solve some cases. A vicious circle, really.

I grabbed the brown shoes and rushed over to my parents" house. Today Dad wore a long brown skirt with a matching brown blouse. He'd replaced the blonde wig with a curly brunette wig. I have to say, he actually looked pretty good for a cross-dressing man, and the skirt was much more flattering because it hid his bowlegs.

"How's the neighborhood watch going?" I asked.

"I caught Callum Bates trying to steal Mrs. Golding's Saab convertible today." He broke into a huge smile.

"Interesting. What happened?"

"I hit him over the head with my handbag."

"That doesn't sound very effective."

"Oh, but it was. I had a brick in it. I wanted to give him a roundhouse kick, but I couldn't get my leg high enough in this skirt. Anyway, he ran off, and the Saab is still in situ. Another crime foiled again."

I handed Dad the shoes. "Great. Keep up the good work."

"Do you want to come for dinner tonight? Your sister's coming, too."

"Sure." I left him gazing at the shoes with delight and headed on to the office.

* * *

"Nice outfit." I glanced at Hacker's black jeans and black hoodie, which said *Gangsta Rapper* on the back. I knew it! "Should I call you Snoop Dogg?"

"Huh?"

I waved my hand. "Never mind. What have you got for me?" I perched myself on the edge of Hacker's desk.

"I checked all of Fandango's bank accounts, and Longshore Holdings made five hundred payments of ten thousand pounds each, all in the last six months," he said.

I whistled. "That's a lot of fashion designs." I added it up in my head. "A total of five million pounds' worth. How does that compare to other payments he received?"

Hacker scrolled down on his computer screen. "Longshore Holdings have paid much more than any other legitimate sales."

"Are we back to the money laundering, then? Longshore Holdings are paying far more than anyone else for Fandango's designs." I paused. "Something kick-started this six months ago. But what?" I tapped my forefinger on my lips. "Have you found out who Longshore Holdings is?"

He nodded. "They're a front company registered in the British Virgin Islands."

"Do they have an address?"

"No address, email, fax, or phone number. Just a PO box."

I narrowed my eyes and scrunched up my face, deep in thought. "What else do you know about them?"

"I'm still checking. Fandango also made a ten-thousand-pound cash withdrawal on the day he disappeared"

"That's a lot of petty cash."

"But that's not all. Wait till you hear this bit."

"I'm listening."

"Umberto Fandango didn't exist until nineteen and half years ago." Seeing my expression of disbelief, Hacker gave me a slow nod that caused his plaits to shake.

"What do you mean?"

"There's no paper trail of him until nineteen and a half years ago. No bank account, no social security number, no driving license. Nothing."

"But he's a famous fashion designer. He must've gone to university or something. He can't just suddenly pop up with a daughter out of nowhere. He must've come from somewhere. And besides, someone must've missed them."

"That's what I thought, but there's no trace of him."

"So, the question is…who is he really?" I said. "Maybe his real identity is the key to this whole thing."

"I'm working on it," he said. "It's a mystery, for sure."

"Yeah, one that doesn't make any sense. Did you find anything about Tia?"

"Apparently Fandango's a very private person. Not much press about him, and nothing about Tia. There are no photographs of them together. It's more than a little odd."

I bit my lip, pondering this for a while. "Maybe she's not really his daughter."

My phone rang again, and I recognized the brisk voice straight away.

"Ms. Fox? This is Heather Brown, Umberto Fandango's assistant," she said.

"Hello, Heather. What can I do for you?"

"I need to talk to you, but I can't do it over the phone," she whispered. "Can I meet you tonight? I have some information for you."

"Okay. When and where?"

"Hanbury Manor Hotel. In the bar, say at eight." Before I could respond, she severed the connection.

I stared at the phone. "The Ice Queen wants to talk," I told Hacker.

"Interesting."

"I need to look around Fandango's house."

"Good idea. I'll go with you." Brad's voice boomed from behind me, making me jump nearly half a mile.

I turned around and smacked him on the arm. "Don't sneak up on people like that. You'll give someone a heart attack," I said, taking in his black army trousers, black sweatshirt, and black steel-toe boots. "Are you having a black day, too?"

This was getting a bit freaky. I felt like I was living in the twilight zone. Any minute, I expected to wake up and realize this week had all been some horrible, surreal hallucination. Suddenly, another thought occurred to me. Maybe I really had choked to death this morning but just didn't know it yet.

"Pinch me," I told Brad.

He raised an eyebrow. "Any particular place you want me to pinch you?"

"I don't care." I squeezed my eyes shut. "I just need to know that I'm still alive."

"Foxy, I'd love to, but not in public," Brad said.

Just my luck—I couldn't get his hands near me when I needed them.

* * *

I drove up Fandango's long, winding driveway with Brad following close behind me in his black Hummer. A silver Rolls-Royce and an SUV sat in front of the gigantic, modern-looking house, which looked to me like a couple of big glass blocks joined together by a very pissed builder. Floor-to-ceiling windows covered most of the front of the house. He must've had a serious curtain bill.

"Have you got a key?" I asked Brad as we approached the frosted-glass front door.

"I don't need a key." He took a small, knobby-looking tool out of his trouser pocket. Ten seconds later the door clicked open.

"You could do yourself an injury leaving that in your trousers." I smirked and followed him inside.

We wandered down the hallway into the kitchen. I opened the fridge and had a nosy inside.

"Nothing but bottles of water and jars of caviar." I pried the lid off one of the jars of caviar and sniffed it. "Urgh! I've never understood the appeal of this stuff. It looks like fly poop." Brad laughed as I shut the door, and we headed on to the living room. It wasn't surprising to see that everything had been trashed. They had slashed paintings, sofas, curtains, and cushions. It seemed a bit like overkill.

"The police wouldn't have left it in this state if they were searching for him, which means someone came along after they were here. Do you think they were looking for something or making a statement?" I said.

"Hard to tell." Brad cocked his head, his tone distracted. He had that peculiar tilt to his head that meant he was concentrating. "What's wrong with this picture?" Brad asked.

I swept my gaze round the room. "That's just it. There are no pictures. Or photographs. There's nothing personal here at all."

He sent a small smile in my direction. "Odd, don't you think?"

I gave him a strange look. "You can talk. You've got nothing personal in your place, either. What does that mean?"

"He's hiding something."

"Everybody's hiding something. Maybe he's just got an obsessive-compulsive disorder about clutter."

"No, he's definitely hiding something."

"I'd expect there to at least be photos of Tia in here." I paused, surveying the scene with a critical eye. "Do both of the vehicles in the drive belong to Fandango?"

"Yes. They're both insured with us, along with the five-million-pound life insurance policy, and the five-million-pound policy for his fashion collection."

I turned to Brad. "Tia said she wasn't driving one of her dad's vehicles because she couldn't find the keys."

"That's a possible explanation. Another one is that maybe she's not really his daughter." He watched me closely as he spoke.

"I'm not sure about her yet. Everything about this case feels strange, and we're missing something vital. If she is his daughter, then the insurance payout is a big motive for having Fandango disappear. If she's not, then who the hell is she?"

"That would be the question of the day," he said as he wandered into Fandango's office.

Computer wires trailed across the floor, but there was no computer in sight. An empty glasses case had been thrown in the corner of the room, and paperwork was strewn across the floor.

"One thing that's bugging me is that if this is a kidnapping, why hasn't there been any ransom demand?" I bent down, studying the documents that littered an antique rug. "And who would want to steal the fashion collection anyway? It's not exactly something that's easily fenced, like drugs or gold."

"Maybe he's already dead. And the collection? Could be it's a rival designer who wanted Fandango and his collection out of the way." He poked around in the desk drawer as I picked the documents up and put them in a pile on the desk.

"There's nothing relevant in here. No will or any other personal documents. Obviously someone's taken everything that might be the least bit enlightening."

Brad nodded. "Let's look upstairs."

We checked out all the smaller bedrooms, but couldn't find anything of interest. When we hit Fandango's master bedroom, we found a huge walk-in closet.

"That's sacrilege!" I stared at the hundreds of shirts, jackets, pairs of trousers, and socks that had been ripped to shreds and left in a heap on the floor. We checked pockets, shoes, and shelves, methodically searching for some kind of clue as to Fandango's whereabouts. Not finding anything, we poked around in the en suite bathroom and found the usual assortment of toiletries—aftershave, toothpaste, Saint Tropez fake tan, tweezers. Nothing exciting and no Fandango.

"I guess that's it, then," Brad said as we headed back downstairs and out to our vehicles.

As I pulled the front door closed behind me, I had a thought. "Don't you think it's a bit odd that Fandango had all this money, but he's the complete opposite of the typical flashy designer? Hacker said there was hardly any press about him, but most people in his position would be paparazzi magnets. Tia, too, for that matter."

"Maybe he's just an eccentric recluse." Brad jumped into the Hummer like a lithe acrobat. "I'll see you back at the office." He did a nifty three-point turn, which was pretty impressive in a vehicle the size of a bus, and sped off.

* * *

Miscellaneous thoughts about Fandango jumped around in my brain as I swung out of his driveway. In fact, I was so deep in thought that I didn't notice the ugly-faced goons were back until they were sitting on my bumper. I sighed. Someone really needed to teach them how to drive properly. They obviously hadn't read up on safe highway stopping distances lately.

I debated whether to just slam the brakes on, but I didn't really fancy having whiplash to accompany my never-ending headache. My only other option was to try and lose them again. I probably should've taken being tailed again as a compliment, but I must admit that it was getting pretty boring and slightly repetitive.

Deciding to take them on a journey around the center of town, I headed in that direction, only to come to a screeching halt.

No, no, no! The weekly farmer's market was in full swing. Traffic sat at a standstill as prospective buyers parked up, congesting the narrow street.

"Come on!" I sounded the horn and glanced over my shoulder. The goons glared back at me. Still, at least they wouldn't try anything in the middle of the town with all these people. Surely they wouldn't.

The traffic crawled along a few feet and stopped again. Out of the corner of my eye, I just happened to notice Paul Clark coming out of the launderette, carrying four bulging bags of laundry in each hand. I grabbed for my rucksack, scrounging around its depths for my camera, but by the time I'd finally found it, he'd disappeared in the throng of shoppers.

"Craparama," I muttered, tossing the camera into the passenger seat as a gap opened up in the traffic in front of me. I floored the accelerator and then instantly slammed on the brakes as another car pulled out in front of me. As I leaned on the horn, they decided to stop in the middle of the road and look back to see who was making all the racket. Giving up, I threw my hands up in frustration, and the car pulled on out, going a few feet and stopping again.

I hammered my fingers on the steering wheel and checked on the goons through my rearview mirror. To my horror, the bald one leaped out of the passenger's side and rushed toward me. He was short, dressed in a badly fitting gray suit that had to be at least two sizes too small. Either he was making some kind of unsuccessful 1980s fashion statement, or he'd been eating all the pies lately. I was surprised by how fast he moved, despite his jelly-wobble blobby gut.

"Agh!" I hit the lock button seconds before he grabbed my door handle.

Blobby Goon pulled on the door, trying to yank it open. When it didn't budge, he banged his fists on the glass and kicked at the door.

Just then, the traffic started moving again and I stuck my fingers up and sped off. I watched in the rearview mirror as he ran back to the SUV and jumped in. In the heavy traffic, it didn't take very long for them to catch up with me. The SUV rammed into the back of my car with a loud crunch.

My knuckles turned white as I gripped the steering wheel. The impact made me lose control of the car, which fishtailed for a second before it went careening into a post on the side of the road. The impact jolted me forward with such a force that the seatbelt cut into my shoulder.

BANG! The airbag exploded, throwing me back against the seat.

I was vaguely aware of the sound of screeching tires as I sat there, stunned, slumped in my seat, wondering if I'd died for the second time that day.

An old guy banged on the window. "Are you okay? Shall I call an ambulance?"

"No, I'm…fine." I looked around for the goons, but they seemed to have disappeared. Rubberneckers stood gawking at me, no doubt hoping to see broken bones and splattered body parts.

"Are you sure?"

I rubbed at my shoulder and winced. My chest felt bruised, my shoulder felt dislocated, and my head felt like I'd been decapitated. My hands flew up to my neck, to make sure it was actually still attached to my body. I slumped with relief when I felt my face, still intact. All in all, it'd been a really horrible day, and it wasn't nearly over yet.

"Thanks. I'm sure." I nodded, easing myself out of the door and gazing at the damage to my car. The front was dented and smashed with some funny green liquid dripping out underneath it. That probably wasn't a good sign, but at least it looked drivable.

Thinking it might be a good idea to call this in, I took my mobile out of my pocket with trembling hands. It took three attempts to tap in Brad's number before I got it right.

"I'm just about alive," I said after giving him a rundown.

"Do you want me to come and get you?"

"No."

"Well, as long as you're okay to drive, take it to the garage that handles my insurance repairs. It's just around the corner from where you are. I'll call and let them know you're on the way. Pick something else in their lot for a courtesy car. And Foxy, be careful."

I climbed back in the car feeling like I'd done ten rounds in a boxing ring with Mike Tyson. As I turned the key, I prayed the car would start. It coughed a few times but finally spluttered to life, and I chugged down the road accompanied by the sound of a high-pitched whirring noise. I turned the radio up so I didn't have to listen to it.

The manager of the garage was waiting for me when I pulled in. He walked around the car and frowned at the damage. "Hmm. It might take a few days to fix, but you're in luck. We've got one courtesy car left." He pointed to a fluorescent yellow Beetle.

I groaned. I could cope with the inconvenience and the pain of the accident, but driving that car? It looked like a giant lemon. People on a space station would be able to see me in that thing, not to mention my street cred would go right out the window. I stared at it for a moment, then closed my eyes with a shudder. I clicked my heels together three times, hoping the car might magically turn into something that looked a lot less like a humongous lemon.

I opened my eyes, only to discover my wishing hadn't worked. "Damn."

"Great color, isn't it?" he said.

I'm not particularly proud of it, but I had bit of a freaky flip-out at that point, and I might've told the man to stick the Lemon up one of his orifices where it definitely wouldn't fit. I'm not one hundred percent sure, though. It could've been some kind of weird flashback, so don't hold it against me. I ended up driving the car, so whatever happened must not have been too offensive.

When I finally arrived back at the office, I limped up the stairs and collapsed in my chair.

"Have you got any painkillers?" I asked Hacker.

Brad rushed out of his office. "Are you hurt?"

"No, I'm having a perfectly normal day, EVEN THOUGH I NEARLY DIED TWICE!" I heard my voice rise to a shriek, cracking on the last word.

"What happened?" Brad's brow furrowed as he stared at me. He ran his gaze over my limbs as I replied, as though making sure I was really okay.

I took a few slow, deep breaths, exhaling forcefully. "It was the funniest thing. I drove past the famer's market, turned the corner, and at that point I noticed a stall selling lions and rhinos. This distraction caused me to lose concentration, and I hit a post." My lower lip wobbled, and I couldn't prevent a teary gasp.

Brad didn't say a word. He just wrapped his warm, heavy-duty arms around me and held on. I let my head sink onto his shoulder, suddenly feeling safe and secure.

"The mob goons were following me again," I finally said when I felt calm enough to talk.

"And then what happened?" Brad asked.

"I don't know. I wasn't looking. I think they drove off, though." I pulled away before I started to enjoy Brad's comfort a bit too much.

Hacker moved up behind me and rested his hands on my shoulders, making a peculiar chanting noise.

"What are you doing?" I twisted my neck around to look at him and winced. God, that hurt.

"Reiki," he said. "It'll get you better in no time."

My eyelids drooped shut. I felt a warm, relaxing sensation flood through me.

"How does it feel?" Hacker said. His voice sounded like it came from a long way off.

My breathing slowed down, and the tightness in my shoulders eased. "Mmm, lovely..." And then I fell asleep.

CHAPTER TWELVE

I woke up at five thirty, stretched out on the sofa in Brad's office, and feeling like I'd slept for a week. I stretched, expecting to hurt like hell, but whatever Hacker had done to me had worked like a charm. Brad stood in front of the window with his back to me, doing some kind of tai chi workout in silence. My gaze wandered over his backside with appreciation as he swept his arms through the air in slow, fluid movements.

"How are you feeling?" he asked without turning around.

"Better." I swung my legs over the edge of the sofa and sat up, rubbing my eyes. "I've got to go have dinner at my parents' house before I meet Heather Brown."

"Keep me updated." He stood on one leg, rested the other foot on the side of his knee like a crane, and lifted his arms in the air, moving into a yoga pose.

I took another look at his rather perfect form and smiled to myself as I slipped out of his office and climbed into the horrible yellow Beetle.

* * *

The smell of marinara pasta, laced with extra garlic, wafted under my nose when I opened my parents' door.

"Hi." Mum stuck her head out the kitchen door. "We're just waiting for Suzy." She had no sooner spoken than the front door opened again and my sister walked in.

"Hi, everyone." Suzy waltzed into the kitchen with her permanent frown locked in place. In fact, I couldn't remember the last time I saw her smile.

"Hi, sis," I said.

"Whose car is that in the drive?" Suzy asked as she sat her Prada bag on top of the cream shaker-style island in the center of the kitchen. She shrugged off her tailored jacket and hung it on the back of a breakfast stool.

"That monstrosity is mine for a while, unfortunately," I said with a grimace.

She just raised her eyebrows, not commenting further. "Where's Dad?" she asked as Sabre barreled into the room and leaped up, planting his muddy front paws on Suzy's pinstriped trousers. "Get off!" She pushed him down, wiping at the mud. "Go to your bed." She wrinkled her nose and pointed to Sabre's half-eaten doggy bed in the corner of the room.

Sabre whined and did as he was told for once. I didn't blame him. Suzy's voice was enough to scare the dead.

"No Romeo tonight, then?" she asked.

I shook my head. "Not tonight."

"Why haven't you moved in with him yet?"

"I'm still thinking about it," I said defensively.

"What's there to think about? It's been over a week since he asked you to move in with him."

"It's complicated," I said.

"Okay, let's diagnose this. You've been romantically involved for a year, which is long enough to make your mind up about what you want, especially when you consider the fact that you were friends, and worked together for a long time before that. It's not like you don't know him well enough to make a decision, is it? And he's been in love with you for years. In fact, Romeo was the one who brought you back to normal after the Brad fiasco. He helped you climb out of the pit that Brad left you in."

"There's no need to get so dramatic, Suzy."

"I'm just trying to establish what the problem is, Amber. Don't you love him?" Suzy asked.

I blushed. "Yes."

"Okay, so Romeo wants you to move in with him. You love him, he loves you, that's good, isn't it?" Mum asked.

I sighed. "Its great...kind of. I'm just worried about him being the one. Not whether he isn't the one, but what if he *is*? Let's just say that he is the love of my life. What if we took the plunge and then something bad happened to him? Then I would've lost the idea, the possibility of Mr. Right. Maybe the anticipation of not knowing is better than losing that possibility. And if something's working, what is the point in changing it? If it ain't broke, don't fix it, right?"

"You're not getting any younger. You could die tomorrow and then you would've missed out on sharing your life with the man you love," Suzy said.

"Gee, thanks for that cheery thought."

She shrugged. "I'm just telling it like it is. You've got classic commitment-phobia symptoms. You don't want to die as a lonely old spinster, do you?" Suzy rested her elbows on the island, trying to catch my eye.

"I'm not lonely. I've got all the voices in my head to keep me company." I plastered a fake grin on my face.

"What voices? Do they tell you to do things?" Suzy asked. In case you hadn't figured it out already, my sister is a psychologist. "If they do, I can help you with that. How does it make you feel when the voices start talking?"

I stuck my fingers in my ears and hummed.

Suzy rolled her eyes at me and exchanged a glance with Mum. She reached over and pulled my hand away from my head. "Are you still feeling depressed?"

A nervous laugh slipped out as I looked between my mum and Suzy. "I wasn't aware that I had been depressed."

Suzy threw me a stern look. "You have to admit things before you can cure them. Not wanting to get out of bed in the mornings, not eating, not tidying up your flat, not bothering with your looks—those are all signs of depression. They all happened after you lost your job."

Mum gave me a hug. "Especially the not-eating part. That's not like you at all."

I stepped out of Mum's grasp and poured a glass of the red wine that sat breathing on the counter. "Well, obviously I was…upset about losing my job." I took a gulp of the dry, fruity liquid. "Anyone would be. But I wasn't depressed. Anyway, my new job is getting a lot more interesting. People are even trying to kill me again. And I've got a cunning plan. If I can solve this Fandango case, I'm hoping the chief constable will offer me my old job back."

"Is that how you measure your job satisfaction, by the amount of people who want to kill you?" Suzy watched me like I was an alien who'd just been beamed down from a spaceship.

"You need to get out and socialize more, Amber. You can't just live for your work. It's not healthy. I should know that better than anyone," Mum said, pouring her own glass of wine.

"You've done all right with Dad, though, haven't you?" I asked.

"I had to accept that he was a workaholic and find other things to fill my life. It wasn't easy," Mum said. She opened her mouth to continue, but just then, a clattering sound came from the hall.

"Ah, here are my girls." Dad wobbled into the kitchen in his brown wedges, wearing the same outfit from earlier.

Mum and I didn't bat an eyelid, but Suzy's eyes nearly popped out of her head.

"Why are you dressed like that?" Suzy asked him. "Are you having some post-retirement issues?"

"He's undercover." Mum stirred the sauce. "For the neighborhood watch scheme."

"Undercover as what?" Suzy looked at us all like we were nuts. "Is there a call for transvestites in the neighborhood, then?"

I shrugged and dipped a spoon into the sauce. "Yummy," I told Mum after I licked the spoon dry.

"He's not using the right accessories, is he?" Mum said to Suzy. "His makeup is getting better, though."

"Do you want to talk about it?" Suzy whispered to Dad.

"Don't try that psychoanalyzing babble on me," he said. "I sectioned a few people when I was on the force, and most of the time you can't tell the difference between the psychiatrists and their patients."

"That's true, actually." I nodded and chugged the rest of my wine.

Suzy rolled her eyes. "Am I the only sane person in this family?"

None of us bothered to answer her.

Dad gazed out the window. "Who's that outside?"

I looked over his shoulder and saw Tia, sitting in her car outside the house. "Oh no."

"Is that a friend of yours?" Mum clapped her hands together with delight. "I'm so glad you've found a few more friends. Shall we invite her in for dinner?"

"No!" I said.

Mum's face fell. "Why not?"

"Because she's a possible suspect in the case I'm working on." And then I thought that maybe it was actually a good idea to observe Tia in a more relaxed environment. Maybe it would give me some insight into whether she was involved in Fandango's disappearance. I relented. "Okay, why not?"

Mum disappeared out of the house faster than I could blink, reappearing a minute later with a smile on her face and a happy Tia.

"Hi! I'm not interrupting anything, am I?" Tia asked. She stood in the kitchen doorway and shuffled from one foot to the other.

Suzy sized her up with a blank I'm-the-therapist-so-I'm-not-giving-anything-away expression on her face. "Are you nervous?"

"N-no," Tia stuttered, as Mum dished out the pasta and sauce into five bowls.

"You should be nervous in this house. Tell me, what do you think of my dad's outfit?" Suzy tilted her head, waiting for an answer. "Just say the first thing that comes into your head."

Tia shifted her gaze to Dad. "You need to accessorize more."

"What did I tell you?" Mum said.

Suzy threw her arms in the air. "You'll fit right in."

We sat at the dining room table, passing garlic bread and salad as Tia talked incessantly about fashion. Suzy, Mum, and Dad hung on her every word, hardly eating a bite. I twirled my pasta on my fork and shoveled it into my mouth with enthusiasm, studying her. I had a hunch about Tia, and I didn't want her following me until I had more information. Luckily, I had a plan to keep her here while I went to the rendezvous with Heather.

I pulled Dad aside as I cleared the table and loaded up the dishwasher. "I've got some job stuff to do. Can you keep Tia talking while I duck out?" I whispered, knowing that I could trust Dad to keep an eye on her.

He winked at me. "No problem."

"Tia, why don't you give Dad some fashion tips on color coordination?" I suggested.

Mum's eyes lit up. "Fantastic!"

"Yes, is it really true that blue and green should never be seen together?" Dad asked.

I nearly passed out when I saw an emotion flicker across Suzy's face. Her eyes lit up, too, and the corners of her mouth curled into a slight smile, but it passed almost as quickly as it had come. It could've been indigestion, though, I suppose.

* * *

Hanbury Manor Hotel was a stately Jacobean country house, set in the middle of two hundred acres of parkland. It even boasted its own golf course and spa. This was the first time I had set foot in the place, and it would probably the last, unless Romeo wanted to whisk me away for a dirty little weekend. And that didn't seem likely, considering he was AWOL with Janice Skipper.

I found the wood-paneled cocktail bar, which was knee deep in wedding guests, and looked around the room. The room was full of party-frocked women and dinner-jacketed men in various stages of drunkenness, but Heather wasn't there. I checked my watch. Eight p.m. dead on.

I jostled my way to the bar and ordered a glass of wine, then moved back to people watch.

"Where've you been all my wife—I mean life?" A short, considerably wasted guy in a gray morning suit swayed to a stop in front of me, blocking my view of the entrance.

I gave him a distracted smile and adjusted my position so I could see around him.

He hiccupped. "Oops. Looking for someone?"

"Yes." I tried to ignore him.

He held his arms out. "Well, here I am, the man of your dreams." He glugged his pint of beer down in one go and belched. "What do you think?"

Not in this lifetime. "No, the man of my dreams is definitely taller." I continued scanning the entrance and sent him silent "go away" signals.

He frowned. "It's because I'm short, isn't it? I always get this. I'm huge in other departments, though."

I leaned in a little closer. "Thanks for sharing, but that's too much information."

"But I am. King Dong's got nothing on me."

"Okay. I'm glad we're clear on that."

He hiccupped again. "Where do you think I'm going wrong with my pick-up line, then?"

I sat back to avoid recycled lager fumes. "I don't think you should just come out with any references to King Dong, for starters. You need to have a bit of mystery about you."

He thought about this for a moment. Then he seemed to get the message and stumbled off to hit on another poor woman who was propping up the opposite end of the bar.

After half an hour, the drunkenness in the bar had turned to rowdiness, so I wandered around to the lobby and restaurants, but Heather still didn't appear. Had I missed her in the crowd? Had she turned up and not seen me because King Dong was blocking her view? I headed out to the car park and checked for her Beemer, but there wasn't any sign of it. Worried, I dialed her mobile, but it went straight to voicemail.

Deciding she had missed me or stood me up to begin with, I left the hotel and did a quick drive-by of the Cohens' warehouse. There were no lights on, and the place looked locked up tight. I drove to the housing estate at the back and parked. With caution, I crept through the darkness to my familiar lookout spot.

Plonking myself down on the cold ground, I strapped on the night-vision goggles and waited, my eyes adjusting to the dark as I gazed at a dim pool of light given off from the streetlamps at the entrance to the industrial park.

An hour later, my eyelids heavy and my back aching, I debated whether to freeze my ass off any longer or go and defrost it in a hot bath. I checked my watch. Eleven p.m. Time to make a move. I could feel the soapy, aromatic suds calling my name. Home it was.

I arrived home to a welcoming party of Brad and Marmalade.

I eyed Brad, who was sprawled on my sofa, his head lolling back against the cushions. He stroked Marmalade, who was curled up in his lap, enjoying the attention.

"Hey, did you pick my lock?"

"I'm not in a position to confirm or deny that."

"What are you doing here?"

"Stroking your pussy." Brad looked up with a wicked grin.

"Ha ha. How did you get in here?" I asked again, wondering if I was actually annoyed or excited at the prospect of Brad slipping into my apartment on a whim. That ability could lead to a rather interesting pre-bedtime fantasy, or it could be extremely embarrassing. Either way, it was a pretty safe bet that Romeo wouldn't be too impressed, and the situation could easily turn into something I might live to regret.

Brad tapped the side of his nose and handed me a glass of wine. "I could tell you, but then I'd have to kill you."

I snorted, sitting down on the edge of the sofa next to him. "You're invading my personal space."

"This is nothing." His fingertip traced the side of my face. "If I was invading your personal space, you'd notice, believe me."

Oh boy! I did believe it.

"What happened with Heather Brown?"

I sipped my wine and moved as far away from Brad as I could possibly get before I did something that was becoming too tempting to avoid. "She was a no-show."

"Strange." He took a sip of wine, studying me over the rim of his glass.

"What are you really doing here?"

"I wanted to make sure no crazy stalkers were waiting for you again."

"Well, that's very nice, but my bath is calling my name, so if you don't mind..." I tilted my head toward the front door.

"I could join you."

I tutted at him and headed for the bathroom. "You can let yourself out."

After a long soak in a hot bath with some lavender aromatherapy oils, I wanted to go to bed and sleep for a hundred years, but when I emerged from the steamy bathroom, Brad was still sitting on the sofa in the living room, stroking Marmalade behind the ears.

"What are you still doing here?" I felt my face flush and pulled my bathrobe tighter around me, painfully aware that I was naked underneath. I could do without a repeat performance of the nipple incident, thank you very much.

Brad's face had a guarded expression on it, and I knew it meant trouble. "I've got a confession to make."

"I'm listening."

"Do you want the good news or the bad news?"

"Come on, Brad. Just spit it out. I'm tired."

"The good news is that Romeo called your mobile when you were in the bath, so at least you know he's still alive."

"And what's the bad news?" I frowned.

"He lost his temper a bit when I said you were in the bath."

"Great! Why did you answer it? Now he probably thinks something's going on between us," I said through gritted teeth.

I pointed toward the door and Brad sighed. He stood up and moved toward the door, and I gave him a little push to encourage him. As I did, my bathrobe fell open. I looked down with a horrified gasp and quickly closed it again, wrapping both arms around my body in case it decided to spontaneously pop open again.

"Don't cover up on my account." He winked, and then left me standing there, hot and bothered.

I tried to call Romeo back, but either he was ignoring me or he couldn't pick up. "Damn it." I threw the phone on the sofa and went to bed.

* * *

I had a feeling of impending doom in the depths of my stomach when I woke up the next day. I couldn't shake it off on the drive to Heather's apartment. In fact, it got worse when I arrived at her building and discovered her car wasn't there. Rain pelted the windscreen through the gloomy sky, and I hesitated for a while, psyching myself up. If there was no answer, I would have to break into her apartment, and I didn't know what I might find. I liked to think I was a kick-ass, hot-shit investigator, but deep down I knew that sometimes I had a brilliant knack for screwing things up.

Heather lived in a run-down apartment complex that was in bad need of renovation. It seemed a world away from her flashy, expensive clothes and car. I wondered about that as I took the lift to the fifth floor, dressed in my navy boiler suit with *Mr. Fix-It Maintenance* written on the front, carrying my matching navy toolbox. There was no excuse for a lack of color co-ordination, even if you happened to be dressed in very unflattering clothes.

I walked down the corridor, found her apartment, and knocked. In the apartment next door, I could hear a couple arguing in what I thought was Japanese. The smell of fried food emanated from the walls.

I waited a few minutes and knocked again, then pressed my ear against the door. I didn't hear a thing coming from inside, so I pulled out Brad's open-sesame tool and picked the lock. I slipped inside and stood there, waiting a moment for my eyes to adjust to the dim apartment.

"Hello?" I called. The sound echoed around the small apartment.

No answer. I slipped inside and turned on the lights.

I figured Heather pulled in a good salary, but it looked like she didn't spend a penny of it on her home. The entrance hall had three doors leading off it, all of which were closed. I opened the first one and found myself in a bedroom. A saggy mattress and threadbare white sheets covered an old double bed, and a battered MDF nightstand lived a solitary existence with no other little furniture friends to keep it company. A well-worn fitted closet with a cracked mirror on the front took up one side of the wall.

I rummaged around in the nightstand drawer and found a yellow sticky note with the words *Carlos Bagliero* scrawled in messy handwriting. Now I was getting somewhere. I rifled through the wardrobe and found the Fandango bag of my dreams in amongst a pile of about fifty. In one of my more shallow moments, I debated whether to sneak it down my boiler suit. Tempting though it was, I'd have a huge guilt trip if I did, and karma was a bitch. I dribbled a bit, lusting after it, and closed the door.

Next up was the bathroom. It was pretty basic—cheap towels, cheap toiletries. I retreated into the hall and found the kitchen.

An ashtray sat on the kitchen table, overflowing with cigarette butts. Next to it was a plate of half-eaten chicken salad on a chipped plate, and a glass of clear liquid. I picked up the glass, studying the lipstick. Dracula red, the same as on the butts. Not a good sign. I sniffed the glass and wrinkled up my nose at the hairspray aroma of neat vodka. Obviously, something had disturbed Heather's meal. But what?

I walked on through to the living room. An ancient stereo system sat on top of a wooden rickety table. They were underneath an open window, which was blowing a draft through the room. The other windows were closed, the tatty blackout blinds drawn. I heard a weird sound through the open window and stuck my head out, looking down to the car park.

Great, just what I needed. The bushy-haired mob goon stood by the entrance to the apartments. Obviously the muscle of the two, he was around six feet tall, with a square jaw, and he looked to be solid-pack muscle. I think he'd overdone it on the steroids. Whatever I needed to do in here, I needed to do it fast.

I hurriedly searched Heather's computer desk. Where was her laptop? Wherever it was, that place was not here. I did find a USB flash drive, though. Woo-hoo! I had no sooner pocketed it than I heard a loud explosion. A bolt of lightning lit up the room and shards of glass flew everywhere.

I dove to the floor, catching the edge of the wooden table with my shoulder. The table jerked backwards, and the stereo unit wobbled a bit and then fell out of the window.

I heard a thud followed by a groan.

Leaping up from the floor, I dusted off the pieces of glass, trying to figure out what had happened. I realized the light was out, and guessed the light bulb had exploded. I moved to the window and peered out.

Mr. Steroid Goon lay sprawled on the pavement below, out cold, with the stereo pretty much buried in his head. I guessed he'd have a rather large headache when he woke up and might want revenge. Since I didn't like the sight of my own blood very much, I decided to not stick around for that to happen.

I ran out of the apartment, swung my ass down the fire exit stairs, and ended up in the car park.

I'd just floored the Lemon up the main road when Romeo called my mobile.

"Where've you been? I've been trying to get hold of you for days," I said, the phone cupped beneath my chin.

"And here I thought you'd been too busy with Brad to even think about me."

A tense silence ensued as I tried to think of what to say. I drove over a bump and dropped the phone. "Damn." I grappled around in the footwell with one hand on the steering wheel until I found the phone. "Sorry, dropped the phone."

"How convenient."

I sighed. "Nothing's going on with Brad. He's just my boss." At least, I thought nothing was going on. "Don't you trust me?" Although to tell the truth, I didn't know if *I* trusted me.

Silence. And then: "Of course I trust you. I just don't trust Brad. It's no secret that he's still in love with you."

I couldn't stop the astonished laugh that sprang from my lips. Brad? In love with me? No. I shook my head, and it occurred to me that I should probably steer this conversation in another direction. "I don't think so, Romeo, but it doesn't matter if he is. Where are you?"

"I'm at your apartment," he said.

"Are you naked again?"

He let out a smooth chuckle. "No, but I could be."

"I'll be there in ten minutes."

CHAPTER THIRTEEN

When I reached my apartment, I rushed into Romeo's arms, partly because I'd really missed him, and partly because I felt bad for having naughty thoughts about Brad.

He buried his lips in my hair, hugging me tight. "I've missed you."

"Me too." I smiled up at him.

"So what's been happening?" He led me to the sofa and pulled me onto his lap.

"Where do I start?" I filled him in on the Cohens' chop shop, the mob goons, and a few snippets about the Fandango case. Until I'd found out which police officer was investigating his disappearance, I didn't want to give too much information away.

"Why didn't you tell me you'd been in an accident?" He pulled me close. "Are you okay?"

"I couldn't get hold of you, remember?" I rested my head on his shoulder. "Anyway, I'm fine now. Hacker did some kind of freaky voodoo stuff on me."

"Don't go poking around with the Cohens too much."

"Why not?"

"I can't tell you. Just take my word for it."

"You can't do that."

"Do what?" He feigned confusion.

"You can't tell me not to do something and then not tell me why."

"The Cohens are nasty. I don't want you going near them without any backup. Just promise me you won't poke around."

"Okay, I promise," I said, knowing I'd do the exact opposite. "So, who's working on the Fandango case?"

He hesitated and shot me a wary look. "Janice is."

My eyes narrowed involuntarily. "Great!" Still, at least if she was working that case, she wouldn't be working with Romeo on his case.

He pulled back, gazing into my eyes as he delivered the punch. "She's helping out on my case, too."

Not so great, then. I did some mental deep breathing.

"She's not that bad, Amber."

I jumped up and paced the room. "She is. You just can't see it. She doesn't show you that side of her. Janice has been trying to get her hands on you for years. She's a sneaky little—"

"You can't keep blaming her for getting you kicked off the force. You did shoot her."

I threw my hands up in the air. "It was an accident! Anyone would think that I aimed that gun at her on purpose and shot her."

He leaned forwards, resting his elbows on his knees. "Well, why won't you tell anyone what happened, if it was an accident?"

I stopped pacing and sat down, staring at my feet for a while as I decided whether to tell him. After a while, I sucked in a sharp breath and spoke. "We were at the shooting range, and she told me she'd slept with you."

"What?" His forehead wrinkled up, a confused, incredulous look on his face.

"Janice told me that she was going to get you away from me and get me kicked off the force if it was the last thing she did. She told me how she was the one who'd stopped me from getting promoted all these years. All this time, she'd been blaming the other promotion board members for my lack of advancement up the career ladder, and it was actually her. Oh, she was ecstatic about what she'd done—hysterical, almost. Then she walked out in front of my shooting booth to retrieve her target, which is totally against protocol, by the way, and I kind of flipped. I didn't mean to shoot her, I just meant to scare her a teensy bit. Who knew I was such a good shot? That's when I popped her one in the ass."

He ran a hand over his closely cropped hair and sighed. It was a couple of minutes before he spoke. "So why didn't you tell me this at the time?"

"Because, technically, it was my fault."

"Yes, but technically, she broke the protocol. The way she tells it, you just shot her when she was walking away from her shooting booth back to the weapons-check area, for absolutely no reason. That's not what happened, apparently."

"And Romeo, who would have believed me? There were no witnesses." I ran a hand through my own hair. "And besides, she's a detective chief inspector, and I was just a detective sergeant. It would have been her word against mine. God, I've been over and over that day in my head a thousand times in the last six months, and I still hate myself for that moment of weakness. And the worst part is that I'm supposed to be an investigator, but I missed all the signs staring me in the face. All the times she made excuses to keep me confined to desk duties, so she could keep me out of the field and get closer to you. All the snide, bitchy comments she made, which I'd heard about through the police station grapevine and dismissed without a second thought. Everything was connected to this sick vendetta she's got against me."

He frowned. "She obviously had this whole scheme of hers planned for a long time, then, Amber. And something else—don't ever doubt yourself as an investigator. You're the best one I know. So, what are you going to do about it?"

I let out an angry snort. "Well, it's too late to do anything now. There isn't anything I can do about it."

Romeo shrugged. "Maybe there is a way. This Fandango case is pretty high profile. If you can solve it before Janice does, maybe the chief constable will offer you your job back."

I looked up sharply.

"I didn't sleep with her." He locked his gaze firmly on me.

"I know. I worked it out later on that the time she said she was with you, you were actually with me. But it wasn't mostly about you. It was mostly about me, and what Janice had been trying to do to me. That's the reason I had a momentary insanity attack—not because I thought she'd slept with you, but because she wanted to destroy me."

He held his arm out and I quickly tucked myself up underneath it. We sat snuggled on the couch for a few minutes, each lost in our own thoughts. Mine involved doing something nasty and painful to Janice Skipper.

Finally, he spoke. "Do you want me to cheer you up?" he asked with that wicked little smile I couldn't resist.

"What did you have in mind?"

"I'll do the nasty thing you like."

I didn't need to be asked twice.

A very satisfying forty-five minutes later, we lay in bed. I traced a finger up and down the defined muscles of stomach, thinking how perfectly gorgeous he was, and how easy it would be to just move in with him and live happily ever after.

But would we? That was the million-dollar question, and I didn't have the answer. Most of the time I thought that "happily ever after" was just a myth spread around by diamond jewelers and wedding dress shops. Okay, so my parents were a good example of a couple who'd stayed together for years, but that was probably because they hardly ever saw each other. And I had inherited their crazy genes, which didn't seem like a good omen.

"Did you hear about Fandango's wife?" Romeo turned his head on the pillow and looked at me.

My finger stopped mid-stroke and I sat up. "What wife?"

"The one he married nineteen and a half years ago."

"Tia said he didn't have a wife."

"Who's Tia?"

"His daughter. Maybe."

"I didn't hear anything about a daughter."

"Snap. I didn't hear anything about a wife."

"What's the maybe-daughter like?" He twisted around, propping himself up on his elbow.

"Quirky, but she actually seems very sweet. What's the story with the wife?"

"From what I heard, Fandango moved to the UK years ago out of nowhere, and married someone named Samantha James pretty much as soon as he arrived. They stayed together for six months and then separated, but they never got divorced."

"Six months?" I shook my head. "I just can't get my head around the fact that Fandango didn't exist until nineteen and a half years ago."

"He's hiding something."

I didn't tell him those were the exact words Brad had spoken.

"Or maybe hiding *from* something, like a wife that isn't quite an ex. But Fandango is a famous fashion designer. Okay, so he's quite private, and there's not much information about him in the press, but even so— anyone who cares to, knows who he is. Only an idiot would try to hide in public," I mused.

"I'm guessing that with a fortune worth millions and the Fandango fashion empire, he's not an idiot."

"Exactly, that's why it seems weird. And now his assistant has gone missing, too."

"I hate to say this, but word on the street is that Fandango is dead. From what you're saying, it looks like his assistant is probably dead, too."

"That's the way it seems. And if he isn't dead, where the hell is he? Maybe the wife can shed a bit of light on something, because I seem to be getting nowhere. Have you got an address for her?" I asked.

He rolled out of bed, strode naked to his jeans, and pulled a piece of paper from his pocket with an address written on it. "Here. And don't tell anyone you got this from me. I'm under strict instructions from Janice not to tell you anything."

I smiled. "Thanks very much. I'll pay you in kind if you want."

His grin lit up his face. "Now you're talking."

We did the nasty thing again, and then shared a shower. While I really wanted to snuggle in bed with Romeo all day, order takeout, lounge around, and forget about everything, I had work to do. I halfheartedly pulled on my clothes, bade Romeo a reluctant goodbye, and headed for the office. It wasn't until I was in my car and on the road that I realized I still didn't know where Romeo was headed. He had very skillfully distracted me from finding out, too, and I had an uneasy feeling that I wouldn't like the answer.

* * *

I waved a pizza box under Hacker's nose when I entered the office. My coffee table had been replaced by a full-sized office desk, complete with file holders, drawers, laptop, and even a pen holder. I found a packet of pens in the drawer with a red ribbon tied around them and a bow on top, along with other stationery paraphernalia. I took it as a good sign that Brad wanted me to stick with the job. In a way it was pretty flattering, but did he want me around because he thought I was a good investigator, or for some other non-work-related, completely sexual reason? And if it was the latter, I wasn't even sure that I felt annoyed about that possibility. I shook my head to clear it of random—and quite dangerous—sexual thoughts about Brad before I had a hot flash.

"What are you doing here on a Saturday? Do you live here?" I said to Hacker as I sat down, swiveling around in my chair to face him.

"I've got no life. What are you doing here?"

"I'm just conscientious." I opened the box and stuffed a piece of pizza in my mouth. "Yum, double pepperoni. I need brain food."

"Do you know what's in that? Refined wheat flour, E numbers, processed cheese—"

I pressed my hands over my ears when he got to the processed cheese part. Processed cheese didn't sound like real cheese and it tasted so good. "Can't hear you." Then I realized that I couldn't eat with both hands tied up, so I took one hand away, pressed my uncovered ear against my shoulder, and resumed eating with the other hand until I got a neck ache.

"You're crazy." Hacker shook his head at me. "I know who EF is, by the way."

"Who?"

"Enzo Fetuccini."

"And who's Enzo Fetuccini?"

"He's the boss of a big mob family in the USA."

"How do you know it's the same EF?"

"I've been checking out Longshore Holdings. They're owned by another company, who are owned by another company, who are owned by Enzo Fetuccini. They covered their tracks pretty well, but not good enough. Fetuccini was in Sing Sing prison serving twenty years for murder, money laundering, and tax evasion."

"You said 'was.' When did he get out?"

"Six months ago."

"Interesting. Also, by the way, I've got something for you to look at." I pushed the pizza box away and handed him the USB flash drive. "I found it in Heather's apartment."

He plugged it into his computer and pulled up the files as I settled myself next to him, my eyes glued to the screen. We sat like that for a minute, astonished at what we were seeing. Whirling around, I grabbed the paper spreadsheets we'd found at Fandango's office and held them up to compare the entries to the financial spreadsheets on the screen.

Hallelujah! We finally seemed to getting somewhere.

"It fits," I said. "The spreadsheets on the USB are the same as the paper spreadsheets, except they mention Enzo Fetuccini by name instead of by his initials EF." I sat back, thinking about this. "So, Fetuccini pays Fandango five hundred payments of ten thousand pounds each, all within the last six months, for fashion designs that can't be worth that much."

Hacker looked at me. "Are we back to money laundering?"

"Maybe. Obviously, Fetuccini has got a prior history of it, but something still doesn't feel right." I pulled out the note I'd found in Heather's office desk. "This note says *CB £5 million*. I found reference to someone called Carlos Bagliero in Heather's apartment, and that would fit with the note. It looks like this CB is paying the same amount of money for whatever it is, as Fetuccini is. Are they paying for the same thing, and if so, what?"

"Drugs?"

"Maybe. Can you find out who Carlos Bagliero is?"

"Sure." Hacker's fingers got to work on the keyboard.

"Oh, and Heather seems to have disappeared. I'm wondering if she made any withdrawals from her bank account lately. She may have done a runner, or she may be dead."

"Maybe she's scared and lying low somewhere."

"I wonder what happened to the ten thousand pounds Fandango took out of his bank account the day he went missing. There was no trace of any money at his home or office."

"Fleeing money. He probably took it and run."

"Yeah, but that's not a lot of cash in the scheme of things. If I was going to run, I'd have taken a lot more than ten grand. Did you find out anything about Tia?"

He stopped mid-tap. "I can't find any birth certificate for anyone named Tia Fandango."

"I think she could be adopted."

"It's possible. I'll look into it."

"That's weird." I looked at the spreadsheets again.

"What?"

"Tia told me this ridiculous thing, and it looks like she was right."

"What did she tell you?"

"Tia told me she had this feeling about pasta, and her dad was being held in an Italian restaurant somewhere. I think she's wrong about the restaurant, but 'Fetuccini' is the pasta connection. Maybe she really is psychic after all."

Hacker gave me a sly grin. "I don't know about psychic, but she's definitely cute."

I smiled. There seemed to be a bit of romance in the air. I hoped Tia didn't turn out to be one of the bad guys.

"There's another file on this USB." He closed the spreadsheets and clicked on another icon. A document with three lines of numbers came up. The first two lines had six numbers and the third line contained eight numbers.

I leaned forward, concentrating on the screen. "What do you think it is?"

"It could be anything."

"Maybe it's a code. How are you at cracking codes?" I asked.

He grinned. "I like a challenge."

"Also, Fandango had a wife called Samantha James." I handed him the slip of paper with her address on it. "Here's her address."

"I didn't find anything about a wife."

"Can you try again? I need to dig up something I can use."

"I'm on it." Hacker typed up a storm, sending the keys jumping and bouncing.

"I think we need to look into Fandango's phone calls as well." I stood up. "I'm going to go try to speak to the wife."

CHAPTER FOURTEEN

Samantha James lived in a sleepy Hertfordshire village called Little Hadham. I programmed her address into the Lemon's GPS and followed the instructions, which were given by an irritating computer-generated voice.

Twenty minutes later, I arrived at a modest, ivy-covered, eighteenth-century cottage. It looked like Samantha had done all right for herself. My footsteps crunched over the gravel as I exited the car and knocked on her door.

A small woman in her late forties answered the door. She had red-rimmed eyes and a wispy bob, and there was a washed-out look about her.

"Hi, I'm looking for Samantha James," I said.

She leaned on the doorframe and wrapped a shapeless gray cardigan around equally shapeless jogging bottoms. "I'm Samantha."

I tried to hide my surprise. She couldn't have looked less like a flashy fashion designer's wife if she had tried. "I'm investigating the disappearance of Umberto Fandango. Can I ask you a few questions?"

"I told the police everything I know."

"I'm not from the police. I'm from his insurance company. It's standard practice to do our own investigation."

She pulled the door open and shuffled back. "You'd better come in."

The cottage was tastefully decorated with antique furniture. Heavy drapes hung at the windows, blocking out most of the light. I followed her into the farmhouse-style kitchen, which had an Aga stove in the center of the room that radiated heat like a furnace.

"Take a seat." She indicated one of the chairs that was clustered around a small table.

"Are you okay?" I asked as I sat down.

She hesitated for a moment, composing herself. "I'm fine, thank you."

"I understand that you and Umberto were married, is that correct?"

"Yes."

"Are you still married?"

"We got married nineteen and half years ago. We were only together for a short time, six months or so, and then we separated."

"I know this is difficult, but would you mind telling me why you separated?"

After much hesitation, she finally said, "It was a mutual decision." She glanced down at the floor and fiddled with the cuff of her cardigan.

"He came to the UK around about the same time you got married. Did you know him when he lived in the States?"

She shook her head.

"How did you meet?"

She let out a soft sigh and sat down in the chair next to mine. "We met in a wine bar."

"And then what happened?"

"We got married six weeks after."

"Wow. That seems awfully sudden."

She looked up sharply. "What are you implying?"

"I'm not implying anything." I smiled, trying to put her at ease. "I just think it's a bit strange that you only knew him for six weeks before you got married." I studied her body language, waiting for an answer. She crossed her arms in front of her and turned away from me. I was pretty sure that she was being deliberately misleading. "Why didn't you get divorced?"

"We were actually just about to. I hadn't had any contact with him since we separated, but then out of the blue, he called me the day he disappeared and…" She trailed off, gazing out the window.

"What happened?"

"He wanted me to sign the divorce papers."

"Did you?"

She kept her gaze out the window as she answered. "Yes."

"Where did you meet him to sign the papers?"

"At his office."

This was growing more and more interesting. "What time was that?"

"About six o'clock."

I thought about the timeline. "You may have been one of the last people to see him alive. Who else was there?"

"Just his assistant, Heather."

"Did you see anything strange? Was anyone hanging around?"

"No."

"Were you in his will?" I asked.

She stood up, walked to the window, and stared out again, her shoulders drooping. "He told me a long time ago that he'd made arrangements for me in his will."

"Do you know what the arrangements were?"

She whispered something inaudible.

"Pardon?" I said.

"I was in his will as long as we remained married," she said, her voice so quiet that I had to lean forward to hear her.

Oh boy. It just kept getting deeper and deeper.

"Do you know where he kept his will?"

She shrugged. "No."

I gave her a minute before I changed the subject. "This is a lovely house." I looked around the kitchen. "Did you buy it yourself?"

She turned back to me, her eyes wandering slowly around the room. "No, Umberto bought it for me." Her voice was wistful.

"Did Umberto have a daughter when you met?"

She stared at the floor for a while as if debating how much to tell me. "Yes."

I let that sink in for a minute. "How old was she?"

"She was six months old. Her name was Tia."

"Do you know who her mother was?"

"No, he never told me."

I stared at her in disbelief. "Okay, let me get this straight in my head. You met Umberto nineteen and a half years ago when he had a six-month-old daughter, but you don't know who the mother was. You got married after just six weeks, and you only stayed together a few months. Then you had no further contact with him until the day he disappeared."

"Yes."

"Don't you think that sounds a bit…odd?" I asked. She didn't answer. I wasn't really expecting her to, so I plowed on. "How do you know that Tia was really his daughter?"

She leaned against the window for support. "Look, he loved Tia. It was obvious to me that she was his daughter."

"Didn't Tia's mother ever contact Umberto?"

"No. Not that I knew of, anyway."

A chill ran through me. "And you didn't think that was also strange?"

She glanced at her watch. "I'm sorry, but I have to go out. I have a relative in the hospital who is very ill, and I need to get back to them."

I took that as my cue to leave, and followed her out the front door. I wasn't ready to end the interview, but short of pinning her down, holding her in a headlock, or applying my thumbscrew technique, I didn't have much choice but to leave. I had a feeling she was a troubled soul with problems of her own, and I needed to keep on her good side. I also didn't think this would be my last visit to see her.

I headed back to the office, mulling over what Samantha had told me, trying to make sense of things. In the end, I gave up and called Brad.

"Speak," Brad said.

"The rain in Spain falls mainly on the plain," I said, faking a posh accent.

"Foxy, what's up?"

I filled him in on the latest and then said, "I think Fandango may have kidnapped Tia when she was a baby."

"I'll get Hacker to look into it. If that's true, then someone must've been looking for them. But why would Fandango be involved with the mob? "

"Maybe Enzo Fetuccini or Carlos Bagliero found out what happened and blackmailed him into doing something illegal."

"That's a possibility, but it doesn't explain Fandango's disappearance, or that of his fashion collection."

The cogs spun around in my brain. "Perhaps whoever Fandango kidnapped Tia from found out and killed him for payback."

"Wouldn't they have contacted Tia?"

"Maybe they're waiting for the right time." I slammed the brakes on when I saw the mob goons pull out of a side road in front of me. They sped down the road on the same route I'd taken earlier that morning. "Oh my God!" I hit the accelerator and kept a sneaky distance between their vehicle and mine.

"What?"

"I'm following the mob goons. I think they're heading to Heather's apartment."

"Don't do anything stupid. Wait in the parking lot and I'll meet you at her place."

As it turned out, waiting wasn't an option. I parked on the road opposite her apartment to keep an eye out for the goons and for Brad. As I watched the parking lot, I spotted her BMW in the lot along with the goons' SUV. I hadn't exactly hit it off with the Ice Queen, but I still didn't want to see her get hurt.

I rammed a can of pepper spray in one pocket of my combats and a stun gun in the other pocket, and hurried across the road. Glancing around one more time, I ran up the fire exit stairs to Heather's floor two at a time.

Adrenaline pumped through my body and my heartbeat rattled in my chest. As I slowly tiptoed toward Heather's door, I developed a sudden case of nervous, bubbling guts.

I could hear the Japanese couple belting out "Girls Just Want to Have Fun" on a karaoke machine inside their apartment. I pressed my ear against Heather's door, trying to make out any sounds from inside, but it was impossible to hear anything over a Japanese Cyndi Lauper.

At that moment, Blobby Goon pulled open the door.

"What the fuck!" he said as I came ear to face with him.

I gave him a dazzling smile. "Er, I was just passing. We're taking karaoke requests. You look like a Blues Brothers kind of guy."

Steroid Goon appeared in the background. He had a bandage wrapped around his head. Tufts of hair poked out between the strips of white material. He narrowed his eyes at me.

"Well, nice talking to you. Bye." My legs suddenly sprang to life, and I took off, running full blast back down the corridor.

Unfortunately, I didn't make it very far before I felt my arm being yanked from behind. I turned around as Steroid Goon dragged me back toward Heather's apartment and tried to dig my heels in the carpet, but

I couldn't get any traction on the threadbare surface. A searing-hot pain shot through my shoulder as he pulled me into the apartment and forced me onto a chair at the kitchen table. My eyes darted around the room as I rubbed my shoulder. I was looking for any signs of Heather. Had they already killed her and dumped her body? I looked at their hands. No sign of blood. I took that as a good sign.

"I was only joking about the Blues Brothers. No need to get so grumpy." I stared Steroid Goon in the eye. Blobby Goon stood next to him and crossed his arms, doing his best menacing impression. I eyed his beer gut and snorted.

Blobby Goon sucked his stomach in. It didn't make much difference.

"I know you," Steroid Goon said. "You're that crummy insurance investigator, Amber Fox."

I didn't exactly agree with the "crummy" part. "While we're doing introductions, who are you?"

"Sally," Blobby Goon said. "And he's Tracy." He pointed his head toward his beefed-up companion.

Tracy slapped Sally over the back of the head.

My eyebrows shot up to my hairline. "Tracy and...Sally!"

Two pairs of black eyes glared at me.

"You mean you're named after a couple of girls?" I couldn't hold back a nervous laugh.

Sally shuffled on his feet, looking uncomfortable. "Sally is short for Salvatore."

I glanced at Tracy. "What's Tracy short for?"

"It's not short for anything," Tracy said.

I could almost feel his pea-sized brain whirring away beneath the surface, wondering where I was going with this. "Did your parents want a girl? Did they dress you up in pink little dresses and make you go to ballet lessons?"

Sally blushed, looking embarrassed. I wondered if that had actually happened to him. "Well, Amber Fox sounds like a porn star." He looked pretty pleased with himself for thinking that up on the spot with no outside help.

"Does not," I said, outraged.

"Does," Sally said.

"Actually, I think the correct term is 'porn queen,'" Tracy said to Sally.

Sally scratched his head. "You sure?"

"Yes." Tracy nodded. "I know because of those awards they have on television."

"What awards?" Sally scratched his head again.

While they were having this peculiar discussion, I took the opportunity to glance every which way around the room, looking for a possible escape route.

"The Porn Queen Awards," Tracy said.

I stood up. "This conversation is getting to be a big fat yawn, so I'll be off now if you don't mind."

Tracy shoved me back into the chair. "Okay, porn queen, where is it?"

"Where is what?" I said.

"You know what." Sally folded his arms, glaring daggers at me.

"If I knew what, I wouldn't be asking, now would I?" I said to Sally. He was obviously the brains behind the outfit. "What have you done with Heather Brown?"

"We're asking the questions." Tracy poked me in the shoulder. It was the sore one, and I couldn't hide a wince.

"You've got something our boss wants," Tracy said.

I snorted at them because I figured they were kidding. Unfortunately, they weren't.

"Yeah, give it to us," Sally said.

"Is it my charm and good looks that your boss wants, by any chance? Judging by the two of you, I'm betting your boss is probably short of those two attributes as well."

Sally caught Tracy's eye. "Did she just insult us?"

Tracy shrugged his shoulders at Sally. "I'm not sure." Then he gave me an ugly frown. At least I think he did—it could've just been his normal face, though. "I'll ask you one more time, and then things are going to get nasty."

"Oo-ooh, I'm scared," I said, hoping things wouldn't get nasty. Nasty was one thing coming from Romeo. Coming from these guys, it sounded quite painful.

"Where is it?" Tracy said.

I grabbed the glass of vodka from the kitchen table and threw it at Tracy. The liquid flew through the air and splashed onto his crotch.

He looked down as half of it soaked into his trousers, and the other half dripped onto the floor. When he looked back up at me, he seemed a tad pissed off for a minute. Then he smirked. "Well, that didn't do anything, did it, porn queen?"

That was when I pulled the stun gun out of my pocket and zapped his nuts.

Tracy let out a high-pitched scream as his nuts caught fire. His eyes nearly popped out of his head as he jerked and twitched, and then he slumped to the floor, unconscious.

"No, but that did." I smiled.

Sally jumped up and down, gazing at his partner's unconscious body in shock. He screamed, grabbed a tea towel, and began flicking it at Tracy's smoking crotch.

It seemed as good a distraction as any, so while there was jumping, screaming, and flicking going on, I thought it was a good time to make a sharp exit.

I ran from the apartment and headed back down the hall. I crashed into the fire exit door with my shoulder—guess which one? I stumbled through the door, sliding down half a flight of stairs at breakneck speed before I managed to gain my footing. I picked up momentum on the way down, and by the time I pushed open the door to the parking lot, I tumbled forward, my body completely out of control. I landed in a crumpled heap on the pavement.

I jumped up just as Brad's Hummer screeched around the corner. Racing for the vehicle, I jumped in on the passenger side.

"Go!" I yelled. "Go, go!"

Brad shifted it into reverse and hit the accelerator, narrowly missing the Goon's SUV as he swung back out onto the road.

My chest heaved up and down. "What took you so long?"

"I thought I told you to wait for me."

I cut my eyes to Brad. He looked hot and bothered. That wasn't good. Brad didn't do hot and bothered. I could almost see steam coming out of his ears. "I thought Heather was in there with them."

"Did you see her?"

I shook my head.

He looked over at me. "Are you okay?"

"I'm peachy." I raked my out-of-control waves off my face.

"Because you don't look okay."

"How am I supposed to look when someone tries to kill me?"

"Not like that. You look...hot."

I didn't know if he meant hot in a sexy way or hot in a flushed, running-for-your-life way. "So do you." And then I realized how that sounded and cringed.

He raised an eyebrow at me. "Are you sure you're okay?"

"You should see the other guy."

And then his face relaxed. "That's my girl."

CHAPTER FIFTEEN

"God, I need a stiff one. No, make that a couple of stiff ones—or ten." I flopped onto Brad's luxurious sofa. "Drinks, I mean, before you get any funny ideas."

Brad poured two large brandies into cut crystal glasses and handed me one. I took a sniff. It nearly blew my head off. Oh well, needs must. He sat in the leather armchair opposite me, elbow resting on the arm, one leg outstretched. He looked relaxed and composed, but I knew the calm was just a façade. Brad never relaxed. Something was always simmering, bubbling away under the surface. The only sign of it was a glint in his eyes, a light that hinted on occasion at the danger that was just below the surface.

"Well, that was fun," Brad said.

"I don't consider that to be fun. On my fun-o-meter scale, it ranks right up there with tooth extraction and kneecapping."

"But it means that someone is obviously rattled."

"Yeah, me. I'm rattled." I sipped the cool liquid, savoring the burning sensation as the brandy slipped down my throat. That meant I was alive, and alive was good. "I don't think Samantha James is telling the truth."

"If Fandango kidnapped Tia, then Samantha won't be telling the truth. She'd have to admit that she knew about it and didn't do anything, which means she's an accessory."

"She knew him for six weeks before they got married. You can't fall in love after six weeks, can you?"

Brad stared into my eyes. "Don't you believe in love at first sight?"

I snorted. "There's no such thing."

He brought his glass to his lips, but didn't drink. He had a haunted expression on his face. "Are you sure about that?"

"Who are you talking about here?"

He took a sip of brandy. "Samantha, of course. Who else would I be talking about?"

"If it was true love, why did it only last six months? I think it was a marriage of convenience. They had an arrangement of some sort."

"If Fandango kidnapped Tia, I don't understand why someone wasn't looking for them before now."

"Maybe they were. Maybe Fandango just hid things well. Hacker said Fandango and Tia were never photographed in public together. There were no photos of them at his house. Seems to me that he was keeping his relationship with her low key," I said. "You hear about it all the time; a father kidnapping his daughter because of custody battles or the like. It's not uncommon."

"You think he assumed a new identity to hide the fact he'd taken Tia away from her mother?"

"That's how it looks."

"Still doesn't explain the mob connection."

I stared into space and downed the rest of my drink. "Unless Tia is from a mob family."

Brad got up and refilled my glass. "He'd have to be nuts to kidnap someone from a mob family."

"Or desperate."

"Or desperately nuts."

"Samantha had a motive for getting rid of Fandango. She told me they were separated for over nineteen years, and then out of the blue, Fandango calls her on the day he disappears and asks her to sign divorce papers. She said Fandango had left her something in his will, but if they hadn't actually got divorced yet, the figure could be substantially higher."

"We're going around in circles. We need to wait and see what Hacker digs up."

I stood up. "Thanks for the drink."

"Where are you going?"

"I'm going to do some observation on the Cohens' warehouse.

Saturday night is nice and quiet. The surrounding warehouses will be empty. It's prime time for a possible arson."

Brad sat his glass down next to mine. "I'm going with you. I don't want those thugs taking another pop at you. Besides, your car is still at Heather's apartment."

* * *

We took the Hummer, parked up in my usual spot, and crept through the trees to the vantage point. A sliver of light from the moon peeped through the darkness, and an eerie silence filled my eardrums. Now this was what I called creepy.

We sat cross-legged, shoulder to shoulder, the heat from Brad's body giving me a warm glow. At least, I thought it was just the shared body heat.

I pulled out the night-vision goggles. "Do you want these?"

"No, I can see like a hawk." He latched his gaze on to the warehouse below.

I pulled the goggles on my head and did the same. A light shone in a downstairs window of the warehouse, but other than that nothing much seemed to be happening.

"Have you heard from Romeo?" Brad asked, staring straight ahead.

"Are you fishing for information?"

"If I was fishing for information, I'd ask if you were in love with him."

I didn't trust myself to speak, so I kept quiet, which was pretty hard for me. Usually the only time that happened was when I fell asleep. I bit my lip to avoid blurting out anything incriminating, and wished I didn't still have feelings for Brad. I couldn't look at him.

"I didn't want to disappear and leave you in the lurch for three months. I just couldn't contact you. It would have compromised my unit and the innocent civilians we'd been assigned to protect." He reached over, pulling my hand into his. A muscle throbbed in his clenched jaw. "The mission I got assigned to was a very delicate one, and secrecy was of the utmost importance if it was going to succeed."

I could see him out of the corner of my eye. He appeared to be studying me carefully.

"Nothing's been the same since you left," he said.

"You were the one who left."

"But you wouldn't let me explain when I came back. You just refused to answer my calls or see me. You shut me out and wouldn't have anything to do with me."

My heart hammered away as I turned to him. "You disappeared without a trace the day after you asked me marry you! What was I supposed to think? I thought I'd never see you again—I thought you'd died, for God's sake. Don't you know what that did to me? Can you even imagine? I couldn't think of a single worthwhile excuse for you to just suddenly up and leave your new fiancée without a word. And believe me, I tried to think of one. I racked my brain for three months to come up with a possible reason."

"I didn't have a choice."

"Don't use that excuse."

"Okay, you're right. I did have a choice. I could risk the lives of thousands of people or risk the life we were going to have together. It wasn't an easy decision, and you don't know how many times I wished that I could take it back."

"But you can't, Brad. One minute you were there with me, and the next you'd slipped into the wind. At the same time that I was basking in the excitement of marrying you, you were boarding a plane for God knows where on some secret SAS mission, and I was abandoned, tossed away without another thought. If you had just told me you had to go, told me you were coming back, I could have dealt with it."

Silence floated in the gap between us.

"I never meant for you to feel like that," he whispered finally, squeezing my hand.

"Well, that was how I felt. Of course I shut you out when you came back, just like you shut me out." I took a deep breath. "Anyway, two years' worth of change has happened since then. I've changed, too," I said, trying to sound convincing. Because if I had changed, why was my heart beating too fast, and why were my palms tingling?

Thoughts jostled for position in my head. *Oh, God, just stop it, Amber. You can't think about this. You can't even talk about it. Bad things will happen if you do.*

An owl screeched above our heads, sucking me back down to reality. I pulled my hand from Brad's grasp. "Something's happening." I pointed to the warehouse as the shutter doors rolled up and the Mercedes, Aston Martin, and BMW I'd seen the other day drove out, disappearing out of the industrial park.

"He's probably moving them somewhere else before they're shipped abroad," Brad said.

Two minutes later, we watched a silver SUV, a black Audi R8, and a gold Porsche 911 drive into the warehouse.

Brad leaped to his feet. "Come on. We'll go get your car, and I'll follow you home. They're not going to torch the place with a batch of new merchandise in there."

* * *

I woke up late on Sunday morning to feel a wet nose prodding my ear, which was Marmalade speak for "feed me." I stretched, dislodging the Fandango file that was scattered on my duvet. It hit me that I was in exactly the same position now that I'd been in when I had fallen asleep. Boy, I must've been pooped.

After hitting the shower, I pulled on some jeans and a sweatshirt, and stuffed my feet into my sneakers. I needed something to kick-start my brain, so I brewed a pot of coffee and wolfed down some chocolate crunch cereal. Suitably buzzing on sugar and caffeine, I took the file to the living room, curled up on my sofa, and went over what I knew so far.

This case seemed to start with the disappearance of Fandango and his fashion collection, but I suspected it really had started long before that. Shots had been fired, blood had been found in Fandango's offices, and a witness had seen Barack Obama driving away soon thereafter in a white getaway van, presumably with Fandango and the fashion collection stashed inside. Heather had suffered a blow to the head, rendering her unconscious at the time, but that could be very convenient or a very strange coincidence. I originally thought Fandango had been kidnapped, but as time went on with no ransom request being made, it seemed more likely that he was dead, especially with the recent disappearance of his assistant as well. Could this case be as simple as a rival fashion designer who wanted to get rid of the competition? I didn't think so. The information I'd found on the USB drive in Heather's apartment certainly indicated otherwise. I had no idea who Carlos

Bagliero was, or what he had to do with the five-million-pound payment into Fandango's bank account. The mob connection to Enzo Fetuccini was unclear, but tantalizing. It could be the result of money laundering, or some other, equally illegal scheme.

All told, there were numerous criminal possibilities for what had happened, and how the mob was connected. The only thing I knew for certain was that the mob goons were looking for something. But what? I supposed they could be searching for Tia. She could be the daughter of a mob family. Was Fandango really her dad, and what had happened to her mother? I pondered the possibility that Fandango had been killed as a revenge attack for kidnapping Tia, but no one had contacted Tia. Or had someone approached her and she just hadn't mentioned it?

There were so many questions surrounding Fandango, I didn't know which one to tackle first.

I maneuvered my head from side to side, massaging the jumbled knot of tightening muscles in the back of my neck, trying to ease the tension. I stood up, stretched, and poured another coffee as I thought about Samantha James. If Fandango had kidnapped Tia, that was a pretty big secret to be carrying around for nineteen and a half years. Surely he must've told someone, and I guessed that someone was probably Samantha. They clearly had an arranged marriage of some sort—what kind was yet another unanswered question. That led me to two possible scenarios. Either Samantha was blackmailing Fandango to keep quiet about his secret, in which case she would want him alive, or she killed Fandango because he wanted a divorce, cutting her off from any inheritance in his will, in which case she would want him as dead as a dodo bird.

A knock at the door interrupted me just before my head exploded with confusion.

I picked up my can of pepper spray, padded to the door, and looked out the security peephole. A distorted view of Hacker's face looked back at me, his plaits sticking up in the air like an antenna. My shoulders relaxed as I opened the door.

"Yo," he said, following me into the living room.

"Yo, yourself."

He grinned. "I've discovered something weird. Guess what it is."

"Fandango was really Elvis in his previous life?"

"No."

I pursed my lips in thought. "Tia is really a man?"

"No, and that would be weird. She's a fine piece of woman."

I moved the file off the sofa and motioned for him to sit down. "I give up."

"Heather Brown was broke. She made lots of withdrawals from her bank account in the last nine months."

"Exactly how much money are we talking about?" I flopped down next to him.

"Seventy-five thousand pounds."

I raised an eyebrow. "Maybe she was being blackmailed, or she was clearing out her account, getting ready to make a run for it.

"Or she had a big spending habit."

I shook my head. "You should've seen her apartment. Apart from all the clothes, which were probably freebies, her stuff looked like it came from a charity shop."

"She could've had a drug habit," Hacker said.

"That's certainly a possibility. Did you find out who Carlos Bagliero is?"

"It's a dead end. I can't find anything at all on Carlos Bagliero."

"Nothing at all?"

"No. I checked social security, passport, driver's license, tax returns, bank accounts, and birth and death certificates. I can't find any trace of him."

"That doesn't make any sense. There has to be a reason why his name was on Heather's USB drive."

"Either she made a mistake with the name, or someone went to a great deal of trouble to wipe all references to him in the databases," Hacker said.

"Did you crack the numbers code?"

"I'm still working on it. Do you want to hear the weird part?"

I sat forward, all ears.

"Samantha James bought a warehouse nineteen and a half years ago, but she never gets any post at that address. No invoices, bills, or merchandise. In fact, she's never owned a business in her life."

"Hmm." On the face of it, buying a warehouse might not seem that odd, unless she had no business to house in it, and she bought it right around the time she married Fandango. Then it would seem pretty high on the odd scale. "It must be a front address, then," I said. "Where is it?"

"It's at the same industrial park where Lennie and Lonnie Cohen have their warehouse."

For a moment, the information stunned me. Then I remembered something. "If it wasn't the only industrial park in the area, I would've thought that was a strange coincidence. I'll need to check Samantha's warehouse out." I stood up and headed for the door.

"I'll come with you."

I gave Hacker a suspicious look as he followed behind me. "Why?"

He averted his eyes. "No particular reason."

"What's going on?"

He picked up one of my fluffy cushions and hid his face behind it.

I moved to stand in front of him and pulled the top of the cushion down. Peering at him, I waited for him to spill the beans. I could wait all day if necessary when I was in stubborn mood.

I sensed him wrestling with his conscience for a while before he finally answered. "Okay, Brad asked me to keep an eye out for you." He threw the cushion on the sofa.

Before I could decide whether to be flattered or angry, my mobile rang.

"Hi, Amber," Dad said.

"Hi, how are you?" I asked.

"Pretty busy, actually. I caught Callum Bates trying to nick a Porsche last night."

I chuckled. "Did you hit him over the head again?"

"No, this time I managed to get in a roundhouse kick to the head before he cried like a baby and stumbled off up the road. I don't think he'll be back in my neighborhood again."

"Good for you."

"How's the case going? Are you still being followed?"

I didn't want to worry him. "Er…a little bit."

"Don't worry, dear. I've got your back if anything happens—oh, I've got to go, I'm teaching control and restraint techniques to the over-sixties neighborhood watch group. Bye."

I hung up and rang Callum Bates. "Got a headache this morning?"

I tried not to giggle, but I couldn't help it.

"What's it to you, bitch?"

"Oooh, tetchy! Someone got up on the grumpy side of the bed today." You had to hand it to him, though—at least he was consistently abusive.

"What do you want, Miss Piggy?"

"What are you up to, Callum?"

"That's none of your business, Porkster."

"This is your last chance. Are you ready to do the lie detector test about your alleged stolen van?"

"No."

"Okay, your loss." I said, hanging up.

CHAPTER SIXTEEN

The roads were quiet, due in large part to all the Saturday-night drunkards still sleeping off their hangovers. If I had a life, that was what I'd be doing, too. Since I still needed to get a photo of Paul Clark to prove his injury claim was false, we took a quick detour to his house.

The curtains were closed behind the bay windows, and there wasn't a peep out of anyone from inside the house. Not even a mouse stirred in this joint. Maybe they'd gone to the launderette for a washing fest. I tried the supermarket again, keeping a close eye out for strange-looking insects and kids high on too much sugar. Clark was like the cockroach that hid when a light was turned on.

Giving up on Clark again for now, we cruised into the industrial park, looking for Samantha's warehouse. To my surprise, her address was right next to the Cohens' warehouse, separated by only a six-foot-wide slip road running along the side. It was blocked by a skip, which was piled high with cardboard boxes. I couldn't exactly park the Lemon in the vicinity, since it would attract too much attention, so I parked up in my usual spot in the housing estate behind the park, and Hacker and I returned on foot.

We circled the warehouse, which had the same layout as the Cohens'. The only difference was that this warehouse had a lifeless look about it that smacked of years of disuse. A layer of dusty grime had long since covered the doors of the loading bay, rust had eaten away at the front-door lock, and cobwebs smothered the small window next to the door, quivering slightly in the breeze. The place was silent, with not a soul in sight, and more than a little creepy. I glanced up to the second floor windows and noticed a security alarm box to the side with faded writing. I didn't think it was actually connected to a security company, but worst-case scenario, we'd have maybe twenty minutes to nose around before someone bothered to turn up.

It took about two seconds to pick the ancient lock. Easing it open, we slipped inside. A damp, musty smell attacked my nostrils immediately. As I waved a hand under my nose, I noticed a filthy light switch, hanging partially out of the wall to our left. "You switch it on," I said to Hacker, giving the exposed, blackened wires a suspicious look. I didn't fancy getting a few hundred volts through that. My hair was unmanageable enough already without adding more static.

Hacker examined it carefully, then flipped the switch. Nothing happened. He turned it off and on again a couple of times for good luck, but it still didn't work. I took the flashlight Dad had given me out of my rucksack and switched it on.

"Great," I said when it didn't work. "I could've sworn Dad put some new batteries in." I shook it about, whacked it on my palm, and tried again. Nope, the little bugger still wouldn't cooperate. "Oh well, never mind." The inside was dark, but not a complete blackout. Once our eyes adjusted to the light, we could just about see well enough. I made a mental note to eat more carrots.

Empty shelves covered one wall of the building, and a few plastic tables had been pushed into the corner with a few sad-looking plastic chairs. A small fridge, which looked like it dated from the 1950s, sat in the corner, and a huge rolled-up carpet had been dumped on the floor next to it. The fridge made a loud humming sound, followed by a whirring noise. It repeated itself in a continual, monotonous loop. Nothing in the barren area gave us a clue as to what the warehouse had been used for.

"Cobweb city." I glanced at the floor, which was caked with sooty cobwebs and yet more dirt. I looked at my once-black sneakers and grimaced at the layer of gunk that had adhered itself to them. "I'll have to stick these in the washing machine when I get home."

"There isn't much in here," Hacker stated as he glanced around.

"What have we got here?" I peered inside the fridge, pulling out a carton of long-life milk. I unscrewed the cap and sniffed. "Whoa!" A rank, putrid odor seeped out. Obviously its life wasn't that long. I quickly replaced the cap, shoving it back in the fridge, out of sniffing range. On top of the fridge sat a small first-aid kit, the case around it rusty and crumbling. Inside I found a bottle of saline eye drops, plasters, bandages, and antiseptic cream.

We climbed the metal stairs to the next floor, our footsteps echoing in the silence. The two doors at the top of the stairs were closed. Hacker opened the first one, and I followed him into a large, empty storage area with windows. I was just about to turn around and leave when I noticed something small, glinting in the light. I picked it up between my thumb and forefinger and held it up to the window. It was the same kind of rhinestone that I'd found at Fandango's offices.

"Interesting," I said, pocketing it. "This proves that Samantha lied to me. She has had some contact with Fandango in the last nineteen and a half years."

"Maybe she stole his collection and killed him."

I shook my head. "She's got a motive to kill him, but why steal the fashion collection? It's not exactly the kind of thing you could get rid of easily on the black market, so essentially it would be worthless." I opened the second door, and we found ourselves in an office area.

A battered metal office desk sat in one corner—not much else, unless you counted the bats hanging upside down from an iron roof joist.

"Is there anything interesting in them?" Hacker asked as I opened the desk drawers.

My eyes lit up. "Yes."

"What?"

"A packet of Pacers sweets." I pulled the packet of green and white striped sweets out and held it up. "They stopped making these when I was a kid. I used to love—"

"I meant anything to do with Fandango." Hacker gave me a strange look.

"Er…no." I quickly threw the mints back in the drawer.

"Okay, then. Time's up. We need to get out of here."

We hurried back down the stairs and opened the front door a smidgeon, making sure the coast was clear. We'd just got outside and clicked the door shut when we heard the sound of footsteps and hushed voices coming our way.

Damn.

We could try and pick the lock again, but chances were good that we'd be caught before we got back inside the building, or we could stand still and pretend to be statues.

Hacker pointed to the skip that was parked in the slip road. We ducked behind it as the voices got closer, and the footsteps stopped. I strained my ears, trying to listen to the conversation.

"We've got two shipments going out this week, so I don't want anything to go wrong."

"I've only got a few more vehicles on my list to steal, but there's some crazy old bat who keeps attacking me."

I recognized both voices.

Poking my head around the skip, I caught the back view of two guys. One was Callum Bates, and the other was short enough to be Lennie Cohen.

"How's your mate Dave getting on?" Cohen asked. "Is he kosher?"

"I haven't known him for long, but he's one of the best car thieves I've ever met. He's only got the Lamborghini left on his list to steal." Bates picked his nose.

Ew! And he had the cheek to call me a pig.

"Well, keep up the good work. I'll make arrangements for your fee when it's all finished," Lennie said.

We heard the doors of a vehicle open and close and the engine start. We waited for five minutes after it pulled away before we stood up.

"So, Bates is working for the Cohens now. I can't say I'm surprised. I'll pass the information on to Romeo," I said. "Come on, let's go."

As we emerged from our hiding place behind the skip, I felt a searing-hot pain in my right foot. "Agh!" I screamed loud enough and high-pitched enough to put any opera singer to shame as I hopped on my left foot and inspected the bottom of my right sneaker.

A nail had embedded itself through the sole, and judging by the pain, probably halfway into my foot as well. My eyes watered. I felt a hot, sticky, wet patch working its way around my toes.

"Are you okay?" Hacker asked.

I grabbed his arm, resting my right foot back on the floor on tiptoes. "I think I might need a foot transplant. What kind of idiot leaves rusty nails everywhere? Any willy-nilly nail throwing should be banned, punishable by death." I supposed that at least I wouldn't have to wash my shoes now, but I wasn't too happy about throwing away my favorite pair.

"Do you want me to carry you to the car?"

"If I say yes, will it make me a wimp?" I tried to ignore the throbbing, which felt like someone was blowing up my foot with a bicycle pump. I didn't deal with seeing my own blood very well, and I didn't really want to take my shoe off in case I fainted, which was a strong possibility.

"I won't tell anyone if you don't."

I gazed down at my foot. "Okay," I squeaked. "But I'm not going to the hospital. They might try to amputate, and I'm quite attached to both of my feet. Can't you do your freaky voodoo on it and make it all better?"

"I could, but there's a slight chance it would turn your foot into a chicken's foot."

I pulled a disgusted face. "Don't get me wrong, I like chicken, but I think it would be hard to find decent shoes for a chicken's foot."

* * *

After Hacker dropped me off at my apartment, I lay down on the sofa with a packet of frozen peas wrapped around my foot in a towel. I had managed to pull the shoe off, but that was as far as I had been able to go. As I stared at the ceiling and tried to ignore the throbbing, I wondered if I'd done something really bad in a past life, and someone up there hated me. Or worse—maybe they'd put a hex on me. After ten minutes, I felt bored and fidgety, so I called Romeo. As usual, his voicemail kicked in. I left a message and stared at the wall for a bit of variety. Luckily, I was saved from complete boredom at that point by a knock at the door.

I swung my legs off the sofa and hopped to the door.

"Foxy." Brad swept in and scooped me up in his arms. He kicked the door closed behind him and placed me gently back on the sofa.

"I'm not an invalid, although I might be soon if they have to amputate it," I told him.

"Hacker told me what happened." He unwrapped the towel, pulled down my bloody sock, and examined the bottom of my foot. "It's just a scratch."

"Is it? It doesn't feel like a scratch. Are you sure there isn't a big, gaping wound? I could feel so much blood."

He shot me an incredulous look. "You mean you haven't looked at it yet?"

"Well, I was just about to, but you interrupted me."

He threw his head back and laughed. "You were scared."

I rolled my eyes. "Was not."

"Yes, you were."

"I don't like the sight of my own blood. Other people's doesn't bother me all that much, but for some bizarre reason I'd prefer to have all my blood inside my body, not outside."

"You need to get this cleaned up." He rolled up his sleeves. "Have you got any antiseptic cream?"

I pointed to a kitchen drawer and watched as he busied himself running hot water into a bowl. He grabbed a wodge of cotton wool, a plaster, and some antiseptic cream. I eased myself back on the soft cushions, closing my eyes.

"You need to get a tetanus shot and maybe some antibiotics," he said when he'd finished.

We went to the hospital emergency room and waited along with the other patient people. An elderly woman with a head injury clutched an ice pack to her bruised forehead. A twenty-something woman with long hair sat with her neck drooping to one side. And a young guy with his little finger sticking out at a right angle looked like he was about to throw up.

"What's wrong with your neck?" I asked the younger woman.

"I can't move it," she said.

"What did you do to it?" I said.

"Well, I went to flick my hair like this, and it got stuck." She whipped her head around, flicking her long mane of golden hair, and I heard a loud cracking sound.

I scrunched up my face. That didn't sound good.

"Hey! How strange is that?" She twisted her neck from side to side, up and down, and rotated it in a circle. "You fixed it." She gave me a huge, beaming smile. "Thanks a lot." She stood up. "I hope you don't have to wait too long. Bye." And she teetered out on the highest shoes known to womankind.

"Dr. Kildare, eat your heart out," Brad said.

SIBEL HODGE

The young guy held his deformed finger up at me. "Can you do anything with this?"

Eventually, it was my turn. A nurse cleaned up the tiny scratch, stuck a sterile pad on it, and fixed it with surgical tape. I was just waiting for the doctor to give me a tetanus shot when Romeo called back.

"Hi, babe," he said.

"Hi. Where are you?" I asked. "Oh, hang on a sec."

The doctor waltzed in with a syringe in his hand. "Okay, you'll just feel a small prick," he said.

I looked away, squeezing my eyes shut.

"Where the hell are you?" Romeo said. "And who's giving you a small prick?"

"I'm at the hospital." I opened my eyes and realized the doctor was gone. "I just got a tetanus shot."

"God, what have you done now?"

The exasperation in his voice bit at me. It wasn't like I'd got hurt on purpose. With a firm grip on my temper, I responded. "Nothing much, I just stood on a nail. What are you up to?"

He hesitated. "I can't tell you," he whispered.

"Why?"

"Because I can't."

"Is Janice Skipper listening?" I said.

"Yes. What are you up to?"

"I can't tell you," I said.

"Why?"

"Wow, this is the most déjà vu conversation I've ever had. Have I been beamed up into a parallel universe?"

Romeo sighed. "Sorry, darling, but I can't tell you anything right now. Are you sure you're okay? You sound a bit weird. Well, weirder than normal, anyway." He laughed.

My eyes narrowed, and the grip on my temper slipped a little. "I'm fine, really. Brad drove me to the hospital."

That produced a long silence from the other end of the phone, and I imagined Romeo doing some deep breathing before he allowed himself to speak again.

"How much longer are you going to be on this operation?" I said.

"Maybe a week," he said, his voice tense.

"How's Janice Skipper getting on with her investigation into the Fandango case?"

"She knows we're seeing each other, so she's careful not to give me any leads that might get back to you. The chief constable is on her back about it. He wants it solved ASAP."

I grinned, hoping that I'd made more headway than she had. Then I heard Janice Skipper yelling his name in the background. I felt my blood pressure rise and I scowled down the phone at her.

"Listen, I've got to go. And be careful," he said.

"I'm not that good at being careful."

"That's what worries me." And he disconnected.

After another small prick to administer an antibiotic shot, we eventually got back to my apartment three boring hours later.

"I'm starving. With all this excitement, I haven't even had any lunch yet." I limped inside. The throbbing had subsided to a dull ache. At least I had all my limbs intact, and none of them had turned into pieces of poultry.

"I'll cook. I've tasted your attempts at cooking, and it's not one of your greatest attributes." Brad peered into the fridge.

I looked over his shoulder. I had one onion, a moldy packet of grapes—which I bought when I was having a health kick day—one lonely egg, which looked like it was about to hatch, and two cartons of milk. Not even Gordon Ramsay could make something with that lot. He closed the fridge door and searched the rest of the kitchen.

"Don't you ever go food shopping?" Brad banged around, opening and closing cupboard doors.

"Yes, when I have time. In case you hadn't noticed, I've been very busy working on your cases."

"There's more to life than work." He gave me a suggestive grin.

"Ha! That's good, coming from you. You're always working, too."

"Have you managed to catch out Paul Clark yet?"

"No, but I will this week, even if it kills me."

"How about a strawberry omelet?" Brad said when all he'd discovered was a few bottles of red wine, a can of baked beans, and a jar of strawberry jam.

I pulled a selection of takeaway menus out of the drawer, waving them at him. "Or not. How about a nice, greasy takeaway instead?"

"I'm going shopping. I'll be back in an hour or so." Brad picked up his keys.

"Keep an eye out for Paul Clark," I shouted after him.

When Brad returned, he had all the ingredients to make a roast with all the trimmings, and a bottle of wine.

"You wouldn't be trying to get me drunk, would you?" I asked as he prepared the vegetables.

"I wouldn't dream of it." He opened the oven door to put the chicken in.

"Because it won't work, you know."

"What's this?" He peered inside the oven and pointed to a plastic, blobby mess on the bottom.

"Er…slight accident. The one and only time I ever actually used my oven was to cook a pizza, and I forgot to remove the plastic tray it came in, so I cooked that, too."

When he finished scraping off the plastic goo with a knife, he gave me a glass of wine and a smile. "You really are incredible."

I didn't know if that was a compliment or not, and I wasn't about to ask.

"Did you know that Enzo Fetuccini is on his last legs?" he said, changing the subject.

"No." I adjusted myself on the sofa, making room for Brad.

"He's got lung cancer. My sources tell me that there's some new guy who's taken over as head of the Fetuccini family, and no one knows who it is."

I took a sip of wine. "Someone must know who he is."

"Apparently, this guy has never even been seen or photographed before, by either the FBI or the organized-crime squad in America."

I tapped my glass, wondering about this. "You don't think—no, it's a ridiculous idea."

"What?"

"You don't think that Fandango has disappeared because he's this new godfather, do you?"

"The thought has crossed my mind. We know that he already had some kind of connection to Fetuccini."

"So, six months ago, Fetuccini starts making large payments to Fandango. What if it wasn't about money laundering or blackmail?

What if Fetuccini was paying him for future services, like taking over as the head of the family?"

"But if that's the case, why would the mob be looking for him?" Brad said.

I let this sink in while the nerve impulses in my brain flickered to life. "When I was in Heather's apartment, the mob goons asked me where 'it' was, not where 'he' was. Maybe they're not looking for Fandango because they already know where he is. I think they're looking for something else. If Fandango is this new secret Fetuccini godfather, I can understand why he suddenly appeared nineteen and a half years ago with an assumed identity, but it doesn't explain all this stuff about Tia and Samantha or the fashion collection."

Brad steepled his fingers as he considered this. "I think Fandango married Samantha to become a British citizen. What better cover could there be for a secret American godfather? No one would suspect a British citizen."

"I need to find out if Tia remembers anything about her mother, because either there's a frantic woman out there somewhere who's been looking for her daughter for the last twenty years, or her mother must be dead. If you were Fandango, would you have taken Tia away to an assumed life?"

"My moral code isn't very extensive, but I'd stop short of kidnapping a baby from her mother. Unfortunately, I don't think the mob have much of a moral code about anything. But we only have Samantha's word to corroborate that Tia is Fandango's real daughter, anyway. Hacker can't find any actual proof."

"No, I think Samantha was telling the truth about that part." I downed the last dregs of my wine. "But I don't think I buy this business about Fandango being a secret mob boss. It seems a little far-fetched. Did you hear about Heather's spending habits?"

"She's withdrawn seventy-five thousand pounds from her account in the last nine months. Seems to me she's got some sort of problem. I'm guessing drugs or gambling."

"It's also a possible motive. People who are desperate for money do desperate things. Maybe she thinks with Fandango out of the way, she can take over his empire and embezzle a bit of petty cash."

"It's a possibility," he said.

"I don't think we're looking at this from the right angle. Every time I think I'm getting somewhere, something new gets thrown into the mix. And the disappearance of the fashion collection doesn't seem to fit in with any theory I come up with."

Brad paused, glancing at the floor. "I didn't just offer you this job because you and I had unfinished business, you know."

I should've told him that we didn't have any unfinished business. I should've told him that, as far as I was concerned, our business was definitely, one hundred percent finito. But the wine was going to my head on an empty stomach, and to be honest, a little light flirtation was on my mind. *There's nothing wrong with that*, I told myself, feeling in a playful mood. *As long as I don't actually do anything, flirtation is fine, isn't it?*

"Oh, tell me more." I smiled, elbowing him in the ribs.

He looked me square in the eyes. "I offered it to you because you really are a great investigator, and I hope you stay with Hi-Tec. Not just for my own personal, selfish reasons, but because I know you'll be a great asset."

I threw my arms around his hard neck and hugged him. "That's the nicest thing anyone's said to me in a long time."

He turned his head to face me, and I could sense that this might be the point of no return. I heard him take a deep breath, and the room turned very quiet. Butterflies fluttered in my stomach, and it was one of those strange moments when your senses are heightened and the colors around you seem brighter. One of those moments when you know that if you take that next step, nothing will ever be the same again. And although it would take one tiny moment for me to kiss him, I knew the dangers of giving in to one of those moments. I'd done it before, when I shot Janice Skipper, and the consequences had been dire. Suddenly, I couldn't stare into his penetrating eyes any longer. I quickly detached myself from him and pulled back, mentally kicking myself.

Leaping up from the sofa, I retreated into the safety of the kitchen on shaky legs, astonished at the magnitude of my feelings. Pressing both hands to my cheeks, I stared out the window. What the hell was I doing? Maybe it wasn't Brad who was dangerous. Maybe I was a danger to myself. It wasn't him that I didn't trust, it was me that I didn't trust. I tried to slow my breathing. If I just concentrated on breathing, I could forget about these crazy feelings that I thought I'd finally gotten rid of, couldn't I? Yes, of course it would work, because I'd promised myself a long time ago that this would never happen again. And besides, I had Romeo now. I loved Romeo. There was no way I would ever betray him. I clutched the worktop until my knuckles turned white.

I'm not sure how long I stood there, listening to the sound of my heart thumping around in my chest. Eventually, I poured us another glass of wine. Okay, maybe another glass wasn't such a good idea under the circumstances, but I needed something to distract me. I went back to the living room and handed Brad a glass, then sat on the floor, knees bent, clutching my arms around them. Brad just watched me without saying anything.

I swallowed hard and took a desperate stab at sounding normal. "Samantha James is hiding something." It was my turn to change the subject now.

"You said it yourself—everybody's hiding something. Even you."

What did he mean? How did he even *know* if I was hiding something anymore? I wasn't the same person now that I was two years ago, and Brad wasn't qualified anymore to know me so well.

I conveniently ignored his last comment and carried on. "She lied to me about not having any contact with Fandango for nineteen and a half years. I know, because I found a rhinestone from his fashion collection in her warehouse."

"Are you going to go back and question her?"

"I'd like to get some more information first. I also found out that Callum Bates is working for Lennie and Lonnie Cohen. It sounds like they're getting ready to ship a batch of stolen vehicles out of the country this week. If they're going to torch the warehouse, I'm betting it will be after they've got rid of the goods."

"Good work, Foxy." He winked at me over the rim of his glass. "You can get your reward now for a job well done."

I gulped. Oh, God, what kind of reward did he have in mind?

"Don't look so worried. Your reward is a nice roasted chicken dinner." As he spoke, a timer went off in the kitchen.

Phew! Saved by the chicken.

CHAPTER SEVENTEEN

Luckily, throbbing body parts didn't keep me awake that night. Mine or Brad's—although I was quite sure that Brad would've liked the idea. However, he had left shortly after we consumed our dinner. Random thoughts deep in my subconscious kept me awake instead. There was just something about the disappearance of the fashion collection. Something about it kept niggling away at me. I woke up early with an idea burning in my brain.

I crawled out of bed and toed through the discarded clothing piled up on the floor. I peered in the closet, only to discover that a clothes-stealing troglodyte had been wearing all my clothes and failing to return them, washed and ironed. All I had left in the closet were my girly clothes, which were far too nice and too expensive to wear while chasing criminals. I dug around a little more and finally discovered a pair of camouflage combat trousers and a sweatshirt in my laundry basket that appeared to be recyclable.

I didn't have time for breakfast, so I gulped a glass of orange juice and grabbed a cold baked potato to eat in the car. My foot still felt a bit tender when I stuffed it into my standby pair of sneakers, which I kept in the back of the cupboard for just such an occasion. That proved the theory I'd had for a number of years now: a girl can never have enough pairs of shoes.

My first stop was Heather's apartment. As I pulled into the communal parking lot, I noticed that her BMW was still parked in the same spot. A black and white cat rubbed himself against the tires in ecstasy, like he'd been snorting catnip. I took the stairs to her apartment and rapped my knuckles gently on her door. As I did this, the door swung open a couple of inches. Either I had magic door-opening knuckles, or the mob goons had left it unsecured. My second guess seemed like the most plausible. I suspected they weren't particularly security-conscious guys.

I took a deep breath and pushed the door open all the way. Everything seemed exactly as I'd left it when I ran out on Saturday, minus the goons. I wandered through the rooms with a sinking feeling in the pit of my stomach. Heather still hadn't returned.

Next up, I went by Fandango's office, just in case Heather had been mysteriously transported there in some kind of weird Star Trek-y time warp. The only living thing that greeted me was a solitary sparrow, pecking about on the ground. The doors were still locked. I banged on them a couple of times just in case. While I waited, I peered through the leopard skin curtains, but the place was as deserted as the *Mary Celeste*.

I said goodbye to the sparrow and made my way to Tia's apartment.

"Hi." Tia's face lit up when she saw me. "Have you got any news? The police haven't told me anything." She beckoned me inside.

Her apartment was exactly how I'd imagined it would be. A mix of vibrant colors and textures filled the spacious, open floor-plan apartment, which overlooked the Union Canal. A shrieking orange sofa took center stage in the living room, covered with leopard print cushions. In front of the sofa stood a modern-style chrome and glass coffee table, and a matching chrome and glass TV stand took up a corner wall. She must be Fandango's daughter after all, I thought, as I observed her choice of décor. Again, I noticed the lack of photos or personal items. Maybe it was me. Surely I wasn't the only person in the world with OCD (obsessive clutter disorder)?

"What have the police told you so far?" I asked, fishing for information. If I could learn what Janice Skipper had discovered with her investigation into the Fandango case, maybe I'd be able to beat her to the finish line and solve the case before she did. I got a shiver of excitement just thinking about it.

She brought her arms out to the side and let them fall again, hands hitting her thighs with a slapping sound. "They won't tell me anything."

"I need to ask you some questions. They might seem a bit strange, but if we're going to find out what happened to your dad, I need you to be completely honest with me, okay?"

Tia sat and patted the empty space next to her on the sofa. "Of course. I just want to help find my dad."

I sunk down into the squashy fabric. "How old are you, Tia?"

"Twenty."

"Have you ever seen your birth certificate?"

"No, I don't think so."

"Didn't you see it when you applied for your driver's license or passport?"

"No, Dad always sorts out all that sort of stuff. Why are you asking?"

"I'll get to that in a minute." I gave her my best reassuring smile. I figured the next question would be a tough one for her. "What did Umberto tell you about your mum?"

Her body stiffened, and she glanced down. A clock ticking somewhere in the background was the only sound in the silence of the apartment. She sat like that for a while, picking at her thumbnail. When she looked up again, her eyes glistened with tears. "My mom died when I was really young." She sniffled and fanned at her eyes.

I reached out and gave her arm a gentle squeeze. "Did he tell you what happened?"

"No. He said it was too horrible. Of course, I asked him about it loads of times, but he refused to tell me."

"Did you ever try to find out what happened yourself?"

"I wanted to, but I didn't know where to start looking."

"Have you ever had contact with any other family?"

"No. Dad said that we didn't have any family left."

I let go of her arm and sank back on the sofa. If I'd kidnapped a baby, that was exactly what I would've said, too. "Has anyone tried to contact you, since he disappeared?"

She shook her head and sniffed.

"When I looked around your dad's house, I noticed there weren't any photos of the two of you—or anyone else, for that matter." I glanced around the living room. "You haven't got anything either. Why is that?"

"Dad isn't flashy at all. He's a very private person, and he's not very sentimental. He doesn't keep stuff like that around, and I just never bothered either, I suppose."

I smiled at her. "He's obviously sentimental about you. He's bought an apartment for you, and presumably he paid for your schooling in America. He's looked after you singlehandedly since you were born. Unfortunately, I think Umberto was carrying around a huge secret, and I need to get to the bottom of it if I'm going to find out what happened to him."

Tia gave me a sad smile. "That's all I want, too. I just want to bring him home safe and sound."

"What was your childhood like? Where did you live and go to school?"

"I went to private school in the UK. When I graduated, I went to the States to study fashion at university. I've just finished a three-year course."

"Whose idea was it to study in the States?"

"Mine. Dad wanted me to stay here, but there are better opportunities in the States."

"What about friends?"

She gazed at the floor and rubbed her temples, sighing. "I didn't have many friends. It was kind of just the two of us most of the time. I got the feeling that he didn't want me to go too far away from him."

"He was over-protective?"

"Yes, but in a good way."

"So you didn't have a nanny or someone to look after you? Someone who could've discovered something about your dad?"

"No, Dad looked after me by himself."

"How about a cleaner or a chef?"

"No, Dad did everything."

Wow. A very rich, practical guy who ran a successful business, looked after his daughter singlehandedly, and did the cleaning. I didn't think there were many of those around. From what I'd learned so far about Umberto Fandango, he seemed to be a genuinely nice guy, which made this case even more peculiar. "And no one ever tried to approach you when you were younger? No one ever told you anything strange about your dad or asked questions?"

"No."

"If you went to school in the UK, how come you never lost your American accent?"

"I picked it up from Dad initially, but then the kids were mean to me at school. I got bullied a bit because I was different. But the more they tried to hurt me, the more determined I became to hang on to my accent. It's good to be a little different from everyone else." She lifted her chin and looked me in the eye. "It's strange, you know. We all start off the same, but I can't understand why some people turn out mean."

I sighed. I'd seen my fair share of mean people over the years. "There are beautiful people and ugly people in the world. And I don't just mean on the outside. Unfortunately, that's never going to change, but it really is true that whatever doesn't kill you makes you stronger."

A half-smile flickered across her face. "You're right."

"While we're on the subject of mean people, did your dad ever mention the name Carlos Bagliero?"

"No."

"How about Enzo Fetuccini?"

"Fetuccini? Like the pasta?" Her eyes lit up. "So I was right about the pasta connection, then?"

"Actually, I think you were, but it's probably not the kind of connection you were hoping for. Fetuccini is the head of a mafia family in America. He had some kind of connection with your dad, but I don't know exactly what it is."

"Dad never mentioned it to me, but then I didn't have anything to do with his fashion business yet. I was going to go to work for him when I graduated from my fashion course. But I can't believe he was involved with the mafia. He just wasn't like that. There has to be some kind of rational explanation. Maybe they went to school together, or played on the same softball team when they were kids or something."

I didn't think it was likely. "He never mentioned anything to you about Fetuccini at all?"

"No, Amber. You have to believe me."

I nodded, giving her a minute before continuing on to the next subject. Unfortunately, I didn't think she would take it as well as the previous. "Tia, have you ever heard the name Samantha James?"

Her face wrinkled as she thought. "No, I don't think so. Why?"

I took a deep breath and chose my next words carefully. "You told me that your dad wasn't married, but I've found out that wasn't quite true. Apparently, he got married when you were about six months old.

They only stayed together a few months, but they never got divorced."

Tia shook her head and turned to me, confusion plastered all over her face. "He never told me." A silence ensued as she took this in. "What was her name again?" she said finally, her mouth still open with shock.

"Samantha James."

"So, he's still married to her? She's my...stepmother?" Shoulders drooping, she gazed at the ground, shaking her head softly.

"Ms. James says that your father asked her to come to his office and sign divorce papers on the day he disappeared."

"She saw him on the day he disappeared? Do you think that means something?"

"I'm not sure yet."

"Did she sign these divorce papers?"

I shrugged. "She says that she did."

"God, what else hasn't Dad told me?" she whispered, more to herself than to me.

I watched a range of emotions flicker across her face: surprise, curiosity, worry, and anger. She finally settled on sadness.

"We think he only married her to get British citizenship, and that he was hiding from something or someone because there's no trace of an Umberto Fandango until nineteen and a half years ago, when he came to the UK. We can't find any birth certificates for you, either."

She turned astonished eyes on me. "But that's impossible. And anyway, what could he be hiding from?"

"I don't know, but whatever it is, I'm guessing it's pretty serious. And I think someone else found out about it, too."

"So, who was he really? And who am I?" She folded her arms across her chest and clutched her arms.

"I know this must be a huge shock to you, but don't worry. Hacker is still looking into things. If anyone can find the truth, he can. Do you want me to call anyone for you?"

"I don't have any family to call. Apart from this Samantha James." She sniffed and looked away. "I think I need to think about things for a while on my own. I need to try to get my head around all of this."

Any doubt I had held as to whether or not Tia had been involved in her father's disappearance had vanished. If she was acting, she was one of the best I'd seen, on or off the big screen. I studied her, trying to work out whether she would be able to get through this without falling apart. Grief did funny things to people, and even though we hadn't found Fandango's body yet, she was starting to go through the process. In a lot of ways, not knowing could be worse than actually finding out what happened to a loved one. It was certainly more wearying. When I first met Tia, I admit I'd kind of written her off as a fragile, kooky airhead, but now I realized that she was stronger than she seemed. She was determined and resilient enough to get through this. I just hoped she realized it, too.

She jumped up suddenly and rushed into the kitchen. "I almost forgot, I finally found my dad's car keys, and there's something odd about them." I heard a drawer open and slam before she strode back in the living room carrying a set of keys.

"Where did you find them?" I examined the bundle of keys, which were tied together with a simple key ring.

"It's the weirdest thing. I found them in my kitchen drawer. He must've put them in there for some strange reason."

"Maybe he didn't want anyone else to find them." I held up a gold key that seemed to have no business on a set of car keys. It was thin, with a corrugated ridge running along the entire length of one side and an eight-digit number etched into it. "I think it's a safety deposit box key."

I called Hacker and asked him to try and trace which bank and box the code number related to. "He's going to call me back," I told Tia when I disconnected.

"I had another psychic premonition," she said, "while you were on the phone."

I tried hard not to look skeptical.

"No, really. I'm seeing something about a yellow sheep."

I held up the key. "Maybe it's got to do with this." I traced my finger along the ridge. "It's gold, with a wobbly shape, kind of like a yellow sheep's wool if you look really hard."

She gave me a strange look. "I don't think so—hey, I know! I think you should do a spell for inspiration."

I arched an eyebrow. "A spell? I don't really believe in all that stuff. Why don't you do it instead?"

Tia's shoulders drooped. "I can't. You're the person investigating this, so you have to do it."

I heard the disappointment clouding her voice, and I felt like a grumpy old meanie. Okay, so Tia had been right about the pasta thing, but I still didn't believe in all that hocus-pocus. As if on cue, to stop me elaborating on this subject anymore, Hacker returned my call.

"Yo. The key is for a safety deposit box at Universal American Bank in Canary Wharf. The box number is five-five-one, and it's rented to Umberto Fandango. Tia Fandango is listed as a supplementary name to gain access to the box," Hacker said, sounding pretty pleased with himself.

That was when I knew without a shadow of a doubt that Tia really was his daughter—because otherwise, why would Fandango give her access to his safety deposit box?

"Hey, are you with Tia?" he said.

"Yes." I could sense him grinning on the other end of the phone.

"Tell her I said yo."

I chuckled. "Okay, will do." And I hung up. "Hacker says yo,'" I said to Tia.

Tia blushed and did her snorty little hyena giggle. "He's yummy."

I thought Hacker was plenty of things, but I'd never describe him as yummy. Still, each to their own. The world would be a pretty boring place if we all thought the same thing.

* * *

Tia and I spent forty-five minutes on the train, squashed in between a businessman's sweaty armpit and an elderly woman who had overdone it with what smelled like Listerine. I didn't know which was worse, but I sure was glad when we emerged from the underground at Canary Wharf. I drew in deep breaths of relatively fresh air, not caring that it had a hint of smoggy, London bus pollution.

We walked the short distance to the Universal American Bank and were directed to the basement by a very efficient member of staff. As we descended the final steps to the deposit box vault, Tia stopped in her tracks, clutching my arm.

"I don't know if I want to find out what's in it." She turned to me with anguished eyes.

"You have to know, Tia. Knowledge is power, and whatever happens, the only way to move forward is if you know the truth. Your dad must've wanted you to find whatever is in that vault, because he specified that you could access it."

She gave me a shaky smile. "You're right." She straightened up her back and carried on walking.

A security guard stood in the reception area outside the vault. Another guard stood outside the reinforced concrete vault door, which was cased in steel.

A nervous Tia told the guard she wanted to gain access to Fandango's box and was asked for her ID. She handed over her driver's license and he recorded it in a logbook. Handing it back to her, he escorted us into the thirty-meter-square vault. Fluorescent overhead lights shone down on row upon row of different-sized deposit boxes. The security guard slid his key into the box, waiting for Tia to do the same. When the keys turned simultaneously, the lock clicked open, and the security guard left us to it.

Tia slid the box from the wall and placed it on a steel table in the center of the room. She glanced up at me, her hand gripping the handle of the box.

I gave her an encouraging nod. I didn't know what I expected to find in there, but I hoped it wasn't a severed ear, or any other bits and pieces that I'd heard the mob liked chopping off.

"Here goes." She opened it and peered inside.

I stepped closer, my eyes firmly locked on the table in front of me. The only thing taking up space in the slim steel box was a faded American passport.

Tia lifted the passport out and flicked through the worn out pages. "'Carlos Bagliero.'" She read the name on the passport and handed it to me. "That's the name you asked me about earlier."

I studied the photograph. Bagliero had light brown curly hair, worn collar length with a fringe, which nearly covered his green eyes. He had lighter skin than I would expect for someone of Italian-American origin—not the usual Mediterranean olive swarthy complexion—and he had a neatly trimmed beard. The date of birth showed Bagliero had been born in 1959 in Sicily. That would make him fifty years old today. The passport had expired fifteen years ago.

So, Heather hadn't made a mistake when she'd scribbled Bagliero's name on the note I'd found in her apartment, which led me to my next thought. If Hacker couldn't find any information on him, then this case was bigger than I'd imagined. But what was Bagliero's passport doing in Fandango's safety deposit box?

"Do you recognize him?" I said.

"I've never seen him before."

"And you're sure Umberto never mentioned him?"

"I'm positive." She closed up the box and slid it back into the wall. "I think you should keep the passport. Hopefully it will help you find my dad."

CHAPTER EIGHTEEN

"It could be a fake." Brad leaned back in his office chair, looking through the passport.

"It doesn't look like a fake," I said.

"Hacker said he couldn't find any information on Bagliero, which means either the passport is a fake, or someone pretty powerful has had his records wiped."

"Okay, let's assume that it isn't a fake. Bagliero was born in Sicily but had American citizenship, which smacks of mafia connection. Who is powerful enough to wipe his records? The FBI, CIA, the organized-crime squad, Homeland Security, or a mole in one of those offices who is working for the mob. Take your pick."

"Fandango suddenly appears out of nowhere nineteen and a half years ago, and Bagliero has had his records wiped. Hardly a coincidence, don't you think?"

I grinned. "That's exactly what I was thinking."

"I'll get Hacker to dig into it again. What about Tia?"

"I think that Tia is Fandango's real daughter. I just don't know who her mother is, or how Fandango disappeared with Tia and no one noticed."

"Well, I have every faith in your abilities to solve this case."

That got me smiling at his not-so-subtle piece of flattery. "I've been thinking about the disappearance of the fashion collection as well. Something has been bugging me about it all along, and I finally worked out what it is." My mind raced on. How stupid of me not to have considered it before. "The collection is pretty much worthless on its own because it's recognizable. It's not something you could fence easily, so why would someone go to the trouble of stealing it?"

"You tell me, Foxy."

I held my forefinger up in the air for emphasis. "Because something was being smuggled inside it. Fetuccini paid Fandango five million pounds for shipments of this collection. The note in Heather's apartment points to Bagliero paying five million pounds as well. The money-laundering scenario never seemed quite right to me, but the payments would make sense if Fandango was smuggling drugs inside the clothing. Maybe Heather found out what was going on and wanted a piece of the action for herself. She's broke, so she needs money, and if she gets rid of Fandango, she can carry on the smuggling ring and keep all the profits."

"And how are you going to try and find the drugs?"

I gave him a cocky smile. "I don't need to find the whole shipment. If I can confirm the presence of drugs at Fandango's office, then that will prove my theory. Don't you just love it when a plan comes together?"

"What's the plan?"

"I have a secret drug-detector weapon."

* * *

My parents' house was empty when I arrived. I scribbled them a note to say I'd borrowed Sabre, and then I grabbed his lead and a few meaty tidbits in the hope that I could deflect him from using me as the meaty tidbit.

I arrived at Fandango's flourmill with an excited Sabre in tow. His eyes were bright and shiny, his nose twitched with excitement, and he was practically frothing at the mouth as I clipped on the lead. Once again, the place was deserted, so I punched in the security code on the front door, and Sabre pulled me inside.

"Seek," I said to him as he sat down, looking up at me expectantly.

Nothing happened.

"Find." I pointed around the room.

That didn't get him moving either.

"Look." I tried a more ushering hand action.

Nada.

"Sabre, go."

He licked his lips. Well, that was a start.

I pulled out my mobile and called Dad. It rang and rang. No answer. I left a message and hung up.

Then I called Romeo, who actually answered his phone for a change. "Hey, do you remember what the search command for Sabre is?"

"Do I even want to know what you're doing?"

"Probably not," I said.

"Are you seriously going to use Sabre for a search? You know what happened the last time he did one."

"That wasn't Sabre's fault."

"The poor handler got a broken leg trying to get away before Sabre humped him to death!"

"Sabre was just a bit over-excited about finding some booty, that's all. Look, I can't deny that Sabre has a few quirky mental issues, but he's a brilliant drugs dog with one of the best sniffy noses in the country. And Janice has more resources at her disposal, so I need all the help I can get. I'm counting on him to find something useful to help me crack the case."

He sighed, and I could imagine him rubbing his hands over his face. "Okay, as long as you know what you're doing. I think the standard command is 'search.' But that dog is nuts. No wonder he got kicked off the force for his unpredictable behavior."

"Maybe it runs in the family," I said.

He sighed again. "Maybe it does."

"What's that supposed to mean?" I snapped.

"Nothing," he said in a tone that implied he certainly did mean something.

"No, carry on," I said, not satisfied.

"Look, it's not easy being stuck in the middle between you and Janice. And since we're doing this operation together, she's making my life hell."

"She's doing it on purpose to split us up. Ignore her."

"It's pretty hard to ignore Janice—oh, shit. I've gotta go." He hung up.

Oh, hell! What did he mean it was pretty hard to ignore Janice? Did he mean that in a sexual way or not? Before I could worry about it any more, my phone rang again. It was Dad.

"Hi, Amber. The command for Sabre is 'search'—oh, and make sure you don't use the word 'slipper.' He goes double bonkoid on that one."

"Great. Thanks, Dad." I closed the phone and turned to Sabre. "Search," I said in an authoritative voice.

And he was off, sniffing away like there was no tomorrow as I followed close behind, holding on to his lead for dear life.

We started in the reception area. Sabre's claws clicked on the floor as he zigzagged across the room on his quest. Obviously there was nothing of interest here, because he quickly got bored and pulled me toward Fandango's office.

I opened the door, hoping for a lucky hit. Sabre sniffed around Heather's desk, and then made his way to Fandango's. He wagged his tail a bit but didn't sit down and bark, which would've been a sure sign that drugs were lurking inside. He ran around the curtains, poked his nose in the sofa, and then flew out of the room. His eyes darted around, as if he were deciding where to go next, before he bounded upstairs to the storage area, taking the steps two at a time, and almost pulling me flat on my face. He searched every single inch of the room with heightened interest, but he kept on going until the whole room was covered in wet nose slicks.

He led me back down the stairs and into the runway area, where he haphazardly ran around, diving under the runway and out the other side, but again, he didn't give me a warning signal.

"Damn, damn, damn," I muttered under my breath, following Sabre into the dressing rooms.

And that was where he hit the jackpot.

Sabre made the peculiar whiny-growling sound he was known for as soon as we got in there. He took great care searching around the dressing tables and drawers, which were crammed full of makeup, hair products, and other weird things designed to nip, tuck, and hold bits in. When he approached the lockers on one side of the room, he sniffed for England. Then he sat down, barked, and wagged his tail with fervor.

I was just reaching for one of the locker doors when my phone rang. I almost jumped out of my skin.

"Hey, darling. I'm sorry about earlier. I'm just trying to do my job and getting caught up in Janice's little agenda is not helping," Romeo said.

I stared at the lockers. "That's okay." It wasn't really, but now wasn't the time for this conversation. "I think Sabre might've found something. What are you up to?"

"I'm doing some boring observation. My partner's just gone to get us some lunch, so I thought I'd give you a quick call."

"And who are you partnered with?"

A long pause on the other end of the phone. And then: "Er…Janice Skipper."

I felt my blood simmering away, working its way up to boiling point. "Janice Skipper?" I yelled.

"Ah. So, I suppose this isn't a great time to talk about us moving in together, then?"

But before I could say another word, Sabre had jumped me from behind. He planted his front paws on the back of my shoulders and pushed me down onto the ground.

The wind flew out of my lungs, and the phone slid from my grasp, flying across the floor, as Sabre pinned me down, humping away at my back with his pop-up lipstick. Not a particularly good position to be in, really, although I suspected it might be even yuckier if he'd jumped me from the front instead.

I tried to lift myself up and shake him off, but he was in a severely hyped-up humping frenzy by then and had a firm hold of me with his front paws, pushing me down. He whinnied away, and I felt his hot breath panting on the back of my head. My hair quickly became wet with slobber—at least, I hoped it was slobber. Slobber was more preferable to other kinds of doggy fluids.

Sabre lost his grip for a second, and I managed to maneuver myself into a crawl position, attempting to drag my body along the floor, but this only seemed to excite him more.

Luckily, canine humping lasted nowhere near as long as human humping, and after a few more thrusts on my back, the whole horrible ordeal was over. He climbed off and collapsed in the corner of the room, panting. If I didn't know better, I would've sworn I saw a smile on his face.

I got to my feet and pulled a disgusted face. I didn't even want to imagine what I looked like. My hair felt matted, I could feel a sticky patch on the back of my T-shirt, and I smelled like wet dog. I'd done some bizarre things before to try and solve a case, but this really took the dog biscuit.

Like all males, Sabre decided to opt for a post-humping sleep, so while the coast was clear, I had a look in the lockers.

I didn't really expect to find much, since the crime-scene unit had already been over the whole building, but Sabre had given me all the confirmation I needed about the presence of drugs in his own unique way. However, I figured it wouldn't hurt to look.

I rifled through most of the sixteen lockers and didn't find so much as a single bag of grass or a joint. In the last one, though, I saw a tiny piece of white paper that had slipped in between the strip of metal joints on the back wall of the locker.

I picked up a pair of tweezers from one of the dressing tables and reached inside the locker, grabbing the edge of the paper.

Voila! It was a small piece of paper that had been folded in on itself. I carefully unfolded it and discovered some fine white powder inside. I gave a wide grin, glad the day hadn't been a total waste. I'd found a wrap of what I thought was probably cocaine.

I stuffed it into a plastic bag in my rucksack, grabbed a couple towels from the bathroom, and left. Draping the towels over my seat, I drove back to my parents' house, being careful not to lean on the upholstery.

"You forgot to mention that Sabre goes double bonkoid about words that rhyme with slipper, too," I told Dad when I dropped the dog off. He just shook his head at me, but I didn't care. I pointed the car toward my apartment and rushed home for a long decontamination session in the shower.

Marmalade took one look at me, sniffed around my legs for a minute, and ran under the sofa and hid. I didn't blame him. If I could've hidden under the sofa to get away from me, I would've done the same, and his sense of smell was even more acute than mine. Instead, I dumped my clothes in the rubbish bin, scrubbed myself with apple blossom shower gel four times, and washed my hair three times, just to be on the safe side. I was squirting myself all over with perfume when I had a horrible thought about Heather.

* * *

I drove to her apartment, desperately hoping that I was wrong. I parked the Lemon next to her BMW and tentatively opened my door.

I noticed the flies buzzing around the boot before I smelled the familiar stench of decay and death. Slowly, I reached out and popped the boot catch.

It swung open in a fluid arc, sending a swarm of flies streaming out toward me. I swatted them away with my hand, and that was when I saw her.

Heather had been dumped in the boot, curled up in the fetal position. A Barack Obama mask covered her face. The mask had a hole in it where a bullet wound to the center of her forehead had ripped through it, execution style. Maggots crawled around in the wound, vying for a good feeding spot. I guessed she'd probably been killed shortly before she was due to meet me on Friday night.

I'd dealt with death many times during my career. You got used to it to some degree; you had to. In order to be a good cop, you had to find a way to detach yourself from the reality of it, but it wasn't exactly what I would call one of the most pleasant aspects of the job.

I stepped away from the BMW and called the police control room. I told the dispatcher what I'd found, and they assured me they'd send someone. While I paced furiously around the parking lot in circles, waiting for the coroner's officer, I contemplated just how short life really was. If I knew that my number was going to be up tomorrow, would I do things any differently? Would I say yes to Romeo and move in with him? Or would I do the unthinkable and take my chances with Brad? Would I go running to Janice Skipper, begging for forgiveness, hoping she would give me my old job back? Or would I just put up and shut up, finally accepting that life moves on as, inevitably, it always does? Was anything really how it appeared to be, or was the truth just hidden in layers?

I was still lost in thought when Carol Blake, a coroner's officer that I'd known for years, pulled up and parked on the other side of the BMW.

"Well, well, well. Janice Skipper won't like this, will she?" She flashed me a wicked grin as she slipped out of her vehicle and pulled on a pair of rubber gloves.

"Well, Janice Skipper can shove it up her—"

She cut me off with a throaty laugh. "That's my girl. Don't let the old hag get to you. Remember that famous old saying: what goes around comes around. She'll get what's coming to her one day." She gave me a quick hug. "She tried to get me thrown off the force once, too, back when she was in charge of the coroner's unit, you know."

"I didn't know that!"

"The trouble with Janice is that she can't stand anyone who's good at their job. It makes her look bad because she's so useless. She's one twisted individual. Luckily for me, she got moved to one of the special operation teams, and I don't have to put up with her any more."

"It wasn't so lucky for me, though."

She threw me a grim look. "I know." She wandered over to the BMW, peering into the boot with a critical eye. "Is this to do with the Fandango case?"

"Yes, I'm pretty sure this is his assistant, Heather Brown."

"You know that Janice Skipper is working this case, too?" She lifted off the Obama mask to reveal Heather's wide open, icy-cold eyes and waxy, pale skin.

I sucked in a breath and nodded.

"Someone's taking bets down at the station about who is going to get a result first," she said.

"And who's the favorite, me or Janice?"

"You, of course. That woman couldn't investigate her way out of a paper bag."

That made me smile. "Well, game on, then."

"And may the best woman win!" She nodded toward Heather's lifeless body. "I'll let you know what I find."

"Thanks." I climbed into the Lemon as my phone rang. Romeo's name was displayed on the caller ID.

"Hey, darling. Are you still mad at me?"

I sighed and glanced up, staring through the windscreen at Heather's bedroom window. "No."

"It's just that you don't normally hang up on me."

"I didn't hang up. I was being humped to death by Sabre." I heard a muffled laugh from the other end of the phone. "It's not funny."

"I take it that Sabre found something useful, then."

"That depends."

"On what?"

"It depends on whether we're exchanging information. I'll tell you my news if you tell me what Janice knows. I hear there's a book down at the station, betting on who'll be the first to solve this case."

"Darling, she's keeping everyone in the dark about it. She knows it will get back to you."

"So, have you finished your stakeout with her?"

"Are you jealous?"

"No," I snapped, trying hard to keep the green-eyed monster out of my voice and failing miserably. "But since we're on the subject, why is it so hard to ignore Janice?"

"Because she's crazy."

"A minute ago you implied that I was crazy," I huffed.

"Yes, but you're crazy in a nice way, she's crazy in a psycho way." It was his turn to sigh. "Look, it's just the same as you and Brad."

God, I hoped not. Then I really would have a reason to be jealous of Romeo working with her. "Huh?" I thought I'd try the vague approach.

"Well, why do you think Brad gave you this job?"

I tapped the steering wheel. "Because he needed a good investigator, and I'm really, really good. I'd also like to add that I'm much better than Janice."

"No, Amber. It's because he wants you back."

"No!" I tried my best shocked voice.

"Look, I'm not Brad, you know. I'm not going to leave you, so there's no reason for you to be jealous." He paused. "And I trust you, so neither of us has got anything to be jealous about. Have we?"

I was glad someone trusted me. I didn't know if I trusted me. "Er…no," I replied, not overly convinced by the words coming out of my mouth.

"Great—oh, I've just heard Janice is on her way down to Heather's car with SOCO, so, unless you want to see her, I'd leave now."

I didn't need telling twice. I knew I'd have to give a statement at some point, but right now wasn't the best time for me. Picking up the phone, I put a call in to the office to let them know about Heather, and stepped on the accelerator. I figured it might be a good time to make my way to the Cohens' warehouse for a stakeout of my own.

CHAPTER NINETEEN

Twilight had turned to dusk by the time I'd settled myself in for another exciting night watching the warehouse. I wrapped a fleece around me to keep out the chill and sipped on a super-sized cappuccino. A wave of tiredness threatened to smother me. I guess that's what doggy humping did to a person. What I really needed was some matchsticks to prop my eyelids open. I settled for rubbing them instead.

A Lamborghini drove up to the warehouse a short time later. It was the same drill as before. The door rolled up, and the car disappeared inside. I peered through the night-vision goggles, wishing that the arsonist would just hurry up and arrive so I could catch him and go home to my snuggly bed.

I finally succumbed to weariness as my chin drooped onto my chest, and my eyelids slid shut. I didn't hear or see Brad arrive until he'd sat down next to me. As his body slid in next to mine, bam! I was wide awake.

"Here." He handed me a flask of coffee.

"Thanks. What are you doing here?"

"The same thing you are. I thought you might like some company."

I sipped the hot liquid. "Heather's dead."

"I heard. And the second Obama mask turns up."

"Strange, huh? But was it planted to make her look guilty, was it a message of some kind, or was she really involved in all of this?"

"That's the thousand-dollar question. The woman who witnessed the white van leaving the scene of the crime said the driver wore an Obama mask. If Heather had found out who the perpetrators were, it could be a message to others to keep quiet."

"Or her killers put the mask on her to throw the scent off them and make it look like she was involved." I finished the coffee and poured another cup. "Or she really was involved in all of this."

"Did you find any drugs at Fandango's office?"

"I found a small wrap of coke. It could be something."

"Or it could be nothing. A lot of models do coke, don't they? Models are in and out of that place all the time. A wrap is hardly evidence of a major drug-smuggling ring."

I stretched my legs in front of me, leaning forward to ease the stiff muscles in my back. "It's the only thing at the moment that explains the payments from the mob. But if Fandango was smuggling drugs in with the shipments of his collection, why would the mob be involved in killing him and stealing the collection? Surely they'd want to keep him alive to carry on with their dodgy business."

"Maybe Fandango double-crossed them. Maybe they wanted to teach him a lesson, so they whacked him and helped themselves to the drugs."

"It's possible. But at the end of the day, they're still businessmen. I think they'd be in this for the long-term benefits. It wouldn't be a wise business move to do away with the smuggler. Maybe Heather found out and double-crossed Fandango. She had a motive. She had some kind of financial drain, probably drugs. She needed the money. Just think how much money she could make if she was in charge of a possible drug-smuggling ring." I turned to Brad.

"But then who killed Heather?" He reached out and tucked one of my flyaway waves behind my ear.

I flinched, his touch burning my skin. I adjusted my position on the ground to avoid further hair molesting.

"Samantha James also has a motive," he said.

I nodded. "And she lied to me."

"What about Tia? She stands to inherit his fortune."

"I don't think Tia's involved in any of this. I can't say the same for any family she's got lurking out there somewhere, though. We need to find out who Fandango was and who Bagliero is. Has Hacker come up with anything yet?"

"No, he's still working on it."

A black Porsche drove up to the warehouse and disappeared inside. Brad gazed at me intently.

"What?" Was I wearing a foam mustache from the coffee? Had I got lipstick on my teeth? I wiped around my mouth, just in case.

"Are you hungry?" Brad said.

"That depends." I grinned.

"On what?"

"Are we talking about food or something else?"

Brad feigned surprise. "Food of course. My, my, my, Amber Fox, you have a dirty mind. Nothing's doing here. Let's get something to eat."

"Okay, just as long as it's not me."

* * *

I knew I shouldn't have got up the next morning. I should've just stayed in bed with a pillow over my head, hibernating from the world and thinking about nice things like clothes shopping. How long had it been since I'd done that? I couldn't even remember. I loved investigating crimes, and it was all well and good wearing practical work clothes, but sometimes it would be nice to just have a normal job, where people didn't want to kill me, and I could wear my clinging dresses and strappy shoes that were just gathering dust in the closet. I longed to have time to indulge my feminine side. I could get a massage, have my hair streaked, or get a manicure. Any of the above sounded much more pleasurable at this moment, because all the signs were there that something bad was about to happen: the ominous feeling hovering around the top of my head like a cloud, the sinister notion of approaching disaster fluttering around in my stomach. Yep, I definitely should have stayed in bed.

Instead of listening to the thoughts, though, I drove to the office, followed the whole way by the Goon Girls, Sally and Tracy. And if that wasn't bad enough, they were trying to ram me again. To put the icing well and truly on the cake, I was also coming down with a bad case of grumpy PMS, and that last little straw tipped the scales.

Well, two could play at this game.

I pulled off the main road, grabbed the pepper spray and stun gun out of my rucksack, and pushed open my door so hard that it flew all the way open and then bounced back, slamming shut.

"Hunh!" I opened the latch again and kicked it open.

Right, that was it. I'd had enough. I was going to teach these idiots never to mess with a premenstrual woman. Something happens in our brains to upset the delicate hormonal balance, and boy, were my hormones messed up. I was just about to scramble out of the car and give them another nut-zapping when I saw Tracy wind down his window and poke his arm out. The only problem was that he had a gun in his hand.

"Shit!" I threw the stun gun and pepper spray on the passenger seat and cranked the engine.

Tracy aimed his gun at my rear window.

I hit the accelerator and shot off down the road with my door still half open. A cloud of dust trailed in my wake, and hopefully in the Goon Girls' faces.

I heard a loud crack as Tracy squeezed off a couple of shots.

My rear window exploded and I got sprayed with tiny pellets of glass as I screeched around the corner, narrowly avoiding a ditch. With a bang, my door slammed shut, making me jump up in my seat like a jack in the box.

I floored the Lemon the whole way back to the office. The wind whistled through the gaping hole where my window used to be, licking a draft around the back of my neck and sending my hair flying all over the place.

"Slight problem," I said to Brad when I stumbled into his office, looking like I'd been dragged through a hedge backwards at high velocity.

His mouth fell open. "What the hell happened to you?" He came over and stood picking clumps of glass out my hair.

"The rear window on the Lemon cracked." I slumped down in a chair, feeling like one of those monkeys who are being nit groomed, which wasn't an altogether unpleasant experience, actually. In fact, it was quite relaxing. And if I hadn't been in shock, I'm betting it would've been quite sensual, too.

"Uh-huh. And how exactly did that happen?"

I cleared my throat, buying time. "Er...I don't know. Probably Janice did some voodoo on me. I need sugar to counteract the effects of the voodoo. What have you got to eat?"

Brad finished removing all the glass and walked around to his desk. "Chopped carrots?" he said, pulling his drawer open. "Or falafels?" He held up a bag with some suspicious-looking brown balls in them.

My lower lip trembled as I desperately fought the urge to burst into tears in front of him.

He held a hand up. "Okay, wait there. I'll go out and get you something."

"Thanks," I croaked, then took a big sniff, brushing away the tears that I'd finally given in to. *Come on, Amber, pull yourself together. Don't be such a wimp.*

Brad came back bearing the gift of donut. I ate two Krispy Kremes before I could feel the sugar returning my hormone level back to normal. Well, as normal as it could be, given the circumstances.

"Good choice," I said in between mouthfuls.

Brad watched me eating, a smile curling up the edges of his mouth. "Okay, so what really happened with the rear windscreen?"

"The mob goons shot at me."

He didn't answer for a minute, and a muscle ticked in his jaw as he stared at me. Clearing his throat, he spoke. "You're an accident magnet. Go to the garage and get it fixed before you go anywhere else."

"I think it's a good sign," I said. "We've got them worried about something, so it obviously means we're getting closer."

Hacker bounced into the room like a pogo stick and squeezed his beanpole body into the chair next to mine. "Yo. I've got something juicy for you."

"Cool," I said, exchanging a look with Brad.

"Okay, Fandango didn't call Samantha James the day he disappeared. She called him."

"Ooh, she told me a double lie then." I raised an eyebrow. "She told me he called and asked her sign some divorce papers. I wonder why she called him?"

"Also, she'd cleared out all the money from her bank account before Fandango disappeared." Hacker looked between me and Brad.

"How much money?" Brad asked.

"Twenty thousand pounds," Hacker said.

"Interesting." I thought about that, and figured we were on to something for sure now.

"But what's even more interesting is that Samantha paid ten thousand pounds back into her bank account on the day Fandango disappeared."

I smiled. "Aha! Fandango withdrew ten thousand pounds from his bank account the same day. So, Fandango gives it to Samantha, but why? My hunch is that she was blackmailing him about his little secret."

Hacker stroked his goatee. "But why suddenly start blackmailing him, nineteen and a half years later? If she was going to do it, why didn't she do it before?"

"Maybe she didn't need the money before. It seems to me that Fandango rewarded her pretty well financially for their little arranged marriage. Maybe the money has just run out, and she needs more. Or maybe she was getting a bit greedy in her old age. I think Samantha's excuse that she went to see Fandango to sign divorce papers was designed to throw me off the scent. If she really had signed them, she wouldn't have so much of a motive to kill him." I paused for breath. "But it doesn't make sense. If she was blackmailing him, surely she would want to keep her cash cow alive."

Hacker shrugged apologetically. "I still can't find any children matching Tia's circumstances who were reported missing around the time Fandango appeared with her," Hacker said. "And there's nothing on Fandango or Bagliero. Whoever they all are, they've hidden their tracks well."

I turned this over in my mind as Hacker carried on talking.

"But here's the juicy bit. You remember the coded numbers on Heather's USB?"

"I'm all ears," Brad said.

"It was a password and account number for a Swiss bank account in Heather's name," Hacker said. "Guess how much money she had in her account?"

"I'll go with a wild guess and say five million pounds?" I said.

Surprise registered on Hacker's face. "Guess when it was paid in?"

"The day Fandango and the fashion collection disappeared?" I was on a roll now.

"Hey, you're good, girl." Hacker grinned at me.

I straightened up in my seat. "I know."

"Are you sure that you're not psychic, too?" Hacker said to me.

"Hardly! I was just thinking about the note in Heather's apartment. It said *CB £5 million*. It must've been a payment from this Carlos Bagliero."

Brad steepled his fingers, deep in concentration. "Do you know where the money came from?"

"Not yet. I'm still checking. The payment came via several different accounts in different countries," Hacker said.

"And what was the payment for?" I wondered out loud. "I'm going with drugs. Any other offers?" I glanced between Brad and Hacker. "Going once, going twice." I slammed my hand on Brad's desk. "Drugs it is, then." I stood up. "Right, I'm going to see a scumbag about a van."

But as it turned out, I ended up taking a very interesting and somewhat scary detour.

CHAPTER TWENTY

I dropped the Lemon off at the garage to get the rear window fixed. The manager took one look at it and laughed.

"You're a really bad driver, aren't you?" he said.

"It wasn't my fault."

"That's what they all say. I bet you're one of those women who see loads of accidents in your rearview mirror but never admit to causing them."

I scowled at him. "Don't push it, I've got raging hormones."

Then he looked scared. "Oh, God. My wife gets that. It's scary. Don't worry. I'll have the car fixed in no time." He practically ran off then to get away from me.

"Is my Toyota fixed yet?" I shouted after him.

He mumbled something incoherent and was saved from me pressing him further by my phone ringing.

"I think I've remembered something important. Do you remember when you asked me about my dad's will?" a breathless Tia said.

"Yes, but I still haven't managed to find it."

"Well, I think I've just remembered the name of Dad's lawyer so you'll be able to get a copy from him."

"Great. What's his name?"

"I think it's Bernie Crumpet."

"Bernie Crumpet?"

"I know, it's a crazy name, but that's why I remembered it."

I scribbled it down. "Thanks," I said, and as soon as the Lemon was fixed, I rushed back to the office to find Bernie's address.

* * *

Bernie Crumpet actually turned out to be Bernie Crumpleton, although I thought that both names weren't exactly confidence inspiring in a lawyer.

The only sign of Crumpleton, Crumpleton and Crumpleton Legal Services was a discreet brass plaque that was hanging on the outside of a quaint, red-bricked Victorian house in Hertford, which had been converted into offices. I didn't know the full extent of their clientele, but it looked like they were doing pretty well for themselves.

I licked the palm of my hand and ran it over my windswept hair in an attempt to smooth down the hideous frizz. Checking myself in the rearview mirror to make sure I didn't look as scary as I felt, I applied some lipstick and pulled a few pouty faces before easing out of the car. Getting information from stuffy lawyers who played the client confidentiality card wasn't one of my favorite pastimes, so I wanted to look as enticing as possible. I was going for the sexy seductress, come-to-bed-look, but in reality, it probably looked like a just-got-out-of-bed look. I'd seen Janice pull off the sexy seductress routine countless times to wrap men around her finger and get what she wanted, so why shouldn't I try it for a change? And after all, this was war.

I desperately wished that I'd worn a low-cut top so that I could flash a bit of cleavage as well, as I sauntered through the entrance, swinging my hips for good measure.

"Can I help you?" the receptionist asked when I entered what must've formerly been a dining room. Expensive dark green leather sofas were arranged in an L shape in front of a cast-iron fireplace. The place was empty. The phone wasn't ringing, the fax wasn't spurting out paper, busy lawyers weren't running around the office. In fact, the only sound was the noise of traffic speeding up and down the road outside.

"Hi, my name is Amber Fox, from Hi-Tec Insurance. I wondered if I could see Bernie Crumpleton."

"What's it regarding?" she asked dubiously, looking up from the magazine she was reading like she begrudged the interruption.

"It's about one of his clients."

"I'm not sure if he can fit you in. He's very busy."

I glanced around the empty waiting room. "Really?" A morgue looked livelier than this place.

"Very busy," she repeated, and looked back at her magazine, in case I hadn't got the hint the first time.

"It will only take a moment. It's very important." I smiled, and thought I heard a slight huff as she picked up the phone and murmured briefly into it.

"He'll see you now." She pointed down a corridor behind her. "His office is through there." With that, she went back to her magazine.

I entered a doorway at the end of the corridor and found Bernie Crumpleton, dumpy and round-shouldered, in an expensive suit—which would've looked much better on George Clooney than it did on him. He was seated behind a large desk that was completely devoid of any paperwork. The only thing on the desk in front of him was an open leather briefcase.

Bernie had an egg-shaped head with plump cheeks, and he'd made the mistake of trying to mask his baldness by winding a few strands of hair around his head in a comb-over hairstyle, which was obviously an attempt to try and look more youthful. It didn't work, though. I guessed he was in his late fifties, and no amount of hair rearranging would make him look any younger.

"Hello." He pushed the top of the briefcase down slightly in a hurry and leaped up from his chair like he was grateful to actually see a human being. "What can I do for you?" He held a pudgy hand out and pumped mine with enthusiasm before holding out a wooden chair for me to sit on, and then returning to his side of the desk.

"Thank you for seeing me at such short notice. I'm Amber Fox from Hi-Tec Insurance, and I'm looking into the disappearance of one of your clients." I sat down and pouted slightly. Let the sexy seductress routine begin.

I twirled a curl around my finger and glanced around the office, which didn't have any files cramming up a busy in-and-out tray, and suspected that he didn't actually have that many clients to choose from. "What a lovely office you have." Flattery always worked for Janice. "You must have a thriving business." My gaze cut back to him, and I gave him my full attention, with an alluring smile thrown in.

He coughed slightly. "Er, yes. Now which client are you talking about?"

"Umberto Fandango. As you may have heard, he's gone missing

under suspicious circumstances."

He drummed his fingers on the desk like he was in a hurry and didn't seem to notice the flattery. "Yes, what a sorry state of affairs." He shook his head. "And how can I help?"

I leaned forward, thrusting out my boobs just enough for him to notice them but not enough to look obvious. "I need to find out who the beneficiaries of his will are, because it might have a bearing on what's happened to him."

He didn't take a second glance at my boobs. Not even a mini-batting of eyelids. His Rolex watch appeared to be more interesting, and he glanced at that instead. He tapped on the face. He didn't seem nervous exactly, more like distracted by something, and it certainly didn't appear to be me. "You mean it might be a motive for someone to...get rid of him?"

"Yes, exactly."

"Well, I've already given that information to the police, and in actual fact, that's probably more than I should've done considering our client confidentiality ethics, but they did stress that it could be a matter of life or death."

Damn. How come the sexy seductress routine worked for Janice and not me?

"I'm sure you can get the information from them," he went on, shifting in his chair as he crossed and uncrossed his legs.

Double damn. Janice would never give up that information to me. "Yes, it absolutely is a matter of life or death, and in order to expedite our investigation it would be really helpful if you could just tell me the beneficiary details." I tilted my head and gave him a little-girl-lost smile. "Think of his poor daughter. She's worried sick, wondering what's happened to him."

"I'm sorry, but I just can't, I'm afraid." He slipped his hand inside the briefcase, pulling out a set of keys and jangling them around in his hand. "Now, if you'll excuse me, I'm in a bit of a hurry." He extended his hand again for another pumping.

I stood up and leaned toward him over the desk, ready to shake his hand, and as I did so, I clocked something strange in his half-open briefcase. Something I'd seen before in Fandango's offices the first time I went there to plant the bugs. Under normal circumstances maybe it wouldn't have seemed that strange, but these were far from normal circumstances. I stared at the white Lycra material, studded with rhinestones, that was scrunched up in his briefcase, and my heart raced with excitement.

I was convinced that the thing he didn't want me to see was a Fandango swimsuit.

Bernie caught me looking and slammed the briefcase shut. Then a red flush crawled up his neck. He recovered quickly, though, pumping my hand extra hard and escorting me out of his office and back into the waiting area quicker than you could say "Speedo."

Odd, I thought, as I got into the Lemon. I had parked a few cars down from his office, and waited for Bernie to appear so that I could follow him. Odd that the law firm didn't seem to be busy, and yet it had a façade that oozed wealth—unless he was into some kind of un-lawyerly dodgy dealings. Even more odd, though, was why Bernie happened to have a Fandango swimsuit in his briefcase, unless he was involved in Fandango's disappearance somehow. And although the attorney didn't appear to be nervous, something seemed amiss to me. Lawyers were good actors. They had to be to keep their guilty clients out of jail, so if he were involved in something illegal, he'd be trying to do a good impression of not looking nervous.

Just as I was wondering where all the other Crumpletons from the name plaque were, and what they were involved in, I saw Bernie hurry out of the building and get into a high-spec Range Rover. He looked like a man on a mission to me. Was Bernie off to warn Fandango? If not, was he going to meet whoever was involved in Fandango's disappearance?

I followed him out of town, keeping a surreptitious four car lengths behind him. When he pulled onto the curved driveway of a detached turn-of-the-century house in a secluded location, I kept on driving and pulled up farther down the road.

I approached the house on foot a few minutes later, wondering if maybe Fandango was hiding out here, or whether he was being held against his will. It was a quiet location. The size of the plot and the established gardens meant that it was almost completely hidden from the neighbors' prying eyes. It would be easy to keep someone tucked away on one of these estates.

I walked quietly up the block-paved driveway and made my way to the downstairs window at the front of the house, peering in. The curtains were drawn, making it impossible to see anything. I looked through the stained-glass front door, but I couldn't see any shadows moving around inside. I could hear something, though, and it was coming from upstairs.

Standing stock still, I strained my ears to listen. Yes, there were definitely noises of some kind coming from up there. Noises of…what were they? Creaking sounds, like a rope swinging, and…slapping, and I could hear Bernie's voice now, too.

"Tell me," Bernie said in an authoritative voice.

"No," I heard a voice say in return, but the voice was muffled, so I couldn't tell if it was Fandango or not.

Another slapping sound followed by a creak and a moaning noise made me freeze in shock for a moment. What the hell was going on up there? Was Bernie torturing Fandango?

I stood, rooted to the spot, listening to more groans and moans.

"SAY IT!" Bernie shouted.

"No," the muffled voice replied. It sounded like whoever was up there had a gag over their mouth.

More slapping sounds, and then: "Tell me." Bernie again.

I tried the handle on the front door. Locked. I darted around to the back of the house and found a door leading into the kitchen. I yanked the handle as my heart hammered away, and with a swift click of the latch, it opened. I hastened through the empty kitchen, to the sound of more slapping and groaning, and crept up the stairs, praying there wouldn't be any loose floorboards to give me away.

The noises were coming from a bedroom directly at the top of the stairs. The door was open just enough for me to poke one eye around the gap and see the whole weird scene going on in the bedroom.

I didn't know whether to giggle or run away. Callum Bates was suspended by his arms from some kind of rope-pulley contraption that was bolted to a wooden bar on the ceiling. His feet just about touched the floor, and I could see welt marks where the rope tied around his wrists had dug into his pasty flesh. Callum wore a pair of black PVC lederhosen, a leather studded gag, and a look of ecstasy. But that wasn't even the weird part. The weird part was that Bernie was dressed up in a white Lycra Elvis suit that was studded with millions of tiny rhinestones, topped off with flared collars and trousers. He even wore an Elvis wig, and was humming "Hound Dog" as he smacked Callum repeatedly on the backside with what looked like a wet trout. Honestly, I kid you not!

"Say it!" Bernie cried, swinging the trout with a delighted look on his face.

"Okay, okay! Elvis is the king," Callum yelled from behind the gag, writhing with obvious pleasure.

"And who loves to be whipped by Elvis?" Bernie increased the slapping tempo.

"Me!" Callum's eyes rolled up in his sockets as his whole body shuddered and then slumped forwards, taking all the weight on his arms.

I gazed on in morbid fascination. Which was worse—a sweaty-looking Callum in his lederhosen, or Bernie, with his round body stuffed into the Lycra suit, unzipped to the waist, revealing his wispy chest hair? This wasn't the strangest sight I'd ever come across as a police officer, but it was close. Obviously, what I'd thought was the Fandango swimsuit was in fact the Elvis suit. And although I hadn't been exactly right about Crumpleton's dodgy behavior, I hadn't been that far off either. Crumpleton wasn't into anything illegal, just kinky. No wonder my sexy come-to-bed look hadn't worked. And with Callum Bates, too? Well, who'd have thought it?

I slipped just as quietly out of the house, feeling disappointed that I hadn't found Fandango, but pleased that I could use this little snippet of sordid Elvis-trout sex against Callum.

* * *

A few hours later, allowing time for post-coital Elvis appreciation, I pulled up outside Callum Bates's house. I carefully tiptoed up his path, trying to avoid the fresh oil slick slap bang in the middle of it. I'd already ruined one pair of shoes this week. I couldn't handle ruining another.

I banged on the door and waited. Then I gave it a few forceful thumps for good measure. I was just about to thump again when the letterbox flipped open from the inside.

"What do you want, Porky?" Bates said through the letterbox, which, rather unfortunately, was aimed right at my crotch.

I ignored him and banged harder on the door.

"Hey! Stop it," he yelled. "I'm not opening the door to you."

I bent down and eyeballed him through the letterbox. He had another thing coming if he thought I was going to give him the benefit of talking to my crotch. That was only reserved for a select few, like Romeo…and maybe Brad. I felt a tingling sensation in my naughty bits—oh no! Not Brad. Definitely not Brad. See, this is what raging hormones did to you. They made you go all funny, thinking about people that you really shouldn't be thinking about.

"Go away." Callum's voice jerked me back down from the little on-the-spot fantasy running through my mind.

"What are the Cohen brothers up to?" I said.

"Ha! I'm not telling you anything."

I made a loud buzzing noise. "Wrong answer."

"What makes you think I'll tell you, Miss Piggy?"

"Because if you don't, I'm going to tell them and everyone else I can think of that you're into wild and sordid Elvis-trout sex with Bernie Crumpleton. In fact, I might put an advert in the paper or plaster it in big, bold letters on a banner. Hmm, I can imagine the headlines now: 'Well-known car thief in sex scandal with a wet, trout-wielding lawyer who thinks he's Elvis.' How do you think that would go down in the criminal underworld? I think your tough-guy-thief street cred would be a tad ruined. Why would anyone want to hire you to steal for them when they can hire a completely normal thief?"

That got the door swinging open pretty quick. Callum poked his head out, his little bloodshot eyes darting around nervously. "Shh!"

I stood up, folded my arms, and gave him the evil eye. "Well, what's it to be?"

He lowered his voice to a whisper. "Look, they'll probably kill me if they think I'm a…"

"A what? A freak? And not only a freak—a freak who's fraternizing with the enemy as well. Your days will be numbered, Bates. Getting trouted by a lawyer? Tut, tut."

"But the Cohens would probably hack me up into little pieces if they knew I was seeing a lawyer. You can't do that!"

He probably wasn't that far off the mark, actually. The Cohens looked like the kind of people who would have a variety of body parts stashed in their freezer.

My hands flew to my cheeks. "Oh my God, shock, horror! I'm sure you'll be sadly missed—anyway, where was I? Oh, yes. If you don't tell me, I'll tell the Cohens you're a weirdo-lawyer lover, and if you do tell me, then it will just be our little secret, and I'll approve your insurance claim for the stolen van. It's a win-win situation for both of us."

Callum stared at his feet for a while. Then he said, "The Cohen brothers are dangerous. You don't want to mess with them. They're into all sorts of shit these days."

"And can you elaborate on 'all sorts of shit'?"

"They're shipping out a batch of stolen cars to Saudi Arabia this week, and they're planning on torching the warehouse afterwards."

"See, that wasn't so hard, was it? When are they shipping the batch out?"

"I don't know," he wailed, his eyes filling with tears.

"You'll have to do better than that."

"Really, I don't. You have to believe me!"

I actually did believe him. There was no way he'd take a chance on lying if he thought he'd get whacked by the Cohens for cavorting with a lawyer. "Exactly when are the Cohens going to torch the warehouse?"

"Wednesday night. They've already pre-booked the arsonist."

"Wow, arsonists must be pretty busy these days if you have to pre-book." Today was Tuesday, so I had a day off from warehouse duty before the arsonist turned up.

"What else?"

"Nothing else. I don't know anything else." He shook his head so hard I thought it might fly off.

I glared at him, making sure he was telling the truth while he sweated. When I was satisfied that he didn't know anything else, I turned to leave. Then I whipped back around to face him. "Oh, by the way, I lied about the insurance claim. You still have to take a lie detector test. Have a good day now. See ya."

CHAPTER TWENTY-ONE

"Heather Brown died from a single bullet wound to the head," Carol Blake told me over the phone. "No surprise there. Also, forensics said that the blood found at Fandango's office matches Fandango's blood type. They're still running a DNA test on it to confirm that it's his. "

"Thanks for letting me know," I said.

"No problem. I have some bad news, too."

"What's that?"

"Janice Skipper wants you to come to the police station for a chat."

"Do I get tea and biscuits as well?"

Carol chuckled.

"When does she want me to come in?"

"ASAP."

I'd rather slit my wrists. "Great, I can't wait."

* * *

I stood outside the entrance to Hertford Police Station, gripping the door handle. *Come on, Amber, it's not like you haven't done this a million times before. Hell, you walked the beat here; you were promoted to detective sergeant here. This place has been your home for nineteen years. What's the worst that could happen?*

Yeah, good point, but that was all before Janice Skipper turned up and had her way, wasn't it?

I'd love to say that Janice had a beaky nose, buck teeth, and was covered in spots, but unfortunately she was just the opposite. She was tall and slim for starters, with shiny, straight black hair that hung down to her shoulder blades, and eyebrows plucked into perfect arches. Her hard interior was hidden well beneath delicate features. You'd never guess just by looking at her petite nose, her pouty lips, and her innocent-looking blue eyes that she was really a man-eating she-devil who'd slept her way up the promotion ladder. I was sure she was a wicked witch in a past life, or maybe an android.

I finally swung the door open with a heavy heart, and legs that felt like blocks of steel. Sweat pricked at my palms as I approached the front desk, and my neck twitched involuntarily. I took a deep breath and waited in the queue of people.

"Hi, Amber, how's things?" the station duty officer asked me when my turn came.

"Great," I said with far more enthusiasm than I actually felt. I tried to smile, but it ended up coming out as more of a manic mouth twitch. "I'm here to see Janice Skipper." I debated whether to add the words "the Wicked Witch" on the end of that sentence, but I was trying to be a grown up.

The duty officer leaned forward toward the reinforced glass partition and said, "Oh, you mean the Wicked Witch."

See, it wasn't just me. "You read my mind."

Janice chose that well-timed moment to appear from nowhere behind the duty officer's desk. She cleared her throat, and the duty officer nearly jumped out of his skin, looking uncomfortable.

Janice gave me a sickly, false smile. "What a lovely reunion, DS Fox. Oh, wait. How silly of me. You're not a detective sergeant anymore, are you?" She tilted her head and narrowed her eyes at me.

Dig number one.

The duty officer bent over the desk, pretending to concentrate on his paperwork.

"Let's do this in the interview room," Janice said. "You know the way, don't you? It will make a refreshing change for you to be on the other side of the desk this time. Kind of like a busman's holiday." She turned to make her way out of the enquiry office and added, "Oh, I forgot, you can't gain access into the station anymore. I'll have to come through and let you in."

Dig number two.

Maybe I should stop counting now before I wound myself up any more. My shoulders already felt like a taut elastic band, about to ping at any second. I rolled them around in a circle to ease the tension, wondering what evil little plans she'd been cooking up for me in her cauldron. Whatever it was, I had a horrible feeling that I wasn't going to like it.

She disappeared, returning a few moments later to open the locked door that led to the rest of the station. She turned on her heels and marched up the corridor.

I followed close behind her as she wafted cloying perfume everywhere. "Nice perfume. Is it Poison?"

She ignored me and threw open the door to the tiny, overheated interview room with no windows. "Sit." She pointed to one of the plastic chairs, separated from the other chair by a desk. The walls were stark institutional white.

"Do I get a bone if I'm good?" I sank down on the chair, resting my elbows on the desk and my chin in my hands, just in case my neck decided to twitch again. God, it was hot in here, which made her perfume all the more oppressive. I knew what she was up to. It was a well-known ploy used by some of the officers in the station. I bet she'd flicked the temperature up right before I got there to try and make me sweat, in more ways than one.

"Right," she said when she'd settled herself on the chair opposite. "Why did you kill Heather Brown?"

My jaw wanted to drop to the floor, but I held it up there with my hands before it had the chance. My brain did a silent shriek. At least, I hoped it was silent. The moisture drained from my mouth. "Huh?" I finally managed when I'd got my tongue unstuck from the roof of my mouth again.

She watched my discomfort with obvious pleasure for a few moments as she sat, straight-backed and tight-lipped. Finally, she said, "Number one, you were involved in a meeting with her on the night she died. Number two, you were the last person to see her alive, and the one who found her body. The fact that you were both meeting Heather and were the last person to see her is highly suspicious as far as I'm concerned. I could arrest you now if I wanted to." She looked like she definitely wanted to.

I raised my chin in the air. "With what evidence, exactly?"

"I don't need any. We both know that I can keep you locked up for twenty-four hours without charging you, and then get the superintendent or magistrate to extend the time." She cackled hysterically.

I snorted. "Good luck with that. Heather didn't actually turn up for our meeting, so I wasn't the last person to see her."

"Don't think I'm content with just getting you thrown off the force. I think it's much more amusing to see you lose your new job and your boyfriend as well. I'm not done with you yet. I'm going to destroy you, Amber Fox." She jabbed a finger in my direction.

"You've been eating too many Froot Loops for breakfast again, haven't you?" I said.

Her mouth pursed into an angry little pucker. I made a mental note never to use that expression.

"This is an extremely high-profile case that involves a very rich and famous person, and you're involved in it up to your eyeballs. If you don't tell me what you know, then I'll arrest you for Heather's murder."

"What, so you can get someone else to do all the legwork, and you take all the glory as usual?"

"You've got it in one."

"You've managed to perfect that into a fine art, claiming the credit for all the cases other people have solved while you sit on your backside, filing your nails." I sat back in the chair, folding my arms across my chest.

She glanced down at her nails briefly before beaming back something that was either a smug smile or its close first cousin. "Thanks."

I was gobsmacked. She actually thought I was complimenting her achievements. "Do you know how long Fandango has been a designer?"

She waved the question away with a dismissive hand as if it were a fly. "I don't know. And frankly, it's irrelevant. No wonder you haven't got very far, asking ridiculous questions like that."

I couldn't help raising my eyebrows at that one. "Okay, let's cut to the chase," I said quickly, clearing my throat. "How about this: We both tell each other what we know so far."

"And why would I tell you anything?"

"Because I have a proposal for you: If I solve the case before you, then you admit the truth about what happened at the shooting range.

And you also admit that you've been trying to get me thrown off the force for no good reason for years."

"Hang on. Let me get this straight. You want me to confess that you actually shot me by accident after I broke protocol at the shooting range by stepping out into your line of fire? And you want me to say how I cunningly and constructively manipulated your career advances and purposefully got you thrown off the force? Ha! Good one. And what's in this for me?"

"Well, if you solve the case before I do, I will give up my job at Hi-Tec and finish with Romeo to satisfy the insane jealousy issues you've got going on, and we'll never have to clap eyes on each other again." I felt pretty confident that she'd go for it. Her bigheaded arrogance and vindictive penchant for wrecking people's lives wouldn't allow her to pass it up. I also knew that Janice didn't know diddly squat.

Her eyes lit up. "It's a deal. What do you know, then?"

What I really wanted to do was shoot my mouth off and wipe that smug smile off her face. It was so tempting—almost too tempting—to tell her everything I knew so far, so she would know that I was a better investigator than her. And the temptation was so great that it burned like an infection under my skin. But I knew that giving everything away would only hinder my own chances of solving the case and getting my job back. I also knew that premature mouth-shooting-off was like premature ejaculation. You never knew what kind of mess you might get into. So instead, I fed her tidbits. I told her about Tia, because I knew that the police had already spoken to her. I told her about the witness who'd seen the van leaving Fandango's offices wearing an Obama mask, because Heather had been found wearing the same mask and Janice would never work out the significance of what that was all about. I told her about the existence of Samantha James, because that lead had already come from the police, but I didn't admit to knowing about her warehouse. I didn't tell her about Fetuccini, Bagliero, and the five-million-pound payments to Fandango or Heather. I didn't spill the beans on Heather's financial problems, Samantha's payment of ten thousand pounds from Fandango on the day he disappeared, and my suspicions about Samantha's diminishing bank account. I didn't let on about my theories on the mob connection, the Goon Girls, or the cocaine I'd found. I didn't mention Fandango's missing past, which seemed to me to be the biggest, most pertinent question that related to this case. I talked for forty-five minutes, spinning it out to make myself sound convincing. I didn't think for a minute that she'd stick to her side of the bargain, but I had a secret trick up my sleeve. Well, not quite up my sleeve, but close.

"Your turn," I said when I'd finished.

"My investigation points to Samantha James. She's been under surveillance, and we've seen her meeting with a suspected hit man. Samantha handed him a brown package that we think contained money for the hit," Janice said.

"What's his name?"

"Charlie Biggs. He's got previous for theft, loan sharking, and he's been on trial for attempted murder. The case was thrown out for lack of evidence, but it's only a matter of time before we get enough evidence against both of them. Samantha killed Fandango and stole his fashion collection to fence." She crossed her legs and plastered another smug smile all over her face.

"Who killed Heather, then?"

"Well, obviously Heather's memory must've returned after she was knocked out, and she confronted Samantha, who then killed her to shut her up."

"What about motive?" I said.

"What do you mean?"

"Well, what do you think Samantha's motive is?"

"No wonder you were such a poor investigator. The motive is obvious, isn't it?"

"Is it?"

"Yes. Samantha killed Fandango to get her hands on his fortune. My superior detective skills have already established that he never got around to changing his will after they split up. He left her half a million pounds. That's plenty of motive in my book," Janice said.

I let that information sink in without giving away that it was news to me. "A minute ago you thought I'd killed Heather."

"Don't be impertinent," she huffed.

I held my hands up in the air in mock surrender. "Well, it looks like you've got it just about all sewn up. You didn't need my help after all. I bow to your superior knowledge." I made a couple of bowing motions, just for the hell of it.

She stood up, rested her fingertips on the desk, and leaned in toward me. "You are dismissed."

I shot one hand in the air. "Please, miss, can I go to the toilet before I leave?"

She narrowed her eyes at me.

I lowered my hand. "I take it that's a no, then?"

My shoulders relaxed with relief when I walked out of the police station. I thought Janice Skipper was barking. Barking mad and barking up the wrong tree.

I slipped into the Lemon and called Hacker, asking him to find out what he could about Charlie Biggs, then I headed to Asda, hoping to finally catch Paul Clark in the act. While I was there, maybe I could pick up some chocolate cake, too. No, make that double chocolate cake with chocolate chips, gooey chocolate sauce, and lashings of cream. Hell, after the shocking day I'd had so far, I deserved it.

I scanned the supermarket, looking for shelf-stacking activity. I didn't find any, but I did find the chocolate cake of my dreams. I placed it carefully in my basket and headed over to the customer service desk.

"Hi, I'm looking for Paul Clark. Is he working today?" I asked the lady behind the desk.

"I'm sorry, but he's not with us any longer. He left a few days ago."

"Okay, thanks."

After I'd paid for the cake, I stepped out into the warm sunshine and felt a tap on my shoulder. I swung around and came face to face with Tia.

"So you're still following me," I said.

"Well, the police won't tell me anything." She looked down at her Fandango leopard skin pumps. "And I'm really worried about Dad. I can't just sit at home and do nothing." She eyed my extra-large cake. "Are you going to eat all of that?"

"I was planning to."

"Do you want to share it?"

My heart sank to my feet. Not because I had to share my prized cake, but because I felt really sorry for her. It must be tough, all the worrying and wondering about what had happened to her dad, and even tougher that she may never get to find out who she really was and get closure on all the unanswered questions she must have. "Your place or mine?"

"Awesome! Come to my place." She beamed at me. "That way you can do the spell at the same time."

"Er...I thought I told you that I don't believe in all that kind of thing." I had to admire her determination, though. When Tia got her mind set on something, I didn't think she'd give up in a hurry.

She gave me a watery-eyed puppy look. "Will you do it for me? I don't know anything about trying to find a missing person. I figure I could do with all the help I can get."

I rolled my eyes at her theatrical tone. "Okay." Sometimes I'm such a sucker.

* * *

I ate three pieces of cake while Tia pushed her first slice around her plate. As I munched, I debated whether to tell her that the blood at Fandango's office matched his blood type. Although it looked more and more likely that Fandango was dead, I really didn't want to worry her any more than was necessary until I was completely sure. Plus, I'm a coward sometimes, too.

"Did you find out who Carlos Bagliero is?" She gave up pushing the cake around and put the plate on the coffee table.

"No. It looks like his records have been wiped by someone."

"Who could do that?"

I had a hunch about it, but I didn't know if it would make things better or worse for Tia. I decided to keep it to myself for now. "There are plenty of possibilities. I'm more concerned with why they were wiped. I think it all links to this secret that Umberto was carrying around with him." I scarfed down the final morsel of cake on my plate, then stuffed my hands in the pockets of my combats to keep myself from shoveling the rest of the cake in. "Unfortunately, Heather is dead."

Tia's eyes widened. "Oh my God! Does this mean that Dad is dead, too?"

"I'm sorry, Tia. I don't know yet." I gripped her hand. "But don't give up hope. Hope's the only thing you can cling on to." I silently wondered again about what I'd been mulling over from the beginning. If Fandango was dead, where had his body been dumped, and why hadn't it turned up yet? And if he wasn't dead, where was he hiding, and who was hiding him? He seemed to have disappeared into thin air for the second time in his life. But that was just impossible, wasn't it? Everyone had to be somewhere, regardless of whether they wanted to be found or not. He couldn't just vanish off the face of the earth again.

"This is so awful. I can't believe this is happening. Do you know who killed her?" Tears sprang into her eyes.

"I've just come from the police station. They think that Samantha James was involved." I didn't want to mention Samantha's involvement with the hit man.

Tia stood up, shaking her head. "My stepmother?" She walked to the window and stared down to the canal below. "Do you think she was involved?"

"Well, apparently Umberto left her half a million pounds in his will, so that could be a motive. Samantha had cleared out all her savings recently, which makes me think that something was going on, but I got the impression Umberto looked after her financially all these years anyway. Why would she suddenly decide to kill him? It just doesn't feel right to me."

Tia turned around and gave me a grim smile. "That's Dad all over. He's always been the generous kind."

"Do you think that Umberto could've been involved in drug smuggling?" I told her about the cocaine I'd found at his office.

She looked shocked. "Absolutely not. Dad hated drugs. Of course, the fashion industry is rife with cocaine use. Dad knew that a lot of the models use it as an appetite suppressant to stay thin, and it helps them stay awake for long hours, so they can keep working. Even the stylists and designers use it, but Dad saw what it did to people, and he was always adamant in his hatred for it. I remember him giving me a pep talk about it once when I was young. I'd never seen him get so heated and upset about anything before. He told me how he'd seen drugs ruin the lives of people really close to him. I think it affected him really badly."

Nevertheless, Fandango obviously wasn't squeaky clean. I doubted that this was all some kind of weird and wonderful coincidence. The evidence so far suggested that he was involved in some kind of dodgy criminal dealings. Just how dodgy remained to be seen.

"But people change. You've been studying in the States for a long time. You didn't get to see your dad that often. Don't you think it's possible that he could have got involved in drugs?" I said.

"No. If you could've seen how upset he was when he told me that story, you'd know how disgusted and opposed to it he was."

If Tia was right, then that seemed to knock my drug-smuggling theory right out the window, unless Heather was the mastermind behind it. It also stood to reason that if Fandango felt that strongly about drugs, he couldn't be this new, secret Fetuccini family godfather, because the mafia probably counted drug smuggling as their number one criminal activity.

"Heather had some sort of financial problem as well. In the last nine months, she withdrew seventy-five thousand pounds from her bank account. That leads me to suspect that she had a drug habit. But even more strange is that she had a Swiss bank account with a five-million-pound deposit made on the day your dad disappeared. Do you think he would've been generous enough to give her that money?"

Tia shook her head. "He's generous, but not that generous."

"The money probably came from this Carlos Bagliero, then. I found a note in her apartment with his initials, and it also mentioned the five million pounds she received. It's possible that Heather was smuggling drugs with the fashion collection, but Umberto also received payments from the Fetuccini mob family for something, too." And that brought me in a full circle back to the money-laundering possibility I'd dismissed before. I rubbed at my forehead. Whatever had happened, it was something that had spiraled desperately out of control. This whole case was getting more and more confusing. What had I overlooked? What angle hadn't I considered?

"You need to do this spell. I think it will give you some psychic insight into what happened," Tia said.

I groaned and gave in. "Okay, but don't tell anyone I did this."

She clapped her hands together, relief flooding her face, and rushed into the kitchen. "Come on."

I reluctantly got to my feet and followed her.

She opened the kitchen window, then retrieved an ashtray from a cupboard and placed it on the beech kitchen worktop. Next, she crumpled up a piece of paper and deposited it in the ashtray.

"What's that?" I pointed to the paper.

"We have to burn something connected with Dad. This is an old letter he sent to me." She got some crushed cloves out of the cupboard, sprinkled them in the ashtray, and then added grated nutmeg.

I gave the concoction a skeptical look. "Are you sure this is supposed to do anything?" I didn't think it would achieve much, but Tia seemed to really believe in all this stuff. Maybe it might help to take her mind off things if she thought she was contributing something.

"Of course it's going to work." She pulled open kitchen drawers, searching around for something. "Where are they?"

"What are you looking for?"

"Matches. We have to burn all this."

I rummaged in my rucksack and found a lighter. "Will this do?" I asked as my phone rang. I handed her the lighter and flipped the phone open. "Yo," I said to Hacker. "What have you got for me?"

"Charlie Biggs is a nasty piece of work. He's mostly into loan sharking, but it's rumored that he also offers a murder-for-hire service. He was suspected of carrying out a hit on a wealthy stockbroker a few years ago on the instructions of the stockbroker's wife. The case was thrown out of court on a technicality."

"Great, thanks. Have you got anything else?"

"Nope."

"Okay, then. I have to go and burn things now, bye." I shut the phone with a loud slap and turned to Tia. "Right, what exactly am I supposed to be doing?"

"This is a spell to gain knowledge and overcome obstacles. You have to light the paper, and when it's burning, you have to read these words." She handed me a piece of paper with handwritten notes on it. "After it's all burned, you have to carry the ashes with you until you solve the case."

I read the note and glanced up at her. "And people think I'm nuts."

"What have you got to lose?"

I sighed, lit the paper in the ashtray, and read out loud: "I look deep within me, and call upon the power within me. All knowledge is here for me. I will overcome all obstacles and pass freely through resistance. Everything I want to know is revealed and made clear to me." I watched the paper crackle and burn, slowly disintegrating into ashes along with the nutmeg and cloves. Then I watched as the ashtray cracked into five pieces, and a sudden gust of wind blew through the window, swirling the ashes in the air all over the kitchen. I grabbed a glass bowl from the worktop, trying to collect the remaining ashes in it. It was going pretty well, too, until the bowl slipped from my grasp and smashed onto the floor.

"Uh-oh," I said. "That's probably not a good sign, is it?"

Tia retrieved a small Tupperware bowl from the cupboard and scooped up what was left of the ashes, which wasn't much at that point. "I think it is a good sign, actually. It means there's lots of positive energy around you."

"Mmm," I said, not quite believing her as I looked around the kitchen, which was now completely covered with a layer of ash, not to mention the chunks and splinters of glass. "Maybe I should be going now."

"Here." She smiled as she handed me the plastic bowl. There was just a tiny pinch of blackish-gray powder inside. "Do you want to take the rest of the cake, too?"

Tempting. "No, thanks. I think you're more in need of comfort food than I am."

"Can I come with you? I really don't want to sit around here thinking about things anymore." She did the puppy-dog eyes again and I sighed.

"Sure. Why not?"

CHAPTER TWENTY-TWO

Was this day ever going to end? It felt like it had been going on forever in some weird kind of eternal Groundhog Day loop. I felt the beginnings of a dull ache forming behind my right eye. Had I really been shot and killed this morning, and I'd been transported to some kind of afterlife where I had to finish things off before my spirit could move onto the after-afterlife world? Or maybe I'd been sent to hell. No, hell was probably a lot warmer than this. Either way, I was quickly losing the will to live.

"Where exactly are we going?" Tia's voice broke into my surreal thoughts.

"I have to try and get a picture of one of our clients doing backflips and somersaults."

"Huh?"

I waved a hand. "I need to get a picture of him doing something that proves he hasn't damaged his back."

"Oh no. We're not going back to the washing machine lady's house, are we?"

"Yep. But we're not going to touch anything. We're just going to sit outside in the car, nice and quiet, until I get my photos."

And that was exactly what we did. We sat in silence, listening to the cooling ticks of the engine, until I heard a whimpering male voice coming from inside Clark's house. The sound carried through an open window.

"Can you hear that?" I asked Tia.

"Hear what?"

"I hear someone crying out." I poked my head out of the car window. "I think they're calling for help."

"I can't hear—"

"Shh!" I said, trying to listen. "I heard it again." I pushed open the car door. "You wait here. I'll go and see what's going on. Maybe Clark really has got a bad back, and he's lying on the floor somewhere in need of help." I approached Clark's front door and noticed it was slightly ajar. I paused, wondering if my ears were playing tricks on me. But no, I heard the voice calling for help again, so I pushed the door open. I seriously hoped it wasn't going to be a repeat of the Bates-Crumpleton scene.

"Hello?" I said, entering the house.

"Help!" I heard the voice call out from the kitchen.

"Shut up!" Mrs. Clark told the voice.

I pushed open the kitchen door and stood aghast, taking in the scene. A red-faced washing machine repairman cowered in the corner of the room while Mrs. Clark pointed an antique-looking pistol at him.

"Oh, good, two repair people." Mrs. Clark swung the gun between the repairman and me. "Shut the door," she said to me.

Oh boy. No doubt about it, I'm jinxed. I felt a ginormous lump rise in my throat. "Er…what seems to be the problem?" I asked as I pushed the door closed.

"She's mad." The repairman pointed a shaky finger at Mrs. Clark. He looked like he was about to burst into tears. "She won't let me go until I fix her washing machine."

Mrs. Clark waddled over to the kitchen table and sank down onto a chair. It squeaked, straining under her weight. "Don't you understand? I have to get it fixed today. I can't cope anymore." Her voice cracked. She looked around the room at the piles of laundry. They had grown into a mountain since the last time I was there. The gun in her hand drooped as she loosened her grasp on it and rubbed at her forehead.

"Well, don't just stand there. Fix it," I said to the repairman.

"I don't work well under pressure." He pulled the washing machine away from the wall and pulled off the casing at the back, keeping one eye on Mrs. Clark.

Mrs. Clark's chair started squeaking again as she rocked her pudgy body back and forth, staring at the floor. "I haven't left the house for weeks. I have to wait in for stupid repair people who never tell you when they're going to turn up. Don't they realize that people have lives? They expect you to wait in all day long, and then they don't even turn up. And when you ring the customer service number, all you get is: press one for this, press two for that, press nine hundred and ninety-nine for this. Blah, blah, blah. And after you've spent hours hanging on the phone, trying to talk to a real person, they cut you off. I can't handle it anymore."

"Those fuckwits," I agreed. "Those customer service people should be shot." Oops, probably not quite the right thing to say.

"I don't want to be married anymore. My husband doesn't do anything to help with the kids. Everything was fine in the beginning when we first got married. Now it's like he doesn't care about anyone but himself. It's just like having six kids to look after! Bloody men, why are they so selfish?" she said.

I took baby steps toward her, hoping to get the gun out of her hand. Even though it looked too ancient to actually fire anything, I didn't really fancy getting shot at for the second time that day. "Maybe he doesn't realize that you're a bit...um, overwhelmed with everything. Have you tried talking to him about it?"

She noticed the gun had lowered and lifted it up again in our direction.

I stopped dead in my tracks.

The repairman gasped, dropping his voltage-testing screwdriver.

I glared at him. "You're not helping."

"Well, why don't you fix it, then?" he said to me with a trembling lower lip.

"Yes, you fix it." Mrs. Clark motioned me to get closer to the washing machine with the tip of the gun.

I shuffled toward it and whispered to the repairman, "What's wrong with it?"

He gave a manic shake of his head. "I don't know." He handed me the screwdriver and practically flew back to the corner of the room.

"Why don't you buy another one now, instead of waiting for your insurance money?" I said, knowing that Paul Clark's corned-beef yoga workout in the supermarket meant they would probably never get the payout. "Your husband works, doesn't he? Er...where does he work, by the way?"

"We can't afford a new one yet. My husband lost his job again. Lazy good-for-nothing. He's not working anywhere now," she wailed, and went into rocking overdrive. "Anyway, this one's got a guarantee."

I stood there, staring at the stupid machine, frowning and scratching my head, while I prayed to the white-goods repair fairies to perform a miracle. The chair squeaking got louder, turning into a grinding sound as Mrs. Clark rocked harder and harder.

"Do something," the repairman said to me, wiping away the sweat pouring down his forehead.

I kicked the machine.

The repairman slapped a hand over his mouth.

"This sometimes works when my dishwasher gets stuck," I said, and gave it another kick.

"You're going to get us killed." The repairman looked at me like I'd suddenly sprouted another head.

I shrugged and kicked it a third time for luck. "Best of three."

That was about the time when three things happened at once. Tia stumbled through the kitchen door, Mrs. Clark's chair collapsed—and she fell in a heap onto the floor—and the washing machine sprang to life.

The gun skidded across the floor, landing at my feet. I snatched it up as Tia's hands flew to her cheeks.

"Holy crap!" Tia said.

The washing machine repairman fainted, landing on the floor with a loud whack, and Mrs. Clark sat in a stunned heap on the floor.

Half an hour later, after a few stiff brandies all around, Mrs. Clark frantically stuffed dirty laundry into the machine, the repairman sat at the kitchen table with an ice pack pressed to the side of his head, and Tia and I helped tidy up the kitchen.

"You're going to be blacklisted on the customer service list for this," the repairman said to Mrs. Clark.

I glared at him again. "Can't you see the poor woman's at the end of her tether?"

"She held me hostage! I could've been shot."

"Don't be such a wimp." I looked at the gun. "This thing is too old to be fired anyway." I pulled the trigger to prove my point and accidentally fired a bullet through the kitchen window.

"Double holy crap!" Tia gasped.

"Fuck!" the repairman screamed. Without further ado, he scrambled to his feet and disappeared out the door.

"Uh-oh," I said, grabbing hold of Tia's arm and dragging her back to the Lemon just in time to see the repairman wheel spinning up the road in his van.

"Wow! That was fun. Where are we going next?" Tia said.

"We're not going anywhere. I'm taking you back to your apartment, and I've got a date with Mr. Merlot."

* * *

I returned home on a mission to get absolutely plastered. I couldn't think, I couldn't say hi to Marmalade, I couldn't even stomach food. I was numb to the core.

I dragged myself into the kitchen, poured a huge glass of Merlot, and gulped away on the fruity liquid. After the first glass, I leaned back on the worktop, staring dumbly at the terracotta walls. They stared back at me until the light faded completely. I blinked, realizing that I stood in the dark, and someone had mysteriously demolished the whole bottle of wine. I chucked it in the bin and opened another.

At some point, someone banged on the door, and I nearly knocked over the bottle in my surprise. I ignored whoever was at the door, opting to carry on with my alcohol spree instead. Releasing a deep sigh, I realized that I felt like a complete and utter failure—and a frizzy-haired failure, at that—as thoughts about my two near-death experiences flitted around in my head. Once in a day I could probably handle. But two? That just about tipped me over the edge. I knew I'd probably be fine about it in the morning. I'd probably even laugh about it in a few weeks, but for now, for just a few hours, I wanted to savor the experience of knowing that I'd survived two gun-wielding maniacs. Well, maybe it wasn't exactly fair to tar Mrs. Clark with the same brush as the Goon Girls. Mrs. Clark wasn't a maniac. She was more on the brink of a nervous midlife episode. However, in my euphoric survival daydream mode, she was still a gun wielder. And even scarier was the fact that maybe Mrs. Clark and I weren't all that different. We'd both aimed a gun at someone; the only difference was that I'd used mine.

The knocking stopped just before my mobile rang. I snuck a quick look at the caller ID and froze mid-glug. The last person I wanted to talk to while thinking euphoric thoughts was Brad. I'd heard that people who had near-death experiences did weird things to celebrate being alive. Things like taking risks that they knew they really shouldn't take, things to tempt fate, things like sleeping with people they really shouldn't sleep with.

In the end, the decision was taken out of my hands. Brad used his open-sesame tool to pick my lock again, and the next thing I knew, I'd thrown my arms around his neck and buried my head in his shoulder, breathing in musky pheromones. Brad's strong arms held on to me tightly as he pressed his lips to the top of my head, muttering my name over and over again.

"Hey, who turned the lights out?" I slurred in a drunken whisper and succumbed to a mushy-around-the-edges feeling as my eyelids drooped shut.

I'm not sure how long we stood like that, because the next thing I knew, I was waking up the following morning in bed, completely naked.

"Agh!" I shrieked as Brad strolled into the room and placed a cup of coffee on my bedside table.

"That's a nice welcome."

I sat up, clutching the duvet around me, gawking at him.

"Don't worry, I've seen it all before." He grinned.

"How recently?" I said when I managed to close my mouth again.

"You don't remember?"

Oh, hell. I stared at him. "Er…what exactly happened last night?"

"You cried."

I felt a hot glow crawling up my neck to my cheeks. "Then what?"

"You told me about your meeting with Janice Skipper. Then you mumbled something about how you didn't want your relationships to get stuck in a rut like Mrs. Clark because you might end up shooting someone again."

"Then what?" I turned my head to avoid his gaze.

"You mumbled something about wanting to do the nasty thing with me to celebrate being alive."

The hot glow turned into a tidal wave of shame. "And then what?"

"Let's just say that it was a very memorable night." He gave me a knowing half-smile and tucked a stray curl behind my ear. His fingers were warm against my cheek.

"Can you do me a favor?"

"Name your pleasure."

Uh-oh, nipple arousal alert coming up!

I sucked in a breath and squeezed my thighs together. "Can you leave so I can get dressed, please?" I said, but what I really wanted was to reach out and smother him with kisses, run my hands all over his hard, toned body, and tangle my fingertips in his chest hair.

He gazed at me long and hard. Then he winked at me and left.

What was wrong with me if I couldn't even remember what happened the night before? I lifted up the duvet a smidgeon, checking underneath for any signs of naughtiness. No, apart from my trembling thighs, everything looked the same as it had last night—but that didn't mean anything, did it? I flopped back on the pillows and squeezed my eyes shut. How could I even contemplate doing the nasty with Brad when I was involved with Romeo? Oh, God. I was a horrible, horrible person. And a horrible person who now had to carry around a guilty secret, to boot. Or maybe it didn't count if you did something that you really couldn't remember. Kind of like a temporary insanity plea or an amnesia-induced coma.

Er, hello. Earth to Amber! Of course it counts. Maybe I needed to go and buy a chastity belt.

"Damn!" I shouted, thumping the bed with both fists. I carried on for a while, adding a few choice swear words, until Marmalade jumped on me, blinking at me with his huge green eyes.

I picked him up. "What would you do of you were me? Would you tell Mrs. Marmalade that you cheated on her?"

Marmalade jumped out of my grasp, rolled on his back, and stretched. I envied him. How nice it would be to have his life—sleeping all day, and then strutting around the neighborhood looking for a different pussy every night, with no strings attached and no complications. Yes, I knew what Marmalade would do. He'd keep quiet. He was a lover, not a fighter.

I sank my head into my hands, tugging at my roots. *Oh, come on, Amber! It's not like you committed mass murder or anything. These things happen. It was only a teensy-weensy indiscretion.*

Yeah, right. You just slept with your ex and betrayed your wonderful boyfriend. And you would've enjoyed it, too.

Fortunately, the sound of my mobile ringing tore me away from my thoughts of doubt and self-loathing.

"Hi, sleepy head." Tia giggled down the phone. "Guess what?"

"You think you did something you shouldn't have last night, and you don't know how to tell the person you think you might have cheated on, but then you don't know if you really did the thing that you think you did, so should you tell them anyway?"

"Huh?"

"Never mind." Even I was confused. "I give up."

"I've found the yellow sheep." Her heavy breathing sounded down the phone.

I jumped out of bed. "What?"

"I know, it's awesome, isn't it? See, I told you I was psychic."

"Where is the yellow sheep?"

"Well, I started looking around at the warehouse you were staring at when I met you, and—"

"Hang on a minute. That warehouse isn't anything to do with the investigation into your dad's disappearance."

"Oh well. I found something anyway. I'm down there now."

"Wait in the woods. I'll see you in ten minutes. And be careful."

After I'd raced to get dressed in record time, I actually made it there in nine minutes.

"What have you found?" I asked Tia as we approached the Cohens' warehouse, keeping my eyes peeled for any sign of scumbags. The place was quiet, almost too quiet, and it seemed deserted. The windows had been blacked out, too.

"Look." Tia pointed to a faded sign dumped at the side of the warehouse. "It says *Golden Fleece Shipping*."

"Golden Fleece, as in a yellow sheep."

"Exactly." She grinned at me.

"Samantha's warehouse is next door." I nodded toward it.

"Can we look inside it, just to make sure Dad's not there?"

"I've already checked."

She tugged on my arm, pulling me toward Samantha's warehouse. "Please."

"Okay." I picked the lock again, and we went inside. Everything was exactly as I'd left it on Sunday. "See, I told you," I said as we came out.

She tried to blink away the tears that were filling up behind her eyelids, but it was too late. They snaked down her cheeks, and she threw herself forward, sobbing on my shoulder. Real, shoulder-shaking sobs that rippled through her. I patted her back and waited until the sobs turned to hiccups, then sniffles, finally subsiding into a shudder.

"Sorry...about...that," she said through deep breaths and a blocked nose. "I just don't know if I'll ever see him again."

"You've got nothing to apologize for."

"So, what are we going to do now?"

"I need to look in here." I walked back to the Cohens' warehouse and pressed my face against the blacked-out glass, cupping my hands above my eyes to block out the light. I squinted, and through the ebony darkness I could just about make out...nothing. The warehouse contained nothing at all. It had already been cleared out. The Cohens must've shipped out their batch of stolen cars already.

I quickly dialed Romeo's number, but my call went straight to voicemail. I left a message to let him know. At least I'd done my bit for the good, tax-paying citizens.

"I want to get inside and poke around," I said to Tia, pulling the lock pick out of my rucksack again and fiddling around in the lock. Damn, the door wouldn't budge. "Do a spell." I looked at Tia.

"It doesn't work like that."

"Well, what's the use of magic spells if you can't get them do what you want?" I rattled the door back and forth as I jiggled the pointy tool in the lock again. Finally, it gave way and opened. "See, who needs magic when you have wonderful little gadgets like this?"

We blew in through the door with a sudden gust of wind. The door slammed shut behind us with a loud crack, making us flinch. I patted my thumping ribcage and crept forward, with Tia bringing up the rear. A lovely bouquet of engine oil gave me a high as soon as I walked in. Tia pinched her nose shut.

I assumed that the layout inside would be the same as Samantha's, so I slid my hand up and down on the wall where I thought the light switch might be.

"Urgh!" I didn't know what was on that wall, but it felt like a sticky oil slick. It was the same underfoot as well. I seriously hoped I wasn't going to ruin another pair of sneakers as my feet stuck to the floor. What had they been doing in here, having oily wrestling fights?

I flicked the light switch, but it didn't work. It was no use trying the crappy torch that Dad gave me, since that didn't seem to work either. "I've got a lighter in here somewhere," I said, rooting around in my rucksack, hoping that it hadn't been sucked into the usual giant abyss that lay at the bottom of my bags. "Let there be light." I held up the lighter in front of us.

"Look!" Tia pointed to an oil lamp on a shelf above our heads.

I lit the lamp and shone it around. I didn't really need to go any farther to see that the place was empty, apart from a thick coating of oil on the floor.

As we turned to leave, I felt something heavy land in my hair.

"Agh! Giant spider! Giant fucking spider!" I frantically shook my head upside down, dropping the oil lamp in the process.

All the blood drained to my feet as I heard a whoosh, and a sea of blue flames gushed across the floor.

I couldn't move. We stood in frozen horror, watching the flames lick up the walls.

Somehow, my built-in survival mode took over. I sprinted to the front door like a rabid Rottweiler. Tia screamed, jumping up and down behind me.

I tugged on the door handle. It wouldn't budge. I gave another hard pull, and the handle came off in my hand.

I stared at the handle. *Okay, don't panic. Panicking will get you killed.*

I tried to stop my legs shaking. I sucked in deep breaths. I smelled the smoke. SMOKE!

Too late! PANIC!

"Holy crap. What are we gonna do? Help, Daddy," Tia wailed, then her jaw went slack.

When the smoke began to burn my lungs and sting my eyes, I knew we were in the poop, big time. "Follow me." I scrambled up the stairs two at a time.

We ran to the offices on the next floor. I slid open the wooden window sash, looking down. This was not looking good. We were about ten meters above the ground. Ten meters!

Huge dilemma. We could become char-grilled steaks at our own little barbeque party, or we could launch ourselves out the window and be squished on the concrete. I gulped back a scream of terror.

"What now?" Tia shrieked, her eyes about to pop out of her head.

"We're toast." I swallowed hard, trying to bring some moisture back to my parched throat.

Tia pressed her hands to her ears. "I didn't hear that."

"The skip!" I suddenly remembered, running to the window on the other side of the building, which overlooked the slip road. I yanked on the window catch as I felt the heat seeping into the soles of my shoes. The bloody thing wouldn't budge. "Some idiot's painted over the frame. It's sealed shut."

Tia grabbed the bottom of one side of the window and pushed while I carried on desperately trying to push up the other. They say in times of emergency that people develop superhero powers. I don't know if I suddenly turned into the Bionic Woman, or whether we just managed to loosen the surrounding paint with our tugging, but the window suddenly flew upwards.

I peered down. The skip was still in place. "You go first."

"No, you go first," Tia said with a nervous shake of her head.

"Okay, we'll go together."

We both straddled the window ledge, swinging our legs over in synchronization. I grabbed Tia's hand, and we jumped.

Little white stars exploded behind my eyeballs when I landed on top of the mountain of cardboard with a thud. I lay there, half on my back and half on my side, waiting for my breath to return to make sure that I was still alive.

I rolled my head toward Tia, struggling for words. "Ughf," was all I could manage to croak out in a low, gravelly voice.

Tia seemed to have fared better than me. She sat up in the skip with no effort at all and twisted around to face me. "That was awesome! I've always wanted to jump out of a plane, but that was great. Hey, maybe that spell going wrong was a premonition."

"Ughf."

"Are you okay?"

"I don't know. Am I still alive?" I felt all my limbs to make sure they were still there and not sticking out at any peculiar angles. Yep, all present and correctly placed. A bit tender, mind you, but nothing major seemed to have happened to them. I tried to sit up. It took me a few goes before my body caught up with my brain. When I was completely satisfied that I was still in the land of the living, I shoved my hair out of my eyes and scrambled out of the skip on wobbly legs. Tia jumped out, looking like she'd just had a quick stroll in the park.

We moved back to the spot where I'd been watching the warehouse all those nights and stared down at the towering inferno as I called the fire brigade. Choking black smoke billowed out through the open window, drifting into the sky and turning it a charcoal color.

"Please tell me that the spider's gone," I said, feeling nauseous.

"It wasn't a spider, it was a bat."

"Ew!" I bowed my head toward her. "Did it poop on me?"

Tia peered into my hair. "No."

"Er…if anyone asks, it's probably best not to mention we were involved in all of this," I said. "We'll just tell them that we were nearby, and it spontaneously combusted."

"My lips are sealed." Tia mimed zipping up her lips and throwing away the key.

CHAPTER TWENTY-THREE

"There's no such thing as spontaneous combustion." Brad leaned back in his office chair, swiveling it slowly from side to side, and shot me a you've-got-to-be-kidding-me look.

"Yes, there is. I watched a program about it once where people turned into human wicks and blew up." I eased myself down in the chair opposite him and ran a hand through my frizzy, scarecrow-like hair. Mental note: heat was so not good for curly waves that had a mind of their own. My lips felt dry and chapped, too. I licked them slowly, and then stopped myself in case Brad thought it was some kind of come-on.

"But the warehouse is a building, not a person." Brad raised a questioning eyebrow. I wasn't sure if it was in response to the lip licking or my thoughts on human wicks.

Damn, he had me on that one. "Okay, maybe it wasn't exactly spontaneous combustion. Maybe it was more like an accident. Actually, it was an accident waiting to happen. That warehouse contained more combustible oil than the North Sea. Even if I wasn't there, it probably would've happened anyway, or the arsonist might've turned up unexpectedly at any point and done it himself." I hung my head in shame. "I'm really sorry." Feeling Brad's eyes boring into me, I looked up again.

He gazed at me in silence for a while, giving me a look that had an element of sarcasm in it. Finally, he said, "You're unbelievable."

I couldn't tell if he meant that in a good way or a bad way, but I suspected it was the latter. I opened my mouth. I was about to say that being unbelievable wasn't a crime, and it wasn't necessarily a bad thing either, but then I had second thoughts. I shut my mouth again. I'd already caused enough damage today. Instead, I pretended to be fascinated with the oak flooring, staring at it until my eyes watered.

"If the fire investigation rules it as an accident, I'll have to pay out the insurance claim to the Cohens. But if they rule it as arson, we can tie up any insurance claim by the Cohens for years. Don't worry about it, Foxy. I'm just happy that you got out unscathed," Brad said.

I flushed with relief. "Really?"

"Yes."

I lifted up my legs, showing him the melted soles on the bottom of my sneakers. "Not quite unscathed." I stood up and smiled. "Thanks again." I plodded out of the door and went to seek out Hacker.

I'd just perched myself on his desk when my mobile rang.

"Hey, darling," Romeo said.

I felt instantly nervous. Would he be able to tell that I'd spent the night with Brad from phone vibes? "H-hi."

"I take it you're still alive." He had an edge to his voice, but I couldn't tell if it was concern or whether the phone vibes were working. "Did you have anything to do with the fire at the Cohens'?"

"No." If in doubt, deny everything.

"Thanks for the tip about them shipping out the stolen cars."

I stayed quiet, which was quite an achievement for me.

"Are you okay?"

"Uh-huh," I said, trying to sound like my heart wasn't hammering away with panic, like I wasn't shaking with nerves, like I hadn't done the "nasty thing" with Brad. If I gave itty-bitty answers maybe he wouldn't hear the guilt filtering through my voice. I didn't want to shoot myself in the foot by giving anything away.

"The whole station is talking about your meeting with Janice Skipper," Romeo said.

"Fab."

"What?"

I could sense him pulling the phone away from his ear, looking at it in disbelief. "Fabulous," I said.

"Do you want to know what they're saying?"

"No, thanks."

"Okay, now I know something's wrong."

"Not." I ground my teeth, then realized what I was doing and stopped.

"Is."

"Not!" The words burst out of my mouth a lot louder and faster than I intended.

"Apparently the DNA test has come back, and the blood found at Fandango's office is a match to Fandango. It looks like he's dead."

"Hmm."

"Janice is going to charge Samantha James with his murder."

"Hmm."

"Right, now I know something is definitely wrong. Who are you and what have you done with the woman I love?"

Fuckety fuck! A major guilt trip squeezed at my insides.

"Maybe we need to talk about you and Brad."

Oh, God. *He knows.* My heart froze. I did some deep breathing, preparing myself for the accusation to follow. Where he'd tell me in a hurt voice that he knew I'd slept with Brad, and that it was over between us. He'd tell me that I'd broken his heart, that I'd betrayed him, and that I was a nasty person. Cold horror slipped through my stomach. I didn't want to lose Romeo. But then if I was honest, truly honest, I didn't want to lose Brad, either.

I couldn't take the risk of Romeo quizzing me further, so I made a static noise on the phone. "You're breaking up. I can't—" I snapped the phone shut mid-flow so it seemed more authentic, leaving him dangling on the line.

"Yo." Hacker glanced up at me, staring at my frizzy hair. "Bad day?"

"More like a bad life. My hair is frazzled, I stink of smoke, I'm in desperate need of a shower, and—" I stopped before my mouth ran away with me. "Have you found anything on Carlos Bagliero yet?"

"No, but I think I'm getting close."

"I don't think Fandango was involved in drugs after all, which probably means he's not this new, secret mafia boss. It also means that I'm back to square one. Either Fandango's involvement with Fetuccini was really about money laundering all along, or Fandango did kidnap Tia from a mob family, Fetuccini found out and decided to blackmail him." I rubbed away the tension in the back of my neck. "I've been thinking about Heather's involvement in all of this. Perhaps she was the one trying to smuggle drugs with the collection and Fandango found out about it, so she killed him."

"But who killed Heather?"

"Carlos Bagliero, Fetuccini, the Goon Girls, Samantha James? It could be any of them." I groaned. "I'm going to see Samantha. The police want to arrest her, and I need to ask her a few more questions first."

* * *

Samantha had the same red-rimmed eyes and exhausted demeanor as before. She looked like she was dead on her feet. We sat in the kitchen, only this time she made coffee. I noticed the aroma of brandy emanating from her mug. She probably noticed the smell of stale bonfires emanating from me, but neither of us let on.

"You told me that Fandango called you on the day he disappeared and asked you to sign divorce papers, but that's not true, is it?"

Her lungs deflated, and her shoulders slumped. She stared into the depths of her mug. "No. I didn't want anyone to think that I had something to do with his death, so I made up the story about the divorce papers. I knew he'd left me a lot of money in his will as long as we were married. If the police thought I was getting divorced, then they wouldn't suspect me. I've got enough on my plate without all this extra pressure."

"So why did you call him?"

"I had a few financial problems, and I asked him for money."

"So the ten thousand pounds he withdrew from his account on the day he disappeared was for you?"

"Yes."

"You also borrowed money from a loan shark, didn't you?" I took a sip of coffee and swallowed.

She glanced up at me and rested her mug on the floor. "Charlie Biggs. We made an arrangement, and then all of a sudden Mr. Biggs upped the interest, and I couldn't repay my installments to him. Umberto used to give me cash every month—a monthly allowance, if you like. I was paying the loan back from this, but when I couldn't manage the increase, Umberto gave me the difference to pay off the whole loan once and for all."

"But why didn't you just pay the ten thousand pounds Fandango gave you directly to the loan shark instead of depositing it into your bank account?"

"I tried to find Charlie Biggs to give him the money, but he'd gone out of town for a few days. I didn't want to leave that kind of money around the house, so I put it in my account to keep safe until I could meet up with Charlie and pay off the debt."

"Why did you take out a loan in the first place?"

She retrieved a handkerchief from up her sleeve and dabbed at her eyes. "My son, Andrew, is very ill. He has a rare form of leukemia, and the doctors here weren't getting any results. I took him to a specialist in America for treatment, but it was very expensive. Umberto has done so much for me over the years, so I didn't want to ask him for more money. I tried to get a bank loan. Of course, they wouldn't loan me money for medical expenses. In the end, I went to a loan shark instead. After the treatment, we returned to the UK, but Andrew has taken a turn for the worse, and he's now back in hospital. Then Charlie Biggs raised the interest and I didn't have it. He threatened to kill me if I didn't get it. The only choice I had was to get it from Umberto."

"I'm really sorry about Andrew," I said. "I know it must be incredibly difficult."

"Thank you."

"Is Andrew Umberto's son?"

She shook her head quickly. "No. I don't seem to be very lucky in the romantic department. Andrew was the result of a brief rebound fling I had after Umberto."

"What was your arrangement with Umberto when you got married?"

"I wasn't stupid. I knew that he was running from something or someone, but I also knew that he was a good person. And, believe it or not, I did love him. I fell for him very hard, very quickly. But look at me." She looked down at herself with distaste. "I knew he couldn't be in love with someone like me. I think I just fooled myself into believing that maybe I could make him love me. He wanted to get married so he could obtain British citizenship. I was young. I thought if I gave him what he wanted, in time he would feel the same about me." She laughed, but I could hear the hurt underneath it.

"Judging by his actions, I'd say that he did love you, Samantha. Just not the way you wanted him to."

A rueful smile quivered on her lips. "Umberto insisted that we keep the marriage a secret all these years."

I thought about secrets, wondering if the world would be a better place if we had no secrets, if we were all transparent. Would it just create chaos and anarchy if everyone knew the truth? I guess it depended on what the secret was.

Everybody's hiding something.

"Did he ever tell you what he was running from?" I asked.

She glanced up, staring me straight in the eye. "No. He wouldn't talk about it, but…" "But what?" I prompted her when she'd fallen silent for a few minutes.

"I guessed it was something pretty serious."

"Why did you buy the warehouse?"

"Umberto bought it, but he wanted me to put it in my name so no one would connect it to him."

"Have you ever been there?"

"No, I had no reason to go there."

"The police think you killed Umberto so you could collect the inheritance money from his will."

She gasped.

I locked my eyes firmly on hers, waiting for her reaction. "Did you kill him, Samantha?"

She raised her chin slightly and shook her head without any hesitation. "No."

Over the years, thousands of people have told me thousands of lies for thousands of reasons, criminals and innocents alike. Small lies, white lies, or great big whoppers. An important part of my job was spotting the falsehoods. There are things people do when they lie that makes it a dead giveaway. Averting their eyes, repeatedly touching a part of their body, a nervous tick, or changing the subject are all telltale signs. Of course, there are some people who are so adept at lying, or they truly believe their lies, it makes it hard to tell. But when I looked in Samantha's eyes, I knew she was telling the truth. And not only that, it made sense as well. Samantha was getting a monthly allowance from Fandango so there was no need for her to blackmail him. She had no motive to kill him for the inheritance if he was supporting her financially all these years anyway.

A few phone calls to various hospitals were all it took to confirm what she'd said about Andrew. She hadn't been meeting Charlie Biggs, the hit man. She'd been meeting Charlie Biggs, the loan shark. I just hoped that Janice Skipper had the intelligence to work it out. The last thing Samantha needed at a time like this was Janice breathing down her neck.

* * *

"Speak," Brad said when I called him on my way back from Samantha's.

"What happened last night?" I blurted out.

Brad chuckled. "Are you sure you really want to know?"

Oh, Goddy God. Did I really want to know? I couldn't decide so I hung up.

I checked my watch. Two p.m. Hopefully, I could catch Mum and Dad at home and grab a late lunch with them.

"What happened to your hair?" Mum asked when I waltzed into the kitchen.

"It turns out my hair isn't heat resistant."

Sabre sprinted into the kitchen and tried to stop short when he got to me, but ended up skidding across the laminate flooring and smacking his head on the stove.

"Maybe that's why he's got a few problems," I said to Mum as Sabre sat there for a few moments, stunned, before falling asleep. "If he doesn't wake up in half an hour, he might have concussion."

"Have you been smoking?" She switched the kettle on and scooped two tablespoons of filter coffee into a French press.

"Kind of." I eyed the coffee. "I definitely need another scoop."

She stopped, the spoon hovering over the coffee. "Are you okay?"

I flapped a hand. "I'm fine—no, actually I'm not fine." I sat down at the island and gazed down at my finger, tracing a circle on its surface. "Have you ever cheated on Dad?"

She sat down next to me. "I've thought about it."

I whipped my head up. "Really?"

"Of course. Your dad's a workaholic. There have been loads of times when I've felt neglected or second best. I've had plenty of opportunity to have an affair as well."

"So...what stopped you?"

She smiled at me. "You know that saying, 'love conquers all'?"

I nodded.

"Well, it's a load of rubbish. Love doesn't conquer all, but when you love someone, you love them, warts and all. Honey, no relationship is perfect. It's all the perfect times that make up for the imperfect ones."

"Exactly, so if you really loved someone, you wouldn't cheat on them, would you?"

"Have you cheated on Romeo?"

I had a terrifying image of me and Brad entangled in each other's bodies under my sheets, getting very hot, sweaty, and dangerously passionate. "I don't know."

"What do you mean you don't know?"

"Well, I was a bit drunk, and something might've happened with Brad."

"Ah." She paused for a while, giving this some thought. "I think that whatever's meant to be is meant to be. You need to ask yourself what it is exactly that you're afraid of. Are you afraid to commit to Romeo and take the chance on a happy future with him because if doesn't work with him, it won't work with anyone? Or are you afraid that you're still in love with Brad?"

"Both," I said, wondering if it would've been more healing to have tied up all the loose ends with Brad years ago. Would I have felt more liberated? Freer to move on with my life, and get Brad well and truly out of my system for good? Maybe then I could've committed to spending a happy life with Romeo and stop holding back. But was I really holding back, or was I just being cautious? Caution was good, right? And I hadn't exactly planned on being in this situation again. What if I was wrong about Romeo, too? What if my feelings for Romeo were just lust masquerading as love? Was I just trying to kid myself? I groaned inwardly. I couldn't go on like this forever. I needed to make a decision about my love life. But what if the last year with Romeo had all been a mistake? What if I was supposed to be with Brad all along?

Mum wrapped an arm around my shoulder and hugged me into her. "I can't tell you what the right thing to do is. You're the only one who can decide that. But I'll tell you one thing."

I rested my head on her shoulder, staring glumly at the floor. "What's that?"

"You can't change fate. I know what happened with Brad hurt you deeply, and it took you a long time to get over him. But sometimes you just have to take a chance."

"Yes, but which chance should I take? Brad or Romeo?"

She let out a soft sigh. "You're the only one who can answer that. I think that once or twice in life, you meet someone and feel a mysterious connection that sinks into your soul and takes a hold on you. It seems like your heart races ahead of you while your brain struggles to play catch-up, but by the time your heart finally does catch up, it's too late to recover. Brad left a scar on your heart, but it's up to you whether he's the one to repair it or not."

"Aagh," I groaned, flopping forward and tugging at my roots. "I thought I was over Brad, but now all the familiar feelings are coming back, and I'm scared. Brad's dangerous. Whereas Romeo is solid, dependable, gorgeous, and funny. He's everything a girl could want. And it's working with him."

"Is it working with him? Why won't you commit to him, then, if it's working so well?" Mum raised an eyebrow.

"Maybe you should've been the psychiatrist instead of Suzy." I gave her a grim smile.

We sat like that for a while, me lost in a merry-go-round of thoughts and Mum rubbing my shoulder, until she said, "How about some chocolate cake with that coffee?"

"Hello." Dad walked in wearing brown leggings and a green T-shirt with fabric camouflage netting draped around him, complete with individual little material leaves sewn on.

I did a quick double take.

"I thought you said you wouldn't be back for hours," Mum said as Dad kissed her on the cheek.

"I wanted to catch Amber."

"Why are you dressed like a tree?" I said.

"I'm doing a stakeout in the park. Some little blighters have been vandalizing the children's play area." He did a twirl. "I made this myself. Pretty good, isn't it?"

I nodded because I didn't really know what to say to that. "Have you caught anyone?" I asked him.

"Not yet."

"Did you want to see me about something?" I said.

"I wanted to tell you that I spoke to the chief constable today at the golf club."

That made my ears prick up. Ultimately, the chief constable was the person with the power to give me my old job back. "What happened?"

"He told me that he's getting pressure from the government to solve this Fandango case. I'm certain he'll give you your old job back if you crack it before that nutcase Janice Skipper."

I didn't really know if Dad was actually qualified to call someone else a nutcase when he was dressed up like a tree, but never mind. Janice was indeed a nutcase, and that was erring on the side of a polite description.

"He told me that the Cohen boys torched their warehouse today," Dad said.

I mumbled something non-committal.

"Brad won't be too pleased if he's got to pay out the insurance. How's it going, working for him?" Dad said.

I stole a glance at Mum. "It's complicated." I kissed them both and turned to leave. I'd just got to the front door when I stopped dead as a thought occurred to me. I retraced my steps back into the kitchen. "Dad, how did you know I was here?"

He gave me a sly grin. "I have Amber radar."

Ten minutes later, I sat in the Lemon, which I'd parked a few doors down from Paul Clark's house. Since I'd already stuffed up the Cohens' warehouse today, I was determined to close the Clark file. Although technically the warehouse probably would've been torched anyway, I didn't think I'd be getting an employee of the month badge for my part. I slouched down in the seat and waited.

It had just gone five thirty when a blue van pulled into Clark's drive. Clutching the camera in anticipation, I inched upwards in my seat.

Paul Clark jumped out of the van and walked around to the rear doors. As he pulled the doors open, I aimed my camera and carried on watching through the viewfinder. The top half of him disappeared as he leaned into the van, pulling something heavy toward him.

And then, bingo! David Bailey, eat your heart out.

Snap: A picture of Clark, straining under the weight of a washing machine he'd just maneuvered out of the van onto his forearms.

Snap: A picture of Clark, staggering up the drive as he carried the washing machine.

Snap: A picture of a red-faced Clark, huffing and puffing, as his torso teetered backwards at a forty-five-degree angle with the washing machine resting precariously in his hands.

I should've been pleased with the result, but I wasn't. I couldn't stop thinking about how his injury claim being rejected would impact on Mrs. Clark and her midlife nervous crisis. Then again, we all make choices in life. It's just that sometimes we don't always make good ones, and we have to live with the consequences of our actions.

I waited until Clark had disappeared into the house. Then I stuffed two hundred pounds in an envelope for the damage to their window and scrawled Mrs. Clark's name on it. I snuck up their path and posted it through their letterbox, scurrying back down the path before I got caught.

I was just about to dig the key into the Lemon's ignition when my phone rang.

"Amber, it's Samantha. I'm at the police station. They've just arrested me for killing Umberto and Heather. I don't know what to…" Her voice cracked, as if the strain was too much, and she fell silent.

I stiffened. Damn Janice Skipper. "Okay, I'm on my way."

CHAPTER TWENTY-FOUR

I rushed into the police station and bumped slap bang into Romeo. My heart sank to my stomach and flew back up again. I thought I might actually be sick from guilt.

"Hey, darling." He smiled at me.

I pushed down the nausea, trying my best non-guilty-looking smile. "Hey!"

He leaned in close, his lips brushing against my earlobe as he whispered in my ear. "My case should be finished in a few days. I'm looking forward to spending some quality time with you."

The hairs on the back of my neck rose. I didn't trust myself to speak, so I carried on smiling.

He pulled away slightly, examining me with his warm eyes. "Are you okay?"

"Of course." I smiled wider and flashed my white enamels, conscious that I probably looked like some kind of cheesy commercial for toothpaste.

"Are you here to see Janice?"

"Unfortunately, yes."

"I'll tell her you're here." He grabbed me, squeezing me to him tightly, and planted a kiss on my lips.

I relaxed into his warm body as a tingling sensation ran right through me.

"Ahem." Someone coughed behind us.

We pulled apart and I saw Janice Skipper's eyes drilling into me.

"You've got work to do," she said to Romeo.

He rolled his eyes at me, said goodbye, and sauntered out to the parking lot.

Janice folded her arms and stared at me. "I don't know what you're doing here. I think you should be busy writing out your resignation at this point."

"And why is that, Janice?"

"Because I've already cracked the case."

"You've arrested the wrong person."

She snorted. "Don't be ridiculous. Samantha James is in custody because she's a murderer. She hired a hit man to shoot Fandango at his office and hide the body somewhere."

"No, she didn't. And you've got no evidence to prove it. Don't do this, you'll regret it."

She waved a dismissive hand. "I don't think you're in a position to tell me what to do. Now, is that all? I'm a very busy person."

"Can I see her?"

"Not a chance. Chop-chop, and start writing out your resignation." She stalked off, leaving me standing there with steam about to gush out of my ears.

I turned to leave and felt a tap on my shoulder. Swinging around, I expected to see the return of the Wicked Witch, but it was Carol Blake.

"Hi." Her eyes darted around, as she made sure Janice was out of earshot, before they settled back on me. She pulled me outside, where the walls didn't have ears. "I've found something interesting. The bullets we found at Fandango's office had the same striation patterns as the one used to kill Heather."

"So the same bullets were used in both crimes. Have you got any idea of what type of gun was used?"

"A revolver."

"Right, so we just need to find the gun."

* * *

I dragged my aching, smoky body through my front door later that night. I was dying for a shower, and was heading toward the bathroom when my front door burst open with a wrenching noise and crashed against the wall.

I spun around to see Tracy standing in the doorway with a weird look on his face. I wasn't quite sure if he was giving me an evil super-villain grin, or whether he was in the middle of having a stroke. Either way, it was slightly disconcerting because he pointed his gun at me again. This time I got a good look at it.

With a low growl, he rushed toward me.

I swung my ass around, running toward the bathroom. I was almost there, too, when he grabbed my hair, yanking me backwards.

"Argh!" I fully intended to go through my vast repertoire of various shrieks and yells, but unfortunately Tracy clamped a hand over my mouth at that point.

Fear gripped at my stomach like a hand, squeezing the breath out of me.

"Are you going to come quietly?" he said, relaxing his grip slightly so I could speak through the gaps in between his fingers.

"Now, now, that's not the kind of thing you say to a lady," I managed to squeak.

"You ain't no lady. I'm taking you to see my boss."

"I can't go."

"Why not?"

"I'm washing my hair tonight." Then I realized that the chances of me being alive long enough to ever wash my hair again were about as likely as winning the lottery. All the blood instantly drained from my face and rushed to my extremities.

He peered at my hair. "You need to."

I stomped on his foot and tried to wrench myself free.

He increased the tightness of his grip around me, so I couldn't elbow him in any painful areas.

"What does your boss want?" Maybe I could keep him talking and try to figure a way out of this.

"You've been poking your nose in where it doesn't concern you, and you've got something he wants."

"What, genital warts?" I said.

"You've got…er, genital warts?"

"Yes, and they're very contagious. You can catch them from just touching someone who's got them."

I felt Tracy's grip loosen at that little revelation. I writhed around, trying to get away from him before he regained his vise-like grip again.

"Where is it?" he said.

"I thought we'd already been through this before. I don't know what you're talking about. Go on, ask me a question. You can ask me anything you like. I bet I don't know the answer."

He was just about to turn around and drag me toward the front door when Tia silently appeared behind him with my huge terracotta plant pot in her hands, raised above her head.

Crack! She smashed the pot over his head.

His eyes rolled back into their sockets as he slumped to the floor, banging his head again in the process.

"Wowee!" Tia said as we stood over him. "I've never hit someone before."

"Don't worry, he's a bit accident prone anyway." I gave him a quick dig in the ribs with my foot. He didn't even flinch.

"What are we going to do with him?"

"Did you see a white SUV in the parking lot with an ugly fat guy in it?"

"Yes."

"That's his girlfriend," I said. I doubted if Sally was capable of using a gun without killing himself. He seemed a bit too high-strung to me, but I wasn't going to take any chances. I stuffed Tracy's gun in my pocket. We could always dump Tracy next to the SUV and gently persuade Sally to get lost with a little firepower. "Come on, you take his arms, I'll take his legs."

We dragged him into the lift and out the communal door to the parking lot, banging his head a few times on the floor in the process.

"He weighs a ton," Tia said.

"Too many steroids. I bet his nuts have shrunk too, especially since they've been on fire." I allowed myself a little chuckle.

"Pardon?"

"Never mind." I smirked.

I could see Sally sitting in the SUV, listening to opera music full blast, miming conductor actions to himself. We approached the car from Sally's blind spot and left Tracy next to the rear passenger door. Retrieving the revolver from my pocket, I walked around to Sally's door and pulled it open, pointing the gun at him.

"What the fuck!" Sally stared down the barrel of the gun.

"Have you got a gun?" I asked him.

"No, I'm not allowed one. It's not fair, Tracy gets to carry one," he whined. "Where is Tracy, anyway?"

I tilted my head toward the back of the SUV. "Over there. Now, you're going to get out nice and slowly, put your girlfriend in the car, and drive off. Okay?"

"Huh? I lost you after the first instruction."

"Are you an idiot?"

Sally looked confused at that.

I sighed. "It's okay, you don't have to answer that. I think I know the answer." I beckoned him out with the barrel of the gun. "Out."

"No," he said.

"What do you mean, no? I've got a gun."

"I know, but if I get out you'll shoot me."

"Newsflash! If you don't get out, I'll shoot you, how about that?" I waggled the gun at him. "I'm a good shot, too. I once shot someone in the ass." Not that I was proud of it, but Sally wasn't to know that.

"Oh, shit. I don't wanna get shot in the ass. You might miss and shoot me in the nuts instead. You've got a thing about nuts."

I took a step back as Sally squeezed himself through the door and waddled around to Tracy. "Jesus, lady, you've killed him!"

"No, he's just going to have a bit of a headache. Again," I said.

Sally wrestled Tracy into the back of the SUV. "Now what?"

"Now drive off and don't come back," I said.

Sally shook his head as he squashed his gut behind the steering wheel. "My boss isn't going to like this."

"Tell me something I don't know. Have a nice day, now."

Tia and I watched until we saw them safely disappear into the distance.

"You need to get out of here in case they come back," I told Tia.

"Okay. I just wanted to tell you that the police rang to tell me they'd arrested Samantha."

"I know."

"Do you think she did it? Do you think she killed my dad?"

"No." I squeezed her arm. "Now, go."

"Do you want to come back to my place and lie low?"

"Thanks, but I need some time to think."

After I was sure Tia had left, I ran back up to my apartment. I checked to make sure Marmalade was okay, and since the door would still close, I decided to leave him in the apartment. I fed him then stuffed a few things in an overnight bag and scampered out to my car without having a clue where I was going.

I waited at a set of traffic lights, tapping on the steering wheel, wondering what to do. I could go to Romeo's house, but if he returned unexpectedly things could get a bit awkward. He'd know something was wrong, and I would have to explain that I'd done something inexcusable. I could go to Brad's, but I might end up doing the nasty thing again, and that would make things even more complicated. I could go to Tia's, but I needed some time to myself to think.

No, don't think. If I didn't think about it, maybe it would mean that nothing really happened with Brad. If I didn't think about it, maybe I could develop selective denial, burying the information somewhere in my brain where I'd never find it again.

Bollocks. What to do? What should I do?

I sat, head tilted to one side, waiting for everything to disintegrate in my brain. Nope, it wasn't working. I couldn't bloody stop thinking about it.

A lorry driver behind me, truck laden with beer barrels, sounded his horn as the lights changed from red to green. I pulled off, deciding at that second to spend the night at a hotel, so I could not think about what I was thinking about in peace.

I couldn't afford the plush, expensive kind like Hanbury Manor, so I checked myself into the cheap kind, which was stuck in a 1970s décor time warp.

I peeked out of my room's window. There was a tiny balcony outside, just wide enough to stand on as long as you were slim. I closed the curtains and checked out the ancient bathroom. There were lime-scale streaks everywhere. Lovely. It looked like the cleaners had done the best with what they had, but they hadn't bothered to remove a toiletry bag that had been left on the side of the bath. As "nosy" was my middle name, I unzipped it and peered inside at a bottle of contact lens cleaner, a plastic contact lens storage pot, some saline drops, a tube of toothpaste, and some hemorrhoid cream. Boring. I'd been secretly hoping it might be full to the brim with something exciting, like cash, for instance—or failing that, chocolate.

Okay, first up on my list of priorities was some food, followed by a long, hot shower. I ordered a chicken burger, chips, and a bottle of red wine, then stood under the steaming shower. A groan escaped me as I savored the soothing feeling of the hot water spraying down onto my tense shoulders.

I padded back into the bedroom wrapped in a towel, which was so small that it could've doubled as a postage stamp. The heating had suddenly sprung to life in the bedroom, turning the room into a sauna. I'd just opened the French windows on the balcony to prevent keeling over from heat exhaustion when I heard a knock at the door, and a male voice announced the arrival of my food.

"Just leave it outside, please." Giving him a minute to disappear, I poked an eyeball around the door. Phew, coast clear. I yanked the door open, expecting my food to be on a tray beside my door. Instead, the idiotic man had left it practically half a mile away. I tiptoed up the corridor and then almost jumped out of my postage stamp when I heard the door slam shut behind me.

Why me? Why do these things always happen to me? I rolled my eyes up to the heavens.

I stood there, debating this little conundrum. I could go down to the front desk, flashing off my nether regions, and get someone to let me back in, giving them a good eyeful or a heart attack in the process. Or I could hope that I had a discreet next-door neighbor who'd let me climb over their balcony.

No contest. I knocked on the door to the right of my room, shivering in the freezing hallway. God, it was bum-numbingly cold. They had a serious problem with temperature control in this building.

"Ah!" A little old lady opened the door and gasped at the sight of me.

"Hello." I gave her my best non-nutcase smile. "Sorry to be a pain, but I've locked myself out. Can I just climb over your balcony and get back into my room, please?"

She jabbered away in German to me with a frown on her face.

"Ja," I said, which is the only bit of German I knew.

The woman waved her arms around as her voice went from loud to shrieking volume. I made frantic pointing gestures toward her balcony. After a few moments of finger action, I think she got the drift.

"Ah!" Her face relaxed and she motioned for me to come in.

"Thanks." I rushed toward the balcony.

I gazed out, trying to decide the best way to climb over without slipping and taking a nosedive to splatsville. The balcony was so narrow, I didn't fancy going forward, plus if I did fall, I'd see it coming. In the end, I clutched the tiny towel around me for dear life and backed out, climbing rear first over the balustrade separating my balcony from the German lady's.

Phew! I breathed a sigh of relief when I landed on balcony firma. My first thought as I slipped through the French doors was that someone had ordered a Texas hold 'em poker game in my absence. My second thought was that I'd gotten my left mixed up with my right when I was in reverse mode, and I was in the wrong room.

All six of the burly, incredibly hairy Hells Angels lookalikes sitting around a table in the center of the room turned around and eyed me up.

"Hello, missy. You must be our stripper-gram," a leather-jacketed biker said, looking pretty excited at that prospect.

"Er...no. I'm afraid not." I gave them a vacant smile. "Anyway, sorry to interrupt—"

Another beefy-looking one with a splodge of ketchup stuck to his beard grabbed my arm. "Hey, not so fast. If you're not our stripper-gram, why are you dressed in a mini dress?"

"Yeah," another one piped up.

"What, this old thing?" I pulled the bottom of my towel down farther—not that it had much effect, but psychologically, I felt less naked.

"Come on, let's get the party started, missy." Mr. Leather Jacket leered at me.

"Let's not," I said.

"Why not?" Ketchup Face said to me.

"It will make you go blind."

One of the others cackled. "Hey, we've got a feisty one here."

"I bet I could make your clothes disappear," one of the others said as he twisted a ginormous diamond ear stud around and around. He licked his lips and looked like he seriously wanted my clothes to disappear.

"I hope that's not your poker face," I said to him. "You're giving far too much away. Nice diamond, though. Is it real?" I looked at his stud, twinkling at me as the light bounced off it.

"Yeah, why?" He gave me a suspicious look.

"No reason. Ooh, look at that." I looked at the five-card spread in the center of the table. There were two aces amongst them. Then I pointed at the two aces held in Ketchup Face's hands. "You've got four aces."

Mr. Leather Jacket looked at the cards in the center of the table, frowned, and looked at his cards. "You can't have four aces. There are two on the table." He glared at Ketchup Face. "And I've got two aces right here, so you can't have two aces in your hand." He shot up, sending his chair flying to the floor. "You're cheating." He pointed at Ketchup Face.

Ketchup Face shuffled in his seat, giving the others shifty eye contact.

"I knew it," Diamond Stud said to his neighbor. "I knew he'd been cheating."

When Mr. Leather Jacket flew across the table, grabbing Ketchup Face by the neck, I thought it was a good time to get the hell out of Dodge.

I was working my way through the wine when Brad called.

"Where are you?" he said.

"Not telling."

"Why not?"

"Because I've got a bottle of wine in my hand, and you know what happened the last time I drank too much."

He paused. "What happened?"

"We did...you know what."

"What?"

I rolled my eyes at the phone. "You know. We did the nasty thing." I felt my pulse pounding as I imagined it.

"Did we?" He sounded bemused.

I frowned, realization dawning over me. "You mean...we didn't do it?"

"Foxy, I would have loved to do the 'nasty thing' with you, but it wouldn't be that enjoyable with you in a drunken coma. Believe me, when it happens you'll be very much awake, and you'll definitely remember it in the morning."

I swallowed back a lump in my throat. *When it happens?* Crikey. I felt dizzy and nauseous with a mixture of relief and shame. Relief that I hadn't actually cheated on Romeo, and shame that part of me was actually disappointed that it hadn't happened.

"So, where are you?" he asked.

"I'm still not telling, just in case."

"I've got some news from Hacker on Carlos Bagliero."

"Great."

"There are three mob families who run their crime organizations on the east coast of America—the Fetuccini family, the Lombardi family, and the Rossi family. Needless to say, they hate each other's guts, and they're always trying to muscle in on each other's territory. Twenty years ago, Bagliero gave evidence in a multiple-murder trial against Godfather Ricardo Lombardi, which put him away for a long time. Hacker is still trying to get more details, but apparently Bagliero was an innocent bystander who witnessed Lombardi shoot two members of the Rossi family in the head. After the trial, Bagliero and his wife were murdered."

"Interesting." That got me thinking for a while before I mentally kicked myself. I'd found one note in Heather's office desk with the initials CB that mentioned five million pounds. When I found the other note in Heather's apartment with Bagliero's name on it, I wrongly assumed that it all referred to the same person. If Bagliero was dead, he couldn't be the same person who paid the five million pounds into her Swiss bank account. In fact, he couldn't be involved in any of this at all.

"Hacker said that someone went to a lot of trouble to eliminate any records on Bagliero."

"No wonder. If Bagliero was killed after testifying, it wouldn't make the authorities look very good if they can't protect their witnesses. So, if he's dead, and wasn't the person who paid Heather five million pounds, then who did?"

"Hacker is still trying to trace where the money came from. Swiss bank accounts are very hard to hack into. All those international state leaders and crime lords expect confidentiality and extra security when they're stashing away their illegitimately earned petty cash."

A light bulb suddenly pinged to life in my brain. "Wait a sec. Isn't it an amazing coincidence that six months after Bagliero is killed,

Fandango suddenly appears out of nowhere?"

"That's the first thought that I had, but Bagliero can't be Fandango. Bagliero had green eyes, light brown hair, and fair skin, whereas Fandango had brown eyes, dark brown hair, and dark skin. I know it's easy to change hair and skin color, but they didn't even look alike."

I tucked that thought into my frontal lobe to dissect later. "Well, I have some news for you, too. I don't think that the mob was involved in Heather's murder or the disappearance of Fandango and his collection."

"What makes you so sure?"

"Barack Obama told me."

"Huh?"

"Okay, the witness said that the driver of the getaway van wore an Obama mask. The same mask that Heather's killer made her wear before he shot her. So it stands to reason that the same person or people were involved in both crimes. Also, Carol Blake told me that the bullets recovered from Fandango's office matched the bullet used to kill Heather. Both were fired from a revolver. When one of the Goon Girls tried to grab me again earlier—"

"Hang on a minute. The mob thugs came back, and you didn't call me?" His voice oozed with worry.

"Well...I thought we'd done something naughty, and I really didn't want it to do it again." Oh, God, that sounded really horrible. "Not that I wouldn't want to do something naughty with you if I was unattached, it's just that—oh, hang on, let me take my foot out of my mouth."

"Foxy, your safety comes first. Anyway, you were saying..."

"What was I saying?" I said, distracted by the thought that actually I did want to do something naughty, and that was the whole problem.

"What happened when they tried to grab you again?"

"Oh, yes. Tia and I managed to persuade them to get lost."

"How, exactly?"

"I can be very persuasive when I want to be. That, and the fact that I got hold of their gun, which happens to be a Glock 17."

"Which also happens to be a semi-automatic weapon and not a revolver."

"Bingo! So, the Goon Girls didn't kill Heather or steal the collection and kidnap Fandango," I said.

"So what are the Goon Girls after? We know that the mob is involved in this somehow from Enzo Fetuccini's payments to Fandango."

"Maybe I was wrong about them. They must be looking for the fashion collection, too."

We said good night, and I climbed into bed after checking under the sheets to make sure I didn't have any company of the creepy-crawly kind.

I tossed and turned all night, falling in and out of sleep. I had strange dreams about Tia, Fandango, Bagliero, Heather, the mob, and even the Hells Angels, which actually worked in my favor. I always found that the best time for piecing together all the fragments of clues was during that limbo time, in between sleeping and waking, when my subconscious was working overtime.

I struggled out from the depths of la-la land early the next morning to the sound of the Germans coming through the paper-thin walls. They were rabbiting on in loud voices as they banged around in their room next door. I rolled over, sending the chintzy bedspread to the floor and receiving a blast of icy-cold air on my back in the process. I pried one eyelid open, my sleepy gaze falling on my watch. Five thirty a.m. I groaned and pulled the covers over my head, trying to ignore the noisy Germans.

The bad news was that I'd had yet another very restless night. The good news, on the other hand, was that I was pretty sure I now knew what had happened. This case had been about blackmail and smuggling all along, just not in the way I'd originally thought.

CHAPTER TWENTY-FIVE

I breezed into the office at Hi-Tec, carrying a cup of cappuccino, a family pack of white chocolate muffins with macadamia nuts, and a surprise for the boys. I was in a particularly good mood because I didn't even know that white chocolate muffins existed, and I was a muffin expert. Go figure. I knew Brad and Hacker wouldn't eat junk food, so I bought them a couple of whole wheat tortilla wraps with some wilting green leafy stuff—which looked as appetizing as a lump of mould—and couple of bottles of sparkling water.

Brad was on the phone in his office having a very animated conversation with someone. Tia and Hacker sat at his desk with their heads locked close together, talking about Tarot cards.

"Yo, everyone." I dumped the food on my desk, wriggled out of my rucksack, and handed out the goodies. Tia was a girl after my own heart and nibbled on a muffin while Hacker sniffed his food and tucked in with vigor. Brad came out of his office, ignored the moldy wrap, and perched on the edge of my desk. If I were him, I would've ignored the wrap, too.

"What?" I said to Brad.

"Did the goons come back?" Brad asked.

"I don't know. I didn't go home."

"Next time, tell me where you are, just in case anything happens." Brad folded his arms, and for the first time since I'd known him, he looked rumpled. Like he'd had a bad night of sleep.

"You should tell your boyfriend where you are," Tia piped up, glancing between me and Brad.

I felt my face flush and turned my face to the window to hide my burning cheeks. "He's not my boyfriend. What gave you that idea?"

From the corner of my eye, I could see Brad watching me.

"Oh, sorry." Tia slapped a hand over her mouth. "I just assumed that you two were an item."

"I just got off the phone with Janice Skipper." Brad thankfully changed the subject, his eyes flitting in Tia's direction with a look of sympathy.

I made fake choking noises and mimed poking my fingers down my throat. Childish, I know, but ooh, that woman pissed me off something chronic.

"I have some bad news, I'm afraid." Brad interrupted my outburst. "Janice has charged Samantha with murdering Heather and Umberto. Apparently, the DNA results have come back on the blood found at his office, and they match his DNA."

Tia dropped the muffin, sending it tumbling to the floor. The color drained from her face. She opened her mouth to say something. Closed it again.

Hacker slid an arm around her waist as she rested her head on his shoulder and sobbed.

"Tia…" I licked my lips, running through my options of what, if anything, I could say to make her feel any better. "Janice Skipper doesn't know what she's talking about." I gave Tia a tissue and a weak smile, glad that Hacker was there to give her a bit of moral support.

After a few moments, the deluge of tears subsided, and she grew calmer. She blew her red nose with the tissue, drew away from Hacker, and rubbed her damp eyes with the sleeve of her top.

"So, this is it? He's really gone? I've been trying to hang on to the hope that he's still alive, but if they've charged Samantha, they must be confident that Dad's dead. Sorry, I need to go." And she rushed out, leaving us staring in her wake.

"I'm going to solve this case if it kills me." I sat down, banging my forehead on the desk as I tried to think. I ignored the concerned looks passing between Brad and Hacker and carried on until my forehead hurt. Then I stopped and cracked my knuckles. "Right, come on, Amber." I pulled out the Fandango file containing Fandango's financial spreadsheets, the other financial files I'd printed from Heather's USB, the rhinestones I'd found at Samantha's warehouse and Fandango's office, the notes of Heather's that I'd found, and Bagliero's passport, spreading it all across the desk, and staring at it until my eyes ached. "Have you traced where the five-million-pound payment into Heather's bank account came from?" I asked Hacker.

"I've managed to trace it to a front company in Sicily. I'm trying to find out who's behind it. Give me a few more hours."

"One thing that bugged me about this case all along was the robbery of the fashion collection. Nothing seemed to fit in with it until last night." I picked up the rhinestone between my thumb and forefinger, holding it up to the light, remembering the diamond-studded biker's earring shining at me. "If it looks like a diamond and sparkles like a diamond, then it must be a diamond, right?" I bit it. "I can't believe I didn't notice it before." I handed it to Brad, who examined it.

"A girl's best friend." Brad pulled up a chair and sat next to me.

"These things were all over Fandango's fashion collection. Personally, I've never really been into glitzy clothes, but I assumed that rhinestones were obviously in vogue this year. I think I know what was going on, and it's actually pretty clever." I shifted in my seat to face them. "Fandango was smuggling diamonds. He had them attached to his clothes. Who would think they were anything other than rhinestones, and who would suspect an international fashion designer of smuggling diamonds? Enzo Fetuccini wasn't laundering money. He was paying Fandango for shipments of diamonds."

"Clever." Hacker raised an eyebrow.

"We know that the mob goons weren't involved in the disappearance of Fandango and his collection or Heather's death because of the revolver used and the Obama mask. Also, they seem to be looking for the collection, too. So the only other person who could've been involved is Heather. She must've found out about the smuggling and wanted a piece of the action. She had a drug problem, she needed the money badly, but I'm guessing that Fandango didn't want to split it with her. So, if she double-crosses him and sells the shipment to someone else, she's cleared a cool five million pounds. She staged a robbery where she just happens to be assaulted and can't remember what happened so no one suspects that it's an inside job."

"What do you think happened to Fandango?" Brad asked me.

FASHION, LIES, AND MURDER

"When there was no ransom demand, I thought he was still alive, but it looks likely that he was killed by whomever Heather sold the collection to."

"Why would a well-respected businessman get involved in smuggling diamonds for the mob?" Brad asked.

"Blackmail," I said. "Fetuccini was blackmailing Fandango to smuggle the diamonds for him, which means that Fetuccini discovered something about Fandango's mysterious past."

"But what?" Hacker frowned.

"I have an idea about that." I scribbled away on my notepad, tore off a sheet of paper, and handed it to Hacker. "Have you ever used this?"

"No, but you are talking to the finest computer whiz kid this side of the equator. Leave it with me." His fingers danced over the keyboard.

"Hang on a minute. If the Goon Girls weren't sent by Fetuccini to find the collection, why do they think that you've got something of theirs?" Brad asked me.

I pursed my lips, thinking about that one. "Good point. I haven't got a clue."

"Well, they broke into your car and your apartment, and they said you had something their boss wanted."

"I checked my car when it was broken into. There's nothing in there really, unless they were chocoholics too and wanted my Easter bunny. The only thing missing was my flashlight, but they were probably too tight to buy one themselves, so they thought they'd nick mine instead."

"Have you checked your apartment?"

"No. Maybe they think I found the collection, and I've got the diamonds stashed in my cookie jar."

"Maybe they think you hid them in your knicker drawer." The corners of Brad's lips curled into a sly grin. "Why don't we check there first?"

"Nice try."

"It would be purely for the purposes of furthering this case," he said, his tone innocent, but the heated look in his eyes gave his thoughts away. I just rolled my eyes and ignored him.

* * *

Brad took my key, sliding it into the lock and opening my apartment door without a sound. I followed close behind, my chin millimeters

219

away from the back of his shoulder. We checked that the coast was clear of crazy mob stalkers before we started our search.

"What happened to the plant pot?" Brad stared at the pieces of broken clay scattered across the floor.

"Tia hit Tracy over the head with it."

Brad smirked.

An hour later, we'd searched every inch of my apartment, including my knicker drawer, and we'd come up with nothing.

Brad held up a pair of black cheeky knickers with the words *Are you feeling naughty?* embroidered on the back. He turned to me, swinging them around. "Are you?" His steady gaze held my eyes until I looked down at the floor, embarrassed.

"Am I what?" I gulped.

"Feeling naughty?"

I grabbed the knickers out of his grasp, managing to steer him away from the top shelf of my bedroom cupboard where my vibrator was located before it gave him any ideas. I am a hot-blooded female, after all, and I didn't trust myself anymore.

"Don't you ever tidy up?" Brad glanced around my messy kitchen and into the living room.

I quickly lunged around, snatching up cushions littered on the floor, flinging them on the sofa in an almost equally untidy pile. Next, I hurled bowls and plates in the dishwasher. "Yes, see, I'm tidying up now. At least it looks homey and lived in with a bit of clutter, not like your place, which looks like the invisible man lives there. Anyway, the oven is spotlessly clean and tidy."

Brad opened the oven door. It creaked from lack of use. "It's only clean because I scraped off that plastic mess inside it. Do you actually use the oven?"

"Not apart from that one time I cooked the pizza."

"Well, that doesn't count, then. Have you thrown anything out recently?" Brad asked.

"The rubbish."

He looked at my overflowing bin. "Are you sure?"

"Well, that was next on my list."

"Anything else?"

"Yes, I've thrown out two pairs of damn fine sneakers, which were nowhere near past their sell-by date, but I don't think the Goon Girls take a size six."

"Have you moved anything lately?"

"Nope."

"And nothing is missing?"

"Double nope."

"Strange," he said.

"Stranger than fiction."

* * *

I dropped Brad back at the office and drove to my parents' house. I needed to ask Dad for a bit of advice, plus it was Thursday, which meant Mum would be cooking her regular lunch for Suzy as she did every week, and my mum's cooking was pretty great.

I'm not sure exactly how I missed out on her cooking genes when the stork dropped me off, but I even had trouble boiling an egg. I was pushing thirty-six now, and a girl could only live on junk food for so long before she turned into a blimp.

There was only one thing for it. I needed to wake up and smell the health food, or the coffee, or whatever the saying was. I desperately needed cooking lessons, especially if I was going to live with Romeo.

Oh my God! Where had that thought suddenly popped into my brain from? Had my subconscious made my mind up to move in with him when I was asleep last night? Part of me really wanted to. Part of me wanted to get married and have lots of little Romeos running around. But then my scary thought process took over, and I thought about the what-ifs. What if he wasn't the right one, what if we ended up hating each other, what if he couldn't deal with me squeezing the toothpaste out from the middle of the tube, what if I couldn't deal with him being so tidy? Romeo's two-bedroom house didn't even have a dirty sock left on the floor or the top left off the shampoo bottle, and that was so not normal. What if he ran off and left me with the little Romeos, and I couldn't cope? What if I was really meant to be with Brad? What if I couldn't trust my own judgment anymore? There were so many what-ifs out there, it felt like they were pressing down on my brain, and maybe, eventually, they'd squash the life right out of me, and I'd turn into a shell of my former self, like poor Mrs. Clark.

"Have you got room for another one?" I wandered into my parents' warm, steamy kitchen, which was scented with spices.

A beef casserole sat on top of the oven while Mum pottered around, piling up roasted potatoes in a dish and emptying broccoli from a steamer. "Hi, honey. Of course we've got room." Mum abandoned the food preparation and gave me a hug.

Suzy sat at the breakfast bar, nails freshly done, hair perfectly coiffed, and clothes perfectly tailored. "Hello." She turned her cheek so I could kiss her.

I stared at her cheek. "Nice blusher." I bumped her shoulder with mine. "Hey, sis. What's up?"

Suzy looked at the arm of her beige silk shirt, making sure it hadn't been rumpled in any way. "I've always hated that expression. What does it mean, anyway?"

I shrugged.

"How are the voices?" she asked me through tight lips.

"They're getting louder." I grinned.

"So…" She studied her French manicure. "Has anyone tried to kill you lately?"

"Now you come to mention it, yes. A couple of mafia guys called Tracy and Sally."

She glanced up abruptly. "I hear what you're saying; I just wonder whether you do. Do you seriously expect me to believe that two men from the Italian mafia with girls' names are trying to kill you?" She shook her head and spoke softly to herself. "Didn't you have to pass a mental evaluation when you joined the police force?" she asked as Dad walked in.

I rolled my eyes. "I'm sure that when you were a kid, you must've been body snatched and turned into a Triffid, and you're really being operated by remote control from planet Zyborg. It's the only thing that makes sense."

"Come on, tuck in." Mum sat down at the island next to Dad, ignoring Suzy and me like nothing fazed her.

After we'd devoured all the food, apart from a few lumps of broccoli I left on my plate, Suzy and Mum cleared the dishes and began washing up.

I turned to face my dad. "You did a police exchange visit with the FBI once, didn't you, Dad?"

"Yes, that must've been about twenty years ago. It was fantastic." Dad's eyes lit up as he reminisced.

"Did you spend any time with the witness protection department?"

"I did indeed. Now there was a department who could organize things."

"How did the program work?" I asked.

"It was amazing the lengths they went to giving people completely new identities. They didn't leave a stone unturned. The protection program provided new birth certificates, social security numbers, passports, jobs, even fictitious information about the witness's past."

"Would they go so far as to stage the death of a witness?"

"Why are you asking about this?"

"I think that Umberto Fandango was in the witness protection program."

"Wow." Dad thought about this for a moment. "Actually, now you mention it, I remember there was this one case while I was visiting them. Some mafia boss was on trial for murder—I can't remember his name now. Anyway, this mafia boss was in a tailor's shop, and a couple of hoods from a rival family came into the shop at the same time. The mafia boss shot them in cold blood in front of the tailor. Apparently, the tailor managed to get away and approached the FBI."

"What happened?" I rested my elbows on the island, feeling a chill run through me.

"Well, obviously the tailor was the prime witness in the case, but he would only agree to testify if he was entered into the witness protection program. If my memory serves me correctly, I think the tailor had a wife and small baby at the time. Yes, it's coming back to me now. The mafia boss ended up getting convicted based on the tailor's testimony and was sent to Sing Sing prison. But there was a leak in the FBI office. The mafia found out where the tailor's safe house was and tried to assassinate him and his family in retaliation, but they only succeeded in killing his wife. That was when the FBI stepped up their protection."

"How?" I asked, realizing that I was chewing the corner of my bottom lip in anticipation.

"The top level of command in the FBI staged the death of the tailor and his daughter and secretly provided them with new identities. Rumor had it that they even provided him with a top-class plastic surgeon to change his appearance. It was the first of its kind for the program at the time."

"Was Carlos Bagliero the name of the tailor?"

"Yes!" Dad slapped the palm of his hand on the island, making me jump. "Yes, that was it. You know, I often wonder what happened to him."

And that was when I stopped listening. Pulses in my brain flickered to life, tying together all the pieces of information as I stared at the floor, drowning out Dad's voice while I processed it all.

I felt lightheaded. Oh my God. Fandango hadn't been stealing Tia away from a mob family; he'd been protecting her from them.

"Your phone's ringing." Dad held out my mobile.

"Yo," Hacker said to me when I flipped it open.

"Have you found anything?" I said with urgency.

"You bet I have. I manipulated the facial-recognition software program you suggested, and you were right. Umberto Fandango and Carlos Bagliero are the same person. Fandango underwent extensive plastic surgery so the transformation was really amazing. I've finally managed to crack into the security system at the FBI's top-secret computer files. Fandango was in the witness protection program after an attempted assassination of him and his family twenty years ago. Fandango—"

"Did you find out who paid Heather?"

"Yes, as I said before, the five million pounds paid into her Swiss account came from a front company. I've finally traced who is behind it."

"Who?" My stomach fluttered with anticipation.

"Lennie and Lonnie Cohen."

"Are you sure?" I said. That was the last thing I expected to hear.

"I'm positive."

"But why did Heather's note refer to CB?" And then the fluttering turned into an excited bubbling as the realization punched me in the face. "Everyone knows Lennie and Lonnie Cohen as the Cohen brothers. That's why it said CB. I know where Fandango is," I said, more to myself than Hacker.

I hung up and ran out the front door, leaving my family gawping in my wake.

CHAPTER TWENTY-SIX

I threw myself behind the wheel of the Lemon, stabbed the key in the ignition so hard that I was surprised it didn't snap, and floored it. The suspension groaned as I crunched the gears and screeched around corners, yelling at cars to get out of my way.

I knew the who, what, and how of this case, I just didn't know the why. And I would have to get that information from Fandango.

I crunched the handbrake on while the Lemon was still in motion, skidding to a stop outside the Cohens' warehouse. I jumped out and jogged around to Samantha's warehouse. My hands shook as I fumbled with the open sesame tool, trying to insert it into the lock. "Damn." I dropped it on the floor.

Three attempts later, I pushed the door open and rushed inside.

"I know you're in here, Umberto," I said, approaching the rolled-up carpet next to the fridge. I waited for a sound or a movement, any kind of sign that I was right, but I could only see the rise and fall of my chest and hear the sound of my heavy breathing. "Umberto." I kicked the carpet.

My foot connected with something hard inside it. I heard a yelp.

I unrolled the heavy carpet until it was laid out straight, coming face to face with a disheveled Umberto in the center of it.

"D-don't kill me." He clamped his quivering hands over his face.

"I'm not going to kill you."

"Are you sure?" An eye appeared as one hand slid down, and he stared at me with suspicion.

"I'm an insurance investigator. I'm not allowed to kill people, although sometimes I do get the urge."

"How do I know you're really an insurance investigator and not a member of the mob who's been sent to track me down and kill me?"

"If I was going to kill you, I would've just come in here and shot you through the carpet, or I would've killed you the first time I met you."

Fandango thought about that for a few moments, keeping his wary gaze on me. "Good point." He sat up.

I parked my backside down on the carpet next to him, tucking my legs underneath me. "Okay, let's start at the beginning. Tell me why you got involved with smuggling the diamonds for Enzo Fetuccini."

He ran a shaky hand through his hair. Eventually, he took a deep breath and began. "I was a tailor, for Christ's sake. I didn't have anything to do with the mob. I was just in the wrong place at the wrong time, and then boom! My life is ruined. This guy came into my shop one day with a few bodyguards, looking for a fancy-schmancy suit. I didn't have a clue who he was. I thought he was an actor or something. So I measure him up, then I go out the back of the shop to find some material samples, and I hear the doorbell jingle." He shook his head. "I can still hear it now, you know. It haunts me. I wake up in the middle of the night in a cold sweat, and somewhere in my head, I can hear it jingling. I came out of the back of the shop, and two other guys had come in, dressed in some cheap suits. The next thing I knew, Mr. Fancy-Schmancy shoots these two guys in the head. I nearly crapped myself on the spot, believe me. It was like *The Godfather*." His eyes grew wide. "I ran like the wind, out the back of the shop to my house. I drove my wife and baby daughter over two hundred miles to a motel in New York. We holed up there for a few days, trying to decide what to do. Eventually, I went to the FBI."

"And they put you in the witness protection program?"

"Yes. Mr. Fancy-Schmancy turned out to be Ricardo Lombardi, this big mafia godfather, and the guys he'd killed turned out to be from the Rossi family, a rival mafia gang. Apparently, Lombardi thought Rossi was disrespecting him by selling his drugs in the Lombardi territory. I didn't know what to do, but the FBI convinced me to testify. They said they'd protect me, and I believed them, so I gave evidence against him. Lombardi was put away for life, and I went back to the safe house in the middle of nowhere."

"But there was a mole in the FBI?"

"Lombardi had someone on the inside of the FBI. His guys found out where we were and tried to kill us." He glanced up at me. "They killed my wife." His lips trembled and his eyes shone with unshed tears.

Even twenty years after it had happened, I could still hear the bitterness and hurt in his voice.

"I'm really sorry." I reached out to touch his arm, hesitated, and then changed my mind. No gesture would repair the damage caused to him.

"An FBI agent was shot, too. That was when the director of the FBI stepped in and suggested I leave the States. They arranged a plastic surgeon to change my looks and gave me a whole new identity. I became Umberto Fandango."

"So you began a new career as a fashion designer, and who would think to look for a guy on the run in the middle of the public eye?"

"That's what I thought."

"Enzo Fetuccini was also serving time in Sing Sing prison for murder. I'm guessing he discovered something about you from Lombardi, and when he got out six months ago, he started blackmailing you."

"I don't know how Fetuccini found out that I was Bagliero, but he told me he would turn me over to the Lombardi family if I didn't do what he wanted." Fandango's forehead wrinkled with worry. "I didn't have a choice. The mob has people everywhere. If I didn't go along with it, I was a dead man."

"Why didn't you inform the FBI?"

"Because things were different this time. Tia wasn't a baby anymore, she was a grown woman. It would mean that she would have to go through what I went through twenty years ago. She would have to change her life completely, and I know how hard that is. I didn't want her life to be ripped apart and turned upside down, so I went along with it. Fetuccini wanted me to smuggle diamonds in with my fashion collection, and I just had to accept it."

"Who supplied the diamonds?"

"I don't know. I never met the guy. A package of diamonds would be delivered to my office by courier, and I would hot-fix them to my fashion designs with glue. Some of the clothing would have rhinestones on them, and they would go out to legitimate customers. The clothing with the diamonds on would be shipped to Fetuccini, who paid for the designs as if it was a genuine order. I then had to leave that money in a package at the rear of our offices to be collected by the diamond supplier."

"So, you never saw the supplier?"

Fandango rubbed at his forehead. "No. After everything that had happened in the past, I didn't want to know."

"And somehow Heather found out what you were up to and wanted a cut for herself?"

"Heather worked for me for years. I didn't know she had a drug problem until a few months ago when I found some drugs in her locker at the office. She broke down and admitted it, promising she would get help if I let her carry on working for her. Of course, I agreed. I didn't want her life to be ruined because of drugs, too. But instead of getting help, she found out what was going on and thought she could score a large amount of cash."

"She arranged to sell the fashion collection, diamonds and all, to the Cohen brothers behind your back," I said.

"Right. She staged a robbery when she knew there would only be me and her in the office. About half past six in the evening, Lennie and Lonnie Cohen burst in with guns, wearing Obama masks. She goes straight upstairs with the tall one."

"Lonnie."

"Yeah. Heather and Lonnie load up his van, while the short one keeps me in the office at gunpoint."

"That was Lennie."

"I thought I was going to die again." His voice cracked.

"How did you know it was the Cohen brothers if they wore Obama masks?"

"They've got a warehouse next door. I'd seen them there before, and I knew who they were. I could tell their voices a mile off. Plus their difference in height was pretty distinctive, too. And they called each other by name when they broke in."

"So how did your blood end up in the office?"

"There was a split second when Lennie looked away, and I rugby-tackled him. The gun went off and the bullet hit me in the shoulder. I passed out on the floor, and when I woke up a few minutes later,

Heather was also unconscious, and the Cohens had disappeared with the collection. My shoulder wound only turned out to be a scratch, but there was so much blood seeping into my shirt, I guess they thought they'd killed me."

"And you took the opportunity to disappear."

"I didn't know if they'd killed Heather, or if she'd staged a bump to the head to make her look innocent, but I wasn't hanging around to find out. When Fetuccini realized I'd lost the diamonds, I would be a dead man. This was the only place I could hide. How did you know I was here, anyway?"

I grinned. "The fridge told me."

"Pardon?"

"There are some things that plastic surgery can't change, like eye color. You needed help for that. When I found the saline drops in the fridge, I didn't think anything of it at the time, but I just realized that you need them for your colored contact lenses, don't you?"

"I hate the damn contact lenses. My eyes are really dry, and I always have a problem with them. I need the drops to lubricate them."

"There was only one place to hide in this building, and that was the carpet, which I overlooked the first time I came here," I said, letting all the information he'd told me sink in for a while.

"It was so hard to keep still and stop shaking when you came here before. I thought you were sent from the mob to try and kill me. It was hell, trying not to breathe in this wrapped-up carpet. And when I heard your voice so close to me, I thought I was a dead man."

"But I don't get it. You couldn't hide out here permanently. Where were you planning on going? And what about Tia—weren't you going to tell her that you were alive? She's been tearing herself up about you."

"I thought it was better to let Fetuccini think that whoever stole the collection killed me, too. That way, I could lie low for a while and eventually disappear. I figured it was best for Tia if I wasn't around, and I didn't think the mob would find out about her. I'd always kept my private life a secret. How is Tia?" The worry lines on his forehead returned.

"She thinks you're dead. She needs to know the truth."

He bent over and hugged himself, looking defeated.

"And the mob is still looking for something. I think it's best if you go into protective custody at the police station until we can contact the FBI."

"But they'll charge me with the smuggling."

I shook my head. "I don't think so. You were being forced to do it. Your safety was on the line. I think they're pretty overwhelming mitigating circumstances. And there's one other small detail. The police have arrested Samantha for killing you and Heather."

"Heather's dead?"

"I guess I forgot to mention that part. It looks like the Cohens killed her. I think she had second thoughts about what she did, and she was about to spill the beans on their little operation."

Fandango stood up, pacing the dirty floor. "That's terrible. Everything is a complete mess."

"Actually, 'a complete mess' would probably be an understatement at this point." I jumped up to join him. "But that doesn't mean you can't get out of it." I let him think about that for a while. I could see him agonizing with the decision, and when I looked at my watch, I was surprised that twenty minutes had gone by. "We need to get out of here."

He stopped pacing and fixed his eyes on me. "Okay, I'll go into protective custody."

"Let's go, then," I said, then swung around when I heard the door open behind us.

Tracy flew through the door, a fresh bandage covering his head. He was followed closely by Sally, who didn't realize Tracy had stopped and bumped into the back of him.

Tracy slapped Sally over the head with one hand, pointing his gun at us with the other. "You're not going anywhere."

Fandango hid behind me.

I made a big show of looking at my watch. "I'd love to stay and chat, but I've got a doctor's appointment."

"Maybe we should let her go if she's got a doctor's appointment," Sally said to Tracy.

"Don't be an idiot!" Tracy snapped at Sally. "It won't matter anyway. I'm going to shoot her in a minute."

I made fake coughing noises, doubled over, and started retching.

"Have you still got those genital warts?" Sally asked. "They're really itchy."

I lifted my head. "No, it turns out I've got a very contagious virus," I said in between coughs.

Sally's eyes nearly popped out of his head. He loosened his shirt collar. "I don't want no contagious virus." He looked at Tracy.

Tracy gave me a suspicious look. "Oh, yeah? What's it called?"

"Dodecahedron virus." I added a few more retching noises for emphasis.

"I think I've heard of that," Sally said, tugging at his shirt collar again. "Is it getting hot in here?" His cheeks turned bright red. "Fuck. I think I might be getting the dodecahedron virus. What are the symptoms?" he said to me.

"Coughing, retching, followed by more coughing and retching, red cheeks, feeling hot, followed by more coughing until your brain explodes into twelve pieces, and you die." I straightened up and let out a mini-retch.

"I ain't staying in here till my brain explodes." Sally's chubby little legs moved toward the door. As he reached out to pull the handle, the door flung open, smacking Sally on the head with a loud crack, and Dad burst into the building waving a gun around.

Sally hit the deck, out for the count, as Tracy stood there, stunned into silence by a Shirley MacLaine lookalike in drag, wearing purple leggings and a yellow blouse with pink flowers on it.

Dad pointed the gun at Tracy and adjusted his strawberry-blonde wig. "Drop it."

"Who the fuck are you?" Tracy threw his gun down, frustration in every movement. As soon as it hit the floor, it discharged a bullet with an echoing explosion. Tracy jumped up and down on one foot, clutching his other foot and howling in pain. "Agh! My toe." Tears streamed from his eyes. "You shot my toe."

"No I didn't." Dad gave him a filthy look.

"Yes, you did," Tracy wailed.

"Sorry to point this out, but you shot your own toe. Haven't you heard of keeping your weapon half-cocked so it doesn't accidentally go off, and you end up with half a cock, or in this case, half a toe?" I said.

"Fuck. I'm never going to live this down." Tracy bounced up and down in a zigzag pattern before losing his balance and falling on his back on the floor, still clutching his foot.

"Are you okay?" Dad asked me, although it was quite hard to hear him over Tracy, swearing and groaning on the concrete floor.

"NO!" Tracy yelled.

"Me, me, me," I said to Tracy. "We're not interested in you. It's just a scratch, you big baby."

"But I'm shot! It's not a scratch. It's a big fucking bullet hole!" Tracy glanced up at me with glazed eyes, looking a bit queasy.

"Okay, can we just forget about your foot, you big girl's blouse!" Dad yelled at Tracy.

I bit my lip, trying to hide my smile. "Dad, I'm fine, but how did you know where I was?"

"Ever since you told me that some crazy people were following you, I got worried. When I gave you the torch, I put a GPS tracking device in it so I could always find you in an emergency."

Sally came to and sat up, dazed. "I think I've got that virus. Take me to the hospital, Tracy." Then he noticed the gun in Dad's hand and Tracy lying on the floor, clutching his foot. "You shot him!" Sally said to Dad. "Man, that's embarrassing, being shot by a woman."

"It's hard being a woman, you know. These shoes are really chafing my heels," Dad said.

"Okay, let's get Umberto to the police station," I said, pulling Umberto toward the exit.

Dad picked up Tracy's gun and stood guard by the door until Umberto and I were both safely outside, then emerged from the building.

We all ran to the Lemon and piled in. I cranked the engine just as I saw Tracy hobbling to the SUV, helped by a red-faced Sally.

I sped toward the entrance of the industrial park, closely pursued by the SUV with Sally at the wheel. As I reached the entrance to the main road, a white van swung in. I did a double take when I saw who the driver was.

"We're going to die, we're going to die," Umberto repeated over and over again from the back seat, gripping the door handle so hard his knuckles turned white.

I was not sure if Sally had actually passed a driving test, but if I was his instructor, I would've been severely ashamed of his bunny-hopping technique. As Sally approached the entrance, he swerved over to the wrong side of the road and got rammed by the van.

"Good thing he's so intelligent because he sure can't drive," I said, stamping my foot on the accelerator and pulling out of the industrial park. I glanced in my rearview mirror to see Sally doing his best bumper-car-driving impression as he tried to detach the SUV from the front of the van, crunching and banging against it in the process.

I stopped looking then and concentrated on the open road ahead, praying that we'd all get to the police station in one piece.

"That was weird," I said as we arrived.

"You're telling me." Umberto peeled his fingers from the door handle.

"Did you see who was driving that van?" I said to Dad, tossing my rucksack over my shoulder.

"No, sorry. I was adjusting my shoes at the time."

"It was Romeo. And the doubly weird thing is that the van belongs to Callum Bates."

CHAPTER TWENTY-SEVEN

"Give me one good reason why I shouldn't charge you with diamond smuggling," Janice Skipper said to Fandango half an hour later.

Dad, Fandango, Janice, and I sat, safe and sound, in a secure holding cell at the rear of the station.

Fandango opened his mouth to speak, his skin turning a sickly gray.

"I can answer this one." I narrowed my eyes at her. She was really pissing me off now. "Number one, you and I had a deal, remember?" I held up my forefinger just to ram the point home, although I really wanted to poke her eye out with it. "And number two, there are mitigating circumstances." I held up my middle finger as well. It was really tempting to drop my forefinger and just leave the middle one up there, but I didn't want to stoop to her level.

A flicker of irritation flashed across her face. "You really are a sad, pathetic excuse for a human being. What deal are you referring to, you idiot? Surely you didn't think I was actually going to stick to what we discussed."

I shrugged again.

"And you are a disgrace to the force," Dad said to her.

Janice stared at Dad's attire. "You can talk. Look at the state of you. Who are you meant to be anyway?"

"I'm undercover!"

"How sad. It would appear that neither of you have got to grips with the fact that you're not police officers anymore." Her nostrils flared as she spoke.

Romeo appeared outside the cell. "The chief constable is on his way down."

"Did you catch those goons?" I asked Romeo.

"Did I say you could speak?" Janice's said to me.

I ignored her.

"No, they got away before I could get the van started again," Romeo said. "I've put an attention message out for their vehicle. If they're seen, they'll get pulled in."

"Damn." I stamped my foot.

"I'm going to release Samantha James now." Romeo made to walk off.

"Er...on whose authority? I haven't said you can release her yet." Janice glared at Romeo.

"On my authority." The chief constable came to stand next to Romeo, peering at us over the top of his half-moon glasses.

Janice gawked in shock at the chief constable's ruddy cheeks and thinning hair, still damp from the shower. "Ah, so you're finally back from the golf course, then, sir."

Dad smiled. "Hello, sir."

"Hello, Tom." The chief constable smiled back at Dad, then turned to his attention to Janice. "Detective Chief Inspector Skipper, please leave us."

Her mouth turned into an O shape. "But...but this is my investigation. I solved the case and found Mr. Fandango." She tossed her shiny hair over her shoulder in defiance.

"And how did you do that, Janice, by magic?" I asked. "Come on, I'm sure we'd all love to hear how you solved the case."

Janice's mouth flapped. "Er...um."

I chuckled to myself, making eye contact with Romeo, who tried to suppress a grin, not very successfully. Romeo winked at me, which made my stomach do a triple loop, and he sauntered away to the custody sergeant's desk to organize the paperwork for Samantha's release.

"I said leave us, detective. Go wait in my office." The chief constable's voice rose, echoing in the small, confined space.

Janice stood up, giving us all a nasty little sneer before unlocking the door and striding down the corridor.

The chief constable sat on the chair that Janice had just vacated. "I'm both honored and saddened by your presence here."

Fandango shook his hand with a worried look.

"Now, I've spoken to the director of the FBI, and a high-ranking agent is boarding a plane for the UK as we speak to take you into protective custody once more."

Fandango nodded slowly, still in shock.

"There will be no charges filed against you regarding the smuggling. It's not in the public interest to waste taxpayers' money on bringing this matter to trial. I'm just sorry that your identity was discovered and your safety was compromised," the chief constable said.

"And what about my daughter, Tia?"

"An officer is bringing her here now," the chief constable said.

"Will she have to go into protective custody, too?"

The chief constable nodded at Fandango. "I'm afraid so."

Fandango's shoulders slumped.

When Tia arrived, I met her at the front desk and led her back to the holding cell.

"This is so awesome! I don't know what to say. I can't believe you found him. Oh my God, how can I ever thank you? This is soooooooo good. Dad's alive!"

I stopped walking and rested my hands on her shoulders, looking into her heart-shaped face, not knowing if this was the last time I'd ever see her. I'd grown fond of Tia in the last few weeks, and I didn't envy the hell she'd have to go through to start over again. "Tia, first of all, you don't need to thank me, and second of all, I think you need some time alone with your dad, so he can tell you what's been going on."

"Well, I brought you something as a thank-you anyway." She delved into a furry sports bag looped over her arm, pulling out the famous Fandango handbag I'd been lusting after for years. "Here. I know it's not much, but..."

I stared at it, gobsmacked. This wasn't just any handbag. This was the handbag of a lifetime. "Wow. I love it. Thank you."

"No, thank you." She flung her arms around me.

After I'd left Tia and Umberto alone, I headed out past the front desk and got stopped by the duty officer.

"Hey, Amber. Good job."

"Thanks."

"I've got a couple of messages for you. Romeo says he'll see you at your place tonight, and the chief constable wants to see you in his office." The duty officer raised an eyebrow at me. "You go, girl," he yelled after me as I scurried up the corridor like my shoes were on fire.

I knocked on the chief constable's door, shivering with nerves. I felt like a naughty schoolgirl who'd been called to the principal's office.

"Come in."

Unfortunately, when I entered his office, the Wicked Witch was still there, sitting opposite his desk. The chief constable smiled at me. Janice gave me evil daggers.

I sat down next to Janice. "You wanted to see me, sir."

His gaze rested on Janice. "I've been hearing disturbing rumors about you, Detective Chief Inspector Skipper."

Janice shifted in her chair. "They aren't true." She straightened her blouse and stuck her chest out.

"So, you've heard them?" he asked her.

She fluttered her eyelashes at him. "No."

"How do you know they're not true if you haven't heard them?" I butted in.

"Shut it, big mouth," Janice said to me, her eyes ablaze with malicious challenge. Then she pouted at the chief constable, trying to look seductive, but really looking like a trout with severe breathing problems.

"I think you are the one who needs to shut it," the chief constable snapped at Janice. "You could learn a lot from Detective Sergeant Fox."

"She's not a detective sergeant anymore," Janice said.

The chief constable held up the palm of his hand to silence her. "As I was saying, you could learn a lot from an outstanding investigator like DS Fox. Although her methods are…somewhat unconventional, she always gets results. In fact, I think the only case she didn't manage to solve was the one involving Mike Cross. That's a pretty impressive track record as far as I'm concerned." He cut his eyes to me. "I'd like to thank you for solving this case and getting the press off my back." Then he turned to Janice again. "Now, detective chief inspector, you have one chance to tell me what really happened at the shooting range."

"I've already filed my report on what happened, and I'm sticking by it," Janice said.

I stood up, casually retrieved my voice-activated tape recorder from my bag, and placed it on his desk. "This is a recording of a very interesting conversation that Janice and I had in the interview room on Tuesday." I hit the play button, savoring her haughty expression changing to dread as our tinny voices filled the room.

I tried hard not to grin as Janice visibly squirmed in her seat. It was pretty difficult, but I just about managed to pull it off. Maybe I'd chosen the wrong career all along, and I should've actually been an actress.

Finally, it got to the part where Janice said, "Hang on. Let me get this straight. You want me to confess that you actually shot me by accident after I broke protocol at the shooting range by stepping out into your line of fire? And you want me to say how I cunningly and constructively manipulated your career advances and purposefully got you thrown off the force..."

That was when I couldn't keep my enjoyment at bay any longer. My eyes crinkled up at the corners as I grinned like the Cheshire Cat. Then I strode to the door and slipped out, leaving Janice to get the biggest bollocking of her life.

* * *

Romeo brought around steaks, coleslaw, and potato salad. He even brought a special griddle pan from his house to sear the steaks with. The griddle-pan touch made me smile.

"What happened to the pot?" Romeo asked, popping the cork on a bottle of wine.

"Which pot?"

"You know, the terracotta pot I bought you, which you said you liked."

"Oh that pot. Um...I had a slight accident."

"If you didn't like it, you should have just said."

"I did like it. It was the most superb pot in the whole world, but smashing it was a matter of life or death."

"A matter of life or death involving a terracotta pot?" He chuckled. "The weird thing is, that doesn't even sound weird coming from you."

"I like your pan, too." I watched him get the pan to the right temperature before lifting the steaks onto the griddle with tongs, pressing them down so they sizzled in the heat.

"You can't have a special celebratory dinner without the proper equipment," Romeo said.

I wrapped my arms around his waist from behind. "How about we put dinner on hold and get out your other equipment?"

Romeo flipped the steaks over, switched off the gas, and turned to face me. "That's the best idea I've heard all day." He reached out and slid the back of his hand softly down my cheek, then picked me up and carried me to the bedroom.

"So," I said as we lay in bed an hour later. "Why the hell were you driving Callum Bates's van?"

"I was doing an undercover operation, posing as a car thief to hopefully get enough evidence against the Cohens to put them away for life. I befriended Callum Bates, pretending to be this guy called Dave, and he introduced me to the Cohens. The plan was that Callum and I would steal high-quality vehicles to order for the Cohens to export to Saudi Arabia. We intercepted their shipment and the Cohen brothers at the docks, and I was looking for Callum Bates to arrest him when I bumped into you at the industrial park."

"Why didn't you just use one of the undercover police vehicles during the operation?"

"The Cohens and Bates would've probably recognized every unmarked car we have, and Janice wouldn't authorize bringing in another vehicle from elsewhere because she's nuts, so I told Callum that I didn't have any anonymous wheels at the moment. He loaned me his van to go scouting for possible targets to steal."

"Did you find Bates?"

"No, I think someone's tipped him off that we're looking for him. I checked his usual hideouts, but there's no sign of him. I'm guessing he's done a disappearing act somewhere. But the good news is that after you left the police station, I did charge the Cohens with Heather's murder and the robbery of the fashion collection and diamonds." He stroked my hair.

"Well done, you."

"No, well done *you*. You just solved one of the most high-profile cases we've ever had. I'm really proud of you, you know."

"Yes, but it wasn't exactly the outcome I'd hoped for. I feel so sorry for Tia and Umberto." I exhaled a deflated sigh. "But I suppose at least Brad will be pleased that he won't have to pay out the insurance claim on Callum's stolen van."

"Speaking of Brad…I've been feeling bad about telling you that you shouldn't be working for him. I trust you completely, and I know that you wouldn't…go back to him. It's just that he's obviously still in—"

"I bet I know where you'll be able to find Callum," I said. I didn't want to have this conversation. I wanted to be in denial. "And it's somewhere that you'd never think of looking in a million years."

"Where?"

I gave him Bernie Crumpleton's address.

"How do you know that?" He rolled onto his side, propping up his head in his hand, looking amused. "Do I even want to know how you know that?"

I tapped the side of my nose. "I have my ways."

"Well, I have some news that might cheer you up."

"What, Janice has been suspended, pending investigation?"

"How did you know that?"

"Just a wild guess." I smirked.

"And the chief constable wanted me to tell you that you can have your old job back."

I stared at the ceiling, looking, but not really seeing. My head spun like a twister at a hundred miles an hour.

"What's wrong?" Romeo rolled on top of me. "God, Amber, you've been moping around, biting your fingernails to the quick, willing this to happen for the last six months."

Exactly. So what was wrong? Why did I feel so indifferent now about one of the biggest turnarounds of my life? I should've been ecstatic about this news. I should've been swinging from the chandeliers—although the fact that I didn't have any in my apartment may have been a slight hindrance, but at the very least I should've been skipping around the room, whooping for joy. Instead, I felt like I was a little kid again, desperately waiting six months for Christmas to arrive, only to find that it was a huge anticlimax. I suddenly realized that I'd spent months craving for this to happen and now…now it just didn't seem right. Had I finally moved on?

Maybe I needed to start a new chapter in my life. Maybe I just liked that fact that I had more freedom working for Brad, instead of dealing with all the rules and regulations of the police force. It would be good to make it under my own steam with no one breathing down my neck for once.

Or maybe I just didn't want to face the prospect of never seeing Brad again.

I forced a smile and tried to muster up some happiness. The knife of guilt that had permanently impaled itself in my chest gave a painful twist. "Nothing's wrong. Come on, let's eat. I'm starved." I turned my cheek to avoid him.

* * *

The next morning I got up late. After all that had happened in the last few weeks, I seriously deserved a lie-in. Romeo had already left for the station, mumbling something about arresting Bates.

I pottered around the house, drinking coffee and asking life advice from Marmalade; generally doing anything I could to put off making a decision about whether to accept my old job back. Marmalade's advice seemed to consist solely of sleeping, eating, and snoring, which probably seemed like quite sound advice under the circumstances. It wasn't until he started licking his bits and bobs that I thought he was really on to something. If only us humans could do that, we'd save ourselves a whole heap of trouble with the opposite sex.

Mum rang in the midst of my dilemma. "Hi, honey. I wanted to congratulate you on the good news."

"Mmm."

"What does that mean? Aren't you happy?"

"Yes—no—I don't know."

"Well, you don't have to make a decision right away, do you? Why don't you have a think about things for a while?"

"I have made one decision, though."

"What's that, honey?"

"I think I've definitely decided that I'm going to move in with Romeo. What do you think?"

"Wow! That's fantastic news. What did Romeo say?"

"I haven't told him yet."

Mum paused for a second.

"What?" I asked.

"How can you say 'think' and 'definitely' in the same sentence? And don't you think that it's a bit strange that you're letting me know before Romeo? Surely he's the one you should be telling first."

"Are you trying to get me to change my mind?"

"I'm not even sure you've made up your mind."

"Mmm." I hung up.

* * *

I decided to head in to Hi-Tec. I knew there were some loose ends that needed to be tied up there before I made any decision. Sliding into the Lemon, I turned the key. Nothing happened. Not a chug or a choking noise or even a mini-splutter. I gave up after a few more tries and slammed the door. I thought about kicking it, but I didn't think it would help, so I set off walking to the office.

I toddled down the road with the sun shining down on my back and the birds twittering away in the trees, so completely lost within my own head that I didn't notice when a black limo pulled up alongside me and Sally jumped out of the driver's side, followed by Tracy. Actually, Tracy didn't jump, he kind of hobbled, what with the plaster cast over his foot and all. He looked quite fetching with the bandage on his head, as well. At least his accessories matched.

Tracy grabbed one arm while Sally grabbed the other, and they lifted me off the ground. I looked like one of those cartoon characters as my legs carried on a walking motion in thin air.

"What now?" I huffed.

"My boss wants to talk to you." Tracy glared at me. He didn't look too pleased to see me again, but the feeling was mutual.

The passenger door to the limo creaked open, and I got bundled inside. Sally and Tracy clicked the locks shut and stood outside the door with arms folded and legs spread in a wide stance, looking like they'd watched *The Sopranos* too many times.

"Hey!" I cried, then froze in surprise. Sitting in the other passenger seat was Mr. Hottie Model from Fandango's office. "Who are you?" I asked, thinking that the tinted windows and locked doors made me feel like I was stuck in a crypt with a blood-sucking vampire.

Mr. Hottie held out his hand and motioned for me to give him something.

I frowned. "What?"

"You have something I want." He looked me up and down slowly, then licked his lips.

I gulped. "I'm not on the menu."

"Nobody likes a smartass."

"And nobody likes a clever dick either."

"Give me your rucksack." He snapped his fingers.

I rolled my eyes and handed it over.

I watched with confusion as he tipped the contents out onto the space between us.

"Aha!" He picked up Brad's camera, turned it on, and flicked through the pictures. "Where's the one of me?" He looked up sharply.

"Which one of you?" I said, racking my brains to try and think what he was talking about. That was when I had a sudden brain wave. The photo he wanted was on my camera, which just happened to be safely stashed at the office in exactly the same place where I'd left it to be recharged, which also happened to be a good bargaining point. It meant that he wouldn't kill me, at least not right away.

"Don't play the innocent with me. You took a photo of me at Fandango's office, and I want it back."

"Oh, I get it now. I know who you are," I said.

"I know who you are."

"I said it first."

"Do you want a medal?"

"You're the new secret godfather of the Fetuccini family." I stared him in the eyes. "And no one could identify you because you've never been caught on camera…until now."

He clapped his hands slowly. "Bravo, Ms. Fox. So, where's the camera?"

A sudden thought popped into my head. This was my chance to help Fandango and Tia, and a way to make sure I didn't end up wearing last season's unflattering concrete boots. And it had to work, because otherwise, I might be the first person in history to die from crapping themselves. "Who else knows that Umberto Fandango is really Carlos Bagliero?"

"Only me and Enzo Fetuccini." Mr. Hottie's cell phone rang. He answered, nodded a few times, said "no" and "yes" a few times, followed by "uh-huh," and hung up. "I'll rephrase my answer. Enzo's dead now. I'm the only one who knows about Fandango."

"I've got a proposition for you."

He looked me up and down again.

I shivered.

"Does it involve you lap dancing on me, naked?" He raised an eyebrow.

"Er...no."

"Pity."

"Several copies of the photo are in very safe locations all over the world. Places where you'll never find them," I fibbed. "I promise never to release the photo to anyone as long as you promise to leave Umberto Fandango alone and never tell anyone about his past, so that he can get his life back to the way it was before Fetuccini found out."

Mr. Hottie considered this for a few moments, head tilted to one side, eyes coolly summing me up.

"If Fandango, Tia, or I wind up dead, I've left instructions for the photo to be released to the press, Interpol, the FBI, and the UN."

"Why the UN?"

I shrugged. "Why not? I have a personal hotline to the secretary-general. So, you only have two options, really. If the photo gets released, it will put a stop to your undercover crime career overnight, not to mention that fact that the Lombardi and Rossi families will probably want to accidentally-on-purpose shoot you in the head now they can identify you. On the other hand, if the photo remains a secret, Fandango can get on with his life, you can continue with yours unhindered, and we'll all still be alive to enjoy it. It's a win-win solution for everyone. So, why don't we forget this conversation ever happened?"

He stared at me. Finally, he said, "What conversation?"

"Good choice." I pushed open the door, whacking Tracy on the back of his knees. His legs crumpled out from underneath him, and he fell onto the floor, banging his head in the process.

"Can I shoot her, boss?" Tracy wailed.

"Ha! You could try." I eyed his foot.

"No, you idiot." Mr. Hottie stared with distaste at Tracy, who was struggling to get up without putting any weight on his plastered foot. Then Mr. Hottie looked up at me. "Anytime you fancy doing the lap dance, let me know." He gave me a smile like he'd already seen me naked, and liked what he'd seen.

* * *

At precisely three p.m. Fandango and Tia strolled into Hi-Tec's office, bearing gifts of champagne and a platter of hors d'oeuvres, which included the fly poop.

Hacker pulled out his chair for Tia to take a seat. Tia blushed and gave him goo-goo eyes.

"I don't know how to thank you." Fandango handed me the champagne and passed the fly-poop accoutrements to Brad.

I took the two bottles. "You don't have to thank me."

"On the contrary, honey, I feel like I do." He pulled an envelope from the pocket of his perfectly tailored Fandango trousers. "Here." He handed it to me.

I gave him a questioning look and ripped open the envelope. When I pulled out a check for twenty-five thousand pounds, my jaw almost fell off. "I can't possibly take this." I glanced up at him in shock.

"Gee, honey, I've got loads of the stuff. It's only right to reward someone who's saved your life."

"Dad will be insulted if you don't take it. So it's settled. You have to take it," Tia said.

Brad expertly pried off a champagne cork and poured the bubbling liquid into five glasses.

I managed to reattach my jaw long enough to take a sip.

"Tia's got something she'd like to say," Fandango said.

"Er...I was wondering...um, I've had such an awesome time in the last two weeks with Amber, jumping out of burning buildings and stuff. I was kind of wondering if you had any jobs going here, Brad." She did the snorty hyena giggle again.

Brad's eyes fell on me. "Well, we do need a new receptionist, but that's not really a full-time job. So I guess it just depends on whether Amber thinks she needs an assistant."

"Huh?" I said.

"Let me put it this way: will you be coming back tomorrow, Foxy?" he said, and we both knew exactly what he meant. He attempted a smile, but it sat unsteadily on his face as he witnessed my hesitation.

So here it was: crunch time! And I hadn't a clue what to do.

Because now I had an extra twenty-five-thousand-pound bonus, I didn't have to stay at Hi-Tec until I found a new job. I could leave today. Right now, in fact. But...

But what?

But then, would it really be so bad to keep both Romeo and Brad in my life? And after all, what's a girl to do when she's in love with two people?

Help!

I gave him a soft shake of my head. "I'm sorry, Brad, but no."

He stood there, keeping his eyes on mine, and I saw a shadow pass over them.

"Tomorrow is Saturday. You'll see me bright and early on Monday." I grinned.

ABOUT THE AUTHOR

Sibel Hodge is the author of the #1 Bestsellers Look Behind You, Untouchable, and Duplicity. Her books have sold over one million copies and are international bestsellers in the UK, USA, Australia, France, Canada and Germany. She writes in an eclectic mix of genres, and is a passionate human and animal rights advocate.

Her work has been nominated and shortlisted for numerous prizes, including the Harry Bowling Prize, the Yeovil Literary Prize, the Chapter One Promotions Novel Competition, The Romance Reviews' prize for Best Novel with Romantic Elements and Indie Book Bargains' Best Indie Book of 2012 in two categories. She was the winner of Best Children's Book in the 2013 eFestival of Words; nominated for the 2015 BigAl's Books and Pals Young Adult Readers' Choice Award; winner of the Crime, Thrillers & Mystery Book from a Series Award in the SpaSpa Book Awards 2013; winner of the Readers' Favorite Young Adult (Coming of Age) Honorable award in 2015; a New Adult finalist in the Oklahoma Romance Writers of America's International Digital Awards 2015, and 2017 International Thriller Writers Award finalist for Best E-book Original Novel. Her novella Trafficked: The Diary of a Sex Slave has been listed as one of the top forty books about human rights by Accredited Online Colleges.

For Sibel's latest book releases, giveaways and gossip, sign up to her newsletter at: www.sibelhodge.com

ALSO BY SIBEL HODGE

Fiction

Their Last Breath
The Disappeared
Into the Darkness
Beneath the Surface
Duplicity
Untouchable
Where the Memories Lie
Look Behind You
Butterfly
Trafficked: The Diary of a Sex Slave
Fashion, Lies, and Murder (Amber Fox Mystery No 1)
Money, Lies, and Murder (Amber Fox Mystery No 2)
Voodoo, Lies, and Murder (Amber Fox Mystery No 3)
Chocolate, Lies, and Murder (Amber Fox Mystery No 4)
Santa Claus, Lies, and Murder (Amber Fox Mystery No 4.5)
Vegas, Lies, and Murder (Amber Fox Mystery No 5)
Murder and Mai Tais (Danger Cove Cocktail Mystery No 1)
Killer Colada (Danger Cove Cocktail Mystery No 2)
The See-Through Leopard
Fourteen Days Later
My Perfect Wedding
The Baby Trap
It's a Catastrophe

Non-Fiction

Deliciously Vegan Soup Kitchen
Healing Meditations for Surviving Grief and Loss

SNEAK PEEK
of the next *Amber Fox Mystery*
by Sibel Hodge:

MONEY, LIES, AND MURDER

CHAPTER ONE

When I was about five, I always loved losing myself in fairytales where the handsome prince would come charging up on his white horse and save the fair maiden. I frequently imagined that I was Rapunzel, although there were two problems with this daydream. 1) I wasn't into heights in a big way; and 2) My hair was destined to be more flyaway than flaxen.

Fast-forward thirty years, and now I had an even bigger problem. I had two handsome princes in my life, and I didn't know what to do about either of them. I know, I know—be careful what you wish for, right?

In my thirty-five-year-old daydream, there was Romeo, my boyfriend and all-round Mr. Nice Guy. Then there was Brad, my boss and ex-fiancé. There was a reason for the "ex" word, though.

I sprawled on my sofa, staring at the ceiling and contemplating this little conundrum. Marmalade, my ginger cat, lay next to me. He purred away, mirroring my ceiling stare. I absentmindedly stroked his head, wondering whether he was contemplating a two-pussy scenario.

I know what you're thinking—two gorgeous men after little old moi. Lucky me. I wish! It wasn't lucky, it was way more complicated than you can imagine. In fact, it was as complicated as trying to assemble flat-pack furniture with a stupid amount of screws and no instructions. Not that I couldn't assemble flat-pack stuff, you understand. I'm a very practical kind of girl. But, you know, flat-pack can beat even the most enthusiastic DIYers. Or is it just me who ends up with a big bag of screws left over, wondering what the hell I'm supposed to do with them?

I was so deep in thought that I didn't hear my mobile ringing straight away. When it finally registered in my consciousness, I tumbled off the sofa, dislodging Marmalade in the process, and grabbed it from the wooden floorboards.

I glanced at the caller ID.

Think of the devil. The last person I wanted to talk to when I was doing my contemplation thing was Brad. He might sway my decision about things, and I was pretty easily swayed at the moment.

"Hey, Brad. What's up?"

"Foxy," Brad said, his Australian twang sounding more pronounced tonight. "What are you doing?"

"Stroking my pussy."

"Mmm. Don't give me ideas." I heard the smile in his voice.

"You don't need any ideas," I said. He probably heard the smile in mine, too.

"No Romeo tonight, then?"

I rolled my eyes. Even though he couldn't see it, he'd know I'd done it. "Stop fishing for information." I grabbed a fluffy cushion from the sofa and hugged it to my stomach, as if somehow that could put more distance between us.

His voice lowered. Deep and slow, he said, "I need you."

A tingling sensation worked its way through my spine, not to mention other parts. I tried to ignore it. I didn't really trust myself to speak, so I gnawed on my lip for a moment, thinking of something witty to say. My wit had suddenly upped and vanished for some reason, so I just chose to ignore his words instead and pretended to be huffy.

I cleared my throat. "What do you want, Brad? It's Saturday night, and I'm a very busy girl." My voice came out huskier than I intended as I glanced around my empty, poky apartment, which was very unbusy at this moment.

Yeah, right, Amber. Since when did thinking about Brad constitute being busy?

"I need you for a job," he said.

I didn't know whether to believe him. "Why do you need an insurance claim investigation done on a Saturday night?" Was he just trying to lure me around to his place for some other, totally un-work-related reason? And if so, how much willpower did I have to resist it? "Can't it wait until Monday?"

"I'm afraid not, Foxy." More serious this time.

"Okay, what sort of a job?"

"Have you ever heard of Levi Carter?"

I thought for a moment. "He's a boxer, isn't he?"

"Yes. He's the world heavyweight boxing champion," he said. "He's also one of our clients."

Brad owned Hi-Tec Insurance. He wasn't just a successful business owner, though—he had a mysterious SAS past, too.

"I've been watching Levi's fight tonight on pay per view," Brad carried on. "He's just gone down in the sixth round by TKO, but something about it doesn't look right."

"What's a TKO?"

"Technical knockout. You've never watched a boxing match before?"

"A few, but that was mostly because I wanted to see two fit guys with six-packs and hardly any clothes on. I don't know anything about the rules."

"It's a knockout declared by the referee when he judges one of the boxers unable to carry on with the fight." Brad paused, waiting for me to take this in. My mind was still on the fit guys, though. "It means the other guy won because Levi couldn't continue with the fight."

"So why is that unusual? Doesn't that happen a lot?"

"It's not unusual, but something feels off to me."

"Okay. What happened to Levi Carter so he couldn't carry on fighting?" I sat up on the sofa, all ears. Brad's instincts were as good as my own. If he thought something was off, it probably was.

"He had a bad cut on his eye by a blow from his opponent. He's at the hospital at the moment, and the doctors say he's got a torn retina. It's quite a common injury for boxers."

"And let me guess...Levi's insured with Hi-Tec for any medical expenses due to boxing injuries?"

"Yep," Brad said. "Although the expenses covered by his policy are fairly limited. Any payout we make is pretty low—minimal, in fact. There aren't many insurance companies who would give a boxer high-risk medical insurance."

"Huh?" My brow furrowed. "So if any payout we make to him for medical expenses are negligible, why all the fuss on a weekend? Why not just wait for the medical reports to come in and see if he makes a claim? Aren't you getting a bit ahead of yourself?"

"Let's just say I've got a personal interest in this one."

That got my interest aroused pretty quickly. Brad didn't do personal, unless it involved a few select people—me included. "Okay, I'll play. If he's got a common boxing injury, what is it that doesn't look right with the fight?"

"That's why I need you. I'll have to show you at my place."

"I'm on my way." I grabbed my rucksack, which was filled all sorts of investigatorish tools, like a stun gun, my SIG Sauer handgun, camera, voice recorder, and notepad, and headed out the door.

* * *

Brad's place consisted of a spacious—and very expensive—barn conversion. Huge ceilings and windows, stark white walls, lots of exposed wooden beams, minimal furniture, and no personal knick-knacks gave it a show-house kind of feel. Brad didn't do clutter. I couldn't live like that. Give me clutter and stuff any day. In fact, give me five minutes with this place and I could clutter it to death. The place was spotlessly clean, as usual. A guy who could kill people with his bare hands and do the housework—a rare find indeed.

"Here." Brad opened the door and handed me a glass of red wine.

"Trying to get me drunk?" I arched an eyebrow and dumped my rucksack on the floor.

"Me?" He faked a shocked look. He looked like he was fresh out of the shower—his cropped hair was damp around the edges and he smelled of…I sniffed…I wasn't sure, but it was pretty scrumptious, whatever it was. Something sexy and manly. Pheromones Pour Homme. He wore butt-huggingly sexy jeans and a black T-shirt that showed off his muscular body. I secretly thought that SAS stood for Sexy Arse Soldier.

I took a sip of wine and followed him into the huge downstairs living space. "Okay, what's so important you have to entice me here tonight?" I rested a hand on my hip.

Brad pointed to his humongous flat-screen TV that took center stage on one wall. A freeze-frame picture of a boxing match caught my eye. Two sweaty, well-defined black men took up the whole screen.

"I'll replay it for you," he said.

I tilted my glass toward the TV. "Which one's Levi?"

Brad sat on his black leather sofa opposite the TV and patted the empty space next to him.

Hmm. Probably not a good idea to sit that close considering the last time I'd had a drink in his company. What if I lost control of myself and we ended up doing something I'd regret in the morning? Not that we actually *did* do anything that time, but, well…it was complicated.

I eyed the spare seat. Okay, what was the worst that could happen? We'd just talk about the case and that would be that. Hey, it was Saturday night, after all, and maybe I could fool myself into thinking that a hot-blooded woman should live dangerously sometimes.

I sat down, my thigh close enough to feel the heat from his. He glanced at me, haunting gray-blue eyes seemingly piercing my thoughts.

I coughed and leaned away from him, keeping my eyes firmly locked on the screen.

"Levi's on the left," he said. "The other guy is Ricky Jackson."

Levi looked in his early twenties. He was good looking, unless you counted a nasty bruise around his swollen left eye with blood gushing from a cut above it. Ricky had a few cuts and bruises, too.

"That's the eye with the torn retina?" I asked.

"Yes." Brad reached for a remote control on the arm of the sofa. "Let me show you what happened before the injury."

He rewound the fight at high speed and stopped it. "Okay, watch it from here."

I watched Levi dance around Ricky in the center of the ring. For a guy who must've weighed about two hundred and twenty-five pounds, Levi was very light on his feet. I was mesmerized by his speed and agility. I thought back to Muhammad Ali's catchphrase, "Float like a butterfly, sting like a bee." If Ali had still been in the ring, Levi looked like he would've given him a run for his money. He looked at the peak of physical fitness, too, like he was buzzing with energy, whereas his opponent, Ricky, was more out of breath as he dodged Levi's quick jabs.

Ricky managed to catch Levi with a punch from his right hand, his glove smashing into Levi's left eye and opening a nasty gash just above it. Blood mingled with sweat, trickling down Levi's cheek and spraying onto the ring as he danced out of reach, before coming back and connecting with right and left punches to Ricky's head. A succession of fast blows by Levi followed, with Ricky struggling to move out of reach. Levi backed Ricky onto the ropes with nowhere to go. Levi was in the middle of a bout of short punches to Ricky's head when the bell sounded and each boxer returned to his corner, where frantic activity took place around both of them.

A close-up shot showed a man in Levi's team pressing an ice bag to his cut eye as another man squeezed water into his mouth from a bottle. Levi swirled the water around and spat it into a bucket. The man with the ice applied something to Levi's cut with a cotton bud, then rubbed some sort of gel on his face.

Levi came steaming out of his corner at the sound of the bell, ready for action. He was just about to land a punch to Ricky's head when it looked like he was distracted by a sound from the outside of the ring.

Levi's outstretched arm was aiming well to hit Ricky on the cheek, but his punch seemed to falter through the air, skimming off Ricky's ear. Levi whipped his head around toward a middle-aged man who was now in full frame of the camera behind the fighters. The man stood in front of the ring, shouting something, his arms pointing up at Levi and waving frantically. The man's face had turned a shade of red that was a cross between tomato and eggplant. Levi's face froze in a scared mask, and his ebony skin seemed to lighten several shades in front of my eyes. As the man carried on shouting, Ricky made use of Levi's distraction, taking his chance to land a forceful punch to Levi's left eye, opening the gash farther. Blood poured from the wound, dripping onto the floor of the ring.

Levi sagged to his knees before rolling onto his back. The referee moved forward, ordering Ricky to one of the corners while he took up position next to Levi's head. Then he started counting to ten.

One!

Levi squirmed on the ground, his gloves pressed to his face.

Two!

Levi's right arm came away from his face and, eyes closed, he rolled onto his side.

Three!

Levi removed his left hand from his left eye but kept his eyes closed. Four!

Levi scooted into a sitting position and squinted through his right eye.

Five!

Levi managed to drag himself to a standing position on wobbly legs. He clamped his left glove over his eye again.

The referee got in Levi's face, saying something I couldn't hear over the shouts from the crowd. He whispered something to Levi, who removed the glove, giving the referee a good look.

The noise from the crowd got louder as the referee led Levi back to his corner, where a guy with Doctor sprawled in yellow letters on his jacket was waiting to check him out.

Levi's team crowded protectively around him like vultures circling carrion, blocking any view by the cameras.

Shortly after, the referee declared Levi unfit to carry on fighting due to the deep gash above his eye and pronounced Ricky Jackson the winner by TKO. Ricky bounded around the ring like an excited puppy, punching his arm in the air and smiling so wide I could see his gums.

I downed the last of my wine and Brad paused the playback before pouring me another.

"Okay, did you see that Levi was distracted by that guy who was shouting at him?" Brad said.

"Yes." I thought about the scene I'd just witnessed. "Did you see the look on Levi's face when he heard him? Levi's head whipped around to face the guy, and he looked really shocked by whatever he was saying. Scared, almost."

"That's the impression I got, too. Levi is a professional boxer—he's trained to not let anything going on outside the ring distract him, but he was certainly distracted by that. It doesn't seem right to me." Brad turned to face me on the sofa and stretched his arm along the back so his fingers were within easy reaching distance of me. They radiated heat like a furnace.

"So, what, you think that little scene was staged to make Levi throw the fight and go out deliberately in the sixth round?"

Brad thought about this, head on one side, for a moment. "Probably not. I don't think any boxer would want to risk unnecessary injury by not keeping his defense up. There are easier ways to throw a fight, if that was the intention."

"What, then?" I sipped my wine, staring at the screen to avoid thinking about the crackling tension I could feel through the small gap between us. "Do you know the guy who was shouting at Levi? I recognize him from somewhere."

"You should do. He's Carl Thomas; he and his wife live near your parents."

I nodded. "Yes, that's it. He's the CEO of that bank…what's the name of it?"

"Don't you remember? It was plastered all over the newspapers last week."

I turned and rolled my eyes at him. "When do I have time to read the papers? My boss has me worked off my feet!"

"You love it." A grin danced around the edges of his mouth.

Well, yes, I supposed he had a point there. In between debating my love life, I lived for my job catching bad guys. Actually, no, that wasn't strictly true anymore. When I was a cop, I caught bad guys. Now I investigated insurance claims, but somehow I always managed to catch cases that still involved the bad guys. Lucky or crazy? I'm not sure which. This was precisely why I needed my investigatorish tools of a stun gun and my SIG handgun. I was a good shot, too. I'd even popped a cap in my ex-boss's ass. Not that I'm proud of it, really. Okay, maybe just a little bit. It's a long story and she more than deserved it.

"Okay, I'll help you out," Brad said. "The bank is Kinghorn Thomas, owned by Carl Thomas and Edward Kinghorn."

My eyes widened. "The same bank that had a safety deposit box robbery last week?"

Brad gave me a cool nod. "The very same."

"Romeo is investigating that case."

"What did he tell you about it?"

I tilted my head down and avoided his steady gaze. "Not much. The only thing I know is they haven't caught anyone responsible yet."

Brad raised an eyebrow. "Aren't you discussing cop talk in the bedroom anymore?"

I suddenly found my nails incredibly interesting and stared at them until my eyes watered.

"Well?" Brad said.

Damn. He wouldn't stop until I gave up some information. "Well, if you must know, we're on a break at the moment." I fixed my eyes firmly back on the TV. I really didn't want to get into this discussion with Brad. Bad things might happen if I did.

Slowly he reached out and twirled a strand of my hair around his fingers. "Interesting. And why are you on a break?"

I tried to ignore him, but it was becoming increasingly impossible. I studied him from the corner of my eye. If I had to rate Brad out of ten, he'd be so far off the scale he'd be hitting quadruple figures. There was no denying how attractive he was. All the elements were there: the gray eyes that had a hint of blue when the light hit them just right, lined at the edges, giving him a dangerously sexy look; the solid cheekbones; the toned sleekness of a big cat; the full and particularly kissable lips—lips that at this moment in time looked like they wanted to kiss me.

Did I want him to kiss me, though? That was the question.

I batted his hand away to stop him molesting my hair any further, but he slipped his fingers through mine before I could stop him.

"I told you before—stop fishing for information." I looked up and my eyes caught his.

I couldn't tear them away from his. It was like he'd turned on some kind of invisible magnetic pull.

"I'm not going to give up until I've got you back." His eyes darkened with determination.

I gulped hard. Yes, that was exactly what I was worried about. Brad could win a stubbornness competition easily. Then again, so could I. But who would be the best man/woman standing?

For a moment, I struggled for words, which was very unlike me. Usually, the only time that happened was when I was asleep. Brad was the only person I'd ever met who seemed to have the power to render me speechless.

The sensible part of my brain said, Don't even go there, Amber. The hot-blooded woman side of my brain said, Stop being such a wimp and go for it. They met somewhere in the middle, and I broke eye contact before the hot-blooded side took over and my brain turned to mushy goo.

"We're talking about Carl Thomas, remember?" I released my hand from his and swirled the wine around in my glass to try and take my mind off lusty thoughts before I pounced on him and ripped his clothes off. "So, Carl Thomas's bank had a robbery last week where a lot of safety deposit boxes were ransacked and property was stolen. What's that got to do with Levi Carter?"

Brad shrugged. "I don't know. Maybe nothing at all. But there's something else that feels weird. I'll replay it again. Keep your eyes on Levi's manager sitting in the first row in front of the ring next to where Carl is standing. Watch his face when he hears what Carl is shouting at Levi." He rewound the fight again to the frame just before Carl arrived ringside.

"There." Brad pointed and paused the frame. "That's Levi's manager." He pointed to an overweight guy, around sixty years old with creepy pale blue eyes and a freshly shaven head. He had the face and body of an ex-boxer himself—chunky and squished around the edges.

I let out an involuntary gasp. "Shit! That's Vinnie Dawson. Better known as Mr. V to his friends or VD to his enemies." I chuckled. Childish, I know, but I couldn't help myself.

"You know him personally?"

"Oh, yes, I know all about VD. I put his cousin, Lee, away for armed robbery about ten years ago. Lee and a few other lowlifes robbed the First National Bank." I pressed my lips together, trying to recall all the details of the case. "That kind of pissed Vinnie off. He and his cousin are like brothers." I tucked a stray curl behind my ear. "Vinnie did his own time in prison about forty years ago, too, for manslaughter. He beat someone to death who owed him money. He only served five years, though. He got time off for good behavior." A fake laugh slipped out. "Good behavior?" I shook my head. "Somehow I can't imagine Vinnie getting brownie points for offering to do extra washing up in the prison kitchen."

Brad nodded. "When Vinnie came out of prison he got into the fight promotion industry. He's made a hell of a lot of money over the years promoting boxers, wrestlers, cage fighters, and Thai boxers. In the fight world, he's a powerful guy. He also has a lot of inside connections to other sports like football and rugby."

I snorted. "Powerful and corrupt."

"Did you know that, as well as being the number one fight promoter in the UK, Vinnie is also a manager? In fact, he acts as both manager and promoter for Levi," Brad said.

"So what's the difference?"

"The manager's job is to look out for the best interests of the fighter. The promoter's job is to look out for the best interests of the promoter."

"So what does the promoter do exactly?" I tossed the last dregs of wine down my throat.

Brad nodded to my glass, asking for my approval to refill it as he spoke. I held it out and watched it fill as he spoke.

"The promoter's job is to set up and pay for everything involved in a fight—from publicity right down to the chairs in the corner of the boxing ring and the drinks served at the venue. Because he assumes all of the financial risk involved in the event, he gets a bigger cut of the winning purse than the fighters."

"And what does the manager's job entail?" I asked.

"Well, the manager will usually sort out gym schedules, travel and fight arrangements, approve the contracts for upcoming matches, paying the trainers—that kind of thing. But if a manager isn't on the ball, many fighters could get a low cut from their fights and end up broke after years of fighting."

"Isn't it illegal for a manager to be a promoter as well, then? It sounds like there's a big conflict of interest."

Brad shook his head. "Well, in boxing, as long as the boxer agrees, they can have the same manager and promoter."

"I don't get it." I scrunched up my face. "Why would any fighter agree to having the same manager and promoter if there's such a conflict?"

"Okay, let's take boxing, since we're talking about Levi here." Brad leaned forward, resting his elbows on his knees. "When a boxer is just starting his career and is hungry to be the next champion of the world, I would imagine he's prepared to take the risk. There's a lot of politics in boxing, and some of the top promoters can put obstacles in the way to stop or delay fighters getting a title shot."

"Hmm. A few years ago, when I was working on the special operations squad, there was a big investigation into Vinnie's involvement in illegal sports betting. There were allegations that Vinnie was responsible for football match fixing, as well as rigging various fights. I wasn't involved in it, though, so I don't know what happened—only that they couldn't get any solid evidence against him. Guess who was running that investigation?"

"Who?"

"Janice Skipper." I mimed poking my fingers down my throat and throwing up. Janice and I had history and it wasn't pretty. "Considering she couldn't investigate her way out of her front door without help, it's not surprising that they never found anything to stick to Vinnie."

Janice Skipper was my ex-detective chief inspector and my archenemy. She was also the reason I left the police force. Correction—she had me thrown off the force before I got my job back and quit. I seemed to be collecting exes of all varieties. She was also the one I'd accidentally shot in the ass. Who knew I was such a good shot? She deserved it, though. Big time.

"It's also possible that the witnesses were too scared to implicate Vinnie in anything," Brad said. "Rumor has it he's eliminated a few rivals or people who've tried to stand in his way in the past. But Vinnie is involved in it up to his eyeballs, aided and abetted by Lee, who runs a betting shop,"

That sounded about right. If you looked up the definition of a psychopath in the dictionary, I'm pretty sure you'd find Vinnie's name. "What a great family business. I bet their parents are really pleased. What do you do for a living, son? Oh, I kill and torture people who get in my way. Good work, son. I'm really proud of your career choice." I snorted.

Brad pressed the start button on the remote control, and this time I wasn't watching the actual fight, I was concentrating on what was going on outside it.

I saw Carl Thomas stride down the aisle in between the crowd, toward the ring, stopping inches away from where Vinnie sat. Engrossed in the match, Vinnie unwrapped a toffee and popped it in his mouth, chewing slowly. He discarded the wrapper on the floor. When Carl started shouting and pointing at Levi, that got Vinnie's attention pretty quickly. Vinnie's jaw hung open, his cheeks puffed out and burned red like his head was stuck in a pressure cooker, and he glared at Carl with all the venom of a funnel-web spider. If looks could kill, Carl would've been boiled alive, decapitated, and stabbed with a thousand knives simultaneously.

The next minute, Levi was on the floor, clutching his eye, and security guards were wrestling Carl away from the ring and back up the aisle toward the exit. Vinnie whispered something to a huge thuggy-looking guy with a bald head sitting next to him, and Thuggy disappeared up the aisle as well.

"It looks like Vinnie understood exactly what Carl was shouting at Levi," I said.

"Yes, but what was so important to make Levi lose his concentration and risk injury?"

"I don't know." I tucked my legs underneath me on the sofa, making myself comfortable. "But, anyway, you said yourself that Levi's medical insurance payout would be negligible, so why the big interest in this?"

"Like I said—I've got a personal interest in this. I had a call from Levi's dad tonight. EJ says something's going on with Levi and he's worried." Brad glanced down at the ground, his eyes focusing on something I couldn't see. "EJ was in my unit in the SAS. He's a good guy, and I owe him a favor. I promised I'd do anything I could to help, and I always keep my promises."

I locked my eyes on his and took a deep breath. The air felt cool on my lips. "Not always." I immediately regretted saying it the moment it flew out of my mouth. That's the trouble with me: sometimes my mouth is a hundred miles ahead of my brain.

Brad opened his mouth to say something, but I cut him off before this conversation headed somewhere I didn't want it to go. There was no point going around in circles. Been there. Done that. I was so not doing it again.

"Well, what does Levi's dad think is going on?" I asked.

"EJ said Levi's wife, Letitia, told him that Levi's been acting jumpy and nervous lately and making rash decisions about things, which is apparently not like him. EJ's tried to talk to Levi, in case he's in some sort of trouble, but Levi wasn't giving anything away. Levi and EJ don't have a particularly good relationship anymore."

"I see." My mind whirred away, working overtime. "So you have a boxer, a banker, and a boxing promoter. The boxer gets injured—which may or may not have been staged—the banker has his bank robbed, then suddenly turns up at Levi's fight; the promoter is involved in illegal sports betting, and about a squillion other criminal activities; and his cousin was done for armed robbery fifteen years ago. Interesting." I tapped my lips. "The question is: what do they all have to do with each other?"

"That's what I need you to find out, Foxy."

MONEY, LIES, AND MURDER
available now in ebook and print!

Made in the USA
Las Vegas, NV
22 March 2023